**THE URGE TO LOWER HIS HEAD,
TAKE HER MOUTH—
AND NOT IN SOME SWEET, GENTLE,
GET-TO-KNOW-YOU KISS—
WAS AS COMPELLING AND STRONG A
NEED AS HE'D EVER EXPERIENCED.**

His body had surged quite insistently to life, ferociously seconding that idea. *You were just about to dump her in Noah's cabin and get back to work*, he reminded himself, needing rational thinking to make a swift return. *Don't complicate things.*

Then her gaze dropped to his mouth, lingered there a long moment, and moved slowly back up to meet his own.

"Pippa," he began, knowing he had to nip this off, and quick. But she'd whispered, "Seth," at the very same time, and something about the sound of his name on those little bow-tie lips of hers, with that bottomless sea of blue above them, doomed him to the pull of the moment.

He leaned down just as she arched up to meet him. They were both in it, both wanting, both throwing all caution aside and simply living in that one, singular moment of need and want.

Also by Bestselling Author Donna Kauffman

The Blue Hollow Falls Series
BLUE HOLLOW FALLS
THE INN AT BLUE HOLLOW FALLS

The Brides of Blueberry Cove Series
SEA GLASS SUNRISE
SNOWFLAKE BAY
STARFISH MOON

The Bachelors of Blueberry Cove Series
PELICAN POINT
HALF MOON HARBOR
SANDPIPER ISLAND

The Cupcake Club Series
SUGAR RUSH
SWEET STUFF
BABYCAKES
HONEY PIE

The Hot Scot Trilogy
SOME LIKE IT SCOT
OFF KILTER
"Santa in a Kilt" in UNWRAPPED

The Hamilton Series
"Unleashed" in TO ALL A GOOD NIGHT
"Lock, Stock & Jingle Bells" in KISSING SANTA CLAUS
"Naughty & Nice" in THE NAUGHTY LIST

The Unholy Trinity Series
THE BLACK SHEEP & THE PRINCESS
THE BLACK SHEEP & THE HIDDEN BEAUTY
THE BLACK SHEEP & THE ENGLISH ROSE

The Chisholm Brothers Series
BAD BOYS IN KILTS
THE GREAT SCOT

The Men of Rogues Hollow Series
"Baby, It's Cold Outside" in JINGLE BELL ROCK
"Exposed" in BAD BOYS NEXT EXIT
CATCH ME IF YOU CAN
"Making Waves" in MERRY CHRISTMAS, BABY

Standalone Titles
THE SUGAR COOKIE SWEETHEART SWAP
HERE COMES TROUBLE
A GREAT KISSER
LET ME IN
BAD BOYS ON BOARD
I LOVE BAD BOYS

Published by Kensington Publishing Corporation

Bluestone & Vine

DONNA
KAUFFMAN

ZEBRA BOOKS
KENSINGTON PUBLISHING CORP.
http://www.kensingtonbooks.com

ZEBRA BOOKS are published by

Kensington Publishing Corp.
119 West 40th Street
New York, NY 10018

All Kensington titles, imprints, and distributed lines are available at special quantity discounts for bulk purchases for sales promotion, premiums, fund-raising, educational, or institutional use.

Special book excerpts or customized printings can also be created to fit specific needs. For details, write or phone the office of the Kensington Sales Manager: Attn.: Sales Department. Kensington Publishing Corp., 119 West 40th Street, New York, NY 10018. Phone: 1-800-221-2647.

Zebra and the Z logo Reg. U.S. Pat. & TM Off.

First Printing: July 2018
ISBN-13: 978-1-4201-4547-2
ISBN-10: 1-4201-4547-9

eISBN-13: 978-1-4201-4548-9
eISBN-10: 1-4201-4548-7

10 9 8 7 6 5 4 3 2 1

Printed in the United States of America

Cheryl & Anne
For the conversation, and the crafting,
the support, and the sisterhood,
but most of all, for the laughter.
I love you both.

Chapter One

Seth Brogan scrolled through the playlist of Disney soundtracks on his ancient iPod, trying to find the one that wouldn't make him want to poke his eyes out with a spork. Or his ears. "Here you go, big guy," he grumbled. "Your favorite. You owe me." The opening strains of "Be Our Guest" from *Beauty and the Beast* wafted through the cold, dry air inside the converted barn. Seth's breath formed little crystallizing puffs of air when he added, "Now, I've got to go out and tend to me vines, lad," he added, adopting the brogue of his Irish immigrant grandparents. "Hold down the fort, aye?"

Seth was rewarded with a snort from Dexter, but at least the auld beast didn't spit at him. Llamas were champion spitters. Dex did, however, pin Seth with a steady gaze. Those deep, soulful brown eyes of his were almost as effective as Seth's ma's when it came to eliciting guilt. "You've got feed in your bucket. Music to dine by. And I'm not putting you in a stall. I know better than that." Seth swore Dex ducked his chin to intentionally look as pathetic as possible. Fortunately, Seth was on to his tricks. "I'd take you out there with me, but it's still snowing to beat the band and I'm not up for melting the ice clumps out of your fur. You're worse than the golden retriever I had as a kid."

Dexter lifted his head, and though clearly unmoved by the speech, the music seemed to mollify him enough that he didn't follow Seth when he walked across the sawdust-strewn dirt floor to the makeshift office he'd set up inside the end stall. Knowing better than to look back or make any kind of eye contact that Dexter would immediately take as a change of heart, Seth grabbed his winter gear off the wall hooks with one hand, as he checked his laptop to make sure the Wi-Fi was still back on. He was hoping to see a reply from the new distributor he'd met with the week before. Wi-Fi was a go, but no incoming mail. "Yet," he murmured, still feeling optimistic.

He zipped up his canvas overcoat, tucking his long, reddish-blond braid inside the back before flipping up the collar. Then slid on the mirrored ski-racer sunglasses before tugging on his hat, pulling the furry flaps down over his ears, and tying the straps tight under his chin, behind the neatly trimmed beard that jutted down several inches. His best friend, Sawyer, had given him the hat as a joke, claiming it fit Seth's whole Viking conqueror vibe. It was true that Seth topped out at a good six inches past the six-foot mark, with the sturdy build to match. And though he had tried to point out to Sawyer that it was unlikely Vikings had worn Russian ushankas, as far as he was concerned, the hat was, hands—and ear flaps—down, the best gift he'd ever gotten.

It had been one hell of a winter and it turned out the furry, fleece-lined hat was the best insulation a guy could have. Last on were heavy work gloves, layered over thinner insulator gloves that would hopefully keep his fingertips from freezing off. He had pulled the Velcro wrist straps tight, grabbed the bucket of pruning tools, and taken one step toward the big sliding-panel doors at the end of the barn . . . when his cell phone rang. Setting the bucket back down, he swore quite colorfully as he pulled the layers of gloves and the heavy winter hat off. He knew who that ringtone belonged to, and chances were, he wasn't heading out into the godforsaken snowstorm for at least another twenty minutes.

"Don't be mad at me," his baby sister blurted, before he'd even had a chance to say hello.

"Happy Friday to you, too, Mouse. And don't be silly. I love you." He said that quite sincerely, even as he girded himself for what was to come, certain it wouldn't be anything good. It never was with Mouse. Normally she went for over-the-top ego stroking, mixed with her own brand of adorable, youngest-of-six wheedling, because she knew he was a sucker for it—the latter part, at any rate—so this rather alarmist preamble didn't bode well. Not at all. "Also," he added, "Ma would skin me alive if I so much as ruffled even one of your pretty red ringlets, so you've got that going for you."

"I've cut them all off, so you're safe."

His eyes widened in momentary surprise, even as he laughed. "Well, I'm not the one you have to worry about then. Does Dad know? You might be responsible for making a grown man cry."

"It was for Locks of Love, so he can't say a word. Well, he could, and he probably will, but it was for charity, and if there's one thing he's got a softer spot for than my pretty red ringlets, it's sick children. Besides, I think I've humored him long enough. I've been wanting that blanket off my neck for ages. And before you say it, I looked like an old Irish nanny with it pinned up. I love the new do. I think it suits me."

"Sounds like everybody wins," Seth said, well aware of the benefits of remaining neutral whenever he could manage it.

"Now you've officially got the longest hair of the lot of us, Mr. Man Bun." He could picture the cheeky grin on her pretty face. "As much as Dad loved those red curls of mine that always reminded him of Great-Grandmama, God rest her soul," she said in a dead-on imitation of their old man, "he certainly hasn't been a big fan of your lengthy locks."

"I had my head shaved for ten years while I served in the Army. I'm reveling in my freedom from hair tyranny."

"Well, if you're wondering what to get Dad for Christmas—"

"The man bun and the even more fantastic stout beard stay as is. Anyone with a differing opinion is welcome to try and come at me with the cutting implement of their choice."

"Don't look at me. I get it. It's like my life in reverse," Moira Brogan said, then laughed. "You probably don't want to know this, but every time I post a photo of you on one of my social media accounts, women of all ages get downright swoony. Man buns and beards are total click bait, as it turns out."

"Click-what?"

"Personally, I don't see it, but then they didn't have to grow up with you slathering your face in pimple cream."

"You must be confusing me with Aiden. The only thing I slathered my adolescent face with was shaving cream, being as I was so manly I had to shave by the time I was fourteen."

"You have a very active imagination."

He chuckled. "So, what was it you thought I was going to get mad about? Why the call?"

"Oh," she said, all the cheer evaporating from her tone. "Right."

He lifted his brows, and waited.

"So, remember back when I was pre-law, I got accepted into that program one of my professors was heading up, to do a semester abroad at Oxford?"

"You mean before the douchebag—and I only use that term to preserve your tender ears from what I'd really like to call him—was arrested on felony fraud charges? Yes, I remember that. Almost cost you your scholarship because he was one of your biggest supporters."

"Yes, well, if you recall, it also cost me my semester

abroad as that whole program fell apart when the new department head opted not to follow through on it."

"I do recall. But you're long done with that, and law school. You passed the bar on your first try—for which the entire family, myself included, has showered you with much-deserved praise—and now you're ready to conquer the world."

"Your support, the family's support, has meant everything to me," she said sincerely. "You know that." She paused, as if gathering her nerve, then said, "The thing is, I really thought I wanted to practice law here at home, in Seattle. That's why I came back here for law school. But the truth is, I miss California, Seth. I want to go back. Only I can't afford it. Yet. And California doesn't have reciprocity with Washington, so I have to take the bar there in order to practice. It's one of the hardest in the country, so I'm really going to need to dig in. I told Ma and Dad and they thought it made sense not to incur any further debt while I was prepping. So, I've moved back home for a bit."

Seth was nodding. "Good idea. And good that Ma and Dad support your choice. I know they were happy you wanted to live and work closer to home, but they have always encouraged us to follow our hearts. So . . . what's the problem?"

There was another pause, then a sigh. "I'm twenty-five years old, Seth. With two degrees, one of them from Stanford, and a license to practice law in the state of Washington. Only now I'm back in Seattle, living at home, and it's like I'm sixteen all over again. Dad actually said something about my missing curfew last night at dinner. Curfew!"

Seth grinned, knowing Mouse would give him a knuckle pop to the shoulder if she could see his expression right then. "I love Ma and Dad more than life, but did you ever wonder why I moved across country to Virginia when I got out of the service?"

"I know, I know," she said, sighing. "I'm not ungrateful. I'm truly, truly not. They're being so great about all of this. But I'm the only one of us at home. The focus is pretty intense."

"Dad always worried about you most, Mouse. He knew you were the last one, and I think he wanted to slow things down, make your childhood last a little longer, and that came out as him being super strict. Ma, she just misses having her house full of running feet and squabbling kids. The silence is probably deafening."

"Except when Aiden or Kathleen bring the grandkids," she said, referring to their older brother and sister. "Then it's mass chaos. And about as suitable for studying as my old dorm apartment. Worse, really. I love my niece and all of my nephews to pieces, but it's like a Mickey Mouse frat house when they're here."

Seth chuckled again, knowing it was true. "So, what, you want a plane ticket to London? Isn't it a little late for an exchange program?"

"You remember my favorite Christmas movie, right?"

Having spent the first eighteen years of his life in a house filled mostly with women had taught him a few things, so without hesitation, he said, "Sure." Then prayed like hell she didn't ask him to name it.

"I watched it again over the holidays, and . . . I got an idea." She let that hang, as if he should easily put two and two together at this point. The pause on his end must have gone on a beat too long, because she said, "*The Holiday*? Jude Law, Cameron Diaz?" When he still said nothing, she added, "Kate Winslet?"

"Oh," he replied, when it finally clicked. "The house-swapping one?" What could he say? He liked Ms. Winslet. And Christmas movies. Then he did put two and two together and his brows furrowed. "What have you gone and done, Moira Aileen?"

"Well," she said, the wheedling tone finally surfacing. "I *am* trying to save money like Ma and Dad want me to. I've managed to scrape together the airfare and basic living expenses by working part-time at the pub, so I'm not dipping into my savings."

That also had him lifting his brows. Their folks owned and ran a traditional Irish pub where all six of the Brogan kids had put in countless hours of indentured servitude. Or at least that's how it had always felt to all of them. Except for the oldest, Aiden, who now helped them run the place. Moira, on the other hand, had gone out of her way to make sure she put in as few hours as possible. "Did you now?" he said, a smile in his voice, along with a hint of the old country.

"I did," she repeated, not taking the bait. "I'm being smart about this, Seth. Uncle Sam will come calling on me to start paying my avalanche of law school debt shortly. Once I pass the bar and move to California, paying the bills and paying my student loans will be my sole focus for years to come. There won't be time or money for any travel." She paused for a breath, then the sweet, affectionate cajoling tone returned. "This is my last chance for a little adventure, big brother."

"So, what, you want me to tell Ma and Dad that you've invited a stranger to come and live with them for a bit while you pop over to Europe?"

"Actually, Ma and Dad weren't all that upset when I explained the idea to them."

That had his brow lifting again. "I can't imagine Dad being okay with your going off to stay in some stranger's home—"

"That's just it, she's not a stranger. Well, to me personally, she is, but you do remember Katie MacMillan, right? My first college roomie? You've met her. You know we're still close, even though we're a continent apart now."

"I remember. Straight over from Ireland, going to university in the States," he said. "You brought her home for Christmas that first year. I was back home on TDY." He chuckled. "Nana Aileen talked to her for hours."

"Right, they were both from Donegal," Moira said, talking faster now. "Well, it's her sister I'm trading with. Katie's meeting me there, to get me all settled in. Ma and Dad loved Katie and they're excited because it means I get to go see our homeland. I'll be the first of us kids to go, Seth. You've seen more of the world than any of us, and I know it wasn't in a good way, but surely you can understand my desire to see more of the world than our own backyard."

The excitement in her tone was palpable, and he did indeed understand the itch. "So, are you just calling to get my blessing, then? Because it sounds like you've got it all figured out."

"Not exactly."

"Moira Aileen?" he said, caution in his tone.

She rushed right back in. "So, Katie's sister . . . she's looking for a getaway herself. She's been to the States before, but this time she really wants to just tuck up and get out of the fray. She was hoping for something longer, like three months. But she agreed to the six weeks, eight at the outside, so that's probably all it's going to be."

"Okay," he said, still suspicious.

"Seattle is a great place—you know I love my hometown— but it's not really . . . you know, tucked away." He heard her take in a slow breath. "The Blue Ridge Mountains, on the other hand . . ." She let that trail off.

His mouth dropped open, then snapped right back shut. "You didn't."

"Seth, you've got that big, beautiful place out there and

God knows, it couldn't be more remote. It's perfect! What better place for Pippa to hide out than at a gorgeous mountain winery in the middle of nowhere?"

"Pippa?"

"Katie's sister. And she won't be in the way, honest. She's very self-sufficient. And the very last thing she's going to want to do is draw attention to herself."

Then the other part of what Moira had said sunk in. "Hide out? What is she hiding from?" he asked. "An angry ex? Her family? Legal recourse? What's really going on here, Moira? What did you get yourself involved in?"

"Wow. What happened to you agreeing that I was smart and responsible? You won't be harboring a fugitive from justice. Jeez."

"I'm not harboring a fugitive from anything at the moment. What is she running from, Mouse?" He waited, but when his sister didn't say anything, he said, "You do recall that my stint for Uncle Sam was with Army Special Forces. I'm good at interrogation."

"Okay, okay!" She let out a long breath. "So, it's like this. Pippa is Pippa MacMillan." She paused, but when he didn't say anything, she added, "The Irish singer." Still nothing from him. "Well, she's a much bigger star in the UK, like Bono big, but she's had pretty good crossover success here in the States. She's a folk singer, so not exactly a household name here, but over there she's crazy famous."

"If she's some big-time star, why does she need to swap anything? Sounds like she could rent a place anywhere she wanted to go, for as long as she wants."

"She could, yes, but over in the UK she's been pretty hounded by the press. If she signed any kind of lease somewhere, trust me, they'd find out and stake out the place, and it would all be for naught. When I contacted Katie to tell her my idea on a house swap, I asked her if she knew anyone who'd be willing. She and her sister are very close. Katie knew Pippa was going through some stuff and she thought this might be the perfect way for her to duck out for a bit without it being all official. If she just swaps, she can hop a private plane, come here, and no one is the wiser. I mean, I'm sure she'll tell someone she trusts so no one worries that she's suddenly vanished," Moira hurried to add. "She just needs to get away from everything and everyone for a bit. Katie told me she's had some health issues and—"

"For the love of God, Mouse, please tell me you're not sticking me with some stressed out, spoiled celebrity who's doing her own brand of self-rehab."

"It's not like that," Moira broke in. Then her tone softened, and grew a lot more serious. "She's—she had some problems, but not the drug or drinking kind. She had some kind of surgery on her vocal cords a while ago. I don't know all the details myself, but there's a lot of speculation about whether she'll ever sing again. Hence all the press hounding. Katie swore me to secrecy about her coming to Virginia, so you can't say anything, either."

"That's the least of your concerns at the moment," he said darkly.

"Seth," she said, quietly now. "Please? She needs to rest, and for that to happen, it needs to be somewhere she can be incognito. I need to study, and I want my time abroad before my post-grad, real life as a lawyer kicks in. It's the perfect swap."

"Except for that part where you involved me without even asking."

"I'm asking now," she said, sounding suitably abashed.

"And no one in her inner circle is going to question your suddenly coming to hang out at her place?"

"She has a few places. The one I'll be staying in is in the village where she grew up, which is across the country from where she lives now. Katie said she bought it to have something in her hometown. She only goes there to spend the occasional holiday with her family. No one is there most of the time. Katie is going to meet me there, introduce me around as her friend from college, which is the truth, and say that Pippa was kind enough to loan me her place for a bit to study. It's all good."

"If she's as big a deal in the UK as you say, what's to say someone here won't recognize here? I live in the land of folk music. And social media is global. One tweet and it would be all over in an instant."

"Blue Hollow Falls, Virginia, is even smaller than the Irish village I'm going to. Every single person who lives in your little burg knows you, loves you, respects you. If you tell them to help you help her, they will. You know they will. Yes, she could stay anywhere, but nothing would be as perfect, as completely off the grid, as safe for her, as this. I knew she'd be in the best hands possible with you. Please, Seth?" No wheedling or cajoling this time, just Moira straight out, sincerely and honestly asking him.

Seth shook his head, then rubbed his palm over his nose and down the short length of his beard, squeezing his eyes shut behind the dark sunglasses he still wore. He'd never been good at saying no to her. "When is this big swap taking place?" He had to hold the phone a foot from his ear to keep her squeal of delight from deafening him.

"That's the other part," Moira said, sounding breathless with excitement again. "It all kind of came together really fast—and I did try to call you, but I couldn't get through, the ringtone sounded all weird and your cell kept going straight to voicemail."

"My power got knocked out for a few days. So, you're saying sooner rather than later?"

"Wellll . . . you might say that, yes."

He felt a nerve twitch in his temple. "As in, when? Exactly?"

"Well, it was supposed to be next weekend, so I'd have

enough time to clear it with you and you'd have enough time to make sure your place doesn't look like a frat house."

"My house is tidy, thank you very much."

"I just remember your room growing up, and—"

"Yeah, well, you can thank the U.S. Army for changing my lifestyle habits. And you said this was for six weeks?"

"Maybe eight," she squeaked.

"Moira, that's not a little favor. I've got a million things to do before the sun finally comes out and the vineyard is back in full swing."

Mouse was right in that he did have plenty of room, but he wasn't at all thrilled with the idea of having a houseguest for the next two months. Heck, even two weeks. He didn't mind helping his sister out, but it occurred to him there were other ways to solve the housing problem. It didn't sound like money was an issue, so he'd find his unexpected guest some tidy little rental up in the hills, cash under the table if need be, where she could do whatever she wanted and be as private as necessary, and he'd be on call if she needed help with anything. Win-win. His baby sister didn't need to know about any of that.

"She won't be in your way," Moira hurried to add. "And who knows, maybe she could be of some help. I've never met her, but Katie says she's a good sport and not at all spoiled by her success. Totally down-to-earth. Oh, and Katie said she loves animals, and their grandparents had a farm growing up, so hey, maybe she can keep your exotic house pet entertained and out of your hair."

"Dexter is not a house pet. He's mostly a pain in my ass."

"And yet, you didn't sell him off when you bought that place."

"It was one of the provisions of the purchase."

"Didn't the old woman you bought the place from pass

away a few months after you closed? You can't be legally bound at this point. I could check if you want."

"I made a promise, Mouse."

"Yes, you did, and I know you always keep them," she said, love and affection clear in her tone. "One of the many reasons you're my hero."

"Wait," he said, her earlier statement coming back to him. "You said this Pippa person was 'supposed to be' coming next weekend? When is she actually coming?"

"Like I said, I've been trying to call you for the past two days."

"We're on the tail end of a monster snowstorm. Ten inches and counting and that's on top of all the white stuff we still have piled up from the last snowpocalypse."

"But it's the end of March," she said, stunned.

"I live above two thousand feet. Snow happens. I've had it all the way into April, and I haven't lived here that long."

"It's still snowing now?"

"Supposed to taper off this afternoon."

He heard her swear, which didn't happen often.

"Moira Aileen?"

"Stop calling me that. You sound like Ma."

"I'm going to sound like Dad here in a minute. When is she coming?" he asked again, enunciating each word.

Just then he heard the high-pitched grinding sound of a small engine echoing through the air outside the barn.

"Well, it turns out it worked for her, schedule-wise, to charter a flight out yesterday, so she took the opportunity and got on over here. She was going to find someplace to hole up for the week until our swap started, but that might have tipped off reporters. So, I kind of told Katie she could probably tell Pippa to just go straight to Blue Hollow Falls. Since I'm not directly swapping my place with hers, it doesn't really matter if we go at the exact same time." Moira said this all in a rush without taking a breath. "But if it's storming up there, then she's probably stuck somewhere."

Seth walked over to the barn's sliding-panel doors and nudged one open. He was thankful he still wore the sunglasses so he wasn't blinded by the sudden, blinding glare of white, or the stinging flakes driven by the wind into his face and beard. Through the blur, he managed to make out a sleek, red and white snowmobile as it popped up over the ridge just south of the barn . . . and plowed right into the middle of a huge, windblown snowdrift. "Yeah, she's stuck somewhere all right," Seth said, listening as the sound of the motor instantly died out. "I gotta go, Mouse."

"Seth, wait, I—"

"I'll call you back. I think I need to go dig my new houseguest out of a snowbank. Also? You've just used up every last one of your favors until you're thirty." He thought he saw arms and legs clad in bright aqua blue poking out of the snowbank as someone appeared to be fighting their way out of the pile of white stuff. "Make that forty." He ended the call, yanked his hat back on, and was already running into the storm.

Chapter Two

Seth was halfway to the snowbank before he realized he'd left his gloves and the liners back in the barn. He was used to working in the cold, so that part he didn't mind. Digging a snowmobile out of a drift the size of a small mountain with his bare hands? Not so much. "Hold on," he yelled. "Help's coming." He doubted she'd hear him over the howl of the wind, but he had to try. The last thing he wanted her to do was thrash around and end up sinking herself and the machine in any deeper. He just hoped to God she wasn't injured. Or worse.

He'd recognized the snowmobile as belonging to Mabry Jenkins, who, until about five minutes ago, Seth had thought of as a fairly intelligent man. Mabry owned a big apple orchard just down the mountain from Seth's vineyard. Snowmobiles were an easy way to check on the orchards and the vines, or any other part of their extensive properties during the winter. Seth owned one, too. To hear Mabry tell it, most winters didn't dump enough snow to make it worth taking the covers off the things. This wasn't one of those winters.

Seth was already formulating the earful he'd be giving the older man later, as he moved off the path he'd plowed that morning between the barn and the house and waded into

snow that was hip deep in places where the wind had caused
it to drift. He was wading through it as fast as he could and
had gotten close, when what sounded like a faint shriek
made his heart momentarily stand still. He swore under his
breath and redoubled his efforts, forcing lengthier strides
through the snowpack. He was, first and foremost, concerned with the welfare of his new houseguest. But he'd be
lying if a small part of him wasn't also visualizing a headline
screaming something along the lines of, NEW WINERY OWNER
PERMANENTLY INJURES FAMOUS IRISH FOLK SINGER IN FREAK
SNOWMOBILE ACCIDENT! His business would be doomed
before he even got it off the ground.

His baby sister was right when she'd said Seth had seen a
lot of the world, most of it bad. Given that, his mind could
conjure up in rather alarming detail any number of potential
scenarios that awaited him on the far side of that mound of
snow, all of them grim.

So he was completely unprepared for the sight that
awaited him when he finally made it around to the other side
of the wind-whipped bank.

Standing in the small clearing made by the snowmobile's
entrance into the towering drift stood a mere wisp of a thing,
hands planted on narrow hips, and the biggest, brightest
smile he'd ever seen stretched across her pale, gamine face.
"Well, that was bloody brilliant, wasn't it then," she said on
a hoarse gasp, looking almost delighted by her predicament.

"You're lucky you're not bloody everything," Seth said,
knowing he should be relieved, not irritated, but that faint
shriek had cost him a good year of his life.

She'd already pulled off her helmet, so now she dragged
off her ski goggles and stuck them inside the helmet, then
propped it under one arm. Her smile grew even wider, if that
was possible. "Halloo there," she said cheerfully, as if they'd
just run into each other on a busy street corner. Close up
now, with the wind no longer snatching the sounds away, he

thought she sounded more throaty than hoarse, making him wonder if that was a result of the surgery Moira had mentioned, or perhaps her natural speaking voice. Before he could decide, she surprised him further by dropping into a deep curtsy, complete with ducked chin and her free hand elegantly extended, then popped upright again. Her smile had a wry twist to it now. "I do love making a grand entrance. Performers, we're such a shameless lot." Then she suddenly bent over and set the helmet and goggles on the ground before propping her hands on her thighs as if fighting to catch her breath.

Seth immediately snapped out of his momentary and quite uncustomary stupor, all but leaping through the last stretch of thigh-deep snow and into the small clearing to lend a hand. "If you need air, tip your head back, not down," he said, taking her arm in a steady hold. "I've got you. I won't let you fall."

"I'm okay," she said on a bit of a gasp, "just more winded than I thought from getting tossed on my arse." She slowly straightened, though, and did as he asked, tipping her face up to the sky, holding his arm for balance. She giggled when the snow pelted her cheeks and chin rather vigorously. "I'm not sure this is helping," she said dryly, speaking from the corner of her mouth while sputtering the snow from her lips, but gamely keeping her face tilted up.

Seth found himself smiling. "I think you're okay."

She tipped her chin forward again, then blinked her eyes open as she turned to look up at him, and he found himself once again at a surprising loss for words. When it came to the opposite sex, there were two things Seth Brogan was most definitely not: he was not shy, and he never found himself tongue-tied. Maybe he'd simply been caught off guard by her being the capricious, glib one. At the moment, however, it wasn't her charming insouciance that had struck him silent once more.

She looked like something out of a traditional Irish fairy tale. Fair skin chapped pink by the snow, red hair woven in two simple plaits that fell to just below the nonexistent curve of her breasts, a slight, almost elfin build clearly outlined in her formfitting, bright blue ski jacket and pants. He wouldn't have been at all surprised to find there were delicately pointed tips on the ears presently tucked under her wide, black, fleece headband. It was the not-so-traditional Irish part that currently commanded his rapt attention. Her eyes weren't the bonny sky blue of his sisters or his great-grandmother. No, hers were a downright luminous shade of teal and azure blue he'd only ever seen in the tropical lagoons of Indonesia, deep in the Sumatran rainforest. Exotic rather than Celtic.

"Penguin got your tongue?" she asked, and the twinkle in her smile reached those eyes, setting the deep teal pools to sparkling.

"Sorry," he said, trying to shake off their hold on him. That husky note in her voice, so at odds with her gamine face and petite size, had an equally entrancing effect on him. Maybe it was the unusual feeling of being caught badly off balance, or her rather blithe demeanor given the heart-stopping entrance she'd just made, but he sounded a little testier than was called for when he added, "But what in the blue blazes was Mabry thinking, letting you commandeer one of those things? And where is he?" Seth hadn't heard the whine of another snowmobile, meaning the old farmer had allowed a complete stranger to simply hie herself up the side of a steep, boulder-strewn mountain covered in more than a few feet of snow. It was beyond idiocy. It was downright negligent.

She turned slightly and followed his gaze, down the mountainside behind her, then looked back to him. "I asked Mr. Jenkins, rather politely, I thought, and he said yes." She smiled. "I'm discovering you Yanks are suckers for a lass with an Irish accent."

Seth had to fight the smile that naturally rose to his lips at her droll tone. This wasn't funny. "You could have been permanently injured or worse," he told her. "These aren't toys."

"He offered an escort, but I could see your vineyard from where I started. He laid out the general route, told me to stick to the deer paths through the snow, cautioned me heartily about going off trail, and told me to turn around if I couldn't navigate easily. The only reason I ended up as I did was I mistook the drift for part of the slope incline." She smiled. "Imagine my surprise when I plowed right in." She turned to look at the back end of the snowmobile, which was still visible. "I did a standard eject off the back end and let the engine die in the bank. It should be fine." She looked back to him, as if that took care of that.

"You did a . . . standard eject," he repeated, somewhat hollowly. She'd said it as if it was something she did every day. "What was that shriek then? I thought you were pinned under the damn thing."

"Oh, sorry," she said. "I think half a snowman went down the back of my jacket when I got up. It was a bit of a chilly surprise, I tell you," she added with a grin. "I didn't mean to alarm you."

Unfazed by his continued scowl, she leaned in and lowered her voice, and he found himself bending down to hear her, as if the two of them were about to share a secret. "If it makes you feel a wee bit better, my older brother is something of a professional with these sorts of machines. Anything with an engine, really. He's a professional stuntman. He taught me a fair bit of what he knows where vehicles are concerned. Normally there's a big landing pad when you leap off. Fortunately, I had a nice pile of snow to catch me." She smiled up at him. "If we ever get caught up in a high-speed car chase, I'm your girl."

Her face was just inches below his now. Normally he'd be
having all sorts of thoughts about those eyes of hers and her
mouth with those bow-tie lips, and maybe what would
happen if he just lowered his head the rest of the way . . .

Only Seth's brain was still hung up on "professional
stuntman." She was . . . well, he didn't know what she was.
He did know she wasn't like any woman he'd ever met
before.

He straightened, tempted to smile again. She was engag-
ing, and it was hard not to fall under the spell of her gregarious charm. Hell, he was tempted to laugh right along with
her. But he was still coming down off the adrenaline punch
from the initial wreck, not to mention her cry of alarm
might have jarred loose one or two memories from his time
overseas that he otherwise was pretty good at keeping
buried. And then there was the residual irritation over his
sister's high-handedness mixed in there, too. So, the best he
could come up with was, "Moira did mention you were self-
sufficient."

Her lips curved in a dry smile. "You should trust her."
Then she motioned behind her with a gloved hand. "You
know, that half-buried snow machine notwithstanding."

He did chuckle then, even as he gave his head a slight
shake. He felt like he'd followed Alice straight down the
rabbit hole. Or into the snowbank, as the case may be.

She stuck out her gloved hand. "Pippa MacMillan," she
said. "I promise I won't be quite so much work going forward.
You'll hardly know I'm here."

He doubted that, very much. He took her gloved hand in
his now chapped-pink, bare one and gave a light shake. His
hand felt like a bear paw wrapped around her small, slender
fingers.

"I appreciate your letting me bunk in. Your sister said you
had plenty of room, but I promise I won't be in the way. I'm
happy to lend a hand if you need one." She propped her hand

on her brow and looked around at the drifts of snow, with more still coming down. "I was imagining springtime in the mountains, though, so maybe that's not much of an offer."

"This is springtime in the mountains."

She grinned at that. "I love the snow. Don't get to spend much time in it, so this has been a lovely bonus."

A lovely bonus. "Well, you'll have a fair amount of it to play in, though my heart might appreciate it if we leave the snow-mobile stunts out of it, at least until the storm dies down."

"Deal," she said easily.

"And thank you for the offer of help, but I thought you were here to rest," he said, trying to find his way past their very unorthodox meeting to something resembling normalcy. "Moira mentioned something about throat surgery?" He thought again about that yelp and tried not to wince. He noted she had a thick scarf wrapped multiple times around her neck. She'd had it pulled up over her mouth and nose at one point, as it still had a crust of snow and ice embedded in the front of it, creating a distinct outline from where her goggles had held the scarf in place.

"Nothing to worry about. I'm not an invalid," she assured him. "The surgery was a good while back. I might not sound it quite yet, but my voice is fine. I just needed to get off the carousel of crazy for a bit. I've still got vocal exercises to work on. I probably shouldn't be out in this much longer, though," she added; then her grin came right back.

"What?" he asked, curious despite himself, when she didn't go on.

"That rush of cold air was actually the only part of my race up the hill that was perhaps a bit foolhardy. It was just so . . . freeing. My hired airport transport couldn't get farther up the mountain road, so we turned in at Mr. Jenkins's croft. I was hoping he wouldn't mind a temporary visitor until the plows came through. Then I saw the snow machine parked out back and the next thing I knew, I was asking to borrow it. Don't be angry with him. I told him about my brother, and even gave him a little demonstration. I had planned to drive it on up the roadway, but he said it would be faster and easier to just go on up the hill. I offered to pay him for the rental, if that's a concern."

"No," Seth said. "Out here we do what we can to help those who need it."

"Aye, he said as much. That's how it is in the village where I grew up, too." Her face lit up as she shrugged. "Honestly, I simply couldn't resist. No one looking over my shoulder, no one fussing after me, worrying every little thing to death. It just felt so good, you know?"

"I do," he said. And it was the truth. At least that last part. His entire existence in Virginia could be summed up by that exact same sentiment. "I'll try not to add any more to that chorus then."

She smiled. "And I'll try not to scare the bejesus out of you."

"Deal," he said, smiling briefly as he echoed her earlier agreement. He glanced at the snowmobile. "Did you have any gear? Bags?"

"It's all down with Mr. Jenkins. I figured I could retrieve it once the roads were clear. If you've got a spare toothbrush and a tumble dryer, I'll be fine. I'm pretty low maintenance. Well, I used to be. I'm pretty sure I still am." She smiled at him. "I'm entourage-free, so I have that going for me at any rate."

Seth just blinked. It was like being caught inside a snowstorm with a tornado. A tiny tornado, but still. He was about to lead the way up to the house, figuring they could exit through the waist-deep trough he'd made when he'd plowed through to get to her, when he noticed she was looking at something past his left shoulder, her eyes growing wide.

"Your sister didn't tell me you had your own yetis up here."

Seth heard the snort behind him before he even looked. He briefly ducked his chin to his chest and momentarily closed his eyes, wondering when, exactly, he'd lost complete control of his life. In his rush to save a woman who clearly didn't need saving, he'd obviously neglected to close the barn door. Seth turned to find Dexter standing a few yards behind him, his heavy coat now caked with the heavily falling snow. Small flakes glistened from the tips of Dex's ridiculously long, dark eyelashes as he stepped closer, his soulful gaze fixed on Seth.

"This is Dexter," Seth said. "He's a llama."

Pippa laughed. "Yes, I'm familiar with the breed. Long-legged sheep, my sister calls them."

Seth nodded, thinking it was an apt description. "He came with the winery."

"Of course he did," Pippa said, without missing a beat. "Does he like women? Can I pet him?"

"He's an attention whor—hound," Seth corrected. "He'll adore you on sight if you even look in his direction. But he's a jealous lover, so be careful. He'll spit if he thinks you aren't showing him enough attention. And, full disclosure, no amount of love will ever be enough. So, you might just want to avoid—"

But it was too late. Pippa had slipped by Seth and was already stroking the base of Dexter's long neck, crooning nonsense words to the beast. Seth sighed inwardly, thinking his second call, after barking at Mabry, was going to be to Moira, warning her never to pull a stunt like this again. He had a million and ten things that needed doing and this late-season snowstorm wasn't helping matters any. Having a full-time guest, even one as sharp and gregarious as Miss MacMillan—maybe most especially due to that—was going to add to that load, no matter how self-sufficient she was. She'd only been here a blink and he was already hours behind schedule.

Then Pippa was talking to Dex while leading him back through the snow, heading toward the barn, not the house, her delightful laughter filling the air as Dex nudged her along while trying to simultaneously nibble on her headband.

Everyone else is having a grand old time. Made him feel like he was being a grumpy old man. Maybe he'd let the enormous burden he'd taken on with the winery get to him. Just a little. He remembered his plan to find his guest alternate lodgings, and that brightened his mood. Maybe he'd only lose the one day. He'd get it sorted out, get her sorted away, deal with Dex, and maybe get to one or two of the items on his lengthy to-do list before sundown. Then he could focus on the mound of paperwork that needed attention that evening.

"Are you coming?" Pippa called out. "Last one to the barn gets to defrost a llama!"

He shook his head in resignation, but he was chuckling despite himself as he followed along after the unlikely pair. He'd look back on that moment later and wonder how he hadn't realized right then that nothing in his life would ever be the same again.

Chapter Three

Pippa unwrapped the towel from her hair and breathed in the moist, warm air while she combed the tangles free. The hot shower and the resulting thick billows of steam had thawed her out entirely, leaving her feeling relaxed and warm, through and through. It had felt so good to fly up the side of the mountain, snowflakes pelting her, the wind brushing past. The snow machine—snowmobile, as Seth called it—had been easy to handle, responsive, and one heck of a lot of fun. She'd felt so . . . alive. Alive in a way she hadn't felt, or, more to the point, hadn't allowed herself to feel in far too long.

She knew she was fine, knew her throat was fine, her voice was fine. Or as fine as it was going to be. It had been eleven months since the surgery. She'd done everything the doctors and specialists had told her to, following their guidelines down to the letter. She'd been given the all clear to begin singing again months ago. She had a few precautions she needed to take, but there was nothing to stop her from resuming her old life. With a reduced performance schedule at first, yes, but . . . she should be out there, singing, recording, performing.

Should be.

Every time she spoke, however, she heard a completely different voice come out of her mouth. One that was still foreign and unfamiliar to her. Her doctors said the last bit of throatiness could fade in time, though she might retain a bit of it forever. It wasn't the huskiness she minded. In fact, she thought it made her sound a bit sexy. She giggled at that as she caught the image of herself in the slowly defogging mirror. "Oh, you're dead sexy, you are."

She was a pipsqueak, or so her grandda had always called her, with all the curves of a ten-year-old lad. She hardly thought having a bit of throat in her voice was going to suddenly imbue her with sex appeal. But she didn't mind it. Maybe she'd even get used to it. Some day.

It wasn't really that she was afraid it would change her sound, although that did concern her a wee bit. No, mostly it was that every time she opened her mouth and spoke, and heard that rasp, she was reminded of that day, standing on the stage in London. It was the last day of her first world tour, one that had taken a far greater toll on her than she'd been wanting to admit, even to herself. She'd been singing her heart out, and, as it happened, she'd sung her voice right out, too. She'd known she needed a rest, knew her voice needed a rest, and she'd planned a nice long one, just as soon as they packed up and headed home to Dublin. But it had been one show too many. Her vocal cords had ruptured right there, on stage, leaving her unable to make any sound at all.

Everything had happened so quickly after that, and though utterly terrifying at the time, she'd come to terms with the catastrophe over the painstakingly slow, seemingly endless, weeks and months of arduous recovery that had followed. That was behind her now, too. She could sing again. Finally.

Only she hadn't.

She had a vocal coach who specialized in post-surgical reentry for singers. Only Pippa had never actually had a single session with her. She'd never so much as uttered a single note, not even in the privacy of her own shower. Not because what came out would sound foreign . . . but because she was utterly, if irrationally, terrified it would happen again. She'd come to terms with the fact it had happened once, but her surgeon had told her that if it happened again, she was done singing. For good.

"So, instead, you're just going to bloody end it now by not taking the chance," she said with a resigned sigh. She wanted to take a chance. Wanted to get up her nerve. Wanted to find her way back to the thing that had always been part of her. She'd started singing shortly after she'd taken her first step, or so her ma told everyone who would listen. Song had been Pippa's boon companion ever since, accompanying her through every single day of her life, both good and bad. Music and song were the soundtrack of her being.

She wanted her song back. Desperately. Not for her career, nor even for the fans who had so delightfully and shockingly given her a livelihood she cherished. She wanted it back for herself. She missed her steadfast companion. So much so, she ached.

That little shriek in the snow pile out there had been the first sound she'd made louder than normal conversation since that night on stage. "And look, nothing bad happened," she reminded herself. "You're fine."

And yet . . .

Pippa realized she was caressing her throat, protecting it, and dropped her hand away. She dried herself off and pulled on the T-shirt her rather gargantuan host had kindly loaned her. It literally fell all the way to her knees. The long sleeves hung well past her fingertips. She took it off, rolled up both sleeves, then carefully slid it on again and turned to the mirror. She laughed and struck a few poses. Her towel-dried hair fell in an unruly mass past her shoulders. Not exactly wavy, definitely not straight, nor curly, just . . . unruly.

Her face was still a flushed pink from the cold and now the steam. She did the fish-face model pose, then stuck her tongue out at herself. "Oh aye, you're the epitome of allure, Pippa Mavreen, that you are."

Smiling, she dug her black leggings out from the pile of clothes she'd shrugged out of earlier and pulled them on under the T-shirt. Seth had given her a pair of jogging bottoms, but she didn't even bother trying them on. She'd need a cummerbund to keep them up and would have to roll the legs up so many times she'd need straps around her ankles as well. She'd worn the leggings under two other layers and they hadn't gotten damp, so they'd do for now.

Her socks, however, were soaked. She eyed the nice thick pair of red and gray ones Seth had given her and decided they were better than going barefoot. She pulled them on, then rolled down the tops, making little tubes around her ankles. She looked like she had duck feet. "Glorious," she said with a grin, wriggling her toes in the roomy foot space. But they were comfy, soft, and toasty warm. They'd do just fine. As long as she didn't have to run anywhere.

Seth had taken her jacket when they'd come inside, and her boots. She bundled up the rest of her damp clothes and the damp towels, and walked back through the house to what he'd called the mudroom, where they'd first entered. There was a washer and tumble dryer there, and in short order, she had a load going. The bathroom she'd used was adjacent to the guest bedroom he'd said would be hers. She'd stuck her nose in the two other rooms at that end of the chalet, but they appeared to be guest rooms as well, so she assumed he lodged at the other end of the place.

She walked out into the main room and took a slower turnabout now that she was alone. Seth had gone back out into the snowstorm, back to whatever it was he'd been doing before her ignominious arrival. He'd told her to make herself at home, and that whatever was in the kitchen was *up for grabs*, as he'd put it. She wasn't sure when he'd be returning and had decided it really wasn't her business to know.

He'd made some mention of only being informed of her arrival shortly before it had happened and apologized for not being more prepared for guests. All told, he'd been polite enough. There had been a hint of a smile once or twice when they'd been out in the snow, but otherwise he seemed neither pleased nor displeased by the situation thrust upon him. Maybe a bit nonplussed. Then, after he'd given her those few instructions, he'd headed back outside.

She could hardly blame him. It had been on the tip of her tongue during their trek in from the barn, where they'd left Dexter to defrost on his own, to tell her erstwhile host that she'd make other arrangements for her stay.

Katie was the only person Pippa had confided in about her internal struggles, and her youngest sister had repeatedly encouraged her to get away, completely away, from everyone and everything in her regular orbit. Pippa had come to see her point, but had been wrestling with herself on where exactly she should go, and how she should go about doing it. The world was indeed her oyster these days, yet it felt like there was no place to hide.

When the situation with Katie's old college roommate had arisen, Pippa took the spontaneous offer as a sign, and agreed on the spot. She'd freaked out her assistant and her manager by telling them she was going off grid, promising she'd check in from time to time, then had chartered a flight and had been winging her way across the pond before she could change her mind. It had all felt good. Wonderful, in fact.

Until now. She wasn't going to be an imposition on someone, as that wouldn't do either of them any good. And yet, in the end, she hadn't said anything about finding other lodgings. She still wasn't entirely sure why. Her host . . . intrigued her. Yes, that was one way to put it. But her curiosity shouldn't come before being considerate.

A quick look through the spectacular, soaring, two-story window that fronted the chalet showed it was still snowing like mad. "So, I guess it's not something I'm going to be figuring out today." With that knowledge tucked away for now, she turned and took in the rest of her host's lair. It was hard to think of it as anything else. He was a towering giant of a man, at least from her five-foot-two perspective. At well over six feet, with broad shoulders that had blocked the snow, thickly muscled legs that had trenched through hip-deep snow like it was nothing, and hands the size of . . . she broke off in mid thought as a little zip of awareness riffed through her. It had been a good long while since she'd felt that particular kind of tingle.

Of course, that zip would lead to absolutely nothing, save a few delicious dreams, perhaps. Katie had warned her that Moira's big brother was something of a flirt, though of the heart-of-gold variety. Pippa was having a hard time seeing the former, but given he'd rushed out into a snowstorm to save her, the latter did appear to have some basis in reality. Katie had made a point of telling Pippa she didn't want anything to mar the close friendship she and Moira had shared since their early days at university. Pippa had promised her sister that romance was the very last thing on her mind. In fact, though the gossip rags liked to portray her otherwise, she was still the girl from Donegal, and not at all the type for flings.

Fling or not, however, she was intrigued by the place Seth Brogan called home. She took a slow turn and studied the cozy interior. The central area of the chalet was a big, airy space that formed the base of the two-story A-frame. There was a gorgeous stone fireplace and generous hearth to the left with a large woven rug on the hardwood floor in front of it, and a series of leather and what looked like hand-woven fabric couches, chairs, and ottomans positioned in a rough semicircle in front of it. On the other side of the room was an antique potbelly woodstove that looked a lot like the peat stove her grandda had, and a plank-style dining-room table with bench seating on either side and large ladderback chairs at either end. The tabletop was empty save for a fat red candle inside an hourglass-shaped holder in the center, surrounded by a pinecone arrangement. She wondered if he'd styled that, or if someone had done it for him.

The remainder of the open area was taken up by the kitchen, which was fronted by a wide, angled, granite-topped counter that served as both work surface and eating area. Several comfortable padded stools lined the counter on her side, and she could see that a double sink and grill were inset on the far side. Behind that, galley style, a refrigerator, stove, and glass-front cabinets lined the curved outer wall. It was both rustic and elegant, yet quite masculine, she thought. *As was the owner?* "Too soon to tell," she murmured.

Looking up, she took in an enormous ceiling fan that dropped down from a spot just past the apex of the roof. She spied a loft space up there as well that extended out over the kitchen, with a railing made of hand-hewn tree limbs. It was gorgeous and went perfectly with the place. A quick glance around showed no staircase or ladder up to the loft. She looked past the kitchen to the hallway that led to the far section of the house, but it was dark. His bedroom was there, most likely, unless the loft above was a bedroom. She guessed there had to be a way up, but if so, it wasn't obvious, and it wasn't at her end of the house.

The snow had been coming down more heavily as they'd made their way from barn to house, so she hadn't been able to make out much about the architecture from the outside, other than the soaring peak on the front, and a general idea of the overall size. The barn, though, was a stunning piece of stone and wood design she hoped to explore later. She walked over and peered out the front window again, looking toward the barn, but the chill had created a fog in the air, making it hard to see much more than the hulking outline of the place. She couldn't see the vines from here, either, but she knew from her trip up the hill that they covered at least several acres, stretching out behind the barn and marching down the slope behind it in neat, orderly rows. She looked forward to talking to Seth about it. That is, if he planned on actually talking to her at some point.

Her stomach rumbled, reminding her she hadn't eaten since the bagel and tea she'd consumed after she'd woken up on the flight that morning. Taking her host at his word, she poked into the kitchen cupboards, found the pantry behind a small door past the fridge, then took a little tour through the contents of the refrigerator and freezer.

When Seth entered through the mudroom door an hour later, she had a nice Irish stew bubbling on the stove, a fresh pot of tea on the counter close to the stools, and a tray of scones in the oven. She'd been searching the refrigerator for jam when she heard the side door open and leaned back to look toward the mudroom. "Welcome back," she said with a smile.

He didn't respond, but he might not have heard her. He was busy divesting himself of the mound of outerwear he had on, all of it covered with snow. She watched as he took off several layers of gloves, draping them on a rack that had been positioned above a small space heater. He unwrapped and took off the long wool scarf he'd had around his neck; then came the heavy canvas coat. It was only when he removed the monstrosity of fur that covered his head that she completely forgot she was standing in front of an open fridge door. Though the cool air emanating from the interior was suddenly quite welcome.

He was, in a word, stunning. All she'd seen of him during their stint outdoors was a snow-encrusted beard, dark sunglasses, and giant, furry headgear in a swirl of white. As it turned out, under all of that he was . . . well, Thor, the God of Thunder came to mind. His hair was long, very long in fact. As it was damp, it was hard to tell for certain, but dark blond was her guess on the color, maybe with a hint of red thrown in, like in his beard. He had it evenly plaited against the back of his head, falling in one long rope that hung halfway down his back. His back, now facing her, was wide, and ridiculously muscular. He'd pulled off several layers and was down to a thin, dark, soaking wet undershirt that clung to him, outlining every last one of those ridges. God bless it.

Though his shoulders were broad, his waist was narrow, at least by comparison. His hips were straight lines, but even in the canvas pants he wore, which now clung to his legs, when he bent down to unlace the tops of his boots, it was apparent that his thighs were not only large, but also very well defined, as was his nicely curved bum.

He turned then and caught her, dead to rights, staring straight at his ass. Her gaze jerked immediately to his as he straightened, and heat flashed into her cheeks. However, the stormy countenance she'd expected to find was not only shockingly absent, but the flash of white teeth, along with a pair of the most beautiful golden-brown eyes she'd ever seen, stunned her right into very uncharacteristic speechlessness. With the chiseled cheekbones just above the beard, which in and of itself made his curved lips look oh so very sensual, his eyes fair to glowed as he grinned at her. This couldn't possibly be the same man she'd met just hours ago.

"Penguin got your tongue?" he asked, utterly unashamedly, those dazzling, leonine eyes twinkling.

She snapped her mouth closed, realizing only then she'd been gaping. Who could blame her? Holy mother of angels, but he was magnificent. Even that seemed too mild a description. "Possibly," she finally managed, her normal, easygoing cheek having completely deserted her. Seeing his glance move to the open fridge door she was all but hanging on to, she straightened and closed it. "Jam," she said rather obtusely. "For the scones. Do you have any?" *Get it together, lass.*

"Will apple butter do?"

She wrinkled her nose at that. "I'm . . . not sure," she said, as politely as she was able. She'd never had it, or heard of it, but it sounded absolutely horrid.

He chuckled at that, and the transformation continued. Who was this gorgeous, charming man? Not the abominable snowman who'd made that daring rescue attempt, then grumbled his way through their brief exchange before depositing her here. Those brief glimpses of something resembling a smile paled in comparison to the real thing.

"Let me change into some dry clothes and I'll get it for you. I think you'll be a convert. If not, I'm sure Addie Pearl stashed some of her jam in the pantry the last time she was out here."

Pippa didn't know who Addie Pearl was or why she'd been putting things in Seth's pantry, but that wasn't any of her business either. Maybe Katie had gotten it wrong about Seth's relationship status. She'd said he was single, but he was a grown man, after all, so it was unlikely he shared every personal tidbit with his sister, or his family. She certainly didn't.

"Don't go to any bother," she said. "About the jam, I mean. Not about the clothes. You should get out of those."

His eyebrows lifted; then he laughed outright when she blushed so deeply she felt her face grow hot. *Seriously, Pip, this isn't like you one bit.* And it wasn't. She was the one who surprised other people. She could put the most starstruck fan at ease with an easy smile and fast quip, just as she could put the most overly confident lothario in his place with a swift, devilishly concocted response. The kind that left him unable to determine whether he'd been delicately refused or witheringly emasculated until well after she'd made her departure.

Yet here she was, in front of a man who hadn't made any untoward comments or acted in any way other than honorably toward her, who had seemed, until this moment, more put out with her than anything, and she was completely floundering. *Your hormones aren't. They know exactly what they want.* She ignored that. Or tried to,

Apparently somewhere during his time spent out in that storm doing goodness knew what, he'd had a change of heart. She narrowed her gaze on him then, hoping that change of heart hadn't included a change in any other part of his thinking where she was concerned. Since she'd climbed into the spotlight with her music, she'd become very adept at reading people. She'd read him as the stalwart, savior type, the kind of man who'd be far more likely to defend her honor rather than sully it. She was rarely wrong, but it did happen.

"I think I'll go do that," he said, seemingly unfazed by her stare-down. "Would there happen to be enough for two of whatever you've got cooking on the stove there? If it tastes half as good as it smells, I'll make sure you'll never want for jam again."

She smiled at that and his easy humor helped her find her voice again. "There is," she said. "And you've got yourself a deal."

He sat on a stool in the mudroom and started to work the buckles and the rest of the laces on his boots. She opened her mouth to ask if he needed help, then closed it again. She most definitely did not need to be putting herself in his immediate personal space right at that moment. Or maybe any moment. Certainly not until she got her sudden raging case of dumbstruck attraction under control.

"You said to make myself at home, so I hope you don't mind my commandeering your kitchen. If you'd rather I not, let me know what your schedule is, and I'll simply cook around it."

"My schedule is all over the place. Cook anytime you like," he said, then grunted as he tugged the first boot, then the second one free. He set them by the space heater. They looked huge to her.

She looked back to him and found him watching her, his expression still open and easy, but the smile polite now, rather than ragingly sexy.

"Sorry I wasn't more prepared," he said. "You shouldn't have had to do the cooking, at least not after that long flight, and the—" He nodded toward the window and, she assumed, the snow.

She smiled. "It was no bother, really. Though I hope you didn't have plans for that roast in the freezer. I made a pot of beef stew. My gran's recipe. It'll last you a few days. I thought it was the least I could do since you didn't know I was coming. I was going to make some bread, but couldn't find the yeast. So, I made scones."

"You like to cook?"

She smiled then. "You sound surprised."

"No, I just supposed you had someone who did that for you." He smiled before she could form a reply. "Part of that entourage you mentioned earlier."

"Ah," she said. "Right. I do have a few folks to help me manage my daily affairs, but I fend for myself in the kitchen. I like to cook, so that's okay. There are times I've thought it would be lovely to have someone do the laundry and change the beds, though," she added with a smile. "I tried it once, having a housekeeper, I mean. Lovely as she was, it just felt odd having someone about, living under the same roof." Her smile curved into a grin. "I do have a cleaning service that comes in once a week now, if that sounds a bit more star-ish. I just make sure I'm not there when they are, and we all get on quite well."

"Well, I'm not a star of anything but this vineyard, so I don't know what explains the service I use," he said, his expression one of amusement now, "but I agree on the needing to be out when they come in."

And she blushed all over again. "Here I am, thinking I'm putting you at ease, showing you how normal I am, and I'm just digging myself deeper into the hole I started with that snow machine, aren't I?"

"We're all our own brand of normal," he said easily, apparently not offended by her patronizing little speech about how she handled all of the day-to-day details of her oh so entitled life. He got up and walked down the hall toward the set of rooms at the opposite end of the house. "The jam should be on the third shelf down, inside the fridge door. I'll be out in fifteen."

Chapter Four

Six to eight weeks. That would take him well into May, and the beginning of the busy time of year. It could be worse, Seth supposed as he stepped out of the shower and dried off. She could have come during harvest. This would only be his second one, and the first that would produce anything worthwhile, so he was more than a little anxious about every step, including the vine pruning presently going on.

Emile Fournier, the oldest son of a well-known French vintner, had bought—against his family's wishes—the old Dinwiddie dairy farm. Twenty-eight rocky, hilly acres in the mountains of Virginia, which Emile planned to turn into a premier winery, expanding his family's label to the U.S. Unfortunately, after producing only a single season of grapes, he'd been called back to France to run the family empire, an unexpected inheritance. The property had lain dormant, becoming overgrown and neglected, for close to a decade before he had sold the place lock, stock, and wine barrel, happy to be rid of the tax burden, to Mr. and Mrs. Gilbert Bianchi. Gilbert was second generation Italian-American, descended from vintners, who'd had a dream of running his own place. As it was a retirement endeavor, his plans had been far more modest than Emile's. Six to twelve acres of vines at most, using the rest to keep a few farm animals— alpacas, to be specific, because his wife had a soft spot for llamas and because Gilbert thought they could sell the wool. They planned to add a tasting room and develop part of the property as an event venue.

The event venue had been Gilbert's wife, Sarah's, part of the project. She'd told Seth the two of them had thought it would be lovely to spend their twilight years watching young lovers say their I do's, seeing folks celebrate anniversaries, special birthdays, and other occasions. They had no children of their own and were the last in their respective family lines, so they wanted to watch others celebrate their lives, while happily celebrating their own good fortune in doing what they loved.

Then Gilbert had fallen ill before the project had barely gotten off the ground. He hadn't made it to his first harvest. He'd eventually gone into hospice, before passing away barely a year later. Sarah was brokenhearted, and knew she should have sold the place, but hadn't had the heart. She'd passed on shortly after signing the final papers with Seth. She'd asked far less than the property was worth, but had put in a few other stipulations that had caused other potential buyers to back out. Making a profit from the sale hadn't been important, seeing as she had no one to leave it to, but fulfilling her and her late husband's wishes had meant every-thing, right down to the wedding venue and the alpacas. Or llama, as the case may be, seeing as they'd only gotten as far as acquiring Dexter.

Moira was right in saying that now that Sarah Bianchi had passed on, Seth could very likely get those extraneous contract stipulations voided, if he could show just cause. He had no plans to do that.

He rubbed the towel over his face and stared at his reflec-tion in the mirror. It was all the plans he did have that were causing him to lose sleep at night. He'd fulfill the promises he'd made to Mrs. Bianchi, both personally and contractually. At some point. "First, you have to get a crop going that someone wants to buy, and then one you can make wine out of." If that didn't happen, the rest of the promises were moot.

His stomach grumbled as the scents of Irish stew and freshly baked scones mixed with the steam. He'd already figured out where he could move Pippa, and had made a call to put that plan into motion before coming back to the house. Without naming any names, of course. Once he'd had plan B figured out, his mood had lifted considerably. He'd still be responsible for overseeing Pippa's stay, which was overload enough, but he'd manage. Moira wouldn't be happy about him juggling their guest around, but then she hardly had room to complain, now did she?

He pulled on jeans and a well-worn green Henley, then managed to get the tangles out of his wet hair, deciding to leave it loose so it would dry faster. He grinned then, thinking his baby sister had no idea how often he'd thought of shaving his head again. It was just that he rather liked the whole heathen-up-the-hill and Blue Ridge Viking jokes the folks in town teased him with. He liked the relaxed, unregimented lifestyle of mountain life. It was a far cry from the one he'd led while serving in the Army. Much of his other military training stood him in good stead, and he was grateful for it every day of his life, but he was happy to be free of certain rigid codes of conduct.

He grabbed the damp towel and the clothes off the floor, then headed back out to the mudroom, mentally going over the speech he'd prepared to explain to Pippa her upcoming move. Given her confident self-sufficiency, he suspected she'd understand his reasoning. She seemed a pretty decent sort, all in all.

Pippa was nowhere to be seen, however. She'd set a place for him at the bar, with a napkin, an empty bowl, and soup spoon. The pot of stew was still simmering on the stove, and the basket of scones, along with the butter, sat next to his bowl. If she'd eaten already, there were no signs of it. The kitchen was otherwise spotless. Well, at least she was respecting his space, he thought, annoyed that what he felt wasn't relief, but disappointment. And telling himself it was because he wanted to get his little speech out of the way wasn't all that convincing, either. *You either want her here, or you don't, laddie. Make up your mind.*

It just seemed . . . quiet. And he loved the quiet. Revered it, in all honesty. It was a large part of why he'd purchased the property. He could run a business right from his own homestead, but retreat into the peaceful solitude of his home at any time. There were no bombs exploding, no planes buzzing overhead, no missiles whistling in, or out, no guns erupting in a fusillade of bullets, and there would never again be the constant, twenty-four-seven hum of activity that was base living. He didn't suffer PTSD, as many of his compatriots did, not in any crippling sense. But his military experience, largely spent deployed in some of the worst places on earth, had marked him. Inevitably. It was a life experience unlike any other. Add to that, his life before the military had been growing up in a house with five other kids, two parents, two grandparents, one great-grandparent, and numerous house pets. All of which had trained him quite well for the constant chaos of life in uniform, but only added to his desire for serenity now.

Given that, he was content and quite satisfied to be far out and away from all the noise, the clutter, the daily disturbances that came with life, no matter how normal and mundane. He had his vines, a few farm animals, and no one to bother him unless invited to do so. Eventually he'd have people coming to the winery, in a steady stream, he hoped, but even that would be regulated by establishing regular business hours.

His home was, and would always be, his sanctuary. His life was perfect.

"So, sit and enjoy the stew you didn't have to make, and be happy your chatty little houseguest will be moving on as soon as you can dig your way out," he muttered.

Instead, he checked the mudroom, noted the washing machine was empty, as was the dryer, though it was still warm to the touch. He started his own load of clothes, then noticed her bright blue ski jacket was no longer on one of the hooks by the door. And her boots were gone. "Dammit, Pippa," he muttered. He looked back at the place setting, breathed in the mouthwatering scents of the stew, then ducked his chin and sighed. She was a grown woman, with an apparently surprising skill set. He doubted she'd go and do anything that would put her in an adverse situation—*Buried snow machine notwithstanding*, he thought, and grinned despite himself, recalling her insouciant smile when she'd said the same thing.

Still, it was going to be dark soon, and though it looked like the snow had finally stopped, the wind hadn't. The path he'd plowed out earlier, and re-plowed on his way back in earlier, was likely half, if not already fully blown over again. He had floodlights on the house and barn, but that didn't completely ease his mind. He looked from the stew pot to his wet and muddy boots. He really didn't want to go back out there, hadn't planned on it until later that evening, to see to Dex and the rest of his farm animal crew, before holing up in his makeshift office for a few hours.

Swearing under his breath and planning on getting free legal advice from his baby sister for himself and everyone he knew for the rest of her natural life, he walked to the kitchen and packed himself a thermos full of stew, groaning in deep appreciation as he sampled a bite or two before putting the lid back on and turning the burner off. He tossed a few of the scones in a baggie, then quickly pulled on his now toasty socks, the not-so-toasty muddy boots, then opted for his fleece-lined canvas overcoat with the big hood. He wasn't going to be outside any longer than he had to be.

The skies remained overcast, and it was more dark than light by the time he made it out to the barn. There were more lights on inside now than when he'd left earlier, so he supposed that answered the question as to where she'd gone. Pippa must have headed out the moment he went to take his shower, because any tracks she'd made were gone. The wind was still blowing something fierce, making him wish he'd grabbed a scarf to cover his cheeks and beard. Dexter wasn't the only one who needed defrosting after being out in the snow.

He heard the music before he slid open the door, and found himself smiling. *Well, at least Dexter has found a new friend.* He spent a second thinking maybe he should let her stay after all, if for no other reason than to keep his lovelorn llama distracted and out of his hair. Then he stepped inside and stopped dead in his tracks, all thoughts of anything other than the tableau in front of him wiped from his mind.

Pippa was sitting, cross-legged, in the middle of the dirt-and sawdust-covered floor with a pygmy goat curled up in her lap, fast asleep; one of his three barn cats—the gnarly one—rubbing back and forth against her back; while Dexter sat hunkered down in front of her, his long legs folded under himself, so she could comb the soft hair on his neck. She was bopping her head to the pulsing rhythms of "I Wan'na Be Like You" from Disney's *The Jungle Book*, which filled the cavernous barn interior at such decibels that neither human nor beast had so much as looked his way.

The doors to the three stalls on the far side of the barn that presently held the remaining dozen little goats were closed. He'd already checked the henhouse out back before heading in earlier, making sure the heat lamps were on and the chickens were safely inside out of the weather. He'd also checked the small herd of Merino sheep, who were, at the moment, being housed in the big round barn down the hill for the duration of the storm. They'd been fed and watered as well. The only one who hadn't been fed was him. *Well then*, he thought, and quietly let himself into the end stall he still called his temporary office, despite having used it now for a full year. He set down the thermos and baggie, took off his coat and hung it on one of the feed hooks. The barn was heated, but with the wind howling, it remained pretty drafty. So he turned on the small space heater down by his feet before settling in the big leather chair he'd rolled out there when he'd finally accepted he was more comfortable working in the barn than in the space he'd allocated for an office up at the house. For now, anyway.

The chair was positioned at an angle that had his back to the side wall, and afforded him a view of the barn interior, mostly so Dexter could see him rather than the other way around. He stared at the happy cluster of woman and beasts, then, shaking his head, turned to his computer, poured himself some stew, and got to work. Despite the throbbing decibel level of the music, for once he left his headphones lying on the battered wooden door he'd fashioned into a desktop by laying it across two beat-up metal file cabinets. He'd added a few old phone books on top of each cabinet to create the right amount of knee space, which normal desks did not provide. Apparently, men his height didn't hold desk jobs.

He'd long since lost track of time, and might have been bopping his own head and singing "The Bare Necessities" under his breath when he finally heard the knock on the wood beam that framed one side of his stall. He glanced up to find Pippa standing on the other side of the stall door, Mr. Grumpy in her arms looking for all the world like a cosseted house cat, which he was most assuredly not. Seth had the scratch marks to prove it.

"I don't see any signs posted out here for your care and feeding," she said with a smile.

Her hair was down, falling to just below her shoulders, all soft and kind of wild, looking like dark fire. Her skin was paler now, the pink from the storm having faded, which only served to make those eyes of hers all the more luminous. She'd taken off her jacket and wore a formfitting black fleece pullover, and at least one shirt underneath, a mock turtleneck the same shade of blue as her jacket. Boutique skiwear, he thought, wondering if she'd ever worn them for actual skiing. Then he remembered her stunt-training background and gave himself a mental head slap for making gross assumptions based on gender and income. His sisters would have smacked him in far more tender places had he done the same to them.

He was also forced to admit the outfit looked pretty darn good on her. She might be slim bordering on skinny, but he could see now that her brand of skinny was far more on the wiry than the frail side. She had toned shoulders and arms and he suspected the rest of her was more of the same. *All the better to manhandle that snowmobile with*, he reminded himself. *And possibly you, as well.*

Her smile widened at his prolonged gaze, making those eyes sparkle with a hint of mischief, as if she'd read his thoughts. He found himself still wondering about the tips of those ears as he finally looked away. *Faerie sprite, indeed.* He picked up the now empty thermos. "I think you've done just fine in the care and feeding department. It was really good. Thank you."

She dipped in what he assumed was another curtsy, but he could only see her from the cat up, the lower half of her body obscured by the stall door.

"It was the very least I could do. I hope you didn't mind my coming out here. I thought I'd give you your house back

for a bit, come out here and see how Dexter was getting on.
Do you have any others?"

"Others?"

"Llamas," she said. "Don't they do better in groups?"

Seth saved the work he was doing, then leaned back in his
chair. "How is it you know about llamas?" he asked. "Or are
they a part of that star-ish entourage you left back in Ireland?" He grinned when she did, and added, "Even with
four sisters, I'm afraid I'm woefully behind on my celebrity
gossip."

"Four, is it? You poor man. Katie said you and Moira also
come from a big Irish brood. I'm one of six myself, though
it's the other way around for us. I've four brothers. As to my
celebrity star-ish entourage, aye, well, these days we're all
about the cheetahs and lynxes, you know," she said, not
missing a beat. "Big cats are all the rage." She wrinkled her
petite nose. "Last season it was orangutans. I didn't much
care for that phase."

"Yes, well, they can be moody, or so I've heard."

She giggled at that and the sound was a surprisingly delightful little trill, without a hint of the throatiness that was
there when she spoke, or laughed. He immediately wanted
to hear it again. It also made him curious about her music,
what she sounded like as a singer. He'd purposely not gone
and looked her up when he'd settled in to work, focusing on
his never-ending load of paperwork instead. He suspected
he'd give in to the urge sooner rather than later, now.

"Actually, I've learned more than a little bit about llamas
from my assistant, Julia. Her mum raises a whole herd of the
happy beasts up in Clonalvy, north of Dublin." She smiled
when Dexter walked up behind her and bumped his nose
against the side of her head. "I've never met one in person
until now, though. I hope you don't mind my combing his
coat. I saw the bucket with the brush and comb sitting by the
CD player, and he seems to really like it." Dexter bumped

her head a bit more forcefully with his nose this time and she giggled again. "You've had your time now," she told the beast. "I thought they were woolly, like sheep." She stroked Dexter's soft, reddish-brown coat. "I can't believe how soft he is."

"Different breeds have different coats," he said. "He's considered a classic. Their coat is silkier. The other is the woolly. You can't comb them. They have to be sheared."

"So, he's the only one you have then?"

Seth nodded. "Mrs. Bianchi—the woman who owned this place before me—rescued him from a farm down in the valley on the other side of the mountain range. He'd been severely neglected, half-starved, left in a stall by himself with a lot of filth. Don't ever try to put him in a stall," he added, a little abruptly, out of concern for Dexter as much as for her safety. "He's phobic about that."

"Understandably so. That's awful," she said, her expression stricken. "And I won't," she said. "Thank you for telling me."

"I tried to introduce him to a few others from a farmer down closer to the mill, on the other side of Big Stone Creek. He breeds alpacas. Dexter is on the small side for a llama, and alpacas are a smaller breed than llamas. He's a gelding, and Tom has geldings, so I thought it might be a good fit, and if so, I'd buy a few and bring them up here."

"But . . . no?" she asked.

Seth shook his head. "Not even close. Freaked him right out."

"Aw," Pippa said, turning to give Dexter a gentle hug. "That's awful."

"I don't know his full story, other than what I told you, and unfortunately, Mrs. Bianchi has since passed away, but Tom, the alpaca breeder, suggested maybe I should let Dex work as herd security. He said that maybe having a job of sorts where he has something to do would help him emotionally, and one that establishes a pecking order that doesn't threaten him in any way would be a start. I did some reading on that and thought he might be right."

"You mean he takes care of the little goats?" Her face lit up. "How adorable is that?"

Seth shook his head. "Well, not yet, anyway. From what I read, I thought sheep would work better. They're housed in the round barn down the hill right now because of the storm. Otherwise, though, they're out to pasture, and Dex is out there watching over them for parts of the day. We don't have a coyote issue at the vineyard, at least not since I've been here, so the flock isn't really threatened, but Dex doesn't know that. Otherwise he's in his own paddock or in here with me. He'll eat too much if he stays in the fields all day." He lifted a shoulder. "It's not the optimal setup, for him or for me, but it works for now, and he seems happy enough." He glanced at Dex. "Maybe over time we can find him a buddy closer to his own size."

"So, you didn't already have them? The sheep I mean. You bought him his own herd?"

Seth smiled briefly. "I made a promise that I'd take care of him. It works, and they're not too much trouble. I actually have a few local kids who come up and help out with them. The Bluebird ladies will come do the shearing when it's time, and I let them keep the wool for their projects. It just sort of works itself out."

"The Bluebird ladies?"

"An artists' guild that works out of a restored silk mill down in Blue Hollow Falls. Long story," he said with another smile. "I imagine you'll meet them at some point."

"I'm looking forward to it," Pippa said, and so sincerely he suspected it would end up happening before too long. Pippa turned to the llama and juggled the cat in her arms so she could give him a proper salute. "Sergeant Dexter of the Royal Sheep Guard, sir," she said proudly.

Seth could have sworn Dexter stood a little taller at that, and smiled to himself.

"So, who did you buy the goats for?"

Seth looked at Pippa, a smile playing around his mouth. "What makes you think I bought them for anyone? Maybe they came with the place, like your pal, Sergeant Pepper, there."

Pippa set the cat down, then straightened and folded her arms on the top of the stall door, her smile bemused. "Let's call it a hunch."

He held her gaze for a long moment, then looked back to his computer screen and punched a few buttons. Not for any actual purpose other than to keep her from reading him like a book, which was apparently another one of her super-powers. "They were a Christmas present for the sister of a friend of mine," he admitted.

"The whole lot of them?" Pippa asked, sounding surprised.

He glanced at her and chuckled. "I bought a whole herd of sheep for a llama, but you're surprised I bought a handful of goats for a ten-year-old girl?"

"She's just ten?" Pippa's expression softened. "Why goats?"

"Long story, but Bailey—my friend's step-sister, and my friend as well—has had an . . . unconventional life. She had goats at one point, and Sunny, her half-sister, got her a few small-breed sheep last year, which Bailey keeps at her place. Well, Addison Pearl's place, which is now Bailey's home as well. Addie Pearl sort of adopted Bailey when an inheritance here brought Bailey's existence to light. She was in foster care before that." He smiled at Pippa's look of confusion. "It's an unusual family tree, but Addie, Sawyer—the friend I was referring to—along with Sunny, and Bailey, were scattered all over before the inheritance of the old mill brought them all together. Now they all live here in Blue Hollow Falls. Still unconventional, I guess, but it works."

"Sounds really nice, actually. And Bailey has a true home now. That's all that matters."

Seth nodded. "Bailey and the son of another friend of mine come up here to help with my sheep a few days a week after school and on most weekends. Bailey loves her sheep, and she takes wonderful care of mine, but I knew she missed her little goats, so . . ." He lifted a shoulder. "I have plenty of room, and if you have a few sheep, then what difference do a few goats make, you know?"

Pippa beamed at that. "What difference, indeed. Katie told me you were starting up a winery here. How do you manage that as well as all the animals? You have your hands full, then, don't you?"

He smiled broadly. "You haven't met the chickens yet." Before she could ask, he said, "Those I got for me. And maybe for another friend of mine. He's starting a micro-brewery and he wanted heritage chickens for his hops yard."

"Of course he did," Pippa said, as if that made perfect sense.

"I found a few more than he needed, and I've always wanted farm fresh eggs, so win-win."

She rested her chin on her folded arms, then batted her eyelashes at him. "You know, I've always wanted a Shetland pony. Since I was a wee little lass."

He grinned and shook his head. "I believe you're in a position to have whatever you want. You don't need me for that."

Her expression changed then, though he couldn't have said exactly to what. It was still soft, still amused, but considering now, as well. She regarded him for a long moment like that, without saying anything, then straightened as the music shut off, creating something of a deafening vacuum with the sudden absence of noise. "I'll dig the snowmobile out in the morning," she said, still smiling, but sounding more the polite houseguest now.

It should have been a relief. No point in getting chummy. Especially as he hadn't mentioned her new housing plan as yet. But, like finding the house empty when he got out of the shower, her words had the opposite effect.

"I'll get in touch with Mr. Jenkins, too, to see about returning it," she went on. "Now that the snow has stopped, do you think the roads will be passable sometime tomorrow? Or is there more coming?"

"No, the snow is done. In fact, I was just checking the weather, and it looks like the temperatures are going to bounce pretty hard in the opposite direction." Which would turn the winter wonderland out there into a mud swamp, but one problem at a time. "I expect the roads should be clear by late morning," he said. "The wind is supposed to die down tonight, too, so the drifting should stop. It will anyway, once the snow heats up tomorrow and starts to get heavy with melt. If the road crews don't get up here early, I can plow down to Mabry's place if need be."

"Of course you can," she said easily, dry smile curving her pursed lips again. Her gaze, however, remained contemplative. She stepped back from the stall door. "I'll leave you to your work, then. I've intruded enough for one day. I hope you didn't mind my coming out here. It's such a beautiful structure, reminds me of the crofts around our old farm outside of Donegal. I just wanted to see more of it, see how Dex was getting along with the melt. I thought maybe I could help there."

"No, that's fine," he said. "I appreciate it, and clearly Dex is a fan."

Pippa smiled and turned to look at the llama, who had wandered back to his corner of the barn and was munching on his supper. She looked back at Seth and said, "Good.

Well, I can find my way back to the house." She turned to go, then stepped back to the door. "Are you an early riser?"

Momentarily surprised, Seth nodded. "If you consider six in the morning early. I'll try not to make too much noise."

"Do you like your porridge with currants or without?"

"I like my currants without porridge, actually," he said, his tone dry now. "And you can hold the currants." They both smiled at that, but he went on before she could speak. "You don't need to cook breakfast, not for me, at any rate. You're a guest, and you're here to rest, or unwind, or whatever it was you came here needing to do. I imagine it didn't include helping with a menagerie of farm critters or pulling KP duty for your host."

"KP?"

"Kitchen patrol."

"Ah. Well, I don't mind doing either thing, but that's very kind of you," she said. "Especially when you weren't anticipating my arrival."

"No worries," Seth said, smiling as she nodded and turned to go. He looked back to his computer screen, clicked open the mail program, checking for that reply from the wholesale distributor that still hadn't shown up. *You might want to tell her she's not going to be staying with you much longer*, his little voice prompted him. He decided he had plenty of time in the morning to broach that subject. He was still waiting to hear from Noah, anyway, on the cabin rental.

"The thing is," she said, leaning back so she could look into the stall, "I rather liked cooking dinner. If it's not a bother, I'll put together a big American-style breakfast for you then. What, like eggs, bacon? You Yanks like potatoes with your morning meal, is that right? If you don't mind, it will make me feel useful, and it's one less thing for you to do. You can get right on with your day."

Seth looked at her. It had been on the tip of his tongue to tell her he wasn't in the habit of having a big breakfast.

Normally a strong pot of coffee and an egg sandwich or two and he was good till he came in from morning rounds. But the look on her face was so damn hopeful. And he supposed, if she truly wanted to, it would give her something to do and would allow him the chance to get out the door without her following him out to the barn. "That would be fine then," he said. "I appreciate the gesture. Thank you."

She beamed and she might have curtsied again, being cute. "My pleasure, kind sir."

"Don't worry about the snowmobile, by the way," he called out as she skipped off. "I'll pull it out with the tractor."

She stepped back to the stall door. Again. And he wondered if he was telling her this now because he thought it needed to be said, or because he was putting off her going back to the house. And leaving him in the barn with a now dozing Dexter and a bunch of sleeping goats. Which was normally one of his favorite times of the day.

"With it getting warm tomorrow, the drifts will be heavy as they melt," he told her. "I'd rather you leave it to me."

She nodded. "Sounds like the wise choice. I am sorry for the bother though."

"No bother. When we go down to get your things, Mabry can hitch a ride back up and drive the snowmobile back down to his farm while we still have enough snow to run it."

Her expression fell at that.

"You were hoping to return it yourself, were you?" he asked, unable to keep the smile from his face. She looked so sincerely forlorn. *God, you really are a sucker for a pitiful look, aren't you?*

"I thought it would be the right thing to do," she said. "One less thing for you. I could head down, have a chat with Mr. Jenkins, maybe see a bit of his place. Then you could bring me and my baggage back up when you've the time to come down and round us up."

"That could be arranged, too." He didn't bother to tell her

that Mabry was likely every bit as busy as he was this time of year. He suspected the older man would be perfectly happy to lose a half day's work if it meant he would be entertained by a lovely and lively guest. Heck, the man had given her his snowmobile after knowing her a mere minute or two. *All the more reason to get her tucked up in Noah's cabin, as soon as possible.*

"Brilliant. Thank you," she said; then she popped off again. He heard the sound of the barn door sliding open, then closed. And once again, he was finally, blissfully, at peace.

He stared at his computer screen, but didn't start typing. He picked up his thermos, remembered he'd finished off the whole thing, and set it back down. The scone baggie was empty, too. He thought about getting up to turn on the coffeepot, but didn't. He turned his attention back to his computer again, but a full minute went by and he realized he was staring at the screen. It was just, the sudden peace and quiet felt really . . . quiet. *Maybe you have been living alone a little too long.*

He looked at his cell phone, thinking maybe he'd call Noah and follow up on his earlier message. Noah owned and ran Blue Hollow Falls' only inn, a very popular spot not too far from Big Stone Creek. He'd recently purchased an old fishing cabin from another friend of Seth's, higher up in the hills, not too far from Seth's vineyard. Noah had renovated and outfitted the tiny place as another rental option for guests who really wanted to get away from it all. It was rustic but well appointed, and Pippa wouldn't have to worry about anyone bothering her, or finding out where she was. And it was close enough that checking in on her wouldn't be too problematic. Seth doubted anyone was in it now, with all the late season snow. If his scheme worked out, he could pick Pippa up from Mabry's and take her right on up to the cabin.

Except, he didn't pick up the phone.

Seth looked across the open floor of the barn area to the opposite corner. He'd removed the doors to two stalls and torn down the wall between them, creating a sort of open-sided area that Dexter could claim for himself, without being shut in. The beast was currently giving him a mournful stare.

"She'll be back in the morning," Seth called over to him. "I've a feeling you'll be hard-pressed to get rid of her."

Question was, why was he so hard-pressed to do the same?

Chapter Five

"Fourth generation," Pippa exclaimed, flipping another page in one of Mabry Jenkins's photo albums. "That's a lovely thing, isn't it?"

"It'll go on through the sixth if my daughter has her way," the older man said proudly. "Maggie's talking her husband into moving out here so she can take over for me when the time comes. He's some kind of computer genius, provides real well for his family, but he works from home more than not these days. She's my only one, so it's her or nothing, I'm afraid. My brother ran this place with me his whole adult life. Never did have any kids of his own. He was five years my junior, but he's passed on now. Three years before my wife, God rest them both." Mabry turned the page. "My daughter has two boys." He pointed a gnarled finger at a recent addition to the scrapbook. "That's her there with her husband." He flipped the page and pointed to another photo. "These are my grandsons. Twins, don't you know," he added, his love for them clear in his voice. "I figure one of 'em might want the place when their time comes."

Pippa looked up from the grinning, towheaded young men, each sporting a different university logo on the front of his hoodie, and smiled at Mabry. "You can't ask for a better legacy than that, now, can you?"

"No," he said, "no, you certainly can't." He closed the book and set it back on the coffee table. "Farming isn't like it used to be when I was coming up, but apples are about as sure a crop as you can get around here." He smiled, showing a few gaps here and there, his pale blue eyes a bit faded but otherwise still sharp. "My daughter knows all the ins and outs, of course, seeing as she helped run this place from the time she could walk. She'll do fine. Place runs itself more than not these days."

Pippa seriously doubted that. She knew for a fact that Mr. Jenkins did a fair share himself, as she'd found him in one of his outbuildings when she'd arrived that morning, lying half underneath a tractor he was bent on repairing. He'd finished that and dragged what he'd told her was a hay baler to the middle of the space and set to working on that next, and after that he started on some other engine he had up on a sawhorse. He wasn't a particularly big man, but time had stooped his spine a bit, and the fingers on his hands were no longer as straight as they'd probably once been. Yet he worked along as if he was a man half his age, lifting heavy equipment, dragging it where it needed to go, crawling over or under it as needed, fixing what was broken, all the while keeping up a running conversation with her. After all that, he'd asked her in for some tea as if he'd done nothing more than water a few plants. He'd tired her out just watching him.

She'd offered to park the snowmobile in the barn, but he said he'd be using it later to go out and check on his trees and repair some fencing the snow had knocked down. She didn't doubt for a second he could do all that and more before lunch.

"What brings you out to Blue Hollow Falls?" he asked her. "From the sounds of it, I'm guessing you don't live around here."

Pippa laughed. "No, I don't, but I'm beginning to envy those of you who do. I'm over from Dublin for a bit of an adventure," she told him. "I'm originally from Donegal, though, clear across the country. They've a good farming community there, too. Reminds me a bit of here, at least what I've seen so far."

"Not much to see with all the white stuff out there," Mabry told her. He stood slowly and ran his palms over his hips before stepping out from around the small coffee table. He wore denim overalls with several layers of shirts beneath and a red-and-black plaid flannel shirt as the outer layer. His skin was weathered and wrinkled, and there were age spots as well, but he had a solid look to him, with a shock of white hair on his head and a quick, ready smile.

Pippa had liked him on sight. "I don't get to see snow much, so this was a pleasant surprise."

"It'll be gone soon enough. Weather report's calling for sixty-degree weather and a good bout of rain headed our way. It'll be muddier than a cow herd in a pond before you know it, and we'll be wishing this white stuff was back, covering it all up."

Pippa stood, too, realizing she was keeping him from his work. His place was far more modest than the showcase style of Seth's vineyard chalet. A white clapboard frame with a pitched, tin-covered roof, the house had a small entryway and living room area. The dining room was off to one side, with a little kitchen beyond, and a staircase leading up to what she assumed were a few bedrooms was on the other side of the foyer.

It was all quaintly old-fashioned, tidily furnished and decorated, with the small, floral patterned couch they'd been seated on, a recliner nearby that clearly saw much use, and a coffee table with its fancy bent legs between the two. A basket full of magazines and a standing lamp were positioned next to the recliner and a small bookshelf crammed full of paperbacks and a few hardcovers was just behind it. She smiled at the old-fashioned television with the long antennae going this way and that. It sat on a small, rolling stand next to the fireplace. It was just like the one her grandda had had in his croft at home.

There were framed photos on the mantel and dotting the open spaces on the wall between other framed prints. More photos lined the wall all the way up the stairs. Some were black and white, some in color. She recognized his daughter in many of them and spied photos of his grandchildren at various ages.

Pippa assumed all the knickknacks scattered about had belonged to his wife. Most men she knew weren't keen on gewgaws, much less the dusting they required, so she thought it was sweet that he'd left them all there. And she noted there wasn't a speck of dust around them, either. If she hadn't already liked the man, that would have cemented him as a friend for life.

She picked up their teacups and carried them to the kitchen.

"Just leave those in the sink there," Mabry said. "Thank you."

She came back to the living room and picked up her jacket. "I don't want to keep you any longer than I have already," she said. "Thank you for the loan, and the conversation."

"World would go much better if we all took a moment for a cup of tea and spent a minute talking to each other. Thanks for listening to this old man ramble on about his life. I'm sure you have better things to do."

"It was my absolute pleasure. I'd almost think you had some Irish in you," Pippa added with a smile. "You make a good pot of tea."

He beamed at that. "My wife's ancestors hailed from Wales, so she was a teetotaler herself. Got me to drinking the stuff when I couldn't handle the coffee any longer." His smile spread, making the corners of his eyes crinkle. "Credit for any brewing skills go to her."

Pippa's smile softened. "I wish I could have met her."

Mabry nodded. "Annie would have loved hearing you talk, that's for certain."

Pippa laughed at that, delighted by his frankness, and Mabry chuckled along with her. "Seth should be here shortly," she said. "I truly appreciate your holding on to my bags for me." Mabry had helped her haul them to the porch earlier, where they stood in a neat stack.

"Looks like you're fixing to stay on a bit," he said. "How did you come to know Seth? If you don't mind my asking."

Pippa smiled, thinking that Blue Hollow Falls wasn't much different from the wee village where she'd grown up. Folks back home were sincerely friendly, always helpful, and not a little nosy. She suspected Mr. Jenkins was more interested in looking out for the well-being of his neighbor than motivated by the desire for gossip. But she was equally certain that whatever was said between them here this morning would end up being common knowledge in town, likely before lunch.

Despite her intention to remain "under the radar," as her sister Katie had termed it, Pippa wasn't alarmed by that probability. In fact, she felt surprisingly comforted by it. She had no doubt that if Mabry Jenkins thought she needed safeguarding, he'd be as stalwart a protector as she'd find anywhere. She couldn't say that for certain about the rest of the townsfolk, given she hadn't met any of them yet, but she knew that while her own villagers back home might feast on gossip as heartily and regularly as they did on tea and scones, they also held that same information closely among themselves. Katie had said Moira promised it would be much the same way in Blue Hollow Falls.

"We just met yesterday," Pippa told him, her smile widening when his snowy eyebrows climbed. "I'm doing a bit of a house swap with Seth's sister Moira. She'll be staying at a croft I own in the village where I was raised, and I'll have the privilege of staying here, at a vineyard in these beautiful, snow-capped mountains." She leaned in, as if sharing a secret. "I don't mind telling you, as lovely as County Donegal is, I think I might have scored the better end of the trade."

Mabry chuckled at that. "You might have enjoyed it more if you'd come a month or two from now," he said. "I don't know how lovely it will all look to you when it's covered in mud."

"If I'm lucky, I hope to see it through to the first blooms of spring."

Mabry's eyes widened even further at that, and not a little concern tinged his features.

"Will that be a problem?" she asked. "I know Seth wants to help his sister by making this swap happen, but please tell me if there's something I should know." She smiled. "Truth be told, I don't think he learned about this swap himself until just very recently." Her smile turned wry. "Possibly right before my snow-covered arrival. But I don't want to be a nuisance," she hurried to add. "I can make other lodging arrangements."

She was hoping she wouldn't have to do that, though. She felt . . . better, already. Content. Settled. Or the beginnings of all those things, at least. She was happy for the escape from the chaos, the pressures, and the endless chatter and speculation that was her present day-to-day life.

Mabry waved a hand. "I don't think that will be necessary." Now he leaned forward, as if also sharing a secret, his own smile a bit mischievous, which charmed her right to the core. "It's not for me to say, of course, but I think our Mr. Brogan could do with a spot of sunshine such as yourself. Boy works himself too hard."

Pippa laughed at that, though given what she knew of Seth's acquired menagerie, the news didn't surprise her.

"That's very kind of you to say. I've offered to help out," she added, "but perhaps I'd just be in the way."

"It may not seem it, but this is a busy time for him, too," Mabry told her, "tending the vines, prepping them for spring. Spring, then, is a whole other thing entirely. It's the busiest time, second only to harvest, and I know this season is a critical one for him, seeing as he's just getting the place off and running."

"Oh, I see. I didn't know that," she said, feeling a bit shamed by focusing so strongly on her own needs that she really hadn't truly considered the cost to Seth. "Maybe it's best if I do make other arrangements, then." She tamped down a wave of disappointment. *You're not the only one with life problems that need sorting out.*

Mabry gave her a critical once-over, looking a wee bit disappointed himself. "We've got a nice inn in town that would probably suit you just fine."

"Thank you," she said, resigned to the decision. "I appreciate that." She didn't want to be in an inn with other guests, no matter how lovely it might be. She'd have to do a little research, see if she could find some other rental property that was more secluded.

"But, if you mean what you say," Mabry went on, pulling her from her musings, "about pitching in, well, maybe what Seth really needs is to not look a gift horse in the mouth, if you understand my meaning."

Pippa smiled, flattered by his persistence. "That's kind of you, but, in all honesty, I know nothing about vineyards, much less making wine."

"You said you grew up on a farm? I can't imagine sheep or goats are much different from one place to another. He's got more than a few of both. Two local kids come up to help, but it would free him up a bit not to have to deal with the livestock." He looked at her and she thought that though his eyes might be a bit dim with age, they still saw things quite clearly. "He's not only single-handedly building up his own business, but also helping Sawyer and the others with the silk mill renovation, which put him further behind."

"Silk mill," she repeated, surprised and intrigued. "Out here?"

Mabry nodded. "Long since defunct. They've completely renovated the old place, turned it into what they call an artisan community center, or some such. Thanks in large part to Addie Pearl—I'm sure you'll meet her sooner than later—Blue Hollow Falls has more than its fair share of artists and crafters in residence. She's a weaver, but we've got carvers, musicians, painters, soap- and candlemakers, even a fellow who works with glass blowing and the like. All part of our Bluebird Crafters' Guild."

"That must be what Seth meant by the Bluebird ladies," she said, and Mabry nodded. "He mentioned they come up and sheer his sheep in trade for the wool. So, it's a whole community. How lovely," Pippa said. Somewhere inside her, a little ache formed, or maybe it was a bit of yearning. Life here was calling to her more strongly by the moment.

"I wish my Annie had lived long enough to see that," Mabry said. "She made lace, you see. By hand. Tatting, she called it. Learned it from her Welsh grandmother. She'd have loved having a place to work with others, maybe even sell a piece." He shook his head, but smiled in reminiscence. "It's a worthy endeavor, at any rate. Just opened and it's already bringing some much-needed life to this area, in a way that doesn't compromise what we stand for. My orchard here will benefit from the flow of new visitors, as will Seth's winery once it's up and producing. None of it would have been possible but for Sawyer Hartwell, and folks like Seth, and Wilson McCall, who gave their time, skill, and energy to make it all happen. Now it's Seth's turn to make his own place into something special."

"Sounds like a wonderful town here, with you all looking

out for each other, pitching in. My childhood home was like that." She smiled with her own reminiscence, grateful for those particular memories. It had been a long time since she'd thought about that time in her life.

Mabry looked directly at her. "But a man's life can't be all about work, you understand?"

Pippa laughed then. "Are you trying to play matchmaker?"

"Are you attached?" he asked, and she shook her head, laughing again. He went on before she could gently explain that she wasn't here looking for a beau. "You're a breath of fresh air, Miss Pippa MacMillan," he went on. "I don't claim to know everything, or even a little about most things, but I do know something about family, and life. You're both looking like you could use a bit of each at the moment."

Touched, she said, "That's very sweet of you. We'll see how things work out." She didn't want to get the older man's hopes up, but a bit of life and family sounded just about perfect to her right now. "If I do end up staying on, perhaps you can come up and join us for supper one night? I'd have to check with Seth, but I make a pretty decent Irish stew, and a downright sinful shepherd's pie."

Mabry hooted out a little laugh. "That's what I want to hear. And you know what? I just might do that. You name the night and I'll get myself on up there. Truth be told, I've been itching to see what he's done to the place. I'll admit, I never did cotton to the man who bought Dinwiddie's old dairy farm way back when with an idea to growing grapes there. Not that he bothered to spend a minute meeting any of his neighbors. Then he up and went right back to France before barely harvesting a single crop, leaving the place to go straight to seed. Lovely couple eventually purchased the property. I came around to seeing their vision for the place, and Annie was downright tickled. Such a shame, what happened to them, him passing on before he'd even got his first harvest, her following him so soon after." He shook his head and sighed. "But I believe all things happen as they do for a reason. There's a greater plan going on, and your Mr. Brogan is exactly what that place needed, at exactly the right time. He'll do right by it. I can feel it."

Pippa wanted to tell him that Seth wasn't "her" anything, but she hoped Mabry was right. *Maybe this place is exactly what you need, at exactly the right time, too.* "Sounds like the vineyard is due for some good luck for a change," she said, pushing that thought aside.

Mabry nodded. "You planning on getting yourself a set of wheels while you're out here? I've got an old farm truck you can borrow, if need be."

"Oh, that's very dear of you to offer. I had a leased vehicle all lined up, but then I landed and saw all the snow and decided that sporty little car wouldn't get me very far. All the four-wheel-drive vehicles were gone, so I just hired a driver to get me this far and thought I'd figure it out from there. We drive on the other side of the road back at home, and the truth of it is, these days I don't actually do a lot of driving. And I've never driven in snow. So, maybe it's best to wait and start up when the conditions have improved."

Mabry smiled. "Sun's out for now, and the temperatures are up. Between the plowing and the sun, should be all clear out there shortly. Rain coming will take care of the rest. We don't get much traffic up this way. Would be good roads to get some practice on. I've a feeling after seeing you handle that snowmobile, you'll do just fine." He winked at her. "You come on down when you're ready and we'll go for a spin. I taught my daughter and both my grandsons to drive. I can teach you, too."

Pippa beamed. "You know, I believe I'll take you up on that! If you're sure you have the time." She picked up the pad of paper that sat by the old-fashioned black telephone and wrote down her number. "Call me if or when you do and it's a date." On impulse, she gave him a quick hug, lifting up on her toes to add a peck on his cheek. "Thank you, Mr. Jenkins. My dad would be happy to know I've got you looking out for me."

It was hard to tell on those weathered cheeks, but she was pretty sure he blushed, which charmed her all the more.

"Get Seth to take you on into town, introduce you to everyone," Mabry said. "We always enjoy talking to someone with a story to tell. I'm sure they'll want to hear tales of your home, and they'll share a few of theirs."

"I can't think of a better way to spend an afternoon," she said, meaning it.

The sound of a large truck engine rumbled outside.

"I think my ride is here." She grinned. "Thank you again for the loan, and the driving lessons."

"I'm guessing you won't need but one, but I'm always happy to help. And the offer of the truck loan stands, too. Don't go spending money on something you can borrow. Save your pennies for something you need."

Pippa nodded. "Sound advice." She liked to think that despite her newfound stability where money was concerned, she'd retained the frugal mindset she'd been raised with. Her parents worked hard for what they had, and had taught her to do the same. It had taken a few years before her parents—her father in particular—would allow her to help them along, as she was more than able to do now. She'd explained that they'd given her the foundation upon which to thrive, so the least she could do was thank them in kind.

She was still fairly certain her father was embarrassed by the things she'd done to help her family, but seeing how delighted her ma had been with a new dishwasher, and a car that didn't have faulty windows, he'd succumbed and been gruffly thankful. She would have bought them a whole new house if they'd let her, but understood his pride couldn't handle such a thing.

Pride was a tricky thing. Being here, in Mr. Jenkin's

modest home, seeing how hard he worked for what he had, she knew if she asked him, he'd say he wanted for nothing. What he had functioned, and if it didn't, she suspected he'd fix it until it simply couldn't be repaired again. Her father was exactly the same way. She, on the other hand, could lease an entire fleet of cars if she wanted to, without even having to consult her business manager. That she had a business manager at all said everything that needed saying on that point, really.

While she didn't want to borrow something that Mr. Jenkins might be needing, she understood there was pride at stake here, too. She knew it likely made Mabry feel good to think he was helping out a young lass, as it would if it were her father making the offer to one of her friends. His simple offer also made her realize that perhaps she'd grown more accustomed to her newfound lifestyle than she'd realized. It was humbling, and she thanked him for that reminder, too.

"If you can honestly spare it," she said, "then I'd appreciate the loan a great deal. Perhaps if you need anything in town, I could run errands for you?" She smiled. "I always like to help out where I can, too."

"That I can see. It's an admirable trait that will do you well." He smiled and walked to the front door as they heard Seth's boots on the porch. "I think we might be able to work something out."

Mabry opened the door for her in time to see Seth with two of her bags propped on his broad shoulders, and another under one arm, and two more, one in each hand. Her breath caught a little, surprising her. Not because she was stunned by the load he'd hefted as if it were nothing, but because the sight of him quite literally took her breath away. He was a towering pillar of a man, sturdy-legged, narrow-hipped, and oh so broad shouldered. His long hair was loose today, and flowed in uneven waves down past his shoulder blades. In the bright sunshine, she saw now that the dark blond did in fact have more than a fair share of red in it, which was the main color of his beard. A mountain man, indeed.

Her mind flashed on how it had felt when he'd put those big hands of his on her, so gently supporting her when she'd gotten winded and a bit light-headed. What he'd looked like, fresh from the shower, then later, out in the barn, sitting in that stall he'd converted into an oddball, makeshift office. He'd looked all fierce and focused as he typed things on the keyboard with remarkable lightning-swift speed, eyeing the monitor as if daring it not to show him the results he was looking for.

"That boy could carry the world on his shoulders; I'm fair convinced of it," Mabry said. "I told him they must grow them like the redwoods out west."

Pippa laughed at that, even as other parts of her body were reacting to the sight of Seth with a surge of unmitigated want. "He must have eaten all of his spinach as a boy." She glanced at Mabry, who arched a surprised snowy eyebrow. "We know Popeye over in Ireland. My brothers were big fans of the sailor man. They saw the movie version as kids, and some friends of ours sent them some of the original cartoons on VHS tapes. They watched those things endlessly."

Mabry nodded. "Did you know that the voice actor who did Popeye for more than forty years married the woman who did Olive Oyl?"

Now Pippa's eyebrows rose in surprise. "Is that right? How lovely!" She nudged him with her elbow. "You're a softy, is what you are, Mabry Jenkins. A true romantic. I'm betting your wife would be fast to agree with me."

"Falling in love is one of the best things we do," he told her plainly, blue eyes alight as he did. "You can do a lot in life, but none so great as that." Now he nudged her and gave her another wink. "I'm here to tell you, it's even better if they fall right back."

Pippa was still laughing when she turned to cross the porch, and walked smack into a wall of Seth. He caught her by the elbows and steadied her.

Flustered, and by far more than the accidental collision, Pippa opted to play the ham to cover it. With Seth still holding her, she arched her head back in a dramatic pose and blew a kiss at Mabry. "Until we meet again."

The older man surprised her by sketching a short bow. "I look forward to it, m'dear. You kids enjoy the rest of the day." He looked at Seth. "You take care of this one, you hear?"

Seth looked between the two as Pippa straightened, then gave a slight shake of his head as if he wasn't quite sure what he'd stumbled into, but whatever it was, he'd clearly missed the thread. "I think she does a pretty good job of taking care of herself," he told Mabry kindly, and when the older man just fixed him with a steady look, Seth chuckled and added, "But I'll do my best. I appreciate your helping out like you did."

"Not a problem," the older man said. "Happy to lend a hand."

Pippa waited for Seth to give the older man a hard time about the snowmobile loan, but he merely nodded, then guided her down the recently shoveled and salted front steps, hand still firmly under her elbow. The sun was out in full now, making the snow an almost blinding sea of crystalline white. She noted that Mabry was right. With the sun on them, the plowed drive and road had already mostly melted, revealing the gravel and mud underneath.

Seth helped her up into the cab of the enormous pickup truck, then closed the door and headed around the back before she could say thank you. Instead she waved to Mabry, who was still standing on the porch, then settled her seat belt across her chest and lap as Seth climbed in and did the same. They were on the road heading on up the mountainside a moment later.

"Looks like you've made another friend," Seth said.

"He's a lovely man," Pippa replied as she took in the surrounding countryside. It was breathtaking all covered in white. The mountains had been shrouded in heavy cloud cover and fog the day before. She'd had no idea how stunning the view truly was. "It's incredibly beautiful up here," she said. "The view from your chalet must be impressive indeed."

"Chalet?"

She glanced at him. "All wood and glass, sitting on a mountaintop. What would you call it?"

He shrugged and nodded in conciliation. "I just call it home."

"Was that the house that was there when you bought the place? Seems fairly modern for the older couple who lived on the vineyard before you. Mabry told me about them," she added, when he looked surprised. "Did the owner before that build it? The man who bought the place when it was a dairy farm?"

"You had quite the conversation," Seth said, and she just smiled sweetly at him. He smiled as well, shook his head, then looked back to the road. "Well, the original farmhouse, back when the acreage was used as a dairy farm, is gone now. That happened before I was born. All that's left of it are the stone barn and the round barn, and a few other smaller outbuildings scattered over the property."

"Mabry said he wasn't too fond of the man who bought the farm from Mr. Dinwiddie," Pippa commented. "Said he didn't even bother getting to know his neighbors."

"Emile Fournier," Seth said, nodding. "I don't think he bothered to make many friends in the area. It was strictly a business setup for him, no house on the property. Fournier planted twenty full acres of vines, with plans to expand from there. I think he intended to tear down the rest of the structures, too, but he didn't get that far. When the Bianchis bought the place, it had been sitting for a very long time, more than a decade."

"Mabry told me he and his wife, Annie, liked the Bianchis quite a lot," Pippa said. "Mabry hadn't been too fond of the vineyard plan before then, but said their enthusiasm changed his mind."

Seth nodded. "The Bianchis were the ones who built the house. Chalet," he corrected himself, shooting her a fast grin. "I never met Gilbert Bianchi, but his wife, Sarah, told me he was a big fan of Frank Lloyd Wright. She loved the mountain homes out west where they'd vacationed in the past, so the house was some compromise between the two. Gilbert was a retired surgeon and Sarah was a horticulture illustrator. Some of her work is still in the house."

"Are those the prints in my room? They're lovely. Wow. I'll have to look her up now. That's really something."

Seth nodded. "She was also an heiress, modest money, or at least that's what she said. So, between the two, finances were never a concern. The vineyard was really sort of a retirement dream of Gilbert's, and Sarah had always wanted to play around with event planning, weddings and the like. Gilbert's ideas were far more modest than Emile's. I think the Bianchis envisioned it more as an event venue."

"I'm glad you kept the stone barn," she said. "It's a beautiful structure."

"I think so, too," Seth said. "I have Gilbert to thank for that. He was a history buff and respected the land and what came before. He's responsible for renovating both the bluestone barn and the round barn, or hiring the companies who did. He used local labor where possible, which endeared him immediately to the folks here. I named the winery Bluestone & Vine in part because of that barn. It'll be the tasting room, eventually."

"How perfect," she said, delighted. "And the round barn?

You mentioned it last night. Where is it? I don't think I've ever seen one before."

"Down past the stone barn. It's the original dairy barn, built in the early nineteen-hundreds, when the Dinwiddies came and started their farm. The lower two levels are still designed for cows and milking, but the upper levels have been renovated. Gilbert liked the shape and thought the main levels, which are accessed on the back side, would make unique places to store the wine casks. The top level is built around a grain silo, which is empty now. His plan was to set up that area with the grape press and oak barrels so visitors could stomp grapes as well. I'll follow through on his plan. It's a good one all around."

Her eyes widened. "Is that real? Like, with your bare feet?"

He glanced at her. "Until they developed wine presses, that's how wine was made. Well, that and natural pressing, where they piled the grapes up and let the weight of them force out the juice."

"Have you done it? Stomping?"

He nodded. "I have."

"And?"

He grinned then. "It's . . . an unusual feeling."

She barked a laugh at that, then gasped and quickly covered her throat.

Seth immediately braked the truck. "Are you okay?"

She nodded, rolled her eyes at herself, and waved him to keep on driving, feeling like an idiot. "I'm fine, truly. I'm sorry. It's . . . a reflex. Too many months worrying about sneezing or coughing or doing anything that might set back the results of the surgery." She tried to pass it off as no big deal. When, of course, it was a very big deal. Sitting-in-a-truck-half-a-world-away-because-she-was-too-chicken-to-sing big deal. But he didn't need to know that. Hopefully, other than Katie, no one would ever know that.

Seth drove on up the winding dirt and gravel road. Even

though his property was right up the mountain from Mabry's, the road connecting the two seemed to wind back and forth all over the place. The snowmobile path had definitely been quite a shortcut.

"Moira mentioned you were coming here to rest, but you told me yesterday that it's all good now," he said after a minute or two had passed. He glanced at her, then back to the road. "So, why come all this way then?" He flashed her a smile, lightening the sudden serious shift in conversation. "Leaving your star-ish entourage behind and everything."

She smiled at that. Seth Brogan was, for all intents and purposes, a complete stranger to her. And yet, it was surprisingly tempting to tell him everything. He was a caretaker by nature, of everything from ten-year-old girls to traumatized llamas. Her instincts told her she could trust him. But telling anyone that she was afraid to sing, that she might not ever make another album, or set foot on stage again, thereby possibly putting the entire cottage industry that was "Pippa MacMillan, Singer" in jeopardy . . . she couldn't risk that news getting out.

There was no decision to be made about whether or not she wanted to sing. She loved making music, loved performing. Being personally responsible for the livelihoods of those who now worked for her added to the stress, but she loved her star-ish entourage, every last one of them, like the family they'd truly become.

"Perspective," she said, at length, which was truthful, if not exactly specific. "It's been a roller-coaster ride this past year since the surgery, and I needed to gracefully step away and sort through it all. I can't do that in Ireland, or anywhere in Europe, actually. It's such a bizarre thing, celebrity."

He glanced over at her again. "I can't say I know anything about what that's like. My job before this was as an Army Ranger." He shot her a fast smile. "We worked very hard not to be seen." He looked back at the road. "I imagine it must feel like a kind of out-of-body experience. Like you're just you, but everyone around you suddenly sees someone worthy of the kind of attention a celebrity draws."

"I never thought of it that way, but you've got it exactly right," she exclaimed. "It's true, you know. You're literally the same person you've always been, nothing much special. You can sing a bit, and write a catchy tune, maybe play a fiddle half decently. But through some magical potion of right time, right place, right . . . something, those things catch on with this group, then that, and then it grows and grows, and suddenly everyone knows your name. But not you. Not really."

"A household name and a complete stranger, all at the same time."

"Exactly. Even looking back, I honestly can't track it. I suddenly went from sitting on stage in a dank and smoky pub to walking out on stage in front of more people than I've ever seen in my life. And they are shouting my name and singing my songs right along with me. Words I scribbled on the back of this napkin or that mobile bill, mind you. It's the oddest thing, really, but at the same time, wonderful and amazingly gratifying, to see my music bringing joy to so many."

She shifted her gaze from him back out to the wintry white landscape. "But I still climb into bed at night, as I always have, get up in the morning, wash my face, pour a cup of tea, and I'm exactly who I've always been, at least inside my head. And I think, well then. Okay. This is a bit of fun, isn't it? I can sing and folks can enjoy it. I can actually make a decent living from it all, but nothing much else to see here, right? Then I'll open the morning paper, and there's my face splashed all over the front of it, with some huge headline proclaiming I'm snogging this poor actor—who only stepped backstage to get an autograph for his young daughter, mind you—or I'm pregnant with triplets. Again! Or any other thing that will sell a tabloid, and I shake my head and think . . . who in the world is that girl? That's not me. I'm just Pippa MacMillan from Donegal." She settled back in her seat again. "Out-of-body. That's the perfect way to describe it."

He chuckled and she glanced at him, smiling, too. "I can't say I can even imagine most of that," Seth said. "Is the trade-off of your pleasure in singing, and making a living—a very good one, it seems—worth the intrusion into every part of your life? It must be one hell of a mind game, seeing people making up lies about you, wondering who believes it, or if that even matters, since they don't know you, or you them." He shook his head. "I don't think I'd want to imagine it, much less live it." He glanced at her. "No insult intended."

"None taken," she said honestly. "I must seem like a spoiled brat, complaining, but I'm not really. Complaining, I mean. Just trying to convey it all, and the hard work it takes. Even though it's working at something I love doing, it's still work."

"That part I do understand. I do complain," he added. "Ask Dexter. He gets an earful daily. Just because you love something doesn't mean it doesn't frustrate you. Often, at times. The rewards outweigh that though. That part I can identify with. Or, in my case, I hope the rewards will make it all worthwhile," he added with a short laugh.

"For me the music is the reward. The success, lovely as it is, is a bonus on top of that. I'd still be singing in pubs if the rest hadn't happened." She realized the truth of that as she said it, and it was a bit of a jolt. She filed that away for later examination, too. "I would have said I wasn't spoiled by success, but a few hours with Mabry and I'm not so sure I haven't been more seduced by this new life than I realized," she added with a laugh. "Maybe my coming here will be good for me in ways I haven't even begun to comprehend yet." She looked at him, her words sincere. "Thank you for putting me up. Mabry told me how busy you are at this time of year, and I want you to know, I do plan on helping out. I'd like to cook. Oh, and it's possible I may have invited Mabry over for some shepherd's pie, but no date on that. And I'll help in the barn, too. I'm sure I can find a way to—" She broke off as he turned the lumbering truck into a recently cleared driveway and pulled up in front of a small log cabin. So that's why the drive had seemed inordinately long. She looked from the cabin, to him, then back to the cabin, and felt her shoulders slump. Her heart did a little of that, too. "Oh," she said softly.

"Pippa, I'm sorry." He looked truly chagrined. "I just—"

"No," she said, looking back at him. "I completely understand. Actually, I was going to offer to find a place, but Mabry had me more or less talked out of it by the time you arrived. Maybe I just wanted him to." She pasted on a smile. "It was kind of you to go to the trouble of finding me a spot. Is this yours, too?"

He shook his head. "A friend of mine owns it. Noah Tyler. He owns the inn in town and uses this mostly for clients who come up here to fish or hunt."

She nodded, trying to cover her disappointment. It stung, though, even if she understood why he'd done it. She'd be lying if she said it didn't. "Mabry mentioned him, too. If you'll give me Noah's contact information, I'll handle this directly with him."

Just then Seth's cell phone went off, sending it vibrating across the top of the console between them. She saw the name on the screen before he picked it up. Mabry Jenkins.

"Hey, Mabry," Seth said. "Did we forget something?"

Pippa couldn't hear what Mabry said, but Seth's face went momentarily slack, then he immediately shifted into full on commander mode. He'd mentioned being an Army Ranger, and in that moment, she fully believed it.

"You stay put," Seth told him. "Don't move anything. We're coming right down. No, you're not all right. Stay put, dammit!" he said, his voice rising. "I'm putting Pippa on the phone. You talk to her until we get back down there. Don't hang up. Talk to her."

Seth didn't ask her, he just handed the phone to her, then jerked the truck into reverse. "Mabry. He's gotten himself pinned under part of his tractor. I think he's having a heart attack. Talk to him. Try to keep him calm. Do you have a phone?"

Heart thumping now, Pippa put Seth's phone to her ear and fished hers out of her jacket pocket. "Mr. Jenkins?" she said into the phone as she handed her own to Seth. "If you'd wanted my company for a bit longer, you didn't have to go to these lengths," she said, trying to sound teasing, as if everything would be fine. "I'd have been happy to keep handing you tools, you know."

Seth nodded at her, urging her to continue. He got the truck turned around and they were heading pell-mell back down the curving mountain road as he punched 9-1-1 into her cell phone.

Chapter Six

Pretty much the only thing that could have wiped the image of Pippa's crestfallen expression from his mind was the sound of Mabry's voice wheezing in pain. Somehow, both things were still stuck in his head fifteen minutes later when he pulled back into Mabry's long driveway. There was only a footpath plowed from house to barn, so Seth drove as far as he could go and killed the engine. "Go into the house and get as many clean towels as you can find and meet me in the barn," he told Pippa, who had slipped down from the truck by the time he was out and around the front. What he hadn't told Pippa was that Mabry was pretty sure the tractor had broken a few bones, though he hadn't said where or how badly, so Seth had no idea what they were about to encounter.

Pippa didn't question him, just nodded and ran toward the screened-in back porch, phone still at her ear.

"Keep talking to him," Seth called over his shoulder as he took off down the mud- and snow-packed path to the barn. He could hear the first strains of sirens whining in the distance. *Thank God.* He was one of the fortunate few who, despite having seen more than his fair share of combat, had managed to find a way to make peace with his memories so they didn't haunt his every waking or sleeping hour any longer. However, he'd be a liar if he said the sound of those sirens, mixing with the drumbeat of his own pulse, didn't rouse a few long-buried memories he'd just as soon leave in the past. He tried not to flinch when he heard the screen door to the back porch slap shut a minute later—failed, but kept on running.

"I've got towels," Pippa shouted hoarsely from far behind him, and he flinched again.

He wanted to turn, tell her not to yell like that, to protect her voice, then shook his head and kept on moving. *Not my problem.* But he was coming to believe it was still a problem for her. Something wasn't quite adding up with her tidy little story about being all healed and just looking for a little downtime. A continent away. *Also, not my problem.* Her animated expression as she exclaimed how beautiful the countryside was, excitedly telling him how she was planning to earn her keep at the vineyard, mixed with the sound of Mabry telling him to take care of her when they'd left the house earlier. *I am taking care of her. And myself. The only way I know how.*

Seth made it to the barn, where the sight of the old man, pinned under the side of the tractor, mercifully wiped his mind clean of everything except for the scene in front of him. "Hey, Mabry," he said, panting a little as he pulled up, then knelt beside the man's head. He took Mabry's phone from his shaking hand. "I've got him, Pippa," he said, and hung up, knowing she'd be in the barn in a few seconds anyway. He dropped the phone in the dirt and turned his attention to the old man. Mabry was pale as a ghost and looked as if he'd aged another ten years since they'd seen him less than a half hour ago. "If you wanted to do some weight lifting, I have a set in my basement, you know," Seth told him, keeping his tone light as he quickly assessed the situation.

It looked like Mabry had been working on the axle, or maybe trying to take the wheel off—it was hard to tell—but whatever the case, the jack system he'd rigged up had failed. One side of the tractor had dropped down, pinning the lower half of his body under part of its weight and probably fracturing one or both of his legs. Mabry had said it might have "banged his legs up a bit," and he wasn't kidding. More worrisome, a piece of the jack had impaled Mabry in the upper thigh. The metal shaft was still in the wound, sealing it, and while Seth was no doctor, he had seen his fair share of shrapnel wounds and far worse. He suspected the moment that thing moved, there was a good chance the old man could bleed out in a blink, if the femoral artery had been punctured.

"If you'd just . . . get this thing . . . off me . . . I'd appreciate it," Mabry wheezed, each word sounding labored and painful.

Seth pressed his fingers against the pulse in Mabry's wrist and counted. "Yeah, well, I left my Iron Man suit at home, unfortunately, but we'll have help here in a jiff. Try and take slow, shallow breaths," he told him. "In and out. Does your chest hurt? Any pains in your arm?"

Mabry shook his head. "I told you . . . not having . . ."

"That's okay, don't talk. Save your breath. I believe you." That was the one bit of good news in all this. Mabry didn't appear to be having a heart attack after all.

The sirens grew quite loud as Pippa raced into the barn, her arms full of bath towels, and a roll of paper towels clutched in each of her hands. "I wasn't sure," she said, panting, "which kind you meant."

"I think the cavalry is here," Seth said. "Hold on to them, though, just in case." He'd asked for the towels in case they'd needed them to help stanch any bleeding. Seth had already slipped his belt off on the run in, to use as a tourniquet, only there was no way to get to where the problem was without moving the tractor, and he was going to need a whole lot more than a stack of bath towels when that jack shaft shifted.

Seth closed his eyes in thanks when the siren went silent. He leaned back to look out the open barn doors, and saw the big Blue Hollow Falls volunteer fire truck, followed by their EMT truck, and another emergency vehicle all rumbling down the drive. More sirens howled in the distance, and he suspected Turtle Springs was sending up their finest, too. *The more the merrier*, he thought. *We're going to need it.*

Pippa came around and sat cross-legged in the dirt next to Mabry on his other side. She put her hand on his forehead, then his shoulder. "You've given us quite a scare," she told him, sounding like a cross headmistress, even as she stroked his arm and laid her palm once again over his forehead.

Seth noted she quite pointedly refrained from looking anywhere below the man's chest.

"If this is the sort of thing you Yanks do for attention," she went on, "I'll thank you not to do it again while I'm here."

Mabry smiled briefly at that, then wheezed, followed by a sharp gasp of pain. Pippa's gaze flew to Seth's for a moment, fear and panic quite clear in her big blue eyes.

Seth felt every bit as helpless and scared as she did, but he winked at her, mouthed, "You're doing fine," then got to his feet to go and meet the rescue team so he could fill them in on the situation.

In the end, it took quite a bit of doing, and he aged what felt like years as the paramedics worked to extract Mabry. Seth had climbed on Mabry's other tractor and used it to drag a path through the melting snow, wide enough so the firetruck and the EMT truck could get all the way to the entrance of the barn. Pippa had offered to help, using the snowmobile to tamp down a path, but Seth had told her to stay by

Mabry. She seemed to have a calming effect on him, and Seth could tell that's where she really wanted to be. Other than to allow the paramedics to do their thing, she never left the old man's side.

Once the trucks could reach the barn, things moved pretty quickly.

Seth helped the firemen, all of whom he knew by name, while Pippa was alternately being cheerleader and cross headmistress to Mabry, depending on what was most needed, more than once bringing a surprised smile to Seth's face and those of the emergency crew.

In short order, the tractor was lifted off of Mabry, leaving the jack shaft in place, to be removed at the hospital. The same leg had suffered a bad, protruding fracture that had produced a fair amount of bleeding when the tractor was lifted off it. Too much, to Seth's way of thinking, which had been proven true as Mabry went in and out of consciousness and his vitals began bottoming even as the paramedics rushed to stabilize the wound. All that was left to do after the heavy lifting was to stand on the sidelines and watch. It took Seth straight back to his days in the service. As he had then, Seth felt utterly helpless.

What seemed like an eternity later, Pippa and Seth stood side by side in the open barn doorway as the ambulance carrying Mabry slowly rolled out the driveway.

"How far do they have to go?" Pippa asked.

"The closest hospital is down in Hawksbill Valley, in Turtle Springs. About twenty-five miles from here." At her gasp, he added, "There's no traffic between here and there, and only one major intersection, so they'll get him down there quickly." Or as quickly as the winding mountain roads would let them, but he didn't mention that part.

"I'm so glad the roads got cleared and the sun came out." Pippa was rubbing her own arms as she said this, as if chilled, despite the much warmer temperatures and clear skies overhead. "I don't want to be in the way, but can we go down and see him later?"

"I talked to Mabry's daughter, Maggie," Seth said. "She's already on the way to the hospital. She said she'll call me and let us know how he's doing. I think we should wait until we hear from her."

Pippa nodded, then turned to look back at the barn, to the tractor, now turned upright but still sitting at an awkward angle due to the broken axle. They both looked at the scatter of blood-soaked gauze and torn paper packets littering the packed dirt floor around the pool of blood that had soaked into the dirt. The firetruck had been called to head to another emergency right when the paramedics had gotten Mabry stabilized and into the ambulance. Time had been of the essence for the emergency teams on all fronts, so Seth had assured them he'd wear the gloves they'd given him to put all of the detritus in a trash bag. The EMT driver had also given him the number of a service that was trained and certified to do the kind of cleanup required after such an event. Seth wasn't sure that would be necessary, but he'd taken the card nonetheless.

Seth worked to keep his mind focused on Mabry and not let it drift back. It was a discipline that had taken him a few years to master, but it still wasn't easy. In fact, it was downright exhausting. He started making mental lists of what would need to be done going forward, not just in the immediate time frame, but long term, given the severity of Mabry's injuries, all of which helped to keep his thoughts fully occupied.

"So much blood," Pippa whispered.

Seth glanced at her and saw her own face had gone a ghostly shade of white. He knew that expression. He immediately slipped his arm through hers and turned her away from the interior of the barn, walking her outside into the fresh air and the blinding white of the sunshine reflecting on the rapidly melting snow. He steered her toward the back porch of the house. She didn't put up even the slightest resistance. Seth knew all about working on adrenaline and the mind's ability to stay ruthlessly focused during times of extreme trauma, just as he also knew the severe crash that could happen once the trauma had abated and time started to move forward again at normal speed.

"Mabry's going to be all right," Seth told her calmly, as if this was an everyday conversation they were having. Imprinting normal on a moment that felt like anything but, helped to divert the brain from the recent trauma to something else. Anything else. "He's a stubborn old cuss."

"He's a decent, kind, and loving soul. He doesn't deserve this," she countered, her words thick with emotion.

"It was an accident, Pippa, not a reprimand," he told her gently. "They can happen to anyone." He felt the fine trembling begin to vibrate down her arms. He knew those weren't surface tremors, but the kind that went bone deep and were uncontrollable, shaking a person right down to their core.

He glanced at her just in time to see her eyes go a bit spacy. Ignoring the screaming tension that hadn't quite unknotted the muscles in his neck or down his spine—the result of fighting both the war going on inside the barn, and the one he'd stopped officially fighting several years ago—Seth immediately sprang into action once more. "It's okay; you're all right," he said, keeping his voice gentle, quiet, and smooth. "Up you go," he added, scooping her into his arms. "Hold on."

She was sturdier than she looked, he thought, but he could feel the tremors shaking hard in her legs now, and knew he'd gotten her just moments before she'd have gone down. He hoisted her up a bit higher against his chest. "Put your hands around my neck," he told her as he moved directly toward the house at a steady but unrushed pace. She needed soothing, not more alarm. "Lock your fingers together. Good, good," he murmured, as he bumped the screen door open, then pushed his way in through the rear porch to the back door that led into the kitchen.

He walked through that room, down the short hall to the living room and eyed the recliner, thinking he could lower her there, push it back, then give her a few moments to wind back down. She just gripped him harder when he started to move her. So, instead, he nudged the fancy little antique coffee table aside and lowered his tall frame down to the middle of the small couch, then settled her across his lap.

"Thank . . . you," she whispered through chattering teeth. "Foo—foolish."

He tucked her cheek against his chest, and slowly stroked her back, then her hair, then her back again. She slid her hands from his neck and pillowed them under her cheeks, pinning them there as if willing them to stop trembling. He could still feel the tremors in her torso and legs, but they weren't as strong now. "Not foolish," he told her. "Human. I've been there, too." He tightened his hold just a bit when she tried to move. "Stay put awhile longer, okay? Give yourself a break."

He rocked slightly, but steadily, and continued to stroke and soothe, which might have seemed silly to some, but he knew the feeling of being held, being rocked, was in itself a powerful trigger, taking one back to a time before memories truly began to form.

He felt the tremors slowly ease from her limbs, and her breathing steadied. She took long, slow breaths, and let them out in equally slow, shuddering releases. He eventually stopped rocking her, but continued to hold her, realizing the motions, the soothing, had worked their magic on the knots and tension in his own neck and spine as well.

"I'm guessing," she said at long length, her voice a rough whisper, "that it took a bit more than a tractor accident for you to end up curled in a ball like this."

"Trauma is trauma," he said quietly. "It doesn't really respect or conform to any kind of scale."

She finally lifted her head and looked up at him. "Thank you," she said, simply.

He smiled then, a brief curving of his lips. "It helped me, too."

She looked surprised by that, then smiled briefly. "I'm glad. That makes it easier to accept."

Their gazes caught, held, and quite swiftly another feeling entirely engulfed him. He'd learned about extreme situations triggering all sorts of primal responses, but he'd never found himself experiencing trauma with a member of the opposite sex. The urge to lower his head, take her mouth—and not in some sweet, gentle, get-to-know-you kiss—was as compelling and strong a need as he'd ever experienced. His body had surged quite insistently to life, ferociously seconding that idea. *You were just about to dump her in Noah's cabin and get back to work*, he reminded himself, needing rational thinking to make a swift return. *Don't complicate things.*

Then her gaze dropped to his mouth, lingered there a long moment, and moved slowly back up to meet his own.

"Pippa," he began, knowing he had to nip this off, and quick. But she'd whispered, "Seth," at the very same time, and something about the sound of his name on those little bow-tie lips of hers, with that bottomless sea of blue above them, doomed him to the pull of the moment.

He leaned down just as she arched up to meet him. They were both in it, both wanting, both throwing all caution aside and simply living in that one, singular moment of need and want.

She whimpered, then fisted her hands in his hair when he started to lift his head, and slipped her tongue past his lips, in case he had any doubts that the sound had been one of need. He held her there, suckled her tongue, then slipped his into the wet, hot recesses of her mouth. They instantly fell into a mating ritual of sliding, suckling, kissing, taking a breath, then delving in once again. She writhed against him, and he pulled her up so she could straddle his thighs.

The position equalized the better part of the vast difference in their heights and she cried out when the very softest part of her rode on top of the most rigid part of him. He felt her shudder through an instant climax despite the layers of clothes between them, making his own hips rock upward of their own volition, allowing her to wring every last drop of pleasure from the moment, if not from him.

It had been a very long time since he'd felt the warmth of a woman wrapped around him in the most intimate of ways, a truth his body was screaming at him to rectify. But instead of tearing away the few flimsy barriers between them and plunging himself mindlessly into the sweet, hot bliss he knew awaited him, he broke free of her mouth and wrapped her up against his chest, reaching for any shred of rational thought he could find, a tether back to reality, no matter how tenuous.

She was panting heavily, her cheek and lips pressed against the side of his now damp neck. He rested his own cheek on top of her head while they both climbed back down from the stratosphere they'd just shot themselves into.

Neither of them said a word as their breathing slowly steadied. He didn't loosen his hold on her though, and neither did she try to crawl from his lap. A thousand thoughts raced through his mind, as he weighed all the pros of perhaps doing this again sometime, preferably when sprawled across the wide expanse of his bed, against all the reasons why that would be a very, very bad idea.

He'd known her for two days and already he could call up picture-perfect moments of her in his mind. Her beaming smile just before she dropped into a deep curtsy after her literally over-the-top snowmobile-entry into his life; her sitting on the floor of his barn, goat in her lap, brushing Dexter's coat; her leaning on the doorway, batting her lashes while asking for a Shetland pony. Reflexively grabbing her throat after barking out a laugh, sitting next to Mabry, goading him into staying strong and alert, looking hurt and so very small when she realized he was getting rid of her.

He swallowed a sigh at that last part. She was bold and daring, confident and independent . . . vulnerable and still a little fragile, and she kissed him like he was the last man on earth.

He'd never met anyone quite like her, and he'd be a fool if he didn't admit she was exactly the kind of woman who might sneak in and steal his heart. *Then go traipsing back to Ireland with it tucked deep in her pocket.*

So, that would be a no, then. He had not a single regret in having done it, but he wouldn't be kissing Pippa MacMillan again.

"As a means to getting oneself past a bit of shock," she said a little primly, "I'd have to say that ranked even higher than the rocking and patting." She lifted her head and looked at him. "Though that helped a great deal, too."

Her gaze was direct. Not hopeful, not dismissive, but simply . . . real.

"It's definitely going on my preferred list," Seth replied, perhaps a bit more cautiously. She was still straddling his lap, and his body hadn't quite climbed on board with the whole never-doing-that-again decision. He suspected she'd climb off him soon enough, though, and he found he wasn't in any hurry to expedite the end of this particular moment-out-of-time. If it wasn't going to happen again, then he wouldn't mind having all there was from this one, and he wasn't going to apologize for that.

"I've never kissed a man with a beard," she said, quite contemplatively.

His grin was spontaneous. "And?"

"It's softer than I'd have thought." She lowered her gaze, studied it a bit, then looked at him again. "I quite liked it, actually, and I didn't think I would."

Just like that his body was right back on board. "You'd been giving it some thought then?"

Her cheeks, already pink from said beard and the heat of the moment, deepened in color. "Would it make your ego grow to unbearable proportions if I said yes?"

It was on the tip of his tongue to mention she'd already made other parts of him grow to unbearable proportions, so what was one more? "I believe I can keep it in check. I'll do my best, at any rate."

"Then yes," she said, rather decisively. "I have. Not that I planned on ever doing anything about it, of course. I mean, you're my sister's best friend's brother. And we live an ocean apart. So why start something up, you know? Too much at stake."

It was perverse, but the more she made his argument for him, the more he wanted to play devil's advocate.

Instead, he said, "If it helps, my behavior just now notwithstanding," he added with a smile, "I'm not casual about things like this, either." Which was the truth, and a big part of why it had been a long time for him. "So, I would agree with your assessment." He almost laughed again when a flash of disappointment crossed her face before she nodded in consensus. What, were they each hoping the other would convince them that maybe continuing wouldn't be such a bad idea after all?

"After spending the past four years now with all those out-of-body, instant star experiences going on, can I just say thank you for this lovely, quite in-the-body moment? It was well worth the wait."

Again, he had to swallow the entirely inappropriate comment that rose to his lips, about how much he'd enjoy a lovely in-her-body moment, too. Then what she said sank in and he paused and met her gaze. "Not a casual person, either, then, I assume."

She shook her head. "My life changed pretty swiftly. There hadn't been anyone special for a time back then, because I'd been working all the time, taking gigs anywhere I could get them, traveling a fair bit. Not conducive to the kind of relationship we non-casual types gravitate toward, you know?"

"I do know," he said, then chuckled. "Intimately."

She smiled then, too. "And when things started to take off, it was kind of odd, because if I did have a chance to meet someone who interested me, likely he was part and parcel of the industry side of things, or he was another musician, or possibly just starstruck . . . or something even less savory." She broke off, shook her head, let out a short laugh. "Sounds ungrateful, but it's simply how it is."

"Sounds complicated," Seth replied. "For me, it's the opposite. I moved out here, bought a place up in the mountains." He smiled then. "Just me, my farm animals, and my llama."

"Yes, well, I've heard about men like you, growing up as I did on a farm," she said, then shot him a dry smile.

"Not that lonely," he said on a short laugh. "Not yet, anyway," he added, which made *her* laugh. "Blue Hollow Falls is a smaller than small town. Not much in the way of fellow singles, and I've been a bit too busy since I moved here to look farther afield."

"So I heard. Mabry told me about the converted silk mill. I'm hoping to get down to see it, just as soon as—oh." She broke off, frowned, then just looked sad.

"What?"

She lifted a shoulder. "Mabry said he'd teach me how to drive on the right side of the road, and offered me a loan of one of his farm trucks. I could simply lease a car, but he seemed so tickled about it. I think he's like my dad that way, happy to know he's of help to others. So I said yes. After today, though . . ." She sighed then. "I'm so worried for him. Worried about his farm. What will he do? What will happen?"

Seth found himself stroking her hair again, then her cheek, as if out of long habit, and had to force himself to drop his hand, which was made more difficult by the light that had instantly flared to life in her sad eyes. "It will work out," he told her. "We help each other out here. I suspect Maggie will stay on, at least for a while, to help out with things."

"Mabry said she might be moving back here permanently, taking over the place when he retires. Though, honestly, I couldn't see him ever retiring. At least not before now." She let out a sigh. "Mabry said something about Maggie's husband being able to work from home, and from the looks of the scrapbook he shared with me today, her sons are grown and in college now."

"I hadn't heard that," Seth said, "about her moving back, but maybe this will simply expedite those plans."

"I hope so. Even if he comes back from this, it's going to take a long while. And I can't imagine he'll be fit soon, or possibly ever, to run the place by himself."

"He has help, and he has Maggie."

She nodded. "I know, and that's such a good thing. It's only, he strikes me as being a lot like my grandfather, and my father. My grandfather worked right up to the moment he passed, saying he couldn't imagine what in the world he'd do with himself if he didn't get up with the sun every day. My father is much the same way. I suspect Mabry is, too."

"You're probably right, though it would do him well to slow down a bit, or at least not rely only on himself and the few farmhands he has to keep the place going. If Maggie can move back, I think that might be best for both of them."

"First, he has to heal," she said. "I know more than a little about that." She shuddered lightly. "Maybe not to the degree of what he'll be facing, but—"

"I don't think it's as much apples and oranges as all that.

If it's something that prevents you from doing what you do in life, then one is just as monumental as the other."

She opened her mouth to reply, then closed it again; the corners of her mouth lifted slightly. "Thank you. I don't think I'd ever thought of it like that. It . . . helps."

He wanted to ask her what, exactly, she needed help with, but didn't. Every minute they spent like this was going to make it harder to keep his hands off her going forward. He was attracted to her, yes. But he also really liked her. And that was the far greater temptation, as it turned out.

"Well," she said, "I should probably find my way out of your lap. I'll help you in the barn."

"No," Seth said, brooking no argument. "I'll see to that."

"Okay," she agreed, not bothering to hide her relief, which made them both smile. "I'll be happy to pick up the slack in some other way. I do want to be of help."

He braced his hands on her hips and helped her shift back off his lap and to her feet. He decided he'd wait a few more minutes before doing the same. "You were a big help out there," he said. "It wasn't easy doing what you did, staying by him, talking him through it."

"I felt so helpless," she said. "I wish I could have done more."

"I felt the same way. I'll call down to the firehouse in a bit and talk to the paramedics, see what they know."

"If you'd rather go on down there now, I could just go ahead and borrow one of Mabry's farm trucks as planned. If Maggie or his grandsons need it, I can rent something and get it back to them."

"What about the driving lessons?"

She smiled. "I'll drive around the yard a bit first, get to know the truck. Given the lack of cars on the road up here, I should be able to sort myself out fairly quickly."

Seth nodded. "Actually, I'm pretty sure you will."

"Why, thank you," she said, and performed one of her

little curtsies, which made him chuckle. "If you'll give me directions to Noah's cabin—"

"About that," Seth broke in, his smile fading. "I should have told you—"

"No, I understand," she said, then added, "I truly do. I was forced on you at an apparently difficult time. That's not a good thing for you or for me. The little fishing cabin looks perfect."

She was putting on a good face, and he appreciated that, but he'd seen her true reaction that moment in the truck, when he'd first pulled into the drive. "I could have handled it better," he said. "I apologize. I usually have better manners than that."

She busied herself pushing at her hair, smoothing her clothing, looking anywhere but at him. "I feel bad just leaving you with the mess in the barn."

"It won't take that long. I've had some experience with that kind of thing."

Her gaze flew right to his then. "Oh, right." Her expression fell. "I'm so sorry. I should have thought. This wasn't easy on you, either. And on top of that, you had to deal with me getting all flighty."

His grin was swift and very real. "You'll get no complaints from me."

Her cheeks flushed a bright pink, but she laughed at the same time. "I suppose I could blame my loose behavior on not being in my right mind." Her smile settled into something more sweet than wry, and her voice held a note of honest affection when she said, "But I can't say I regret it, either."

He nodded, but opted to remain silent.

The silence spun out and their gazes remained locked. She finally looked away. "So," she said briskly, "if we can figure out where Mabry keeps his truck keys and which truck you think he'd want me to take, I'll get out of your hair once and for all."

Seth's mind flashed to how she'd fisted her hands in his lengthy locks, how she'd pulled his mouth to hers, no uncertainty at all about what she wanted. His body flashed back to awareness, reminding him just how much he'd liked that about her. *Like I had a chance in hell of ever forgetting.* Seth stood and quickly shifted around her, leading her along the hall to the kitchen, willing his body to settle down. "I'm sure the keys will be in the truck. I know he drives the big Ford Ranger, so I'm guessing he was thinking about his old blue and white Chevy. Not much you could do to hurt that old thing." Seth kept on walking, through the kitchen door, across the porch, and outside, waiting for her to catch the door behind him.

They walked across the backyard toward a second, smaller barn that Mabry used as more of a makeshift garage. The fire trucks coming and going had flattened the bulk of the snow behind the house, and the sun was doing a pretty good job on the rest of it. "It's slippery out here. Be careful," he cautioned, trying to silence the running argument going on inside his head.

This didn't feel right. Not just because it made him a rude host or because he knew she'd been disappointed by the change in plans. The plain and simple truth was, he didn't want her somewhere else. *All the more reason to make sure that's exactly where she goes.* If she stayed under his roof, he was pretty certain, one way or the other, they'd end up in his bed. And hers. And probably every other flat surface in the house. The hunger she'd ignited in him was no small thing. And he was pretty damn sure she'd say the same. It was for both their sakes that it was best if they were in separate digs. He was doing the right thing. For himself, for her, for their respective siblings.

"We don't have to mention this to Kate or Moira," Pippa said as she came to stand beside him. "About my being in the cabin."

They both looked at the truck, an aging aqua-blue and white Chevy pickup whose best years were behind it. In the right hands, it would be a classic, but out here, it was just a beat-up old farm truck. Seth hoped she didn't mind getting her backside dusty, or worse.

"Probably a good idea," he said. "Once Moira is off on her grand adventure, she won't be giving us much thought anyway." He looked at Pippa then. "It was very kind of you to offer up your place to a total stranger."

She smiled easily. "Not exactly a stranger. We've not met, but she's Katie's dearest pal, and that makes her family. I was happy to help. And, honestly, it wasn't like I was using it, so it really wasn't much of a favor to grant. My oldest brother, Garrett, owns a pub in the village there. I've instructed him to keep an eye. He's done that much and more for me and Katie over the years, so she'll be well looked after." She laughed. "Probably more so than she'd like, actually. He's quite the daddy hen."

"I'm liking the man better by the minute," Seth said. "So, there's a pub in your family, too? My folks started ours right after they married. We've all worked there when we were younger. My older brother, Aiden, runs it with them now. My oldest sister, Kathleen, takes care of the books. She and my mom have a small bookkeeping business."

"Sounds lovely," Pippa told him. "Ours isn't a family business. Garrett is the first tavern owner among us. Katie has worked for him, though."

"Where do you fall in the family lineup?" he asked.

"Katie is the youngest at twenty-six, the baby of the clan, like Moira, which is likely why they bonded so closely. She's four years younger than me. Then my brother Cassian, who is right in between us, then me, then our three older brothers. Garrett is ten years older than I am, Brian eight years older, and Braedon five. He's the stuntman." She grinned. "My folks had three, then took a break, then had three more. What about you?"

"In the middle. Aiden is forty-one, then Kathleen, who is thirty-nine. Both married, both keeping my parents out of our hair by giving them plenty of grandkids. Then Catriona, who is thirty-six. She's an engineer, engaged to an engineer, so a match made in heaven," he said with a chuckle. "Then me, thirty-two, my sister, Branna, twenty-eight. She's an elementary school teacher, wrangling third graders this year. And Moira, twenty-five, lawyer."

"That's an impressive lineup," Pippa said, smiling.

"No less than your own," he said with a nod.

"Even with our age differences and me and Brae being all over the world at any given time, we're still close. It sounds like it's the same for you."

He nodded. "It is. It's hard for folks to understand how united a large family can be unless they come from one."

"Oh, aye, it's true. I often wonder how my parents did it and remained married, without doing away with any of us during our teen years."

Seth chuckled and their gazes caught, held, then held some more.

Pippa ended the moment by walking around to the driver side of the truck. "Brae would never let me live it down if I couldn't manage a simple truck," she said, looking through the driver-side window.

"It's a stick," Seth mentioned. "Clutch."

"I know the lingo," she said dryly, then opened the door and hoisted herself up on the seat, not so much as glancing at the dust, straw, and other farm detritus littering the interior. Of course, she was already dusty and dirty from sitting on the barn floor earlier, which hadn't seemed to faze her, either.

She pulled the seat belt across her lap, then undid it and reached under the front of the seat to move it forward, then forward some more. Seat belt back on, she turned her attention to the steering wheel and dash. The keys were, in fact, dangling from the ignition. "Okay, laddie, I'm sure you want to do me proud today," she murmured in a soothing tone as she pushed in the clutch and started the engine. "There you go," she purred, then shifted into first gear. "Let's see how you—" She broke off as the truck lurched forward, and promptly died.

To his credit, Seth had simply stepped back calmly when she'd started the engine. "I think you're in third."

"It's backwards," she called out. "We have the clutch the same, but I'm used to the gears being on me left." And to her credit, after two more tries, and a few leaps forward, she pulled off as smoothly as if she'd driven the truck for years. She did a circle around the yard, then stopped, backed it up, and went forward again, then repeated the whole maneuver twice more. Then with a wave to him, she carefully pulled out onto the road and was gone.

It wasn't until Seth was halfway through cleaning up the barn, trying like hell to ignore the echo of utter silence that surrounded him once again, that he realized he'd never given her directions to Noah's cabin.

Grinning, and knowing he had no business being happy for the excuse, he closed the barn doors to keep the critters from getting inside until he could get back and finish the job. Then he hopped in his truck, and headed out after her.

Chapter Seven

Pippa sat on the small wood bench outside Turtle Springs Memorial Hospital, waiting. There wasn't nearly the amount of snow down here in the valley as they'd had up in the mountains. There were a few small piles here and there from previous plowing, and still some snow cover in yards that had more shade than sun, but otherwise, it looked more like the wet pavements and sidewalk puddles one saw after a good rain.

She hadn't gotten lost. Not really. Once she'd headed up into the hills and realized she had no idea where she was going, she'd initially kept on driving. There weren't that many roads up there, so she'd thought, how hard could it be? She hadn't remembered Seth making any turns when they'd gone to the cabin the first time. Or not many, anyway. When that plan hadn't worked out, she'd thought if she got high enough in the hills, her mobile signal would miraculously come back, and she would do a quick search to find the town's only inn, contact Noah directly, and be on her merry way. Worst case was she'd use the map system to find her way back to Mabry's or the vineyard.

Unfortunately, the long day had taken its toll on more than just her body and her ability to think clearly. Somewhere during her trip higher into the hills, her phone had died. Even if she'd had a charge cord on her, which she hadn't, the old truck wasn't exactly equipped with a USB port.

So, she'd taken the next turn that headed down out of the mountains, hoping she'd come across a sign that would lead her into Blue Hollow Falls, where she could ask directions to the inn and Noah. Instead, she'd found herself all the way down in the valley, at the two-lane highway her driver had taken to head up to the vineyard in the first place. There wasn't a helpful sign for the vineyard, of course, but there was a sign telling her she was five miles from Turtle Springs, where they'd taken Mabry. So she'd headed there instead, to see how he was doing.

The rest could wait.

Part of that "rest" was, of course, finding her way to her new lodgings. The second part was dealing with the other big thing that had happened that day. On the couch. Right there in Mabry's house. It would be handy, and not entirely untrue, to blame her out-of-character behavior on the extraordinary stresses of the day. But she knew that was only half of it. Seth Brogan had ignited a long dormant flame inside her from the moment he'd stepped inside his own mudroom, looking like a conquering warrior, just in from the storms of battle. At best, her reaction to Mabry's heart-pounding rescue had simply lowered her defenses enough to do what she'd wanted to do all along. *You mean, jump him?*

She propped an elbow on one knee and lowered her forehead to rest on her hand. *Not two days out on your own, untethered from the world, and you're making bad decisions like it's your first semester at uni.* She took a deep breath and let it out slowly, hoping her good sense would return. *It's going to take more than breathing exercises to handle this one.*

That was the core reason she hadn't given Seth a chance to backpedal on the cabin rental. Because no matter how many deep, steadying breaths she took, no matter how lost she got herself up on those beautiful, snowcapped hills, or how long she locked herself away in a tiny cabin built for one . . . the truth was, she wanted to jump him again so bad she ached with it.

"Well, I guess I can tell the sheriff's department to call off the search teams."

She whipped her head up so fast she had to blink several times and look down again when the setting sun half blinded her. "My phone died," she said, as if that explained everything. Shielding her eyes this time, she looked up—way up—at the man presently towering over her. "I'm sorry I worried you," she said sincerely. "I drove off without thinking to ask for directions, and foolishly thought I could figure things out." She relayed the rest of the story, adding, "I haven't been in to see Mabry. He was in surgery when I got here. I talked to Maggie, though. She's inside, in the waiting room. I came out here because . . ."

"You're probably not a big fan of hospitals," Seth said, finishing for her.

And that right there was why he was such a danger to her. Her libido wanted to jump his impressive frame, yes. As often as he'd let her. That she could deal with. Probably. Possibly. If she wasn't anywhere near him. Her heart, however, was already looking for ways to wrap him up for keeps. He was a good, kind, caring, funny, sexy-as-hell man. How was she supposed to talk her heart out of wanting that? Who wouldn't?

Two days. What would it feel like in two weeks? Or two months?

"I'm not a big fan of them, either," he said.

"Oh, no," she said, feeling instantly ridiculous. "I'm so sorry. Were you injured in the war? Wait, that's not my business." She shook her head. "I must seem so foolish to you. You're out risking your life defending your country, and I'm out here shivering because I had a little surgery once and the smell of a hospital makes me queasy."

"Like I said before, I don't think it much matters why," he said. "We feel how we feel."

We do, indeed, she thought, wishing he'd stop being so damn perfect.

"Your little surgery sounds like it was the result of a potentially life-changing injury. It would be odd if that didn't affect you, potentially quite powerfully," he said plainly. "And no, I wasn't injured. I was one of the very fortunate ones. But a great number of my buddies weren't so lucky. I spent a lot of time with them afterward. So, the less time spent anywhere around a hospital these days, the better."

"I'm so sorry," she said again, further abashed. "I don't have any experience at all with that, or what your life was like while serving." She smiled briefly then. "The closest I've come is playing music and singing for the troops. The British troops."

"I can't imagine they weren't appreciative for the break," he told her. "A chance to not think for a little while and simply enjoy a few hours of life outside our mission was a big deal. I know I'd have been glad for it."

"That's kind of you." She smiled. "I'm not an American, but we are your allies, so I think it's okay if I thank you for your service." She looked up at him. "I mean that."

He nodded. "I won't say it was my pleasure," he added with a brief smile of his own. "But I felt it was my duty."

"I'm truly sorry I worried you," she told him. "I honestly didn't mean to. Maggie said she'd talked to you and you were coming down to see Mabry, so I thought I'd just wait here and we'd figure things out then." She gave him a partial smile. "Besides, you have the cabin key, and all of my luggage is in the back of your truck, so I wouldn't have gotten very far even if I had managed to find the place again."

Seth glanced over to where he'd parked his truck, and it

was obvious from his expression that he hadn't put that part together. "Right," he said, but saw her knowing smile when he looked back at her, and smiled sheepishly. "As soon as I realized you didn't have directions, I took off trying to find you. I didn't want you to get lost. Then I couldn't find you anywhere up there, or back at the vineyard, or back at Mabry's." He glanced at the hospital. "I should have known you'd be resourceful."

She nodded. "It's nice to know someone is looking out for me all the same." She grinned then. "Garrett and my dad would be relieved to hear it."

"Does your family know you're here? In the States? Other than your sister, I mean."

Pippa nodded. "We've gotten a bit far flung over the years, especially Brae and me. But Brian is in London now, and Cass travels often. So, we've a rule about Mum and Dad always knowing where we are. They don't need to know the specifics, of course, but they know I'm staying at a vineyard owned by Moira's big brother. Katie spent years gushing about your family, so they feel like they know you. I know they're excited to finally get to meet your sister."

He smiled, nodded. "That's nice, your giving your parents that peace of mind. I know how much my parents worried when I was overseas, more so once I became a Ranger and couldn't tell them exactly where I was."

"I bet they're happy you're back in the States now."

He nodded. "They'd be even happier if I was growing grapes on the other coast, but yes, they're happy I'm home and that I'm doing something I feel passionate about."

"Why wine?" she asked. "Is it in your family?"

He shook his head. "My commanding officer, who happens to be Sawyer Hartwell, part owner of that renovated silk mill I told you about, got very interested in microbrewing when we were overseas. He's opened a gastropub as part of the mill. That wasn't something that called to me, but he talked about it endlessly, and so I learned a great deal whether I wanted to or not." He grinned. "We ended up stuck at a vineyard for ten days after a mission that I still can't talk about in a place I can't mention. We'd been in rather confining quarters for quite a bit just prior to our unplanned stay, so I spent as much time outside as possible." He shook his head, still smiling. "Partly for the fresh air, and partly to get away from Sawyer, who was always talking to the family who owned the place, about his grand plans once he returned home. I spent hours walking the rows of vines thinking that if I was going to do anything with spirits, it would be as a vintner." He shrugged. "I ended up talking to the patriarch of the family at great length. He showed me how to prep the vines, talked to me about the old ways of pressing grapes, about the value of table grapes versus wine grapes, about having a variety of stock, how many acres to plant if you wanted to make a profit, and ways to supplement income if the acreage wasn't available to fill in the bottom line."

"Sounds like he made quite an impression on you."

"Oh, he was a fount of information." Seth chuckled. "He also thought any ideas I might have had about starting my own place were foolish and quite misplaced. He loved talking about his own achievements, but he was fairly bigoted about the idea of an American growing grapes that were worth turning into wine. He was of the mind that you had to be born to it."

"And yet, here you are, with winery and llama in tow."

Seth nodded. "It's funny, but the more he told me I couldn't, the more I wanted to try. It probably wouldn't make him happy to hear it, but if I have any success at all at this, I owe him a great debt of gratitude."

"And probably a shipment of a case or two of your finest label."

Seth laughed. "That, too."

"So, did Sawyer have anything to do with why you ended up in Virginia?"

Seth nodded. "I'd actually returned home to Seattle and had a very good job offer in the technology industry. That was my strong suit when I served. I would have been all set."

"Just because you're good at something, doesn't mean that's what you should be doing."

He tilted his head at that, gave her a crooked smile. "I thought stability was more important than being thrilled with going to work every day, but Sawyer kept after me, saying I'd risked my life for my country, so giving a winery a try would be child's play in comparison."

"The only thing you risk getting shot with is grape juice."

He chuckled. "Exactly. The technology sector will still be there if I turn out to be an abject failure. It was also important to spend some downtime away for a bit, too. I needed to reconnect with myself after serving. Something else Sawyer is very good at understanding. I love my family, but being smothered by them was the last thing I needed. They support me, want me to be successful." He studied her. "So, I take it singing and playing music wasn't the career path your folks had in mind for you, either?"

She shook her head. "Believe it or not, with all the MacMillans running around County Donegal, I'm the only one in our particular line who plays an instrument. And the only singing done by any member of my family is in church. And not in the choir," she added drily. "Trust me."

Seth chuckled. "What was it they hoped you'd become?"

"There was never much discussion about that. I knew from the moment I heard music, the moment I realized I could make beautiful sounds like that, what I was destined to do with my life." She laughed. "You'll never know how relieved I was, after standing between my mum and dad at church, when I discovered I could actually sing."

Seth laughed with her. "They tried to dissuade you?"

She shook her head. "Not so much that. They could see it was my passion. I sang in church from the time I was old enough to be in the choir. Taught myself how to play an old fiddle one of my friends had in her attic."

"Impressive."

Pippa laughed. "I didn't say I was any good at it. I think my parents finally agreed to real lessons just to keep their sanity and their hearing intact." She smiled up at him. "I enjoyed every part of learning to play that lovely old thing. I still have it, in fact. When I got old enough, I played fiddle at Garrett's pub the nights he had music and dance, sang a little there, too, when I got brave enough. My parents didn't dissuade me from doing that. It was more that they urged me to find a 'real' occupation as something to rely on. They saw music as more of a hobby pursuit than something I could support myself doing. I don't fault them for that, because they were right." She grinned. "I just didn't care if I starved. Singing was all I wanted to do." She shrugged. "So, I kept at it."

"And look at you now," Seth said, smiling with her. "I'm sure they're beyond proud of you."

Her smile flickered a little then. *More worried than proud these days.* "They are indeed. I'm very fortunate to have their support. I'll love them always no matter what, but without their strength, and that of all of my siblings, I don't know that I'd have gone on to do as well as I have." A simple statement, but containing more truth than she could convey. If anyone could understand that, though, she imagined it would be the man standing in front of her. Odd, what a comfort that realization was. Or maybe not so odd at all.

Seth shook his head, smiling. "I try to think what my folks would do if one of us wanted to travel the world as a musician, while another of us wanted to risk life and limb as a stuntman. I don't know that they could manage it."

"They managed your going off to war," she said.

Seth nodded. "That is true, but they didn't manage it very

well." He smiled. "Perhaps I should introduce them to your folks. Then they'd see how fortunate they are that the riskiest thing any of us is doing these days is trying to start up a winery from nothing."

"Hardly nothing," she replied. "You've got acres of vines, a stunning home, a beautiful stone barn, another round one I've yet to see, and a view beyond all measure. I'd say you were well on your way."

"Yes, well, all of that only works if I actually grow grapes, and enough of them to amount to anything. Those vines have been left to their own devices for far too long." He laughed. "If it would stop snowing sometime before June, that would help, too."

She laughed with him. "See, folks can't imagine how someone can even think about wandering the globe, playing a bit of the fiddle, singing a little tune, and hope to support themselves with it. But I know my abilities; I know my perseverance will pay off. At least enough so I can get by." She grinned. "If I don't want much. Or that's how it was for me for far longer than I can recall. What I can't imagine is starting up an entire enterprise that relies, in large part, on the whims of Mother Nature. I can't pretend to know what your frustrations must be like."

"Suddenly I'm wishing I was better at playing an instrument," he said, and they both laughed.

"Do you play?" she asked.

He shook his head. "Not a lick. I can move these big stompers around to music fairly well though," he said, lifting one booted foot. "Full disclosure, I can't say as I was a big fan of folk music when I first moved here."

"More a Disney soundtrack kind of bloke, are you?"

He barked out a laugh at that. "Oh yes. A regular slave to that rhythm."

She giggled, and noticed how it made his golden-brown

eyes flash in awareness. And that, in turn, made parts of her flash right back.

"I'm more of a jazz and blues kind of guy," he told her. "But living here for a few years now, I've come to develop a deep appreciation for the music of these mountains. We've got some amazing musicians in the Falls."

"I'd love to meet them," she said sincerely. "Hear them play."

"Oh, I imagine it would be a dream for them to have you join in. I still don't follow folk, so I can't say I know your music, but I can guarantee you the folks at the mill will have."

"I wouldn't presume to intrude on their—"

"Intrude?" He laughed. "If you can pluck a string or bang on something with anything that comes close to a decent rhythm, you're expected to join in. The rest of us show our appreciation by tapping our toes or doing a little dancing. It's our community sport."

She grinned at that. "Sounds like Blue Hollow Falls is a great deal like the villages back home."

"I wouldn't be surprised by that. One thing we respect here is privacy. If you ask folks to keep your presence here to themselves, they will. Or I'll ask them for you if you'd like."

Her smile softened. "Thank you. That's both kind and generous of you. And I don't doubt the truth of it. We would do the same back home. That's why I know you won't have to worry about your sister. She'll be looked out for."

He nodded; then his gaze turned more contemplative. "I probably shouldn't be presumptuous. You fill arenas, so Moira tells me, and deservedly so, I'm sure."

She laughed outright at that. "That's kind, but trust me, I'm no prima donna. Far from. It would be an honor to play with the folks here. I'd be the grateful one," she said. She looked down for a long moment. Her voice was quieter when she finally looked up at him and the truth just came out. "It's just, I'm not really here to sing or play, Seth."

He looked at her for a very long time, then said, "Aren't you?"

She heard her own soft intake of breath, and it felt as if her heart paused for a long beat, and then another, as their gazes caught, then held. *How is it that you know me?* she wanted to ask him. *Maybe it's because he does know me, that I told him in the first place.*

The moment was shattered when the hospital doors whooshed open and Maggie came out at a fast stride. She was a tall woman, with long hair that was naturally wavy, part brown but mostly gray. She wore jeans, hiking boots, a floral-print turtleneck and green fleece vest, and looked both worried and in control, all at the same time. In the short time they'd spoken, Pippa had felt enormous relief. Maggie took on the mantle of being in charge like it was second nature. She'd make sure Mabry received all the care he needed, no doubt.

At the exact same moment, a good-looking guy in an SUV pulled around the loop drive in front of the hospital and paused. "Greetings," he said with a broad smile. "Noah Tyler, your inn host with the most, and shuttle guide. Pippa MacMillan, I presume?"

Seth waved to Noah and went over to talk to Maggie while Pippa walked over to the curb where Noah's SUV idled. "Hello, yes, that's me," she said with a little wave. "A one-woman pain in everyone's backside." She did a little curtsy bob, making him laugh. "I'm guessing Maggie didn't get hold of you to let you know not to come down after all. I'm so sorry for all this. I didn't realize Seth was coming when I asked her to call you. Then she tried to call you back, but I'm guessing she didn't get through?"

He shook his head. "I've been out running errands, in and out of cell signal. I had to come down here anyway, so don't worry."

"You're very kind," she told him, then smiled. "Everyone

here is very kind. I'm just sorry you all are having to be so kind to me. Maggie told me all about your inn. I'd love to see it, see the rest of Blue Hollow Falls, too."

Noah Tyler was a very attractive man with dark hair, dancing brown eyes, and a flashing grin. Pippa knew from Katie's gossip sessions with Moira that Noah was involved with Stevie, who was the best friend of Sawyer Hartwell's significant other, Sunny. Who, Pippa now put together, was the sister of the ten-year-old Seth had given the goats to. *Everyone connected to everyone*, she thought, just like in her village growing up. She felt more at home in Blue Hollow Falls by the minute.

"Blue Hollow Falls would love to see you, too," Noah said. "Not that I've mentioned your name to anyone," he added, then did the little zipped-lip-turn-the-key action, making her smile. "You'd love the mill, though, the artists, the musicians. I'd be happy to introduce you around. I can promise you they'd be thrilled and not a little protective. You wouldn't have to worry."

"Seth just got done assuring me of that very thing," she told him. "I appreciate that, and the offer. Once I get settled in, I'll let you know."

He nodded easily. "Sounds like a plan."

No penetrating stare, no seeming ability to read her mind, to see past her polite excuses. Pippa sighed a little in relief, and yet her gaze flickered toward Seth, as if needing to confirm their connection. He was hugging Maggie, who was wiping tears from her eyes, but smiling, so Pippa hoped it was good news.

Noah noted the direction of her gaze. "I heard you were really good with helping Mabry today. We all appreciate that."

Pippa looked back at him. "I didn't do anything. I felt so helpless."

"That's not how I heard it," Noah replied kindly. "Mabry's like a local treasure. It's such a shame what happened, but it could have been so much worse. We owe you for being there for him." He grinned. "See, yet another reason for us to protect your privacy. Are you sure you don't want to swing by the mill on the way up to the cabin? I'm heading back to the inn. You can follow me up if you want."

"Thanks, Noah, but we've already run you all over. I'll see that she gets up there."

Pippa turned to find Seth standing behind her. "Where's Maggie?" She looked behind Seth in time to see her heading through the doors back inside the hospital. She turned back to Seth. "How's Mabry?"

"Maggie said he came through the surgery really well. They removed the jack. It just missed the artery, so they repaired damage from the puncture, and that all went well. It turns out they had to do a little bit more work on the fractures than anticipated, but the prognosis is full recovery, followed by some lengthy physical therapy."

Pippa winced. "I know that's supposed to be good news, but I feel so bad for him. That's a lot to handle."

"His grandsons are on their way. Thankfully it's spring-break time for them, so they'll be able to pitch in for a few days. Maggie is already making arrangements to move in for the duration. She didn't say, but I suspect this will be the nudge her husband needs for them to go ahead and commit to moving back to the Falls full time."

"I wish it were under better circumstances," Noah said, "but I am really happy to hear they're coming back. I think it will be good for all of them. And all of us, too."

Seth and Pippa nodded; then she said, "I'm so glad he has family to support him."

"He has all of us to support him," Noah chimed in. "We'll all make sure he's doing okay, and check in on Maggie and the boys, too."

Pippa nodded, then looked between the two men. "You've got a special place here. With some special people." Before she could change her mind—*or run and hide*—she added, "I'd like to take you up on your offer, Noah, when you've the time. See the mill, meet some of the artists."

Noah beamed. "We can make that happen." He looked at Seth. "Listen, why don't I take her on up to the cabin and show her all the ins and outs. I know you've lost a full day with the vines, and that's on top of the snow. You've got to be behind. Go on back to work. I'll take care of our new guest."

Seth looked ready to argue the point, but Pippa said, "It's okay. I'll just follow him up."

Seth nodded then, and said, "I've got her bags in the back of my truck. Let me move them to the back of Mabry's Chevy."

"Oh," Pippa said, suddenly concerned. "I forgot to ask Maggie if they'll be needing it back now. For her sons to drive?" She looked at Noah. "Maybe you should just give me directions and I'll go get a rental while I'm down here in town."

Seth shook his head. "They've got their own wheels. Don't worry. We'll shift things around later if needed."

"Unless you'd rather be driving something a bit spiffier," Noah said. "She's a classic, but you're probably used to something with a bit more giddyup."

She watched as both men glanced at the old Chevy, clear longing in their eyes. "Bluebell and I have become pretty well acquainted on our jaunt through the hills. If they don't need her back, I'll hold on to her. I offered to run errands for Mabry in exchange for the loan. I'll keep my word on that and talk to Maggie, see what I can do."

Noah grinned and nodded. "See? You're part of the community already."

"Bluebell?" This from Seth.

She looked at him. "There's a little brass plate screwed into the dashboard with Bluebell engraved in it. It's been there a long time by the looks of it. I figured that was the truck's name."

"If not, it is now," Noah said with a grin.

"You still have some things up at the house," Seth mentioned.

"I know." Pippa looked from Noah to Seth, and the words were out before she could think better of them. "Would it be okay to come by tomorrow? I could get my things, maybe give Dex a little grooming session. I'd be happy to help the kids with the sheep and the goats if they're coming by. I wouldn't be in your way."

Seth held her gaze again, in that way he did, so penetrating. He was probably weighing the pros and cons of their being in close quarters again. With that lovely chalet right there, and several beds nearby. Offering them complete privacy from any prying eyes. Heck, the old door he used as a desktop out in the barn might be at risk, if the way he was looking at her right now was any indication. Pippa tried not to shift her weight as her body responded with a very enthusiastic *Yes, please!*

Pippa could feel Noah's gaze on her, and knew it was probably on Seth as well. She'd just met Noah, but he struck her as being a pretty sharp guy. No doubt he was reading all kinds of things into the sudden, stacked-with-tension silence between her and Seth. All of those conclusions likely being correct.

"That's okay—" she began, wishing she'd kept her mouth closed.

"I just saw Bailey and Jake at the mill when I was by earlier," Noah said at the same time, an oh so helpful smile plastered all over his handsome face. "They were home last week on snow days, so I think Addie Pearl was about done having Bailey stuck in the nest. Bailey, too," Noah added with a laugh. "I heard her say she was going to pick up Jake and bring both kids up to your place tomorrow to burn off some energy."

Pippa glanced at Noah and saw the way he was smiling at her and Seth. *Oh yeah, he knew. Oh, boy.*

To her, Noah added, "I'll draw you a little map of how to get from the cabin to the vineyard, and down into the Falls. It's easy."

"When you know where to turn," she said on a laugh.

"That does help, yes." Noah turned to Seth, as if it had all been decided. "Do you need help with those bags?"

Seth looked at Pippa, then to Noah, then shook his head. "I've got it."

Pippa watched him as he walked off toward his truck without saying anything further. She hadn't missed the part where he hadn't answered her question. *Which is answer enough, isn't it?*

"So," Noah said when she finally looked back at him. His eyes were on full twinkle now and his grin was as wide as was humanly possible. "That's interesting."

Pippa could have played coy, or pretended she had no idea what Noah could possibly be referring to. But perhaps it wouldn't be such a bad idea to have someone on her side where Seth was concerned. She glanced at Seth, who was doing his Viking bellman impression again with her luggage, then back at Noah. "It has definitely been that," she said, and shot him a direct smile.

Noah's eyes widened in delighted surprise. "Well, well. Miss Pippa MacMillan, I think I like you."

"Good to hear," she said, then grinned and leaned her folded arms on the bottom edge of his open window. "Because it's quite probable I'm going to need some advice before this adventure is all said and done, and you've just been nominated to the position."

Chapter Eight

Seth slogged through the mud to the last row of vines and continued clipping. It was a gamble, knowing which parts to cut off, which buds to leave, hoping for the right end result. Cut too much, no grapes. Leave too many, not enough nutrients to produce a full grape bunch. Have a late frost in the spring, or an early one in the fall, lose too much of your crop and you'd wish you'd left a few more buds as backup.

He glanced upward to the clear, vibrantly blue sky and wiped the sweat from the back of his neck. Even at 2,700-feet elevation, it was seventy-four in the shade, and hot as blazes out in the sun. Which was now making his job like one long, continuous mud-wrestling match. He wasn't sure which was worse, trying not to fall on his ass every other minute—and not being entirely successful—or having to clear away two feet of snow from each and every vine so he could see what to cut, as he'd had to do all the week before.

He crouched back down and continued working. "It would be helpful if you'd hold steady for, oh, a week at a time there, Mom Nature," he grumbled. Seth had been having an ongoing conversation with her all winter, and now into the spring. Clearly, she wasn't listening. He suspected they'd be having many more conversations just like it.

The sound of someone shouting "Mr. B! Mr. B[...] Seth straightening and walking to the end of the ro[...] looked down the slope toward the round barn and spied Jacob McCall racing up the hill. *And not slipping around at all*, Seth noted. "Ah, the agility of youth," he said under his breath, feeling twice his thirty-two years at the moment. "Slow down, slow down," Seth called out as the out-of-breath thirteen-year-old reached the edge of the field at a dead run.

Jake skidded to a stop a few yards away and walked the final few steps, breathing in big gulps of air. The smile splitting the boy's face was on par with the excitement Seth had heard in Jake's voice, which was a good thing. Seth didn't think he could handle anything traumatic at the moment. Mabry's accident was still haunting him.

"Do you know—" Jake began, still sucking in air, then pausing to brace his hands on his bony knees to catch his breath. His grin never abated. "Do you know who is in the stone barn? Right now?"

Seth cast his gaze toward the house, then to the stone barn, then down the hill to the round barn. He didn't think he'd been so deep in thought he'd have missed the sound of a car or truck driving up, and since all he saw was his truck and the old blue and white Chevy, clearly, he hadn't. Addie had left after dropping Jake and Bailey off a few hours ago. Pippa had decided to take his non-answer the day before as a yes and had shown up not long after Addie. Seth didn't have any pregnant goats or sheep at the moment—praise the Lord—so he wasn't quite sure what Jake was so wound up about. "I guess I don't," he said. "Why don't you tell me?"

"None other than the best fiddle player ever put on God's green earth. And that's a direct quote from Miss Addie Pearl. But I second it. And third it." The normally quiet, shy young man was literally bouncing on the balls of his feet. "Right in your barn," he said, enunciating each word.

Seth felt silly for not knowing immediately whom Jacob was so excited about. It was just, he thought of her as Pippa. Not as Pippa MacMillan, the best fiddle player ever put on God's green earth. "You've met Pippa, then. I told you she'd be here."

"You said a 'friend of your sister,'" he said, making air quotes to accompany that last part. "Your sister knows Pippa MacMillan? And you never said anything? I've been out with the sheep moving them to the upper field. And all that time, she was right here." He said the last two words like they were individual sentences.

Seth chuckled then. Jacob McCall was, by nature, a quiet, reflective kid. Newly a teenager just a month ago, he was tall for his age but not all that awkward. He had a thick thatch of dark hair sprouting off his head this way and that, with more cowlicks than waves, serious green eyes like his dad, and a work ethic every bit as etched into his DNA as it was in his father's. Jake got his quiet and calm from his father, Wilson, who was as good a man as there was. Maybe Jake was even more taciturn by nature. All of which made this exuberant display that much more amusing.

"Actually, my sister was college roommates with Pippa's sister, Katie."

"Still, that's like only one degree of separation." Jake raked his hand through his hair, making it stand up on end even more. "I got done and walked into the stone barn just now and there she was, sitting on a stool, brushing Dexter's fur. Like a regular person. And he lets her!"

Seth laughed. "She is a regular person. And those two formed some kind of bond right off. Which is a good thing," he told Jake. "Dex can make goo-goo eyes at her now. Everyone wins."

Jake let out a laugh that was half boyish giggle, half new-teen croak. His voice was changing, which charmed all of the adults, and routinely mortified Jake. "I didn't say anything or interfere, I swear. I just stood there staring. She didn't see me."

"Go on and introduce yourself. She's a very nice person. She'll enjoy meeting you."

Jake blushed bright pink at that, which was when Seth realized what else was going on here. He didn't tease Jake about it though. Seth remembered his first crush all too clearly, and how much glee his older siblings took in torturing him with the knowledge. He could still hear their good-natured mocking to this day.

"Do you know her music is pretty much the only fiddle playing my dad still listens to?" Jake said.

Seth had become good friends with Wilson and admired him and his son a great deal. But even though Seth knew he could count on Will for pretty much anything, Seth couldn't say he knew much about the man personally. "Does he, now?" Will was also a military vet, but he hadn't served with Sawyer and Seth. In fact, he never talked about his time in the service, and Seth and Sawyer respected that. Seth knew Will had lost his wife when Jake was little, and that Will's mom had helped to raise Jake after that, while Will remained in the service. When she passed, Will had processed out and moved to the Falls full time. Seth only knew this because of Addie Pearl's close relationship with Will's mom. Will never spoke of it. "Is he thinking about taking up the fiddle again?" Seth asked, trying to keep the question light, but quite curious despite himself.

According to Addie Pearl, Will not only was an amazing fiddle player, but at one time, he'd made his own instruments and was quite the craftsman. Given the beautiful work Seth had seen Will do as a stonemason, he didn't doubt it. But he would never have known about that, either, if Addie hadn't told him. Seth thought it had something to do with Will's time in the service. Sawyer thought it had to do with Will losing his wife. Probably they'd never know for sure. If Will hadn't talked about it by this time, it wasn't likely he ever would. So, this bit of insight was very interesting news, indeed.

"I don't know," Jake said, quietly now, back to his normal, more subdued self. "He's never said anything about it." Jake glanced over to the stone barn, then down at his feet. "I saw Pippa and I thought . . ." He broke off, looking away from Seth and the stone barn.

"You thought maybe if your dad knew she was here, he'd want to play?"

Jake still kept his gaze averted. "Maybe."

Seth put a hand on Jake's shoulder, gave it a comforting squeeze, then let go when the young boy finally looked up at him again. "It's good that you're thinking about your dad like that. He'd be proud of you."

Jake let out a brief snort. "I don't know about that."

"Caring about people who matter to you is always positive. Wanting to do things that will make them feel good, also positive."

Jake's expression cleared, and some of the excitement returned. "I just think if he knew she was here, maybe . . ."

"Maybe," Seth conceded, "but I have to be honest and tell you she's not here to play or sing, Jake. At least, that's what she told me. She's taking some time off."

"Because of her surgery," Jake said. When that earned him a surprised look, Jake said, "Everybody knows what happened." He gave a little shudder.

"You mean about her injuring her vocal cords?"

"They weren't just injured—they totally ruptured," Jake told him. "Right in the middle of singing 'Call Down Your Heart.' That's her biggest hit. It was the third encore on her last tour stop in London."

"How do you know all this?"

"There's a video of the whole thing on YouTube. I only

watched it once." Jake made another face and shuddered again. "It's pretty freaky."

Stunned, Seth said, "There's a video? Why would they leave that up there? Someone should report it."

Jake just rolled his eyes. "It wouldn't matter. It was a huge concert. Tons of people recorded it on their cell phones. No way could anyone keep that from going viral. It was—" He made a face, like he'd just tasted something sour. "It was a long time ago, like a year almost. I guess she's better now. But she hasn't put out any new music since it happened."

Seth smiled again, even while part of his brain was still processing all of that information. He remembered telling Pippa more than once that anytime something life-changing happened to a person it was a big deal, no matter the cause, and he'd meant it. But knowing this definitely altered his perception about what she must have gone through. "You really must like her music," he told Jake. "You follow her pretty closely."

Jake let out a short laugh. "I like her music a lot, but I don't have to 'follow her' or anything to know all that," he said, making air quotes again. He looked up at Seth, propping his hand on his forehead to shield his eyes from the sun. "You know she's a pretty big deal, right? Like—"

"The Bono of folk music," Seth answered, remembering Moira's description.

"I guess," Jake said, scrunching up his face. "He's kind of an old guy. I was going to say more like Katy Perry. Or Beyoncé. Okay, maybe not as big as her," he conceded. "But definitely pretty big."

Seth supposed he should count himself lucky that he at least knew the stars Jake was referring to, so he didn't have one foot in the grave quite yet.

"So, go on over and introduce yourself to her," Seth urged. "But no sharing on social media, okay?"

"I know. Noah told me she was here on the down low. I won't blow her cover. I'd never do that."

Seth smiled, knowing Pippa had yet another white knight looking out for her. First Noah, now Jake. She seemed to recruit them without even trying. *Like she did with you?* He ignored that, or tried to. "I really appreciate that." He glanced down to the round barn. "Why don't you go grab Bailey? She might like to meet Pippa, too." And Seth thought that might help break the ice a little for Jake, who was clearly as crush-struck as he was starstruck.

Jake rolled his eyes. "Nah, she's hosing down the sheep. She didn't even know who Pippa was." He said it in a tone that made it clear how incredible that was. "Bailey doesn't listen to current music. At all. She likes old stuff. She talks all the time about some seriously old dude named B.B. King, who died a few years ago. And another one, Miles some-body."

"Miles Davis," Seth said and grinned. "I knew I liked that kid."

Despite the gap in their ages, it hadn't taken long after Bailey's arrival for her and Jake to strike up a friendship. There weren't too many kids in Blue Hollow Falls. But theirs wasn't just a friendship of convenience. Addie said the two were thick as thieves when Jake was over there helping Bailey with her own sheep, whispering and laughing one minute, squabbling like family the next. Seth thought both kids had benefited from forging a bond. Bailey's life up to very recently had been spent mostly in foster care and Jake, of course, was growing up without his mother, and now his grandmother was gone as well. Addie Pearl had been a blessing for him, too.

"I know she'd like Pippa's music," Jake went on, "if I could just get her to listen to it. I wish my dad was picking us up today, but he's working on a stone chimney over in

Buck's Pass. He'll be blown away to hear Pippa MacMillan is here."

"I'm sure she wouldn't mind meeting him, too, if you think he'd like to," Seth said, wondering if Jake was right, or if it was wishful thinking. "She'll be staying in the area for a little while."

"Thanks, I'll ask him," Jake said. He looked over at the stone barn, then down to the round barn. "Well, I should go help Bailey finish with the sheep. We've got to go to the stone barn after, to feed the goats. If Pippa's still there, I'll get to meet her then."

Seth hid his amused smile. Jake was clearly nervous. It was very charming, and though Seth had no doubt Pippa would put the smitten young teen instantly at ease, Jake didn't know that.

"If you'll help me with this last row," he told Jake, "I'll walk down to the round barn with you. I'm going to move the sheep to a different field tomorrow because their regular one is a mud pit. So I wanted to talk to both of you about that anyway. Then, if you like, I'll introduce you to Pippa."

Jake's relief was palpable, and his grin swift. "That'd be great." He turned to the vines. "I didn't bring my snips with me."

"I've got an extra pair in the bucket over there. Snip low, leave high on that row."

Jake nodded and set straight off, not needing more guidance than that. Seth nodded in approval. Jake had shown an interest in the vines from the first time he'd come up to help with the sheep and Bailey's goats. Seth had shown him a few things, talked to him a little about it, thinking Jake was just being polite. But the boy's interest was sincere. More than that, he picked up on what he was shown as if it were second nature. Jake had helped Seth with his first harvest, and Seth let him keep his hand in whenever possible, after his other work with the livestock was done.

Seth watched Jake work, nodding in approval as the boy

trimmed off the dead and withered, examined the good buds, made his choices, and snipped off the rest. Jake didn't know it yet, but Seth had been giving Jake the same section to work on during the off season for a reason. He planned to let Jake harvest that section, press his grapes, and see what he could come up with. Not all grape juice had to be fermented into wine. Grape juice in and of itself was a viable product, though it didn't command the same price. He thought Jake might find it a fun challenge. It was a good place to start, Seth thought, then chuckled to himself. *Or is it the blind leading the blind?* Either way, they'd both enjoy themselves.

A half hour later, they were walking up the sodden strip of grass that lined the center space between the rows of vines, with Jake alternately chattering on and on about how amazing Pippa's music was, and flaming beet red at the thought of actually talking to her. Jake said more in the time it took them to get to the end of the row than he had said to Seth in the entire time he'd known the boy. *The power of a pretty, talented woman*, Seth thought. Made even the young ones lose their cool.

They'd just stepped from the end of the row, both of them looking like the creatures from the mud lagoon at this point, when they heard Bailey's laughter echoing from the open doors to the stone barn. "Looks like we won't have to worry about introducing Bailey to Pippa," Seth said. A short glance at Jake showed the teenager looking suddenly vulnerable and uncertain. Seth put a hand on Jake's shoulder, gently squeezed. "You'll be fast friends in the blink of an eye. I can guarantee it. She's just like you and me, just another person. I grow grapes, she sings songs. We're all the same, Jake."

"Maybe," Jake said, sounding entirely unconvinced. Jake set the tool bucket down and helped Seth with the pull tarp he'd dragged along behind them with some of the chunkier bits they'd trimmed from the vines. It would all go into the burn pile. Then Jake glanced down at his hands, and his muddy pants, and Seth suspected Jake knew he had just as much of the stuff on his face and in his hair, which was true.

"Go on up and shower," Seth told him.

"But we still have to feed the goats."

"I'll help with that, or Pippa will help. She grew up on a farm." If Seth had thought Jake's hero worship where Pippa was concerned had reached its zenith, he'd just been proven wrong.

"That's awesome," he said and Seth couldn't help it, he chuckled.

"We'll take care of that, then I know Bailey's going to want to shower off, so go get yours out of the way. Then she can jump in while you're talking to Pippa."

Seth had built a big outdoor shower off the back of the house right after moving in and used it year-round to wash off the muck of the fields before heading into the house. It was paneled on three sides with tall cedar planking and had a bench and row of hooks in addition to the shower stall itself. All private, it had an entrance directly into the bathroom at the back of the house. Jake and Bailey always brought a duffel with a spare set of clothes so they could get home without trashing Addie or Will's vehicles with their mucky, stinky clothes after an afternoon or full day playing with livestock or out in the vines.

"Okay, thanks." Jake glanced to the stone barn again, all nerves and anticipation, but Seth could also see he was relieved that Seth had arranged it so Bailey wasn't there when Jake met his idol. Seth understood that, too. It wasn't so much that Jake wanted to have Pippa and her friendship all to himself. Jake wasn't like that. It was that he was probably certain he was about to totally geek out and make an utter fool of himself in the presence of someone he'd admired for so long, and he'd rather his best friend not be a witness.

What Bailey didn't see, she couldn't tease him about for years to come.

"Just put the tools on the bench. I'll get them later." Seth waved Jake off toward the house and dragged the tarp over to the burn pit, which was in an open space halfway between the vines and the stone barn.

Bailey's laughter echoed out from the open door of the barn again, mixed with Pippa's giggles this time. He smiled, thinking how much Bailey had changed since coming to Blue Hollow Falls. She'd been a pretty stoic young lady herself, but in a far different way from Jake. Wise far beyond her years from a life that demanded she grow up way too fast. Since Addie had taken her under her wing, Bailey wasn't any less wise, but the child in her had truly blossomed.

Seth paused outside the open doors, then took a slow turn and looked out over his operation, his farm, at the view beyond it, which he never tired of seeing. He let it sink in, settle inside him, something he made a habit of doing every day. His smile grew as the sounds of Bailey and Pippa, chattering like magpies, filtered through and blended with the rest. He felt . . . happy. Sincerely, down-to-the-bone happy. Sure, his business wasn't off the ground yet, and there were a myriad of stresses facing him on a daily basis as he moved closer to that make-it-or-break-it moment. None of that was the point though.

It struck him, in that moment, that perhaps serenity and inner peace came in a variety of forms. That what he'd needed to soothe his soul, and his psyche, after leaving the Army, wasn't so much having utter solitude or getting away from the frenetic pace of city life. Maybe it was simply a matter of finding exactly the right spot in which to plant himself.

Who knew that keeping the company of sheep, goats, chickens, and a lovestruck llama would go hand in hand with tending endless rows of vines and more vines. It wasn't how he'd seen it all coming together while walking those endless rows of vines in a distant country, what felt like light years ago now. Far from. But it was turning out to be perfect for him.

"Penny for your thoughts."

Seth turned to find Pippa standing in the open doorway to the barn, leaning against the side beam, her arms folded over the dark green T-shirt she wore. She had on black jeans that now showed more dust and dirt than denim and a pair of army-green, knee-high rubber farm boots that looked a few sizes too big, and probably were as they were one of the pairs he kept for his day-laborers and part-timers to use as needed during harvest season. Her pretty face was free of makeup and her hair had been combed close to her head and tamed into tightly woven pigtails. The curled ends rested just below her shoulders, each pigtail held in place with bright red elastic that somehow added to the overall perky vibe she already exuded just by breathing.

"Taking a moment between chores," he said, smiling at her. Because he'd already learned it was just damned impossible not to. "What are you two up to in there? Sounds like my sisters when they were cooking up something sure to stretch my parents' patience." He grinned. "Or their bank account."

"No plotting or planning. Just girl talk. She's a sharp one," Pippa added, referring to Bailey. "I like her."

"She's a likable kid."

"I don't know about the kid part. I feel like she's seen a lot more of this world than I have, and without ever leaving the States."

"Likely true," Seth said. "She's an old soul, as Addie says."

Pippa laughed. "Yes, I've heard a lot about Miss Addison Pearl Whitaker today. The patron saint of Blue Hollow Falls, as far as I can tell."

Seth chuckled. "You wouldn't be wrong about that. We

all owe her a deep debt of gratitude, and it would irritate her something fierce if she were to hear me say it."

"I gathered that as well."

Bailey came out just then, carrying in her arms one of three baby pygmy goats in residence. Bailey was lanky for a ten-year-old, with freckled skin that tanned surprisingly easily, which made her pretty red hair and serious, bright blue eyes all the more striking. Seth didn't envy the adults in her life, himself included, when she got old enough to be interested in boys. Or, more to the point, when she got old enough for boys to be interested in her.

"I'm thinking this one," Bailey said to Pippa.

Pippa's eyes widened, then went instantly moist. "Truly? Are you sure?"

Bailey looked from the goat to Pippa, then back to the goat. She smiled. "I'm sure." She handed the armful to Pippa. "I've posted his regimen on the nursery stall. You have to follow it. If you have any questions, text me." Her smile spread to a lopsided grin. "You also have to name him."

Pippa looked down at the goat in her arms. "I do?" she said, then sighed softly.

Seth knew she was a goner right then. *What is it about girls and goats?* They were cute enough, he supposed, and these stayed little, which meant they didn't outgrow their cuteness. He liked them because they could plow through and chow down an overgrown field better than a tractor, and he didn't have to be there while they did it, which freed him up for other things. He doubted Pippa was thinking about their usefulness at the moment.

"I don't name the babies I don't plan to keep," Bailey said. "It's a special thing, like a bond. It should be between the two of you."

Seth frowned. "Bailey, she can't—"

"She knows I can't take him back to Ireland," Pippa said,

breaking in before Seth could get any farther. "Bailey just wanted me to have a special companion and connection to this place. She'll find him a good home after I'm gone." Pippa looked at Bailey. "I'll support him of course. And presents on holidays. And if you think he needs a playmate, that, too." She lifted the goat's face to hers, then giggled when he licked her right across the face. "You have to make sure they'll send photos," she told Bailey. "Videos, if possible. And that they'll keep his name. Will that be okay?"

Bailey shrugged. "We'll make it okay." As if that was that. And knowing Bailey, it would be. She looked at Seth. "Sunny gave me my Little Bo-Peep sheep, and you gave me my first three baby goats. It made me feel like I belonged here, like I was connected to something long term." She shrugged again, but the look in her eyes was anything but casual. "I wanted to do for Pippa something like what you did for me."

Seth could have told Bailey that Pippa had both a childhood home and a huge family and probably more feeling of belonging and connectedness than she needed. Pippa wasn't adrift, as Bailey had been. But then Pippa was handing the baby goat to Seth and wrapping Bailey—who wasn't much shorter than Pippa—into a tight hug. Pippa's eyes were squeezed shut, a single tear trickling down her cheek as she expressed her sincere thanks to Bailey. A second later the two of them were giggling again, this time in mutual excitement.

Seth looked down at the baby goat, who was busy chewing a button off the front of his shirt. "I think you just won the baby goat lottery," he told the little nibbler. "Don't blow it."

"So, are we cool?" Bailey asked Seth after he'd handed the kid back to Pippa.

"They're your goats to breed, sell, keep, whatever. That was our deal," Seth said. "I provide the space and the feed in return for the help you give me with the sheep. Any money you make from selling them goes to Addie for your college fund."

"I'm not selling him to her," Bailey said.

"That's your prerogative, too."

"Bailey, I'm not letting you give him—" Pippa began.

Bailey cut her off with a shake of her head. "This isn't about business. This is about belonging."

Seth noticed that Pippa shot him a quick glance, as if trying to gauge his reaction. She quickly looked back to Bailey, her expression one of sincere affection. "I think this is perhaps the loveliest gift I've ever received. Thank you."

Bailey nodded, smiled. "You're welcome."

Seth felt out of the loop. Well, partly out. He knew Pippa wasn't here so much to rest as she was to search. Seth just hadn't figured out the "for what" part yet. Whatever it was, Bailey had apparently pegged it after just an hour or two. *And you don't need to figure it out, remember? Her journey is her journey. Yours has already been decided. Those paths will diverge soon. That's why you're sleeping alone in your bed at night, remember?*

Seth noticed Jake coming in their direction from the house. He stifled a smile when he noted Jake had tried to tame his wet hair into submission and was staring hard at his feet as he walked. "Hey, Bailey, I think Jake is done with the shower. Why don't you head on up for yours?"

Bailey glanced toward the house—which Seth realized he'd started thinking of as the chalet—then looked right back at Seth, her expression smooth, open, easy. Jake might want a solo meeting in case he geeked out when meeting Pippa, but if he could see Bailey's face right now, and the automatic protectiveness she had for her good friend, Jake would know that he had nothing to worry about.

"Will do," she said. She looked at Pippa. "I'll come back

before I go." She smiled. "In case you have any questions. See how the naming thing is going."

"That would be great," Pippa said happily, without a trace of anxiety. Apparently, there were no second thoughts about her new acquisition.

Bailey stepped past Seth, then turned back. He'd been watching Pippa walk back into the barn, and noticed Bailey hadn't missed that, either. But she didn't say anything about that. Instead, she tugged his shirtsleeve and he ducked his head down closer to hers. "Jake is super freaked out about meeting Pippa. He worships her music. She's like . . ."

"The Beyoncé of folk music?"

Bailey rolled her eyes. "More like Bono. Anyway, can you just . . . hang around a few minutes? Help him out if he gets totally geeked? I know she'll be great to him, but he'll beat himself up forever if he fanboys all over her."

"Fanboys?"

"Makes a fool of himself over her." Bailey looked up into his face and smiled beatifically, then batted her eyelashes. "Not that you'd know anything about that."

Seth coughed on a surprised laugh. Bailey didn't rib or tease very often. When she did, it was usually for a purpose. "Very funny," he told her, but he was smiling and there might have been a faint trace of heat in his cheeks. *Outed by a ten-year-old.* "You know Pippa will be heading back to Ireland before too long," he told Bailey, hoping to nip in the bud whatever little matchmaker plans she might have.

"I know," Bailey said blithely. "The world isn't that big a place these days. That's all I'm saying." Then she headed on up to the house, waving easily at Jake when they passed, then turned around and ran back a few steps so she could hug him from behind. She brushed off the dust and dirt she got on the back of his nice clean shirt, then when he turned around, she reached up and whispered something that Seth was too far away to hear. Whatever it was, it made Jake laugh.

Seth saw the rigid set of the boy's shoulders relax a bit and shook his head. *Bailey to the rescue.*

"Some guy out there is going to be a very fortunate man one day," Seth said under his breath. *And that girl should be at least thirty before anyone gets any ideas. Maybe forty.*

Bailey ran the rest of the way up to the house while Seth waited for Jake. "You clean up good," Seth said, then winced when the tips of Jake's ears went scarlet. *Some wingman you are there, sport.*

"Is that Jake?" Pippa's voice echoed from inside the barn.

And the rest of Jake's face now matched his ears.

Pippa came bouncing out, no baby goat this time, a huge smile on her face. "Hullo," she said. "Bailey has told me so much about you, I feel like we're already friends." She held out her arms. "I'd hug you but I'm still covered in baby goat." She turned and headed inside, assuming Jake would follow, which he did. As did Seth, wishing he knew the trick to being a pied piper.

"I've a new goat," she told Jake excitedly. "Bailey gave him to me just now. I have to name him, and I have no idea where to begin. You've probably named loads of animals. Would you help me?"

"I—uh, sure. Yeah. I mean, yes. I'd be happy to, Miss MacMillan."

Pippa giggled at that. "You sound like you're talking to my mum. Just call me Pippa. Is it okay if I call you Jake? Or would you rather Jacob? Or Master McCall?"

Jake laughed at that, the high-pitched kind that broke and croaked in the middle. Seth winced, which Pippa noted as she glanced past the boy to him. Without missing a beat, she leaned in closer to Jake as she so often did, as if sharing a secret. "I've had that going on with my voice now for about eleven months. It's so annoying." She straightened and grinned. "I'm told I'll grow out of it, too, but it doesn't help much in the interim, does it?"

Rather than being mortified, Jake shook his head and grinned back at her. "Not at all, no." They walked over to the goat stalls together.

And just like that, Pippa had another heart tucked neatly in her pocket.

Seth had thought to stay in the barn, work in his office a bit, just to be on hand for moral support if Jake needed it. As that didn't seem to be the case, Seth opted to head on back to the chalet and scrape a few layers of muck off his own person.

It wasn't until he was stepping under the shower that he thought back to his earlier reaction. *Yet another heart tucked in her pocket.*

He'd been thinking of Jake's and Bailey's, of course. And Noah's. And Mabry's.

"Right. That's exactly what you were thinking." He ducked his head under the spray. Then, just to make sure he shut down all thought paths that led to Pippa, he turned it to cold.

Chapter Nine

Pippa drove Bluebell down the road that led from the vineyard, past Mabry's apple farm, down into Blue Hollow Falls. The town proper was small by any standard, but it was a bucolic little place, tucked away as it was in the hills. She'd seen it once before, the day she'd followed Noah from the hospital up to her wee cabin.

The town wasn't more than a few blocks long, with several side streets at staggered intervals. She passed a post office, a church, Bo's diner—which she'd heard raves about from Bailey—a hardware store, bookshop, and several offices touting various services. There were a few cute little shops tucked in here and there, a large antique store on the corner at the one main intersection. That two-story shop was diagonally across from a rather important-looking redbrick building with fat, white pillars holding up the small portico that shaded the wide brick steps leading up to the big oak doors. She noticed the little redbrick library next to it that she'd missed on her first pass through, and took the time to glance down the side streets, which appeared to be mostly residential. Then their little caravan was through the town and out the other side, back into the winding twists and turns that led through hills and more hills.

Today, instead of continuing on down to the main highway that went to Turtle Springs, they took a turn onto a narrower track that reminded her of the single-track roads at home, only there wasn't much, if any, room to pull to the side to allow an oncoming vehicle to pass. Pippa followed Addie's dusty green Subaru through a charming covered bridge that spanned Big Stone Creek. She knew from Jake that Big Stone Creek's headwaters were up near the peak of the mountain known as Hawk's Nest Ridge. Addie's home was up in that area, as was Sawyer and Sunny's place.

Up there the creek seemed more aptly named, as it was little more than a trickling stream of spring water. It picked up steam quickly as it traveled steeply downward, however, drawing in more and more water from other springs that seeped out between tumbles of boulders—some easily the size of Addie's car—as well as any number of feeder streams. The creek tumbled and wound its way down through the hills, the high point being the one spectacular waterfall drop, right where the mill was located, which she'd get to see today. Then on down the mountain it went until it fed into the Hawksbill River below, which ran like a long, winding snake through the valley of the same name.

Pippa knew Turtle Springs was tucked into one of the curves of the Hawksbill, which had a wide span and a steady, almost lazy flow to it, as it also wrapped around the hospital where Mabry was still a guest. She hadn't been allowed in to see him yet, which worried her, but Maggie had said she'd let Pippa and Seth know the minute he was out of intensive care.

Pippa downshifted as their little procession wound through more twists and turns, higher into the hills once again, proud of how well she'd adapted to the different driving conditions and opposite rules of the road. Of course, it didn't hurt that she was playing follow the leader. She gasped in delight as they popped out of the trees and there was a sudden, railed drop-off to her right, affording her a view of some of the most breathtaking scenery she'd seen yet. There was still some snow at the highest peaks, outlining every ridge and crevasse. Below that it looked as though someone had cloaked the timeworn hills with a blanket of pine trees, undulating over each curve in a deep, rich, emerald green, accented here and there by protruding ridges of granite and stone.

Pippa could see Hawk's Nest Ridge from there, too. She'd get to see it up close that Sunday. Addie had invited her to supper, where she'd meet Sawyer and Sunny, as well as Bailey's wee Herdwick sheep that she'd heard so much about. Seth would be there, too, which might be the first Pippa would get to see of him this week, despite her daily trips to the vineyard to visit with Dex and care for her baby goat.

Pippa knew Seth wasn't keen on Bailey's having given her the baby goat, whom Pippa had named Elliott that same day, much to everyone's dismay. Apparently, that wasn't a goat-worthy moniker. When she'd explained she'd taken the name from the young boy in the movie *E.T. the Extra-Terrestrial*, which was all about connections and home and family, Bailey and Jake had simply looked at her, no comprehension on their young faces. Seth, however, had said, "El-li-ott," in the same gravelly voice E.T. had in the movie, making Pippa giggle. They'd shared a private grin, and her body had leapt so eagerly in response, she'd had to pretend the baby goat had nibbled somewhere he shouldn't as an excuse to look quickly away.

They hadn't been in close proximity to each other since, which hadn't seemed to dull her desire for him one whit. The opposite, if that was possible. Pippa had promised Bailey and Jake a movie and popcorn night up at her cabin. Seth had been invited, too. She'd hoped with the kids there as chaperones maybe he'd relent and allow himself to be in the same room with her. She was still awaiting his decision. Bailey had agreed out of sheer politeness, Pippa knew, while Jake's ears had turned bright pink before nodding and asking if he could bring anything. Pippa had promised Bailey she wouldn't regret attending, and privately prayed she was right.

And Pippa and Seth hadn't shared so much as a wave since.

When Pippa had gone to the vineyard the following day, Seth had been on the far side, still working his way through the vines, and hadn't moved much closer to the barns by the time she said good-bye to Dex and Elliott for the day. It had been the same the next two days as well. Come yesterday, Thursday, he'd been gone altogether. He'd stuck a note to Elliott's stall door, saying he'd gone down to Turtle Springs to check in on Mabry and run errands, and to let her know that Bailey and Jake wouldn't be up that day. She supposed she should be happy he'd felt compelled to do that much.

Pippa hadn't been stung by his removing himself from her orbit so much as she'd been . . . curious. He could have told her at any time—including the day she'd asked him directly—that he'd rather she not come, but he hadn't. To her mind, she and Seth were grown adults, and despite their apparent hormonally driven desire to jump each other, she was fairly certain with proper sleep and three squares a day for stamina, they could reasonably expect to control themselves even when standing within five feet of one another for more than a minute. So why such an extreme reaction?

She'd been careful to stay out of his way, to not interfere with his work. Of course, she could have steered clear of the vineyard altogether, but the way she saw it, she kept Dex occupied when he wasn't on sheep guard-patrol, and she'd taken on the care and feeding of the baby goats. She wasn't eating Seth's food or sleeping under his roof, so certainly he could stand her doing that much.

Yesterday, with him gone, the kids off for the day, and Dex back in the field with the sheep, Pippa knew she could have fed and played with the goats for a bit, then just turned around and gone back to the cabin. Or down into Blue Hollow Falls, as she'd been promising herself she'd do every day that week . . . but always ended up at the vineyard instead.

What she'd done, however, was go exploring. Seth hadn't specifically told her not to go into the rows of vines, so she'd taken the afternoon and strolled through a goodly number of them. With the showers that had passed through early in the week, and the continued warmer than average temperatures persisting all week, the snow was gone completely now. The unrelenting sun, coupled with a strong breeze, had dried out the ground so that what had been mud and muck was now more like malleable dirt.

Pippa stayed on the still somewhat spongey strip of turf that ran down the center of each row, though she had waded into the soft soil here and there to study some of the vines, looking at the cuts Seth had made, looking at what he'd chosen to keep. She'd still been mostly flummoxed by how he made his choices when she'd finally climbed into Bluebell several hours later and headed back to her lovely little cabin for a nice, long soak.

Pippa had fallen in love with her wee cabin in the hills the moment she'd stepped inside it. It wasn't anything like the chalet, but she loved what Noah had done with the small space. Rustic was the theme of the day, but the cabin wasn't merely serviceable. The innkeeper in him had made sure it was comfortable and cozy too. Handwoven rugs covered the hardwood floor, overstuffed cushions plumped up the small couch, and a lap throw had been folded and draped over the back. There was also a padded rocking chair, which matched the pair on the little front porch.

The one main room served as living area, dining area,

and kitchen, all of which could fit in the space of her living room back in Ireland, and her place was modestly proportioned. The round breakfast table sat two comfortably and four if they didn't mind moving for folks coming in and out of the kitchen area. The kitchen, though well-appointed with new appliances, was just big enough to get things done with one chef at a time. The bathroom had been the biggest surprise. Small, with a tiny commode and sink, so the rest of the space could be devoted to a nice, big, spa-sized tub. Pippa had texted Noah her personal thanks. It felt like her own little nest before she'd even unpacked.

Overhead, the open-space room soared to a second story peak, from which hung a large ceiling fan on a long pole between two skylights, much like the one at Seth's chalet, though much smaller in scale. If the cozy ground floor room and spa tub had charmed her, her heart had gone completely around the bend when she'd finally climbed the wide, flat, ladder-style steps up to the loft. Tucked into the eaves of the steeply slanted roof was a big, wide queen-size bed, a small nightstand, a small dormer window at the far end facing out the front of the house, and a stunning giant window that served as the headboard and filled most of the side wall.

It was a wonder she ever left the bed at all. It had fast become her favorite spot. The view she had from there, lying on her stomach, arms folded on her pillow, was beyond breathtaking. She was above the trees up there, like being in a treehouse, and could look straight down the peak of the mountain ridge, with other ridges snaking off to the left and right and ripple upon ripple of mountaintops for as far as the eye could see.

At night, the view shifted from the mountaintops up to the star-filled sky. That particular light show was one she'd never tire of for the rest of her days. She'd yet to see her first shooting star, but she felt certain that was only a matter of time. Pippa made a mental note to ask Addie when they got to the mill if there was a place she could get a map of the stars. Her father was an avid stargazer, and Pippa smiled to herself, thinking she might surprise him with a new wealth of celestial knowledge upon her return home. Maybe that would help erase the worry lines she'd seen feathering the corners of his eyes when she'd stopped in to see everyone just before hopping across the Atlantic.

Home. She missed it. Missed her family, her team. But she wasn't ready to leave. She'd just gotten here, just settled in, begun to find her place, to fit in. *It's about belonging.* Bailey's words from last weekend echoed through her mind. Pippa smiled, thinking she hoped to be as wise as that little girl one day.

Addie turned off the mountain road onto one that was gravel and dirt, drawing Pippa from her thoughts as she continued to follow the little car over the bumpy, pitted road to the site of the mill. Even knowing where they were going and hearing endless descriptions of the place from Bailey and Jake didn't prepare her for the reality of it. She braked the truck so fast the moment she first saw it, she stalled out. There wasn't anyone behind her, so she simply sat there and took it in as Addie drove on ahead and parked in the little gravel lot near the side entrance.

The mill was tucked up on the side of a hill, in a crook of Big Stone Creek. Pine trees soared behind it, giving off their unique, blue aura, and beyond and above that was Hawk's Nest Ridge, creating a spectacular backdrop. The mill itself was gorgeous, built from wood and bluestone with a new slate roof and two stacked stone chimneys. Sawyer and his friends had done a spectacular job giving it new life. Dignified, and quite large in scale, it somehow managed to seem intimate and cozy at the same time, built into its own little nook. If that wasn't enough, it sported a huge, freshly painted red waterwheel on the side, steadily turning as it churned the rushing waters of Big Stone Creek after they came tumbling over the boulder ridge that gave the town its name.

"Blue Hollow Falls indeed," she breathed, then jumped when a knock came at her window. She turned to find a grinning Bailey smiling and waving at her, making hand motions for her to lower the window. Pippa did so and simply said, "Wow."

"I know, right? It's like, you think you're going to get used to it, but you really never do. Can you hear it?"

There was no way not to. The sound of the falls was a thunderous rhythm that worked perfectly in sync with the low, growling groan of the waterwheel. Pippa nodded. "It's brilliant. All of it. Truly spectacular."

"Hurry up and park. I can't wait to show you the inside." Her expression turning serious, Bailey put her hand on the open window frame as Pippa started the truck up again.

"What is it?" Pippa asked, surprised at the sudden shift.

"It's going to be okay," Bailey told her. "You know that, right?"

Pippa smiled, knowing exactly what she meant. "I wouldn't have come if I didn't think it would be."

"Good," Bailey said, looking relieved. "So, hurry already!" And she was off and running over to help Addie.

Pippa shook her head and grinned, amazed at how her life had changed so suddenly to include all these people who were already dear to her. She turned the wheel and bumped over the ruts so she could pull in next to Addie. Addie and Bailey were dragging large, soft, woven baskets the size of laundry hampers out of the back. They didn't seem heavy, and Pippa intended to offer them a hand. But she'd made the mistake of looking over at the creek first and found herself drawn toward the water, and the falls, almost as if by an unseen hand.

She stood at the edge of Big Stone Creek and let the thunder of the falls and the steady groan and swish of the great waterwheel serenade her, lulling her senses until she felt their rhythm fill every part of her. From somewhere inside the mill came the faint, rich sounds of a mandolin, its sweet notes somehow threading through the maelstrom of thundering water and churning wheel, adding just the right lyrical footnote, the perfect underscore. And for the first time in so very long, so long she'd begun to truly fear she'd never experience it again, that feeling rose inside her, squeezing her heart, making her throat tighten with emotion, and her eyes grow a little glassy. She let it in, let it fill her, right on up, until she thought she would burst with it. *Oh, thank God.*

"Ha'penny for your thoughts," came a deep voice from just beside her.

She'd been so lost in her triumphant moment of reconnection, she hadn't heard Seth approach. She turned to him, so broad, so tall, with his hair down around his shoulders, the Viking thrust of that beard, the perfection of his mouth, and those beautiful golden-brown eyes of his that focused instantly when he saw the emotions playing across her face. He looked at her with care and concern, as sincere and true as she'd ever known. That was Seth. And the words simply tumbled out of her. "I can hear music again," she said, part gasp, part sob.

He looked confused and more concerned than before. "That's Drake Clarkson. He's a magician with a mandolin." The last part of his words had clearly been an automatic response. His gaze took in all of her. "But you're not talking about that music, are you?" he asked gently.

It was her moment of truth. She was tired of overthinking, tired of worrying, just . . . tired. She'd come here to change that, hadn't she? And Seth Brogan was already part of that change. No matter what she told herself. *Say it, or walk away from him, Pip.* She shook her head, and her breath caught as the emotion rose up in her throat again. "I can hear *my* music."

"That's why you're here then," he said, almost more to himself than her.

She nodded, and pressed her hand to her lips, trying to get a grip, but the sheer relief alone was overwhelming. "I thought I was here to get over the fear of performing, the fear of it happening again, a rupture." She looked up at him, and his handsome face was a blur now as her eyes swam. "I couldn't come back from it a second time, Seth. I couldn't." Her breath caught again and she looked away, back at the water, at the falls, at the wheel, willing their rhythm to find their way inside of her again, soothing her, smoothing her, supporting her. "I am afraid. Terrified. Of that."

She felt his blunt fingertip brush away the tear from her cheek, then gently, oh so gently for a man with hands so big, he turned her face to his. "So either that fear swallowed up your music, or your music was too risky a thing to hear. Either way, without your music, there's no temptation to sing. No music, no risk."

It made such perfect sense, so clear, so obvious now. "You're right," she said. "You're absolutely right."

He stared into her eyes for the longest time, and she thought any moment he'd lower his head and kiss her. She saw the want there in his gaze, knew he had to see the same in hers. She'd just started to rise up on her toes, unable to stop herself, when he said, "I don't know why you get to me the way you do," he murmured. Then he surprised her by smiling. "Well, I do know. I could give you a list." His voice was husky, private, his words just for her, and she wanted to grab the collar of his shirt and yank his mouth down.

"I came over here to apologize," he said. "For being an ass this past week. For ducking out." He searched her eyes again, and now it looked like it was his moment of truth and she found herself holding her breath. "But this thing, whatever it is between us, at least for me, it's just—a lot. Maybe too much."

She tried to ignore the tight squeeze of disappointment that clutched at her heart. "I know," she said. And she did. He was right. Her rioting emotions at that very moment were proof positive of that. She ducked her chin then, moving back slightly until he lowered his hands. She instantly wanted them back, in case she needed more proof. *Too much, indeed.* She needed to be honest, let him know he wasn't alone, put that out there. So she looked up at him and smiled. "I have my own list, if that helps."

His lips curved at that. "I'm not sure it does." His gaze remained steady on hers.

"I know, right?" she said lightly, though nothing about this was light. She looked down for another moment, then met his gaze again. "The one who should be apologizing is me. For the past week, I mean. I knew when you didn't answer me, when I asked you about coming back to the vineyard the day Mabry got hurt, what your answer was." She smiled. "I mean, you moved me to a cabin miles away for a reason, and it's not just because you have a lot of work to do."

"Pippa—"

"It was the right thing to do," she broke in, before he could apologize again. Then smiled a little more broadly. "Clearly."

Rather than the dry smile she'd expected, he looked abashed. "I should have—"

"Done exactly what you did," she finished for him, not letting him apologize again. "I agreed with the decision, so it's not on you. It was selfish of me to keep coming to the vineyard," she said. "I made all kinds of excuses to myself as to why that was a perfectly fine thing to do. But it wasn't, and I shouldn't have. I guess I just . . ." Now it was her turn to trail off.

"Wasn't as good at burying your head in the vines as I was?" he finished for her, a hint of that wry note there now.

"Aye," she said, feeling foolish for putting them both through this. "I promise I'll leave you in peace from now on."

He didn't say anything to that, and his expression was unreadable.

"That is what this is about, right?" Her heart actually skipped a full beat when he didn't answer right away. She suddenly felt stretched in too many directions. She wanted to go off somewhere, examine her big discovery. She wanted to sit by that creek for hours and let the music fill her until she was drowning in it. Having her music back was enough. It was everything.

Or should be. So how was it that her huge, overwhelming rediscovery didn't diminish one bit the fact that she wanted the man standing in front of her so badly she burned with it? *Take the thing you came here to find, and let the other one go,* her little voice schooled.

"From now on, it's me at the cabin, you at the vineyard," she said, taking the lead if he wouldn't. "I'm pretty sure we can control ourselves if we happen to bump into each other in public. We're managing it right now."

"Just barely. I want to kiss you so badly my teeth ache," he said in a husky whisper that thrilled her right down to her toes.

She stood there, stunned by the heat in his declaration, rooted to the spot, every nerve ending in her body screaming at him to just *do it.*

"But I know if we do, there will be no closing the barn door after that," he said. "And none of the other considerations have changed."

The silence stretched out, as if each were willing the other to just go ahead and do it anyway. "You're right," she finally said, looking down. Their locked gaze had been so intense that breaking it felt like breaking a physical bond.

Still looking down, she said, "Is it okay if I think reality sucks, though?"

He let out a low, raspy chuckle. "Yeah, I'm right there with you."

Another moment passed, then another, with neither of them making a move to say anything further, nor end the conversation and walk away.

"I'm sorry I intruded," he said, at length, finally drawing her gaze back to his. "On your epiphany moment."

"Honestly, you were the perfect person to share it with," she told him. "Your insight was . . . also perfect."

He nodded, and she smiled, and it wasn't awkward, but it wasn't good, either. Finally, she smiled again ruefully and said, "Is it weird to feel all sad and devastated, like we just broke up, when we never began?"

A fast grin flickered over his lips, looking almost like relief, but his eyes were still a little bleak. "Not weird at all." A moment later he turned away from her and faced the creek and the falls.

A moment later, so did she. It felt like a chasm had opened up between them, even though they weren't any farther apart now than they had been a second ago.

"So, what happens for you now?" he asked. "With your music, I mean."

"I'm . . . not sure." She smiled briefly. "You might find me sitting next to this creek a lot."

"Well, if there's one thing I know for sure, it's never to underestimate the power of Blue Hollow Falls."

"I believe you're right about that," she said softly, thinking he didn't know the half of it. She watched the waterwheel for long moments as it slowly churned along, pulling up water, pushing it onward, pulling up water, pushing it on again, and let the slow, steady rhythm fill her, as if she was pulling up her own courage, then pushing it over and out. "I like being your friend," she said abruptly. "I like spending time with you, very much, and I wanted to believe we could leave it at that." She looked from the wheel, to the water rushing over the falls, and let the rest tumble out. "But you're right. About that barn door. About this being too much. About me being temporary here." She wanted to look at him then, but went on and simply finished the rest of what she had to say. "I just wanted you to know I value the friendship you have shown me. Your insight has always been spot-on, and that's helped me." She smiled. "And the laughter. I needed that more than I knew."

When he didn't say anything, she finally sneaked a peek from the corner of her eyes, but he was still looking at the falls, and what little she could see of his expression was unreadable. She noted he'd slid his hands in his pants pockets, and wondered—far too desperately—if maybe that was a measure he'd taken to keep from reaching for her, once and for all.

Then Pippa saw Bailey was heading their way. "It looks like my mill escort is wondering where I've gotten off to." She waited a moment, but when Seth still didn't say anything, she took a deep breath, squared her shoulders and thought, *Fine then.* "I guess it's time to see where this next step takes me," she muttered under her breath, not sure if she was more annoyed with his continued silence, or her inability to just stop talking.

"Anywhere you want it to go," came just loud enough for her to hear.

She glanced back to him, wanting to know if she should be reading anything into that, but he was still facing the creek. "Thanks," she replied quietly, as he'd sounded sincere. Then she turned and walked away. There was, after all, nothing more to say. Except, *Good-bye, Seth Brogan.*

She lifted her hand in a wave to Bailey, willing her eyes to stay dry, her throat to stay relaxed. Her heart not to break. "You don't ask for much," she murmured.

Then, mentally kicking herself even as she did it, she glanced over her shoulder for one last look just before Bailey reached her. She was so surprised to see that Seth had turned to watch her walk away that her step faltered, just for a moment. She was too far away now to see his expression, but his stance was steady, the set of his broad shoulders resolute. He looked right at home, fitting in so perfectly with the spectacular backdrop behind him, and yet somehow managing to dwarf it, all at the same time.

And maybe you don't ask for enough, her little voice prodded. Ignoring it, and the urge to turn around and run right back to him, she resolutely shifted her gaze forward, for good this time, and found a smile for Bailey.

"You ready?" Bailey asked, a smile of excitement on her face.

"As I'll ever be," Pippa said, and they walked hand in hand toward the mill.

Chapter Ten

Seth didn't see it as being a glutton for punishment when he followed the two, at a distance, and headed toward the mill as well. He'd been at the mill for a reason, but had detoured when he'd seen Pippa standing beside the creek. He'd had his little speech all prepared for when she came to the vineyard again, but just as well to get it out in the open sooner than later. He'd concluded just that morning that it was both silly and childish—not to mention impractical—for him to continue to find ways to be as far away from his own barn as possible when she was there. He'd confess she was a distraction, put all the blame on himself—where it rightly belonged, as obviously she wasn't having any of those issues herself—and ask, as kindly as possible, if she could refrain from spending so much time at his vineyard. Or any time at his vineyard.

He'd even planned to offer to talk to Addie to see if maybe they could keep Elliott up at Addie's and Bailey's cabin, so Pippa could go visit him there. Dex would mope, but the sheep were back outside, back to their regular routine, so Dex would be too busy to mourn too much. Seth would play him Disney marathons if he had to.

He walked over to the creek, mentally rehearsing it again,

but then she'd turned to him, those brilliant blue eyes of hers drenched with raw emotion, a sheen of tears, and what looked like relief, joy, and terror, all rolled into one. And all his carefully rehearsed explanations had dissipated like the mist that hung over the falls.

That they'd eventually had "the talk" anyway was of little solace to him now. Because now he knew she wasn't at all nonchalant about this . . . thing, they shared. The more she'd danced in and out of his barns, cheerfully chattering with him as easily as she chatted with Bailey and Jake, the more he'd become convinced that he'd been blowing what happened at Mabry's into a way bigger thing than it had been for her. He'd told himself that for all her down-to-earth nature, the truth was, she was a well traveled, worldly woman. She'd told him there hadn't been a romance in her life since her swift climb to fame, and he believed her, but that didn't mean she hadn't gleaned a lot of life experience from her globe-trotting lifestyle. Maybe she was just better equipped to handle a surprising attraction.

You've trotted the globe, too, you know, gleaning all sorts of life experiences. How's that working out for you so far in the relationship department?

He ignored the question, because the thing was, he'd made himself believe it was all in his head—and various other parts of his body—and he'd be doing them both a favor by just laying down the necessary ground rules so he could move on with his life. Instead he'd discovered he didn't know jack squat about anything when it came to how Pippa felt about him.

He paused inside the door to the mill and took a moment to try to shove all of that from his mind. It had been said; it was done. Over. Just because it had taken every ounce of willpower he had not to scoop her up like some Neanderthal and carry her off to his mountain lair the moment he realized he wasn't at all alone in this raging attraction, that changed nothing. If anything, it should be more of a relief. He'd never have to see her again. *I guess it's time to see where this next step takes me.* He swallowed several very succinct swear words. "Anywhere I want it to," he muttered. Now all he had to do was make himself believe it.

Seth scanned the interior of the mill, realizing he was looking for her, and swore under his breath. *Get a grip, man. It's done.*

The mill was a bustle of activity, as it had been since it had opened, way ahead of schedule, just before Christmas. It hadn't been completely finished back then, but enough that they'd been able to get things going. Seth, Sawyer, and Jake's dad, Will McCall, had been the driving force behind the bulk of the renovation, with an enormous amount of help from a few local contractors, townsfolk who wanted to pitch in for the greater good, and all of the crafters and their families as well. They'd gutted the interior and put in three floors. The basement, which had a walkout around back, was where Addie and Sawyer each kept an office for overall mill and guild business. The furnace and electrical grid were down there as well.

The main level, which opened on the side of the building via a large sliding panel door, featured a catacomb of individual booths, studios, and nooks, that had been added organically as each artist created a spot to display his or her wares, along with space to create and demonstrate their art. It made for a market-like feeling, inviting visitors to wander through the aisles, in and out of each artist's domain like a folk-art-oriented bazaar.

The third floor, accessed by a staircase built into the wall opposite the one that housed the mechanics for the waterwheel, was a series of shared classrooms where artists could teach seminars, conduct demonstrations, or hold lectures.

Different classroom spaces were set up for different types of art or craft; one for music, one for painting, one for sewing, weaving, and needlework, and a large generic space that leant itself to any number of other classroom needs.

There wasn't any one spot a person could stand on the main floor and see more than a few of the booths or studios, but the chatter of the artists and the patrons filled the air, giving it a friendly neighborhood vibe, and everyone could hear the music that echoed forth from the rear of the building. Sawyer's brewery and gastropub were back there, along with a small stage where the musicians in residence could play, alone or together, oftentimes inviting other local or visiting musicians to join them. That was something that happened throughout any given day, as was happening now with Drake on his mandolin. He'd been joined by someone on a Dobro as well, from the sounds of it. Folk music, sometimes lively, sometimes soulful, lent the place a joyful vibrancy that was the perfect complement to the creative energy that abounded from studio setting to booth display.

Seth wandered down one of the aisles along the west side of the building, intending to take the most direct path back to Sawyer's place, but admitting he was still looking about for a glimpse of Pippa. It wasn't so odd, he told himself, given the moment of self-revelation she'd had by the water, that he'd want to see how she was doing. She would be meeting people who were quite likely fans of hers, as well as being confronted with their urging her to join Drake on stage to play or sing.

He had a brief thought that he should have come through first before going out to talk to her, had a chat with the guild members, asked them not to pressure Pippa to perform . . . then shook his head. *Not your problem.* Besides, she could handle herself, as she'd proven time and again. He really needed to let go of this protective streak he seemed to have for her. One he knew damn well had nothing to do with Pippa's connection to his sister.

He was halfway to the back when he heard her unmistakable laughter. Not the giggle that Bailey so easily elicited from her. This was a full-bodied, throaty laugh, and he knew she was probably busy putting a nervous fan at ease or making someone feel they were the center of her attention. And they would be, in that moment. A more real or genuine woman than Pippa MacMillan he'd yet to meet.

"Oh boy," came a deep voice behind. "Brother, I know that look."

Seth turned to find Sawyer standing next to him. Seth topped his former commanding officer by an inch or two and was a bit broader in size, but Sawyer was still a commanding figure in both stature and attitude. He was relentlessly positive and the most outgoing guy in the room. Folks tended to gravitate toward Sawyer, and he ended up in leadership roles time and again, mostly because everyone around him happily waited for him to direct them. Seth had long since given up trying to figure out the source of his best friend's magnetism, and simply accepted it as Sawyer's due.

"There is no look," Seth told him. "Therefore, your pity is misplaced."

Sawyer chuckled. "Oh, this isn't pity, my friend." He clapped Seth on the shoulder. "This is a welcome to the party."

Seth threw him a side eye, even while part of him was half straining to hear what Pippa was saying as he and Sawyer drew closer to the sound of her voice. "I'd ask what party, but I'm very sure I don't want to know."

"The party of lovesick fools, still trying to tell themselves they can manage it, control it, put it neatly into a little box labeled 'things I am definitely never going to do,' then stick it on the shelf. Like it has a hope in hell of staying there." Sawyer laughed. "Learn from my mistake, pal. Stop torturing yourself. You're wasting precious time."

Seth kept walking without giving Sawyer the benefit of a response. It irked him that he was so obvious. "I'm the laid-back, not-a-care-in-the-world kind of guy. If you don't count the huge winery I'm trying to get off the ground," Seth said, as they ducked through the swinging panels between the pub's kitchen and the tiny office Sawyer used for pub business. Seth nodded hello to Hudson, Sawyer's new chef, then closed the door behind them once Sawyer was inside. "Not the fall-apart-over-a-woman-who'll-be-an-ocean-away-in-a-few-weeks kind of guy."

The performers on the pub's small stage had grown to a trio now, and though the music was more lilting than thumping, the stage was just beyond the other wall of Sawyer's office, close enough that Seth sat on the corner of Sawyer's heavy old oak desk so they could talk without having to shout.

Sawyer sat in the old leather swivel chair behind the desk and studied his friend for a long moment. Then he laughed and said, "Yeah, you really should just give up and give in now."

"I didn't come here to talk about Pippa," Seth said, deciding Sawyer was having way too much fun at his expense. "I wanted to touch base with you before I talk to Addie. With spring finally making an appearance, I was thinking about adding on to the pens we built for Bailey's sheep last fall. So she could house her goats up there and not have to make the trek to the vineyard all the time."

Sawyer's smile slipped. "Is there a problem with her going out there? Or Jake? Did something happen?" They all cared about Bailey as if she were their own, but none so much as Sawyer. Bailey had bonded with him straight off when she'd first come to town the previous fall. "Because you have to know she doesn't just go out there to play with the sheep and the goats. She's out there babysitting you."

Seth's brows shot up in honest surprise. "Babysit me? What on earth for?"

Sawyer shook his head, the smile back. "And here I thought you knew how her mind worked by now."

"I thought I did. Illuminate me."

"When she first got here, we were finishing up the mill, Sunny had just started in on renovating that monstrosity of a greenhouse out in the woods, and I set to work getting the brewery up and running. So Bailey had all her mother-hen tendencies tied up in overseeing the mill, overseeing me and the brewery, and Sunny with the greenhouse. And making sure Sunny ended up with me, too, now that I think about it." He leaned back in his chair and tucked his hands behind his head, the teasing glint back in his bright blue eyes. "The mill is done now, my brewery is coming along, Sunny's got the greenhouse up and going, so . . . it's your turn, my obtuse friend." His smile widened to a pleased, satisfied grin. "And apparently Pippa's turn as well. I heard Bailey gave her a goat."

It's about belonging. Bailey's words echoed through Seth's mind as he stared at his friend, wishing he could ignore the blatant truth staring him right in the face, but . . . no. "Well, I don't need mother-henning. And, before you say anything more, I'm not saying I don't want Bailey there. Or Jake. I love having them around. I rely on them. What I was getting at was that now that she's breeding the goats, and is thinking about finding ways to show them, maybe sell them—which Addie has said she'll oversee, so don't worry—it would be smarter for her to have them closer to home."

Sawyer unlaced his hands and sat forward, propping his elbows on his desk and pressing his lips against his folded fingers. "So, this is about Pippa, then," he said at length.

Seth just swore under his breath and stood up. "I should have just gone straight to Addie."

"You want the goats at Bailey's place because then Pippa will be at Bailey's place. Are you sure you don't want me figuring out how to move Dex there, too? I understand he's taken quite a shine to your Irish songstress."

"Irish song—she's not my Irish anything."

"Oh, I think there's a good chance she's your Irish everything, but you're just too stubborn to admit it."

Seth shocked them both by saying, "No, I'm not too stubborn to admit it. I just don't know how to make it work and keep her, and I don't think I could stand watching her walk away if we let this go any further."

Sawyer recovered from his surprise first. "Further?" He grinned, unrepentantly. "So, it's gone . . . somewhere then? When? You booted her out to Noah's cabin like a day after she got here. Chicken-shit move, by the way." He flapped pretend wings.

"Bite me." Seth turned to go.

"Seth," Sawyer said, all teasing gone. He waited for Seth to turn back around. "Teasing aside, if she's it for you, don't spend your energy on finding ways to shut it down. Spend that energy on figuring out how to give it—give her—your best chance." He stood now, and the commanding-officer aura overtook the best-friend ribbing. "You stepped in when Sunny and I couldn't figure things out. When I thought the obstacles were insurmountable, as did she. We owe you. We want you happy."

"Sunny lived hours away, not an ocean and a continent," Seth reminded him. "And one of you isn't a world-famous singer."

"And yet, in the end, I would have been willing to work with that, too, to have what we could have, versus having nothing at all." Sawyer sighed when he saw he wasn't getting anywhere. "All I'm saying is, when we started working toward something, instead of against it, solutions were found."

"And if we don't find a solution?" Seth asked him, quite sincerely. "What then? And if you're about to say, 'be thankful for what time you had,' save your breath. We're not cut out for that. I wouldn't do that to her, and I sure as hell am not going to do that to myself. I didn't risk my life every single day for years on end and miraculously survive, just to come home and torture myself over what any sane person would assess and say is a no-win situation."

"We're Rangers," Sawyer said. "You wore the green beret, same as me. We made it our business to run toward no-win situations, and get the win anyway. What happened to that guy?"

"That guy is no longer serving his country. He's serving his desire to build something worthwhile with his own two hands. Something that has a chance in hell of being a success. We didn't run into situations we knew we had no chance of winning, Sawyer. Which is why we're both standing here right now. I'm not about to change that rule now."

"And I think the very fact you frame it that way, like it's life or death, should be telling you exactly how important it is to find that win. If you can't get that this is also life or death, the life being the one you might have, and the death being the one you'll never know, well . . . I don't know how else to make you see it." Sawyer sighed, and said, "As to the other, if Addie okays it, I think we can figure something out with the goat pens. But at least be honest with yourself about why you're going to all this trouble."

Seth looked at Sawyer then, and knew that while his friend and former CO looked resigned, what he felt was disappointment. In Seth.

"You're also going to have to be the one to explain it to Bailey," Sawyer reminded him, as if the disappointment wasn't enough of a direct hit. "And you know damn well she's going to see right through it, too. So, good luck with that. You'll either piss her off because you're using her so you don't have to face your own problems, or hurt her feelings for pretty much the same reason, or—and this gets my vote—she'll be both."

"I'll figure it out," Seth told Sawyer. "Don't say anything to Addie."

Sawyer chuckled then, and the tension between them evaporated, as it always did. "Oh, trust me, if you decide to go that route, it's going to be all you, brother."

Seth put his hand on the knob, paused, and turned back. "I appreciate what you're saying," he said. "And that you're returning the favor you think I did for you and Sunny. I mean that. If I screw this up, that's on me. But, end of day, it's my life, my future. Hers, too. I hope you can respect my choices, even if you don't agree with them."

"Always," Sawyer said, without hesitation. "I'm standing on the other side of that hurdle. I just wish you could see the view from here. If you could, you'd do whatever it took to jump over."

It wasn't until Seth opened the door that he realized at some point during their conversation, the music had stopped. He knew that partly because of the silence, but mostly because Drake Clarkson was standing on the other side of the door.

Seth also realized that he and Sawyer hadn't modulated their conversation at all, and standing beside Drake was Pippa. From the look on her face, she'd heard way too much.

"Sorry, man," Drake said, looking miserable. "I thought Sawyer would want to meet Miss MacMillan. I . . ." He trailed off, because what was there to say?

"It's okay," Seth told Drake. "I'm sure he would." Seth stepped back so Drake could go on into Sawyer's office, then Seth moved through the doorway, pausing beside Pippa. "Pippa—"

"It's okay, Seth," she said, no bite in her tone, nor embarrassment. In fact, it was the utter lack of emotion that gutted him. "You'd already made it clear outside, earlier. And you don't have to talk to Bailey. I'll take care of it. And she'll be good with it. I promise you. Addie and I will see to that."

He simply stared at her, feeling like he was the small one, and she was the one towering over him.

"If you don't mind," she said, "I really would like the chance to say hello to Sawyer."

Seth stepped aside and she moved into the office, then turned, and very quietly closed the door between them.

"I thought I told you to take care of that girl." Mabry's voice was still hardly more than a rasp following two additional surgeries to finish repairing his leg. "Good dang thing I can't get out of this bed."

"You're doing fine from right where you are," Seth said resignedly. The past four days had included a call from Addie on Saturday, disinviting him to Sunday supper, saying she only wanted "folks who had the sense God gave them" sitting at her table. Then there'd been the brief conversation with Sunny on Monday when he'd gone out to the greenhouse with some leftover lumber he was donating for use as shelving. She'd been more sad than annoyed, which somehow felt even worse. She'd told him she wished she had the right words and wisdom to share with him, as he'd had for her when she'd been grappling over whether or not to start a serious relationship with Sawyer.

Then there was the glare he'd earned from Bailey yesterday when she'd come to tend her goats. Apparently, Pippa hadn't been quite as successful in keeping her promise there as she'd hoped, though Seth could have told her that. Shoot, even Hattie Beauchamp, the older woman who owned and ran Bo's, the only diner in town, had shaken her head and made a tsking sound when she'd stopped by his booth to top off his coffee just that morning. The only one who hadn't castigated or counseled him at this point was Will, and that was probably only because Seth hadn't seen him as yet.

"I won't even ask how you heard," Seth said, pulling up

a chair so he could sit beside Mabry's hospital bed. It had been a week and a half since the accident, and the old man had finally been upgraded to stable and was out of intensive care. Seth had been by to talk to Maggie numerous times, both at the hospital and the farm, to see if there was anything he could do to help, as well as get updates on Mabry's condition. Today was only the second day Mabry had been allowed to have visitors. Maggie had kept it to just her and his grandsons for the first day. Seth had been the next one on Mabry's request list.

"Maggie told me," Mabry said. "Pippa's been helping her, running errands in exchange for using old Bluebell. They talk. Maggie likes her." He smiled then. "That was my wife's buggy, you know. That's what she called that old Chevy. Her bluebell buggy." The old man paused to clear his throat, his voice sounding a little thicker when he continued. "I'm happy to see it in use again. Haven't let anyone drive it since Annie passed."

"I'm sorry, Mabry. I didn't know. We just thought—"

Mabry waved a hand. He looked frail now. The liver spots on his hands stood out in stark relief, and the lines in his face, earned from decades of working in the sun, seemed even more deeply grooved. "No, I intended her to use it. Annie'd be happy. Probably cross with me for not getting her buggy out and about sooner."

"Well, that's very kind of you. I can tell you that Pippa loves that old Chevy." Seth's smile grew. "And I promise she's driving it on the right side of the road. In fact, you'd think she'd been driving around here all her life."

Mabry smiled, then coughed again. Seth picked up the cup of water on Mabry's bedside table, but the old man waved it away. Seth had always thought of Mabry as being timeless, but he looked every one of his eighty-four years right now.

"Once I saw her toot around on that snowmobile, and

hearing about her brother, I knew she'd be fine," Mabry said. "A stuntman. Can you beat that," he went on, wonder in his voice. "Did she tell you about him?" He shook his head. "Made me wonder what a fella had to do in life to land in that kind of occupation."

"Be half crazy?" Seth offered with a chuckle, then leaned forward in alarm when Mabry's laugh led to a long, watery bout of coughing. "Can I call the nurse for you?"

Mabry shook his head, but this time he did motion to the cup of water with a bent straw sitting in it. Seth picked it up, and angled the straw so Mabry could take a sip.

"Damn tubes they put down my throat," Mabry said. "Feels like they scoured the inside with sandpaper. Can't get that tickle out. Tried to tell them if they'd let me have something stronger than water, with a little body to it, I might heal a darn sight faster." He motioned for another sip, then leaned back on his pillow once Seth had set the cup down. "Think I've got the twins talked into smuggling me in a nice chocolate milkshake. We'll see how that pans out."

Seth grinned. Mabry might look like he was one step away from death's door, but Seth knew the old man was too stubborn to go quietly. "I'll see if I can lend a hand there." And he would, just as soon as he consulted with Mabry's team of nurses.

"I appreciate that," Mabry said. He rested for a few moments, and Seth sat back in his chair again. "So," he said, at length, "is it that you're blind, or just plain stupid then?"

Seth let his head drop back and closed his eyes. So much for getting around that particular lecture. As a reply, he said, "Pippa and I agree on this. We're adults, and in charge of our personal lives. I'm sure she appreciates, as do I, that everyone is so concerned about our well-being, but—" Seth broke off as Mabry's earlier words came back to him. "Wait, are you saying Pippa talked to Maggie about me? About us?"

"As I understand it, there is no *us*. And if you and Pippa

were really being so gosh-darn adult, you'd be talking to each other like normal people do—and by normal, I mean people who don't have their heads stuck up where the sun don't shine." Mabry shook his head. "It amazes me that you kids today manage to procreate at all, given how scared you are by the least little thing."

"I hardly think living an ocean apart, leading lives that couldn't be less alike, is a little thing," Seth said, then swore under his breath for being drawn into defending his choices. Again. "She hasn't been here two weeks yet. We hardly know each other."

Mabry waved a frail hand. "Sometimes it takes years to see it. Other times, you know it the instant you lay eyes on one another. That's how it was for Annie and me. I knew the first night I kissed her I was going to marry her. Shoot, I knew the first time I made her laugh."

Everything about Mabry's statement resonated in a place so deep inside Seth he couldn't refute it. Memories flashed like a series of rapid-fire photographs through his mind. Pippa laughing with him, Pippa doing her little curtsies, Pippa scolding Dex, giggling with Bailey, batting her lashes at him and asking for a Shetland pony. He'd known her less than twenty-four hours then, and his heart had definitely already felt a wobble.

"All I know is," Mabry went on, drawing Seth reluctantly from his thoughts, "back in my day, when a man met a woman who turned his head sideways and his heart upside down, he didn't go whining about how unfair life was. He went after her and the world be damned."

Seth sat there as Mabry's words settled way down deep inside him and took up permanent residence. No amount of pretending, ignoring, or distracting was going to shake them loose. The truth was like that. Seth smiled, both amused and resigned. Amused that he'd ever really thought he was going to forcibly manage his feelings about Pippa. And resigned for the exact same reason. "You know, Mabry, I've been talked to and glared at all week about this, but that's possibly the frankest, most direct advice I've been given yet."

"You gonna take it?"

Seth stood and picked his jacket up off the back of the chair. "If I was going to listen to anyone, it'd probably be you."

"So, I take it that's a no, then." Mabry shook his head. "Remind me on my hundredth birthday, when you're old enough to look back and wonder what in the hell you were thinking, letting something this good pass you by, to kick you in your behind with my good leg, and tell you I told you so. And believe you me, I won't take any pleasure in it, but I'm damn well gonna do it."

Seth chuckled. "I don't doubt that for one second." Seth offered the old man another sip from the cup, then set it back on the table.

"Young people these days," Mabry muttered just as a nurse bustled in.

"Visiting time is up, I'm afraid," she said kindly.

"I was just heading out," Seth told her.

"Don't forget that other little matter we discussed," Mabry told Seth.

Seth frowned for a moment, then remembered. The milk-shake. "I won't," he said, then intercepted a warning look from the nurse that Mabry couldn't see from behind her. Seth winked at her, then nodded to Mabry. "Don't give these ladies a hard time now. They're the only thing standing between you and freedom."

"They love me here," Mabry told him. "Don't you, Miss Frieda? Best patient they ever had."

"Of course, we do," the nurse said, smiling indulgently at Mabry as she looked over his chart and consulted the tray she'd brought in lined with a row of little plastic cups, each filled with a variety pills.

Seth let himself out, then let out a long, relieved sigh

once he was back outside in the parking lot. Partly because he was free of the hospital itself, but mostly because despite how perilously old and infirm Mabry had looked, Seth had no doubt that if a full recovery could be made, Mabry would make it happen. "Stubborn old people these days," he murmured, then smiled.

Seth glanced at his phone to check on the time and nodded. He was set to meet Will up at the vineyard to go over some stone repair work. Will had done much of the stonework restoration on the mill himself, which had been a monumental task. He'd also been the one to talk Sawyer into redoing the mill's roof with slate shingles rather than the metal roofing that had been original to the century-old building. Seth had agreed with Will and pitched in when he'd made his argument to Sawyer, then wished he hadn't when all three of them and a handful of other locals had spent days up on that roof under a blazing sun tacking them all into place.

Seth was going over in his mind the list of things he wanted Will to look at, so he didn't see Pippa leaning against Bluebell, which she'd parked right next to his big pickup, until he almost tripped over her.

"How's Mabry?" she asked without preamble. "Tell me the truth," she cautioned him. "I want a frank appraisal. I'm going in to see him this afternoon and it's making me nervous. Maggie said he asked to see me. She also said you were going to visit him this morning. I know you and I aren't supposed to be talking or whatever, and I kept my promise about not being at the vineyard. But Mabry was in intensive care for so long and with the extra surgeries, I've been worried sick about him. Maggie doesn't show it, but I sense she's been worried, too, and I knew you'd give me the straight truth." She lifted her hands and let them fall. "So, here I am. I didn't know what else to do."

"Slow down, slow down," Seth said gently, and started to

reach for her without thinking. She sidestepped away before he could touch her, which startled him. "Sorry. I was just . . ." He shook his head. "Never mind." He took a short breath, then looked up to find her standing several feet away now, arms crossed, but with an intent, worried look on her face. If there was any doubt she'd come here to discuss anything other than Mabry's condition, that resolved it. This wasn't about him, about them. *Do I want it to be?*

"He looks his age," Seth said, stepping back until he leaned against the side of his truck. *Just two friends, sharing some much-needed information.*

"Have they said anything about whether he'll be able to walk again? Maggie told me about the second blood clot, the emergency surgery. And that after the first one he had to deal with an infection that wouldn't go away." She shook her head. "I keep thinking he's just going to bang his way through this, but it seems like things keep stacking up against him." She sighed and wrapped her arms more firmly around her waist.

"I think when you first see him, you're going to feel your worries are spot-on. But—" He lifted his hand when her gaze flew to his. "But," he repeated calmly, "as soon as you start talking to him, you'll realize he's got this. And I truly think he does. If anyone can overcome such awful injuries and get back on his feet, it will be Mabry Jenkins. Mark my words on that."

Pippa let out a shaky sigh of relief. "That's more or less what Maggie told me, but I worried that she's just projecting confidence to make herself feel stronger for her father's sake, you know?" She rubbed her arms, then finally let her hands fall by her sides again. "I knew you'd be straight with me, and I just wanted to be prepared. I'm so bad at this. He doesn't need to see me being all fluttery and freaked out."

"He's happy knowing you're driving Bluebell. Turns out his wife named the truck. It was hers."

"Oh!" Pippa gasped, and her expression crumpled a bit. "That's so lovely." She looked and sounded truly touched. "Are you sure he's okay with that?"

"Very sure."

She nodded. "Good. Okay. I love that old heap," she said. "I truly do."

"I told him as much. It made him happy and he said Annie, his wife, would be happy about that, too."

Pippa smiled, nodded, and let out a little sigh of relief, but the worry and the nervousness were still clear on her face.

The two stood there for another few moments, the growing silence not uncomfortable, but not entirely comfortable, either.

"Pippa—"

"Seth—"

They both spoke at the same time, then smiled. "You first," he said. He thought she might do her little curtsy and was more disappointed than he should be when she didn't.

"Nothing, I just thought . . . what I mean is . . . I want you to know, I didn't come here to say anything else . . . I truly didn't." She folded her hands together in front of her and stared at them for a moment, then looked back up at him. "I know we agreed it's best to stay to our own paths. But this is a small place, and I also know that everybody knows. About us. About us choosing not to be an *us*. And I feel like the whole town is waiting with bated breath for something to happen." She smiled then. "You have no idea how much Blue Hollow Falls has in common with the village I grew up in. I'd forgotten just how deep into everyone's pocket everyone could be."

"I know you were hoping for more privacy," Seth said, unsure what else to say.

"No, it's not that. Surprisingly, it's not. Actually, now that I've met so many people, I'm more at ease. They're all so lovely, and so kind. It reminds me of home. People from my village will make Moira feel the exact same way. I know that, so I know I'll be fine here."

"Good," he said, meaning it. "I'm happy to hear that." Which was true, but he felt oddly left out, knowing she was establishing an identity for herself in town, and he wasn't going to be any part of that. He would have enjoyed seeing her discover his newly adopted town, enjoyed sharing her thoughts and reflections on how the place struck her, in comparison to how he'd come to love it. He'd have enjoyed watching her with people, and vice versa. And he'd be lying if he said he didn't feel remiss in watching out for her, even if she didn't need him to.

He couldn't shake the look on her face that day beside the creek, the trust she'd put in him. Trust he knew damn well she didn't just go handing out. And he'd turned away from her. "I'm sorry for making this more complicated than it has to be," he said quietly. "That day, by the creek, you said some very kind things, about the friendship we'd begun. I couldn't say it then." *Because I was still reeling to learn I wasn't the only one falling.* "But, I appreciate that, and I feel the same way."

She glanced up at him then, looking uncertain.

"What I mean is, I'm here to support you, any way you need. If we need to talk . . . like today, right now . . ." He lifted his hands, let them drop by his sides. "Then we should talk. I'm glad you're happy here, glad to know this place is working its magic on you, in whatever way you need it to."

He watched as she took a steadying breath; then she nodded. "Thank you. That's . . . a lovely thing to hear. I appreciate it."

She looked small, and vulnerable, and he was making things harder, when he'd been trying to do the opposite. He curled his fingers into his palms to keep from doing what he wanted to do, which was to say the hell with all this and reach for her. That wouldn't help either one of them. So, he said what he had to say, not what he wanted to say. What he'd wanted to say since she'd walked away from him at the mill. *Don't leave.* "I don't want you to feel pressured by other people's opinions," he said, and winced when she let out a dry, humorless laugh. "At least you're getting the supportive gestures. I'm the one getting all the lectures."

Her eyebrows lifted at that. "Are you now?"

He frowned. "Are you getting them, too? Because I'll make sure—"

"You'll do no such thing," she told him. "People express themselves—it's what they do. That they care about you and your happiness is abundantly clear and I know that's at the core of all this, so it doesn't bother me so much. It speaks well of you, and well of them, that you're all looking out for one another." She smiled briefly. "Even when you wish they wouldn't."

He smiled back, and it was on the tip of his tongue to ask her if she'd begun writing any music, if she'd found herself wanting to play up on that little stage at Sawyer's place. He knew she hadn't yet, or it would have been the talk of the Falls, but he wanted to ask about it anyway. She'd trusted him with her big revelation, and he felt he was letting her down by not following through. He wanted to tell her that when folks weren't giving him the side-eye for not sweeping her into his arms and riding off into the sunset, they were gushing about what a lovely young woman she was, and how they couldn't believe she was so down-to-earth, as normal as you please. Her surgery was common knowledge, even to the folks who hadn't known who she was at first, and everyone understood she'd be ready to sing and play when she was ready. Though it didn't keep them from urging him to urge her to give it a go.

"I'd better get on with my errands, then," she said, breaking into his thoughts. "I'm glad we talked. I've felt . . . not bad, but not good, either, about how we left things, by the creek. If that makes sense." She paused, looked up at him. "Thank you for letting me know. About Mabry." She pulled the set of truck keys from her pocket and offered him a smile. "See you around, Seth."

"Yeah," he said, "see you around." But she was already in the truck, starting the engine, then driving away. He supposed he should feel better now. They were on the same page. Even though the entire population of Blue Hollow Falls was seeing scattered rose petals and hearing wedding marches, he and Pippa could and would handle this. "Like the adults we are," he grumbled, climbing into his own truck. He tried not to ask himself why, if things were so damn great now, he felt even more like absolute crap than he had before.

Some of Mabry's truth-telling played through his mind. *Back in my day, when a man met a woman who turned his head sideways and his heart upside down, he didn't go whining about how unfair life was. He went after her and the world be damned.*

"Yeah, but that doesn't explain what happens when the world comes calling, demanding that life go on," he muttered. "What then, Mabry?" He put the truck into gear, then barked out a laugh as he listened to himself. "Sure sounds like whining to me, Brogan." *So, what are you going to do about it?*

Chapter Eleven

"Okay." Bailey sighed, dabbing the corners of her eyes with a crumpled-up paper towel. She leaned back against the fortress of pillows she and Pippa had piled on the floor in front of the couch. "You're right. Elliott is the perfect name."

They looked at each other, sniffled, each lifting a hand until the tips of their index fingers touched, and said, "'E.T. phone home,'" then rolled their eyes and collapsed back on the pillows in a fit of giggles.

"We're so hopeless," Bailey said. "I'm sorry Jake got sick and couldn't come, but now I'm glad. He'd never let me live this down."

Pippa rolled her head to the side and looked at Bailey. "What, you think he'd have been unmoved? I think you'd have had equal ammunition. That's all I'm saying."

Bailey turned her head and looked at Pippa. "Yeah. You're probably right." Then she grinned.

Pippa rolled herself up to a sitting position, then leaned forward until she could reach the coffee table they'd pushed into the middle of the small space. She clicked a button on her laptop and made the screen go dark, then picked up the empty popcorn bowl. "I'm glad you liked it. I was six when my oldest brother let me watch it for the first time. He was babysitting us at the time. It terrified me. I had nightmares for weeks. My mum was so upset with him."

"Yeah, six might be a little rough."

Pippa sent her a worried glance. They'd talked about the movie beforehand, and Pippa had okayed it with Addie first, but still, perhaps she'd made the wrong call. It was hard to remember Bailey was only ten. "You were okay with it, though? I'd forgotten about the language. Sorry for that bit."

"I loved it," Bailey said. "And it's not like I haven't heard those words before." She smiled and put a palm over her chest. "I promise I won't use them in public, or out you as being a terrible influence on a minor." She finally nudged Pippa's shoulder. "Stop worrying. I'd have told you to turn it off. I wouldn't have tortured myself."

Pippa smiled, relieved, then laughed. "If only I'd taken that reasonable approach with Garrett."

"You were six," Bailey reminded her.

"I imagine you would have, at any age."

Bailey thought about that for a moment, then nodded. "Probably. Or left the room, more likely. But I'm a special case."

"A special girl, more like," Pippa said, then leaned over and kissed her on the cheek, making Bailey roll her eyes. So, she kissed the girl's cheek again, loudly this time. "A special girl who needs to learn that PDA between friends is a good thing, not icky." Then she wrapped Bailey up in a hug, making her squeal, and they both fell over, with Pippa still hugging and Bailey grappling about until she could grab a pillow. Bailey swung first, which did make Pippa let go, but only so she could grab her own pillow. "I'll have you know I have six brothers and sisters," Pippa told her as they crawled around, swinging, ducking, and laughing so hard they were gasping. "I'm a pillow fight veteran."

"I was raised in foster care," Bailey shot back, taking a

wickedly aimed swing at Pippa's clutched pillow and knocking it behind the couch. "Pretty sure I can hold my own."

Pippa raised her hands in mock surrender, and Bailey lowered her pillow, only to have Pippa grab it from her and swing, making Bailey's eyes pop wide in surprise. Pippa merely shrugged, then grinned as she swung the pillow over her head like a lasso.

"Oh, it's like that, is it?" Bailey said, grinning like a fiend and lunging for another pillow while simultaneously ducking Pippa's swing. "Game on."

It was Bailey's retaliatory fling that caught a very surprised Seth square in the face as he entered the cabin. He grabbed the pillow and kept it clutched in his fist. "I knocked," he told them, "but it sounded like you were being attacked by banshees, so I thought I should come in and offer my assistance."

Breathless, Pippa wrapped her arms around her pillow and held it against her chest, and Bailey collapsed back on the piles of blankets that had been the basis of their pillow fort. "Banshees are the heralds of death," Pippa told him, still gasping for air. "And the only thing dying here are these poor, poor pillows." She swung hers at Bailey, who took the hit with arms open wide. Then both she and Pippa fell back into the pile in another round of giggles.

"Draw?" Bailey said at length.

Pippa just nodded, then squealed when Bailey lunged over and planted a sloppy, wet kiss on her cheek.

Pippa finally looked back to Seth, who was a towering Viking inside her wee, wee cabin. It did all kinds of things to her insides, finally seeing him here, things she'd imagined in great detail, late at night, burrowed in her big bed, all alone, staring out into the night sky. The kinds of things she had no business thinking about with a child lying next to her. A very impressionable one at that.

"Are you my Uber?" Bailey asked him, before Pippa could say anything.

He nodded. "At your service."

"I thought Addie Pearl was coming to pick her up on her way home from the mill," Pippa said, when she finally had her breathing, if not her hormones, back under control.

"Addie's weaving class ran long," Seth explained. "She had a couple of students who had their class dates mixed up. Showed up on the wrong night, but they'd driven a long way, so she included them. That put her behind. Sawyer would have come, but he and Sunny are out having a date night in Turtle Springs. I was by the mill to talk to Will, and Addie pegged me since I was coming up this way to go home." He looked at Bailey. "I've got to go by my place first; then I'll take you on home. Addie should be there by then, but if not, I'll hang out until she arrives."

"I could have taken her," Pippa said. "Addie should have just called and let me know. It seems silly to have put you out."

"I'm not put out. Addie asked, and I said I'd be happy to do it." He shrugged. "No big deal."

"What?" Pippa asked, as she turned to gather up the pillows and caught the satisfied smile on Bailey's face.

"Nothing," Bailey said, suddenly the picture of innocence as she started to pick up the blankets. She put the heap on the couch, then collected their sodas and the empty popcorn bowl from the coffee table and carried them to the kitchen. "I'll just be in the kitchen cleaning up. You adults talk amongst yourselves," she added with a little bow, that same pleased smile back on her young face as she looked at the two of them.

Pippa looked back at Seth. "Do you know what's gotten into her?" she asked, truly curious. Then she spied the dawning look on Seth's face. "What is it? What am I missing?"

"She thinks Addie played us," he said.

"Played—" And then it became clear. "Oh," she said. "I see. Do you think?"

Seth nodded. "Fair bet."

"Not Addie Pearl, too," Pippa said with a sigh.

"Yes, Addie Pearl, too," Bailey chimed in from the kitchen.

Pippa and Seth both shot her a quelling look, but even though Bailey lifted her hands in surrender, the smile didn't waver. She turned and continued washing the cups and the bowl, started whistling a little tune too, as Seth and Pippa turned back to each other.

"Could I speak to you a moment?" Seth asked. "Outside? Away from adorable Eagle Ears over there?"

"It's fine by me," Bailey said over the running water in the sink.

Pippa smiled at that, even as she wondered what he was about. "Certainly."

Seth stepped outside onto the tiny front porch. Pippa followed, glancing over her shoulder at Bailey with a wry smile and wiggling eyebrows.

Bailey just shot her a sudsy thumbs-up and continued with the housekeeping.

"What's up?" Pippa asked, as she moved out into the warm April evening, closing the door behind her. The unseasonably warm spring had continued unabated, but the temperature still cooled off fast at night, especially up here in the hills. Pippa wrapped her arms around her waist, thinking she should have grabbed one of the blankets.

The porch was as wide as the cabin, meaning not wide at all, and not very deep. Seth took up the lion's share of it, so Pippa sat down on the first step and turned to lean on the porch's support beam. Seth walked down the three steps to the stone walkway, then sat down on the bottom step and leaned against the railing on the opposite side. "So, it's not going away," he said without preamble.

"What? The town's plan to see us get together?" Pippa waved a hand. "I'm getting used to it. Don't let it get to you. They'll figure it out in time."

It had been a little over a week since they'd spoken in

front of the hospital. Spoken at all, actually. Another week of not going to the vineyard, which she'd known she would continue to miss, but she missed it more each day, not less. And not just because she missed Elliott or Dexter, both of whom were still housed there. Bailey had been firm about keeping the goats at the vineyard, more or less holding Elliott hostage, saying if Pippa wanted to see him, she should just tell Seth and make it happen.

Pippa smiled, remembering the conversation. *If only it were that simple.*

Pippa had spotted Seth here and there when she went down to the mill to meet with more of the artists, soak in the creative energy that fairly hummed inside that magical building, but they'd never even made eye contact, much less spoken. Then she'd all but bumped into him out at the magnificent old greenhouse that Sunny was still restoring, amidst the amazing work she was doing with endangered orchids. But they hadn't spoken there, either. Pippa had spied Seth and Sawyer building shelves and tables in the rear of the place. She also hadn't missed the speculation on Sunny's face when she'd caught Pippa staring at Seth while he wasn't looking.

It was true that Pippa was getting used to the knowing looks, the whispers, because they were all couched in affection. His friends wanted Seth to be happy. And they thought she was worthy of him. It was flattering, really. What she wasn't getting used to was her own yearning. And not just for more of what they'd started that day on Mabry's couch. Pippa felt like she'd made a dozen or more new friends in the few weeks she'd been in Blue Hollow Falls. Kind, decent people whom she knew would be there for her if she were to ask for anything, need for anything. She knew there was an element of her celebrity at play, but mostly they'd welcomed her because she'd arrived as a guest of Seth Brogan, and that made her a guest of the town.

And every day, as she developed those relationships, learned and experienced new things in and around the Falls, she found herself wanting to turn to him to share this thought or make that aside, to ask him for insight about this person, or share a laugh with him about that funny thing that happened. She could ask general questions of anybody, but that wasn't the same as sharing those moments with somebody. And no matter how hard she tried to make it otherwise, he was her somebody.

"I'm not getting used to it," Seth said, quietly breaking into her thoughts.

She looked at him and her heart clutched at his honesty, then glanced down at her hands. She'd taken to rubbing the tips of her fingers together in recent months, as if she still couldn't get used to the fact that they weren't callused any longer. She'd been away from the fiddle so long, they'd gotten soft again. She wanted to be honest with him, too. Tell him that it was true she didn't mind the well-wishers, but she did mind not being with him. Only he looked so miserable, and that would only make things worse for both of them.

"Maybe I should go then," she murmured instead, not knowing what else was left to say. She looked up. She hadn't made the offer lightly. In fact, she'd been giving it a lot of thought.

To his credit, he didn't respond right away, but took her offer as it was intended. "Are you finding what you came here looking for?"

His insight always surprised her. Even more surprising was that it never felt intrusive, or made her feel vulnerable. Quite the opposite. She nodded. "It's funny. I didn't come to Blue Hollow Falls for anything, of course. It was merely a spot to be in while I contemplated . . . everything."

"But?"

She smiled briefly then. "But it's turned out to be quite specifically the right spot."

He listened to her, then tipped his chin down, studying his own fingers, which were laced on top of his bent knee. "Are you finding all the answers you need?"

She lifted a shoulder. "I don't know yet." She looked at him. "But I think I could, yes."

"Then you should stay."

"Seth," she began, but he spoke over her, calmly, but with purpose.

"Moira said you'd originally wanted to stay longer. Now that you're in the cabin, there's not really a limit on the swap. So you should stay however long you want. However long you need."

"Not if it's compromising your life here," she replied, without hesitation.

He looked at her then. "I'm not asking you to leave."

She studied his face. "I know you aren't," she said softly. She thought about what he'd said, wondered if she should just go anyway. Only that would make him feel bad, too. Finally, she said, "If it's okay, I'll stick to the eight weeks Moira and I agreed on."

"Actually, I had a different idea."

Her eyes widened. She hadn't expected that response. "Oh?"

He shifted his seat so he could look at her more directly. "So, it was watching that house-swap movie, *The Holiday,* that gave Moira the idea to do this whole thing to start with. Did Katie tell you that?"

"Yes," Pippa said, even more confused now

"There's another movie, with Julia Roberts and Dennis Quaid."

Pippa frowned. "I know it. The one where he cheats on her, she kicks him out, then suddenly questions everything about her life and goes to live with Kyra Sedgwick. *Something to Talk About,* that's the name of it, right?" Her mouth dropped open. "Are you suggesting that one of us should be seen in the company of another potential beau so folks know we're not interested in each other?"

Now it was Seth's turn to open his mouth to speak, then close it again. "That wasn't my plan at all, actually."

"It might work, though," she said, now that she'd gotten past the shock of the suggestion. "If it's really bothering you that much, I guess we could try that." She instantly hated everything about the plan. The very last thing she wanted was to see him with another woman. But she was trying to be supportive, be a good friend to him. "Um, did you have someone in mind?" she said, not sounding so much like a friend, as like a woman trying not to be consumed with jealousy. Which was exactly what she was. She cleared her throat, tried again. "You are planning on telling the other woman it's a ruse, right?" Then another thought struck her and any attempt at being casual about this escaped her entirely. Her expression fell. "Or is there really someone? Is that what you're trying to tell me?"

"No," he said without hesitation, and seemed suddenly very interested in her reaction. "I also don't think it would be wise to bring anyone else into this."

Pippa tried not to look as massively relieved as she felt. Failed just as miserably at that, too, she was certain. She pulled up her knees and wrapped her arms around them. *Like that's going to protect you.* "So, what is your idea then?"

"I only mentioned the movie because the title came from an old Bonnie Raitt song."

Pippa nodded and without thinking sang the refrain about a woman wanting to give people something to talk about. "Yes, I know it," she said absently, her mind still fixated on this plan of his, on how kind he was being, and how badly she was blowing this "just be friends" moment. "Bonnie's a brilliant musician. We actually performed together at a benefit once."

When Seth didn't go on, she finally glanced over at him,

only to find him staring at her, almost as if he was transfixed. "What?" she asked. "You are aware I know some famous people, right? It's not like we go shopping together, or go on holiday, but I have bumped into one or two."

"Pippa," he said, sounding quietly stunned.

"You sang."

They both turned to find Bailey standing in the open doorway, staring at Pippa in much the same way Seth was.

"What?" Pippa said. "No, I was just—" Then she broke off, and immediately cupped her hand around her throat. She looked from Bailey to Seth. "Oh my God. I did, didn't I?"

"You have a beautiful voice," Seth said.

"Haven't you heard it before?" This from Bailey, who looked rather disgusted with him.

He shook his head, but his gaze was on Pippa. "How did it feel?"

Pippa let out a little gurgle of stunned laughter, but kept her hand protectively wrapped around her neck. "Just fine, apparently. I wasn't even thinking. I was just in the moment, like I used to be, and . . ." She leaned back and squeezed her eyes close, then shook her head, still dumbfounded. Then she laughed, and kept laughing.

"What?" Seth and Bailey asked at the same time.

She finally opened her eyes and looked at both of them, her mouth curved in a deep, wry grin. "It's just, as you might imagine, over the past eleven—well, I guess it's closer to twelve months now—I've given this moment a great deal of thought. What would be the first note I'd sing? What song would it be? Where would it happen? Would I be alone? In a studio? In the privacy of my own shower, perhaps? I've played it out so many times, so many ways." She shook her head and tipped it back against the post. "Never once did I think it would happen and I wouldn't even notice."

Seth smiled with her, but there was still concern for her in his gaze, and that made her heart squeeze a little, too.

Concern for her, not simply her voice. He wasn't worried about her career, he was worried about how she felt.

"Did it hurt?" Bailey asked.

Pippa shook her head. "No. I'm healed. If I wasn't, I wouldn't be laughing, much less singing. And I couldn't do that, either, for a very long time." She reflexively continued to massage her throat anyway. How could she have spent almost a year all but paralyzed in fear, then gone and done it, and not even noticed? It made her feel even more ridiculous than before.

"So, why have you waited so long to try?" Bailey walked over and sat down cross-legged on the porch, right next to Pippa, her blue eyes as baleful as Pippa had ever seen them. "You're afraid it's going to happen again."

Pippa nodded and felt the sudden sting of tears at the corners of her eyes, which was silly. It was over now, and about as anticlimactic as it could possibly have been. "Maybe not from singing one song, or two, or even a whole record of songs. But singing one song will lead to another, and someday another album, because that's how my job works."

"And a new album means touring, or at least performing, and not in the controlled environment of a studio," Seth said. "But up on stage."

Pippa looked at him, and their gazes met, held. She should have felt exposed in that moment, naked for the world to see, her deepest fear finally revealed. Instead, she felt . . . protected. Seth understood, truly understood. He'd understood the moment she'd gotten her music back, too. He knew how monumental this was for her. And he was neither babying her nor bullying her. He was simply listening to her, being there for her. And that felt like the safest place in the world to her. "Aye," she said.

"Like before," Bailey said quietly, drawing Pippa's attention back to her.

Pippa nodded. "It's silly, mostly," she said, not wanting

Bailey to be afraid for her. "I mean, it could happen, but it takes a lot to do that kind of harm. I'd take better care, not strain my voice so badly. It's not like I'm going to walk out, launch into a song, then—" She broke off as that moment flashed through her mind again, making her heart lurch in a painful squeeze, and her stomach to do a queasy little flip.

Bailey leaned over and clasped Pippa's shoulders in a fierce hug. "I'd be afraid, too," she whispered in Pippa's ear before sitting upright again. "It would be weird if you weren't."

Pippa gave a watery little laugh at that. *From the mouth of babes.* "True, I suppose, when you put it like that." She reached for Bailey's hand, squeezed it. "Thanks," Pippa told her.

"So, maybe you start slow," Bailey said. "Maybe you record songs as you write them so there's time in between. And you don't have to do tours, right? I mean, you could just make records."

"Yes, I could," Pippa said. "But what feeds me as an artist, what pushes me to write music, to find the words to sing, the notes to play, is the performing. Not so much to stand up on a stage, but because that's the only way to join together with others and let the music unite us. It's hard to explain, but I don't play or write music for myself. I do it to share with others, and I want to be part of that sharing."

Bailey sat there and thought about what she'd said and Pippa took that moment to risk glancing at Seth. He had the same fierce, contemplative expression as Bailey and she smiled, thinking how lucky she was to have found two souls so intent on helping her save her own. *And that should be enough, shouldn't it?*

"I'll find my way," she told Bailey, not wanting them to feel they had a responsibility to help someone who was still trying to figure out how to help herself. "That little bit just now was a bigger step than you know." She smiled. "Who knows what's next?" she said, wiggling her eyebrows. "Maybe a whole advert jingle while washing dishes."

Seth smiled at that, as did Bailey, but Pippa knew they didn't buy her casual nonchalance, because she wasn't buying it. She had some major thinking to do, but for that, she needed to be alone.

Something of that need must have shown on her face, because Seth pushed himself to his feet. "Why don't you go grab your things," he told Bailey. "I'm sure Addie Pearl is home by now. I'll just take you there directly."

Bailey nodded, scrambled up and turned to go into the cabin. She stopped in the doorway and looked back at them. "I'm really glad I got to hear it," she told Pippa. "Your voice is even prettier now than on the songs Jake played for me. I promise I won't tell anyone, about you singing again, okay?"

Pippa hadn't even thought about that. It was a measure of just how deeply Blue Hollow Falls had lulled her into feeling safe and secure. It made her heart catch, thinking she had this little warrior looking out for her. "Thank you," she said with heartfelt sincerity. Then she smiled. "It wasn't much to listen to, but I'm glad you were here, too." And she meant that, too.

Bailey flushed with pleasure, then ducked into the cabin.

Pippa stood and turned to find Seth standing on the step two down from hers, which brought their gazes level for the first time. Well, the first time when both of them were standing, anyway. She tried not to think about that, but it was hard not to because she was already all caught up in those soul-deep eyes of his, and thinking about what his hands had felt like on her, and that beautifully sensual mouth.

"What did you mean?" she asked, grasping for any conversational thread, trying to ignore the wobble he put into her knees, heck, her heart, when he looked at her like he was right now. "About Bonnie's song, I mean," she added. "We got off track." She tried to run through the song lyrics in her head, but he'd lifted his hand to gently pull hers away from her throat. She hadn't even realized she was still massaging it.

In response, he slid her hand to his shoulder, then took her other one in his, sliding his free hand around her waist. He swayed their bodies in a slow rocking motion, then lowered his mouth to her ear, his soft beard brushing the side of her neck, and stunned her speechless by quietly singing a stanza from the song. The one about how the singer thought that if folks were going to talk about her and a particular gentleman she knew, then maybe they should silence those rumors by . . . *giving them something to talk about.*

Her mouth dropped open in a silent "oh" as she turned her head just enough to meet his gaze, which put his lips so close to hers he had only to lean the tiniest fraction closer to mate them together.

It was as if everything else stilled around them, and there was only that moment, and only them inside of it. She searched his gaze, as he did hers, wondering if he meant they should pretend to—or if he meant he'd changed his mind and really wanted—but instead of waiting for answers, she decided to give him a few of her own. So she closed the space between them and kissed him gently on the lips.

In response, he slipped his arm around her waist and slowly pulled her fully against him, then kissed her back, until she melted into him and let all the rest drift away.

Behind them, standing on the porch, her pillows and hoodie clutched against her chest, Bailey smiled. "Finally," she said under her breath. "Adults are so dense sometimes."

Chapter Twelve

"I'm sorry, what?" Sawyer set the blue cheese and smoked pepper-bacon burger he'd been about to bite into back on his plate.

Seth went ahead and sank his teeth into his Vermont cheddar, glazed onion, and beer-mustard burger, then groaned in appreciation. "This is a definite yes," he said, and made a pencil mark on the paper Sawyer's new chef, Hudson Walker, had laid on their table when he'd delivered their first taste-testers. "Seriously, I can't believe Noah let you hire that guy away from him."

Sawyer grinned at that. "I think Noah realized early on that Hudson was destined for greater things than his inn kitchen. Besides, I didn't steal him so much as swap him. Bert was the perfect hire for the glorified food-truck type menu I thought I'd launch with, but the moment Hudson dropped by and began riffing ideas about turning my expanded food-truck theory into a full-blown artisanal menu, locally sourcing all the food and pairing it with my craft beers . . ." Sawyer shrugged. "It just came together. Bert is happy at the inn. He's a very charming guy, so he gets to mingle with the guests directly, which is more his style anyway than being stuck back in the kitchen. Noah says everyone loves him. Win-win, really."

Seth traded their plates and took a bite from Sawyer's untouched burger over his protests, then closed his eyes on a slow groan of pleasure. "He's a genius. You've hired a genius." Seth reached over and marked the box on Sawyer's sheet. "I don't think this taste test is necessary," he said. "Just let the man cook. It's a safe bet anything he puts on a plate is going to be a home run."

"This was his idea," Sawyer said. He glanced around at the handful of other tables and got numerous thumbs-up from the guild artists that Hudson had invited for that afternoon's private "menu development meeting" as he called it. "He's just trying to pare down to the best ones."

Seth noted everyone was either busy eating or scribbling enthusiastically on their response sheets. He grinned at Sawyer. "I don't think this is going to help narrow it down much. It's going to be a ten-page menu before we're done."

"And this is just for the burger section," Sawyer said, then picked up Seth's burger, turned it around, and took a bite from the other side. His reaction was pretty much the same. "You might have a point," Sawyer conceded as he set the sandwich down and wiped his chin with a napkin. "Also, you're not going to just drop that bomb in my lap and pretend it's business as usual. What do you mean, you and Pippa are going to 'give the people what they want'? What does that even mean?"

Seth took a sip of beer, then tried to explain. "I was in my truck heading into town the other day and heard that Bonnie Raitt song 'Something to Talk About.' You know it?"

"Who doesn't?" Sawyer said. "So, you're saying you got this crazy idea from a song? Because that's even more insane."

"It's not insane. It got me thinking, if the folks around here thought they'd gotten their wish and Pippa and I were together, they'd move on to some other mission in life."

Sawyer frowned, pushed his plate back and folded his arms on the table. "Please tell me that Pippa actually knows about this."

Surprised, Seth said, "Of course she does. What, you think I'd lead her on?"

"I honestly don't know what to think. Why not just let people want what they want and you stick to your principles," Sawyer said. "Such as they are."

"What is that supposed to mean?"

"Just that if you're so dead set on beginning something with the first woman I've ever known to turn you completely on your head—and your ass, if you want my opinion—then this screwball idea seems to be playing with fire. Like, of the inferno variety." He made an explosion motion with his hands.

Seth picked up a French fry and popped it into his mouth, grinning as he chewed and swallowed, then said, "Yes, well, see, that's the other part of this plan."

Sawyer closed his eyes, only it wasn't in food rapture this time. "I'm afraid to ask."

"What? Who got your butt out of that very tricky sling that time in Jakarta? And who, might I ask, thought up that very incredible tactical retrieval in Mumbai? Both successful, need I remind you, given we're sitting here talking about them. I'm a great planner." He grinned and bit into another fry. "Everyone says so."

"Yes, well, despite the fact that your mood seems to have made a remarkable recovery, for which we're all thankful, I'm afraid even your admittedly brilliant military strategizing can't conquer the Blue Hollow Falls gossip grapevine. So why bother?"

"Do you want to hear my plan or not?"

Sawyer waved his own fry. "Go on. Let's hear it."

"It was something Mabry said, actually, that made me finally realize I might be trying to fight this thing a little too hard."

Sawyer put his fry down. "Wait. So you're saying that I—
the man who has also saved your bacon on more occasions
than need mentioning here—have a heartfelt conversation
with you, urging you to follow your heart, and that doesn't
get to you. But a man old enough to be your grandfather
says, 'go get her' and *that* is what makes you rethink things?"

"First off, Mabry Jenkins was married to the love of his
life for more years than we've been alive, so I think he's got
you beat there, and secondly, who better to listen to than my
elders?"

Sawyer lowered his fry, then popped it into his mouth.
"Okay. Point taken." Sawyer folded his arms. "So, are you
saying this was Mabry's idea? This big plan of yours?"

"No," Seth admitted. "But after talking about his wife, he
said something about how, back in his day, if a man met the
right woman, he didn't whine about the obstacles, he just
went after her and let the rest sort itself out."

Sawyer lifted his hands, then let them fall in his lap.
"Pretty sure that's exactly what I told you."

Seth grinned. "I guess it was something about his delivery. Anyway, I ran into Pippa in the parking lot that same
day, and Mabry had already gotten me to thinking and
then there she is, and we hadn't spoken in a while and . . ."
He shook his head. "I think part of this is how fast it's all
come at me. How real can that be, right? And she's connected to Moira and her life is half a world away, and let's
remember that, oh, she happens to be this rock star of the
folk music world, which is easy to forget here when she's
just being Pippa MacMillan, but we all know that's going to
be a thing."

Sawyer shook his head, as if trying to keep up with him.
"It's scaring me that I followed all that, but okay, so, what
did Mabry say about that?"

"It wasn't about our situation specifically, it was just
something he said about how you can't gauge how real

something might or might not be based on time alone. Sometimes you just know." Seth looked at Sawyer. "He made a comment about how he knew his wife was the one for him the first time he made her laugh. And I had all these instantaneous flashbacks to every single moment Pippa smiled, or I made her laugh, or her reaction to something else that I recalled. I didn't even know there were that many, or that I'd obviously internalized every last one of them. Mabry saying that, it was like . . ."

"A punch right to the gut?" Sawyer said.

Seth just nodded.

Sawyer grinned then. "I might know something about that." He leaned back in his chair. "It's true, sometimes you just know. Though Mabry's a better man, or a more courageous one anyway, for just going after her right from the start. I did exactly what you're doing. Fought it tooth and nail, using logic as my defense, when nothing about attraction is logical. But it's what we do to keep from getting our hearts stomped on and handed back to us in a basket." He rested his forearms on the table again. "The thing is, it's always going to be a risk, no matter who it is. Obstacles or not. You don't take that risk, then you never reap the far, *far,* greater reward. And if Pippa isn't worth that risk, then who is?"

Seth nodded in agreement. "That's where my head has been these past few days as well. Seeing Pippa in the parking lot right after talking to Mabry was like a one-two punch. Then I heard that song, and it got me to thinking."

"Wait." Sawyer pushed his plate aside. "I'm confused. So you're saying you do want to pursue things with her after all? But you're going to do that by having a pretend relationship? What am I missing here?"

"Okay, I'll start from the beginning."

Sawyer sighed, but waved another fry. "Have at it."

"We agreed—Pippa and I both did—early on, that it was

a bad idea to start something. I knew—I think we both knew—that living under the same roof was going to prove a very bad plan if we hoped to keep our hands to ourselves. So, I leased Noah's cabin. Then Mabry had his accident and we spent a very intense day dealing with that. And after it was over . . . things might have happened."

Sawyer's eyebrows climbed halfway up his forehead. To his credit, this was not paired with any kind of knowing grin. More . . . concern, which Seth appreciated.

"Nothing like that," Seth quickly added. "But we did give in, momentarily, to things. I'm not a kiss-and-tell guy, so—"

"And I'm not asking for details. I get the gist. A line was crossed."

Seth nodded. "And I think it's safe to say we both then realized that my plan, about the cabin, was absolutely the right idea, because . . ." He shook his head, blew out a long breath.

Sawyer did smile then. "I'd launch into the you're-an-idiot speech again, but since it looks like you finally got that memo . . ." He made a sweeping gesture with his hand. "Proceed."

Seth smiled at that. "So we're living apart, but she continued coming to the vineyard, seeing Dex, helping Bailey and Jake. She gave me plenty of space, but otherwise didn't seem all that bothered by our being, you know, in the same vicinity."

"Unlike yourself," Sawyer said, then raised his hand. "Just a guess."

"Ha. Yes, I was having a harder time with that than I thought she was. So I put increasingly bigger distances between us, but that wasn't working out too well either. Then we had a pretty big moment by Big Stone Creek, which I can't explain, but the end result was that I found out she was just as affected, which was why she wasn't staying away. But she promised she would, and I stood there like an idiot and let her walk away. Then I blew any chance of pulling my head out of my ass when she overheard my conversation with you in your office that day and *boom*, it should have been over. Only it wasn't. Because now I knew we both thought there was something, a big something. And then I talked to Mabry, and he said what he said, followed by me walking outside, straight into Pippa. We dance around each other, reaffirm the decision to steer clear, but agree we should at least be able to talk, and she drives off and I'm left standing there asking myself what in the hell is wrong with me? I get in the truck, and I hear the song." Seth leaned back in his chair. "My point being, at every turn, rather than consider giving it a chance, I've just driven my decision to not have this relationship into the ground, then smacked it a few more times with a pile driver, for emphasis."

Sawyer didn't say anything and Seth knew he was processing, so he sat back and waited. "So, what you're saying is that you can't tell Pippa you've changed your mind and flip-flop on her, because she'll feel she can't trust you to know what you want, and she'll be worried that you could flip right back the other way again."

"Bingo," Seth said, tapping the table with the flat of his palm for emphasis. "Hence the plan."

Sawyer rubbed a hand over his face. "Which is, exactly?"

Seth leaned forward and lowered his voice. "Pippa made the comment that the townsfolk didn't seem to be moving on to another subject; they still want to see us together, and they make that pretty clear at every opportunity, even if they're kind about it. Pippa said she was getting used to it. The truth is, I think she's kind of charmed by it."

"Because you think she's not so averse to the idea after all." Sawyer made it a statement.

"I know she's not," Seth said, then leaned back in his chair. "She said she was sorry it was bugging me so much.

I countered with the idea that maybe we just give them 'something to talk about.'" He laughed then. "She thought I meant one of us should be seen around town with someone else." Seth specifically didn't mention the singing, nor would he, even to Sawyer. That was Pippa's news to share. "Then she wondered if I was trying to tell her I was interested in someone else. Her reaction to that was interesting."

"Well, that's good then, right?"

Seth nodded. "I told her I meant we should just let the locals think we're a thing. Then they can move on and focus on the next big to-do."

Sawyer laughed as the light finally dawned for him. "And you think that if you pretend to be together, you could just innocently-not-so-innocently let things progress naturally from pretend to real, like it was just this great plan back-firing on both of you?"

"You say that like it's a bad thing."

Sawyer rolled his eyes. "I say that like a guy who thinks that sometimes the hard part of being a brilliant strategist is that you tend to overthink things *way* too much."

Seth smiled. "I thought this was kind of brilliant, too."

"I think it's an utterly insane way of approaching a fairly straightforward concept. There's this wild new thing the young kids are doing called dating. You should try it. Take her out to dinner. In fact, bring her here for dinner. Do a little dancing. Take a nice long drive. Hell, walk the vines together holding hands."

Seth grinned. "You missed your calling. You should be running a dating service." He was not remotely put off by Sawyer's reaction. In fact, he'd expected it. This was how Sawyer had reacted to every one of his successful plans to get their missions accomplished and their butts safely back to base camp. To Seth's way of thinking, this reaction meant he was on the right track. He popped another two fries in his mouth, then pointed a third at Sawyer. "Sunny is a very lucky woman."

"She is," Sawyer agreed, grinning despite his clear irritation with his best friend.

Seth was okay with that. "The thing is, if I ask her out, try to go the normal route, there's all this pressure and worry. Like, should-we-shouldn't-we, what if he changes his mind again, what should I think about this, how should I react about that. All of the crap that dates are so fraught with when you're trying to get to know someone, trying to find out if this is the one you're meant to be with."

Realization began to dawn. "Ah. But if you're just pretend dating, for the sake of getting the locals off your back, then there's nothing to worry about, because it's not real. So you can just be yourselves."

"Exactly," Seth said. "We let our guards down, just act naturally. Actually, even planning how we're going to put on this little song and dance is a thing that will probably draw us closer together. We'll have some laughs, and in the meantime . . ." He lifted a shoulder. "Things will sort of figure themselves out. We'll either go from pretending to real, or we'll figure out we were right to nip it in the bud. But at least we'll know."

"*You*'ll know," Sawyer countered.

"We'll both know," Seth said. "If she decides to still keep her distance, I'll respect that. I have no choice but to respect that, but at least we'll have tried. I've given up pretending if I ignore it, it will go away."

Sawyer must have seen something in Seth's expression, because he leaned forward immediately. That had been his skill as a commanding officer. No one could read a situation, or a person, better than Sawyer. "But you don't think she will back off, do you? Because, perhaps, this little charade has already begun? And maybe it won't be a charade for long?"

"Last night I went up to the cabin to get Bailey. They

were having movie night. Pippa and I sat outside and talked
while Bailey was inside cleaning up. And yes, I told her
my idea."

"How'd she take it?"

"We were dancing at the time," he said, by way of expla-
nation.

Sawyer lifted his brows again. "Okay."

"So, I thought it went well," was all Seth said, not com-
menting on the kiss. Then both his smile and all of his
bravado dimmed. "Only I haven't heard a word from her
today. Maybe she assumes I'm taking the lead, since it was
my idea."

"But you're worried she's having second thoughts."
Again, Sawyer didn't make it a question.

"Not worried so much as . . . well, okay, maybe worried
sums it up. It's possible I could have put the plan into motion
in a less . . . emphatic manner."

"Ah," Sawyer said, his lips twitching. "Hard to be in a
pretend relationship when only one of you is pretending."

"Yeah. I might not have thought that part all the way
through."

Sawyer grinned widely then. "No pain, no gain."

"Kiss my—"

"So, what did you think of the burgers, mates?"

Seth and Sawyer looked up to find Hudson standing
beside their table. He was as tall as Sawyer and as solidly
built as Seth, with a flashy grin, a mop of wild curly hair on
his head, and the kind of swagger one would expect from an
Aussie with his extraordinary culinary skill set.

"Which one was your favorite?"

"Yes," Seth said with a grin, handing his scorecard to
Hudson, showing every box checked. "When is dessert day?"

Hudson laughed. "I'm still working on it, mate. But
you're on the invite list, I promise."

"These were amazing, Hud," Sawyer told him. "Let's go

with the top four vote-getters, and if it's a ten-way tie, then chef's choice."

"I knew I liked you," Hudson said, then moved on to chat with the artists and crafters seated at each table.

"Smart move, making the guild your lab rats," Seth said, watching Hudson work the room as well. "They'll be raving about this to everyone who stops by the mill for weeks."

Sawyer smiled. "That's the idea. All for one—"

"Burgers for all," Seth finished, and they both chuckled.

Drake and a few other crafters got up and went over to the stage. They'd stowed their instruments there earlier and Drake climbed up on stage and stepped behind the mike. "Okay if we play a little, work off those amazing burgers?" Drake called out to Sawyer.

Sawyer waved his hand. "Please do."

Moments later the sound of a fiddle being tuned and riffs from an accordion punctuated the lively chatter populating the dining area, as did the laughter coming from whatever table Hudson was visiting.

"You know, you've created something really special here already," Seth said, taking in the scene. "I can't believe it's all come together so quickly."

Sawyer smiled. "Tell me," he said. "I feel like my head is spinning every day, trying to focus on the brewing, and get this up and going at the same time. Hudson has been a god-send in more than one way. He's been interviewing sous-chefs and kitchen help. I'm going to have to hire a restaurant manager soon so I can focus on the brewery side of things." He shook his head. "Not complaining, mind you. I'm so grateful this has blossomed like it has. Not just the brewery and pub, but the whole mill. Addie Pearl held a meeting last week with all of the crafters and artists in residence so far, and everyone's saying the same thing. It's been an over-whelming response since we opened our doors with that big holiday open house. In the dead of a pretty brutal winter, too.

We're all excited to see how things grow over this coming summer."

"You build it, they will come," Seth said. "It's got everything going for it, and this place, where folks can sit, chat, linger, and enjoy the whole mill vibe, it's just the icing on the cake."

"Get that winery of yours going and we'll be sending the crowds right up the hill to you. Maggie was by here yesterday to give us an update on Mabry and she said she and her husband have decided to move here for good. Apparently, her husband is thinking he might retire and work with Maggie and the boys to open a cidery to go along with Mabry's apple orchards."

Seth's eyebrows shot up. "Truly? That's a fantastic idea."

Sawyer nodded. "Create something of a destination location, what with your farms being side by side. And you've got Ansted on the other side of the mountain with his pumpkin farm. I think you all could make the fall harvest months a huge event time. Then, when you get the event venue up and running, you'll have wedding season to balance that." He grinned, leaned back in his chair. "Hard to believe when we started working on this rundown place and your horrifically overgrown fields, that we'd get here just a few short years later."

"Speak for yourself," Seth said, chuckling. "I still feel like I have such a long way to go. If this crop of table- and stock grapes happens, then next year I'll start pressing and fermenting."

"I'll be serving the Bluestone & Vine Llamarama Label here before you know it."

Seth chuckled. "Fingers crossed." He'd named his label long before he'd harvested his first bunch of grapes. He'd done it partly for Sarah Bianchi, and partly because it just suited the way he thought. He'd thought he'd go on to have a herd of llamas back then, but Dex was worthy of the label all by himself, even if he would forever be the only one.

"Now all you have to do is get the girl," Sawyer said.

Seth shook his head. "I don't know," he said. "The more I listen to myself explaining it to you, the more I think maybe you're right, about all the planning." He checked his cell phone, then tucked it back in his pocket. "And maybe all this is moot. Maybe she's going to make the decision for me."

"Maybe so," Sawyer said, then looked beyond Seth's shoulder. "Whatever the case, I think you're about to find out."

Seth turned and saw Pippa entering the room. Jake was with her, and he was carrying an old fiddle case.

Pippa waved and Seth started to lift his hand in response, then he realized she was waving to Drake. In fact, he didn't think she'd even noticed he was there. He thought about getting up, going to talk to her, but then Drake was crossing the room and he, Pippa, and Jake disappeared back through the doorway.

"What's that all about?" Seth wondered.

"There's one way to find out," Sawyer said, then made a shooing motion. "Go see." He grinned. "Maybe you'll get the chance for a little PDA. No better place to put your grand plan into motion than at the mill. Before supper, every man, woman, and sheep will know the two of you are making more than googly eyes at each other."

Seth shook his head, but looked at the now empty doorway. "I don't want to intrude on whatever she's got going on. I don't even think she saw me." He turned back to find Sawyer leaning back in his chair, arms folded across his chest, a very satisfied smile on his face. "What?"

"Nothing. Other than this is going to be a very gratifying time in my life." He lifted his hands and gestured around him. "My brewery is taking off. The guild has the mill hopping. Sunny just got her new grant approved for her next research proposal." He folded his arms again. "And I finally get the chance to see you make a complete fool out of yourself over a girl."

"Har, har," Seth grumbled, wondering why he'd thought it was such a good idea to tell Sawyer anything in the first place.

"Fair is fair, after all," Sawyer added.

Seth thought about that and a smile creased his face. "Yeah, well, there is that." He pushed his chair back and stood. "You were pretty spectacularly awkward in your pursuit of Sunny. It's a credit to her she saw through all that to the stellar man underneath."

Sawyer stood, too. "Thanks, I think," he replied, chuckling. "I'm sure Pippa will do the same. Eventually. I'll be happy to have a chat with her if you think it will help."

Seth just gave him a quelling look. "I think I can handle this on my own."

"Yeah," Sawyer said with a laugh, "because you're doing an awesome job of it so far." Sawyer walked around the table and clamped a hand on Seth's shoulder a little harder than was necessary. "Just don't go hurting her and make me have to hurt you. Don't screw this up." He let his hand drop away.

Seth rubbed his shoulder. "Gosh, thanks, Dad. I'll do my best." He snagged his fleece off the back of the chair. The unusually warm spring weather had taken a dip back toward the frigid that morning. "I'm going to head back up to the vines. I've got a distributor coming by later this afternoon. It looks good that he'll be able to handle getting my table grapes sold this fall, along with bulk stock grapes to other vintners."

"That's great news," Sawyer said, though Seth could see that he was disappointed Seth wasn't going to go track Pippa down right that instant.

"It's not a done deal yet," Seth said.

The trio of musicians on the stage, still sans Drake, started up a lively tune featuring a folk guitar, a bass, and the accordion. Folks immediately started tapping their toes and the couple who ran the photography studio in the mill got up and started an impromptu little dance.

"Sunny has been playing Pippa's music over the greenhouse sound system that Noah helped her and Stevie set up," Sawyer mentioned, out of nowhere. "She says the orchids like it."

"And why wouldn't they?" Seth asked, suddenly needing to get out of the mill, back in his truck, and on up the road. Back to his winery, his vines, even his dang llama. *To the life you understand.*

"You listen to her music?" Sawyer wanted to know.

"That's a story for another day," Seth replied. "I really need to get on the road."

Sawyer nodded, finally conceding he'd done all he could.

Seth got his fleece on, but never made it out to his truck. Will intercepted him as he was heading out the main door to the side parking lot.

"Have you seen Jake?" Will asked, looking none too happy.

Seth stopped, frowned. "Yeah, he's with Pippa and Drake. Is something wrong?"

Will was older than Sawyer and Seth, just shy of forty. He topped out right about six feet and his wiry build belied the fact that he tossed bluestone and granite around all day like they were pick-up sticks. "Where are they?" he asked, prompting Seth to put his hand, gently, on Will's shoulder.

"What's wrong? Has something happened?" Then Seth recalled what Jake had been carrying when he'd stepped into the pub. "Is this about the fiddle?"

Will had been about to push past Seth, but his green-eyed gaze swiveled right back. "So he does have it?"

Instead of relief, what Seth thought he saw in Will's eyes was a flash of—grief? Regret? He wasn't sure. Whatever it was, this was no small thing to him. He'd never seen Will this disturbed. "I'm guessing he didn't have permission?"

"I don't know what's gotten into him lately. Ever since he met up with Pippa MacMillan, he's been a changed kid."

Seth smiled then, thinking maybe he was beginning to understand, but kept it gentle. "He's a brand-new teenager, with brand-new hormones. He's got a little crush on her. It's okay, Pippa knows just how to handle it. She's great with him." At least in as much as Seth knew.

"So great that she's talked him into taking one of my fiddles without asking?" Will asked. "I think we might have different interpretations of great, then."

He went to push past Seth again, and this time Seth put his hand on Will's arm, not as gently, but not in anger. Not yet, anyway. "Whoa, whoa, hold on. Tell me what's happening."

"This is between me and Jake. And Pippa, apparently."

"I know you're angry," Seth said, realizing now he'd clearly misread just how upset Will was. "But I promise you, there's nothing nefarious going on here. Pippa is one of the kindest, most generous people I know. She'd never encourage any kind of dishonesty. Maybe Jake wanted to impress her, I don't know, but I don't think it's worth—"

"This doesn't have anything to do with you, Seth," Will bit off. "Let me pass."

If it has to do with Pippa, it does, was the first thought that ran through Seth's head. "Fine," he said, "I'll go with you."

Seth thought he heard Will swear under his breath, and still confused by what would send one of the smoothest, most even-tempered men he knew into such an agitated state, Seth decided he'd take the lead. Not that he thought Will intended to do any physical harm to anyone, but why take chances?

Just then the squeaky, rusty notes of a fiddle echoed down from the upper floor, followed by a mix of male and female laughter. Will turned around and was up the stairs before Seth could stop him. "Wait," he called, knowing he should save his breath.

Will strode right into the music studio classroom without knocking.

Seth was right behind him. "Sorry," he said. "I tried to—"

"Jacob Wilson McCall," Will said to his son, stopping just a few feet into the room, his tone far calmer than Seth would have expected, which, in turn, made it feel that much more portentous.

Drake sat on a stool in the front of the room, his fiddle in one hand, bow in the other. Jake sat on a stool next to him, in a mirror pose, with his fiddle and bow—or Will's fiddle and bow—in his hands in the same position. Pippa sat on a folding chair facing the two, her hands clasped. Or they had been. She'd risen immediately to her feet and turned to face their surprise guests.

"You must be Jake's father," Pippa said, smiling and extending her hand, as if Will wasn't standing there, glaring a hole right through her. "It's a pleasure to finally meet you. Jake talks about you nonstop."

"Dad," Jake croaked, fumbling to stand up, almost knocking the stool over. His ears were tipped in bright scarlet. "I can explain."

Pippa turned then. "Oh, Jake, no," she said softly, as awareness dawned.

Will was already past Pippa, having ignored her outstretched hand. "Pack it up. We're going home. Where you'll be staying for an indefinite period of time when you're not at school. You're grounded."

"Will," Drake began. "He just wanted to learn—"

Will turned to Drake and though his expression was still tight, he seemed to be realizing that he was making quite a scene, so his tone was more modulated when he said, "I don't have a beef with you, Drake. This is between me and my son."

"Mr. McCall," Pippa said. "I'd like to—"

"Jacob?" Will said, cutting her off, and Jake, who'd already hastily packed up the fiddle, walked quickly toward his father.

The two turned, leaving Pippa standing there, her mouth hanging open in dismay, only to find Seth in the doorway, blocking their exit. "First," Seth said very quietly to Will, "you'll do me the favor of turning around and showing your son how you treat a lady. Pippa clearly didn't know. This isn't on her."

Will stared down Seth for a long moment.

"Dad," Jake began, but stopped when Will shot him a quelling look.

Real concern etched Seth's features then. He'd never, not ever, seen Will like this. An outburst was one thing, but this was so out of character it was alarming. Something else was clearly going on here. Something that involved far more than Jake's borrowing a musical instrument without asking.

"Jake," Seth said kindly but firmly, "why don't you go on out and get in your dad's truck. Your dad will be out in a minute."

"Seth—" Will began, a warning tone in his voice.

Seth waited until Jake had cleared the room and his footsteps could be heard on the steps leading down to the main floor, then he stepped closer to Will and lowered his voice so it didn't carry past the two of them. "I don't know what in the hell has gotten into you," he said, his tone calm, his gaze far from it, "but I know you well enough to know you're going to regret how you're handling this."

"You don't know a damn thing," Will said, but didn't move away.

"I get that. Whatever the hell this is about is your business. You don't want to tell me, fine. At the moment, I'm just trying to keep you from making a bigger ass out of yourself than you already have." He held Will's stormy gaze with his own steely one, then said, "If you think you have it in you, apologize to Pippa. That'll be one less regret you'll have later."

Will held his gaze a moment longer, and that's when Seth saw what was lurking behind the anger. Fear. The bald, uncontrollable, crumple-to-the-knees kind of fear. Seth knew that look, because he'd seen it on the faces of his comrades many, many times, and on his own face as well. He also knew the fury was so big because anger was the only emotion potent enough to quash that kind of terror. He saw the twitch at the corner of Will's mouth, the throb in his temple, and knew if he were to shake Will's hand right then, he'd feel a tremor there, too. The kind pure force of will couldn't control.

Seth was just about to make his excuses to Pippa and Drake, and get Will the hell out of there so he could fall apart in private, when Will sucked in a hard breath and turned to face Pippa and Drake. Neither of them appeared angry. Concern was the only emotion etched on their faces.

"This has nothing to do with either of you," he said stiffly. He looked at Drake. "It's kind of you to offer, but Jake will not be learning how to play the fiddle." He glanced at Pippa then, and Seth saw his jaw tighten and his throat work. "Jake talks about you nonstop," he told her, sounding neither complimentary nor damning. Simply stating facts. "I've never seen him quite like this." He took a moment and his throat worked, but none of the rigidity went out of his frame. If anything, Will seemed so stiff, he looked brittle rather than hard. "I've appreciated your music for a very long time." Will paused, then added, his voice hardly more than a rasp. "It reminds me of . . ." His voice quavered, badly, and when he finished, he sounded like he'd swallowed a handful of gravel, the emotion in his voice was so thick. "Someone I loved. Very much. I'd, uh . . ."

He stopped then, and Seth could see Will was visibly

trembling now. Seth wasn't sure how to comfort him, or help him, or if it would be welcome if he tried. All he could do was let Will say his piece.

"I'd appreciate it," he managed, the words being ground out through a world of emotion, "if you'd leave Jake be. It's not about you. I just . . . please."

Seth looked from Will to Pippa. Tears were making tracks down her cheeks, and he could see it was costing her to not go to Will, to try to comfort a man who was clearly in a great deal of pain.

It was a humbling moment, for all of them.

"I promise," she said, her voice thick with tears. "If in time, you ever reconsider, you've only to—"

"Thank you," Will said, then turned and exited the room, his stride determined but no longer rigid.

Pippa looked at Seth. "I didn't know," she said, her eyes huge with sorrow, her voice trembling. "I'm so sorry."

Drake, who had packed up his own fiddle, walked over to Pippa and put a hand on her shoulder. "I think we all know this is about Will. Don't take it personally. You just wanted to help."

She nodded, swiped away a few tears, and smiled. "Thank you for being willing to help, Drake. It was very kind of you."

Drake shrugged. "I'll always support a budding musician." He walked to the door, pausing by Seth. "Sorry, man," he told Seth. "Thanks for sticking up for her, though. It was the right thing to do."

Seth just nodded; then Drake left the classroom, too.

"He was speaking about his wife, wasn't he?" Pippa asked, tears glittering on her eyelashes again.

Seth turned to her. "I think that's a pretty safe bet, yes."

"Does he ever talk about her?"

Seth shook his head. "Not in the time I've known him. He's a quiet man. But a good one, despite what you just saw.

This was so far out of character for him," Seth began, feeling he needed to defend Will, who'd been nothing but a good friend to him.

Pippa nodded. "I could see that. Jake is such a great kid, and I don't doubt his dad is responsible for that. Jake told me that his mom died when he was little, that he doesn't remember her. Do you think Will talks to him about her?"

Seth shrugged. "Don't know. But given the fact Jake took that fiddle—which clearly has some history behind it—without asking, indicates there's some kind of disconnect there."

Pippa sighed. "I feel so bad for both of them. Will is still hurting, and so is Jake. I wish there was some way to help them. If they'd just talk about it."

"As a rule, my gender isn't big on that."

She smiled then. "I don't know, you do pretty well."

"I grew up in the estrogen ocean—I had no choice."

She let out a short, surprised laugh at that. "Maybe we just need to stick Will and Jake in a house with my sisters and your sisters for a month."

Seth chuckled. "There's an idea."

"Are you going to talk to him? Or try?" she asked quietly when their smiles faded once more. "I will honor my promise, about steering clear of Jake, but I can't help feeling that's not going to help matters any. If this is about his wife, Jake's mum, and it looks to be, then Will's sticking his head in the sand won't make this go away. If he doesn't want to confront his painful past, he doesn't have to. Only Jake's not a little kid anymore. And he clearly wants to pursue things that Will wants to keep dead and buried." She lifted her hands, let them drop. "Forcibly keeping Jake from exploring that part of his life, whether it's about his mom, or his interest in music . . . that's going to eventually drive a wedge between them. My parents didn't understand me at all when it came to my passion for music. Fortunately, they supported me anyway, but if they hadn't? If they'd forbidden me?" She blew out a breath. "I don't even want to guess what measures I'd have been willing to take. I mean, it would be one thing if I—or Jake—wanted to pursue something illegal, or that could get me killed or something. But it's music we're talking about. I don't think Jake fancies himself a career musician. He just wants to play music like his mom and dad did."

Seth looked at her. "Jake's mom played?"

"You didn't know? I don't know if she played, but she was a singer. That's how she met Will, back when he was in the military. He played the fiddle at some local place near whatever base he was stationed on and she asked to sing with the band." Pippa lifted her hand. "That's all I know. I'm not sure what all Jake knows. That's all he told me."

Seth nodded. "I'll talk to Will. At some point. I think we need to, for Jake's sake, if nothing else. I'll talk to Sawyer, too. And Addie Pearl. Will's mom was a good friend of hers, from childhood, I'm pretty sure. I don't think she knew Jake's mom. Jake didn't come to live here until his mom passed, but I can see if Addie Pearl has any insight into what happened."

"Good," Pippa said, sounding relieved. "That's really good. If there's anything I can do—"

"I will let you know," Seth said.

Silence fell again, and just as Pippa turned to retrieve the purse she'd left leaning against the folding chair, Seth heard himself blurt out, "Have you given my proposition any thought?"

Clearly surprised, Pippa turned to him and let out a little laugh. "I thought I made my answer to that pretty clear on the porch steps last night."

Now it was his turn to look surprised. "I hadn't heard from you today, so I wasn't sure if you'd had second thoughts. Bailey hasn't said a word to anyone, by the way. She texted me this morning to make sure I knew the secret was safe with her."

Pippa rolled her eyes, but her smile was filled with affection. "I wonder how much she heard."

"Hard to tell," Seth said, "but she seemed pretty happy with the end result."

Pippa frowned. "I didn't think about—isn't it wrong, letting her think we're . . . you know?"

"She's been raised with barn animals. I don't think she's squeamish at the idea that we might be having—"

"I didn't mean that!" Pippa laughed, looking a bit shocked. "She's ten."

"She's helped birth more goats than the average midwife."

Pippa covered her eyes. "Aye, and I could have done without knowin' that, couldn't I?"

Seth grinned. He liked it when she went full Irish. "Aye, that I do," he said, his own brogue fairly dead-on, given his grandparents had been straight over from the old country.

"What I meant," Pippa said, "is that it's not fair to let her think we're happily involved, then I take off and—" She lifted a shoulder. "I mean, I know it's not her heartbreak, it would be mine, but she's still a young, impressionable girl and . . . I hate to set her up to be sad. It's wrong."

Seth nodded. "That's true." He closed the distance between them, lifted Pippa's chin with his fingertips. Her beautiful blue eyes were swimming with emotion again, but he wasn't sure he fully understood the source. *Only one way to find out.* He had been bold enough talking about how Will should face his fears; the least he could do was man up and tackle his own. "Would it be a heartbreak? For you?" he asked, his voice barely above a rumble.

Her bottom lip quivered, just the tiniest bit, and he was

rubbing the pad of his thumb over it, soothing it, before he could think on the wisdom of his action.

She searched his gaze, then whispered, "Would it be for you?"

It was a pivotal moment. He could feel it like a gravitational surge, rooting him to the spot, wrenching her question into tight focus. There was no backing down now, no big, elaborate plans meant to save them from themselves. Just this moment. And this woman, asking him for his honest response. "I think it will be, aye," he said, the brogue gruff, as was his voice.

"Me too," she whispered, then made a sound like a half laugh, half sob. "We're so hopelessly bad at this staying apart thing. And I'll be honest, Seth, I don't want to pretend to be with you." She took a deep, shuddering breath and held his gaze as directly as she ever had. "I want to truly be with you," she said simply, and yet so boldly. So bravely. "Whatever that means, wherever it goes."

Chapter Thirteen

She was standing in a classroom, surrounded by music stands, folding chairs, and a small, makeshift stage. But Pippa might as well have been standing on the edge of a cliff, with one foot slipping perilously close to the edge. Her heart was thundering that hard.

"And when you leave?" he asked, his eyes dark with the kind of want that made her toes curl inside her boots and every pleasure point in her body tighten to the point of pain.

"Then we'll either come up with a plan . . . or we'll be idiots and say our good-byes, deserving whatever heartbreak we get."

He surprised her by smiling. "You Irish are a rather maudlin lot."

She let out a watery laugh. "For all we know, we'll have parted ways long before I hie myself out of here. It's quite possible we'll wonder what on earth we were thinking, getting tangled up with one another."

"Speak for yerself, lass," he said, then pulled her into his arms, folding her up close as he tipped her head back and closed his mouth over hers as surely, as rightly, as any man ever could.

It was as romantic as any windswept romance she'd ever read, and everything she'd wanted him to do that day standing beside Big Stone Creek. They'd wasted so much time. With that thought, she gripped his shoulders and gave herself fully to his kiss.

This wasn't the teasing exploration of their sunset dance on the porch, nor was it the emotional, exhaustion-fueled tempest that had erupted the day of Mabry's accident. This was the pure, unvarnished mating of two souls with like wants, like desires, absolutely intent on letting things progress as they would. No more caution flags, no more wondering what he meant, or she wanted. This felt like . . . well, like a proper beginning.

"One of these days, I'm going to kiss you somewhere private," he said, as he finally lifted his head.

She wiggled her eyebrows. "Promises, promises."

When he realized the double entendre, he laughed and this time he kissed her hard and fast. "Yes, well," he said, dropping another kiss on the corner of her mouth, then moving along her chin, then nipping the curve of her neck. "That, too."

She shivered in utter delight. "It's good to have goals," she said, then let out a little squeal of laughter when he scooped her up as if planning to carry her off right then and there. "I'm sure you've something important you should be doing," she said, giggling and swatting at his shoulders.

He let her feet slide back to the floor, but held her against him a moment longer. "I can't think of a single thing I'd rather be doing at the moment. Well . . . maybe one thing."

"We'll see about that," she said, playing prim to his bold, then giggling when he just winked. "Perhaps a nice meal, a little conversation, a dance or two. I've been wanting to try Bo's. Bailey keeps raving about the breakfasts she and Sawyer have there."

His grin went from bold to full-on Viking. "Breakfast it

is then." He started to scoop her up again, but she laughed and batted his shoulders.

"Quite sure of yourself, aren't you then?" she teased. "I'll have you know I'm not a breakfast-on-the-first-date kind of girl, Mr. Brogan."

"I'm not sure of much," he told her, still smiling, but with a serious note in his gaze as well. "But I'm certain I'll be wanting to share as many meals with you as you'll allow me to."

Her heart simply melted. Every time she thought he'd tease her, he'd go the other way and say something unbearably sweet. "Why don't we begin with dinner. Tomorrow evening, perhaps?" she asked. "If Bo's suits you, that would serve the purpose of putting the town on notice that we've succumbed to their demands and have forced ourselves to pursue this romance they all seem so certain we should be having."

"Well, when you put it like that, how's a bloke to resist?"

She reached up on her toes and brushed a kiss against his mouth. "It's a date, then." She smiled up into his face. "I rather like the man bun on you, by the way."

She was charmed further when she saw a bit of heat climb into his cheeks. Surely, given his looks, and his stature, he'd had women tossing much more lascivious comments his way. It made teasing him that much more fun. "Although, to be honest, it makes me want to reach up and yank it all down again."

He reached out and tugged at the end of one of the braided ponytails she'd taken to wearing back when she was out in his barn every day. "Well," he said, the corner of his mouth curved in a wry grin, "if dinner goes well, maybe we'll both let our hair down. I'll do yours if you'll do mine." He gave an exaggerated eyebrow wiggle that made her laugh all over again.

A buzzing sound went off in his pocket and he abruptly

pulled his cell phone out, then swore under his breath. He punched the button to answer it. "Mr. Denton, I'm sorry. I got unavoidably detained. A friend in need. I'm on my way. I appreciate your patience." He hung up. "Meeting with my potential distributor. I was on my way there when the whole Will thing blew up."

"Go, go," she urged him. "We'll talk later."

Nodding, he pocketed his phone and started for the door. "Sorry to ravish you and run," he said with a grin and a wink, then crossed the room right back to her, framed her face in his broad hands, and kissed her so tenderly, it made her eyes sting. He made her feel desirable just by looking at her. This, however, was what she thought it might feel like to be loved.

"Thank you for being the brave one," he said, looking down into her eyes. "I'll try to live up to your example from now on." He flashed a smile. "But feel free to give me a swift kick if I don't." He was gone before she could reply.

Pippa had been pacing the main room of her cabin for so long she was surprised she hadn't worn a track in it. It would be easy to be all unicorns and moonbeams over the new turn of events between her and Seth, and to be truthful, she was tempted to smile like a loon, dance a little jig, and revel in the thrill of it all. She wanted to endlessly replay every touch, every kiss, every word, to the exclusion of all else. At least until it was time to see him again, and add new memories to the loop.

And she'd done that pretty much nonstop since she'd left the mill the day before. But now it was a brand-new day, and her thoughts were once again on Jake, and on Will. The excitement, the anticipation, along with the attendant nervousness she felt about seeing Seth again that evening for their first real date, was outweighed at the moment by her concern for a sweet boy and his anguished father. She wanted to do something to help, but everything she came up with held the risk of doing more harm than good. Based on what Will had said, it seemed to her that she had been a large part of the catalyst that had sent him barging into that music room.

She kept replaying that emotion-choked confession he'd started to make, and was fairly sure what he'd meant was that she, Pippa MacMillan, sounded, to him, a lot like his late wife. It had been wrenching to hear that note of raw pain in his voice, and know there was nothing she could do to change the memories her singing apparently brought to the surface.

And yet, on the other hand, Jake had told her that Will listened to her music, that her songs, her fiddle playing, were the *only* folk music he listened to. She realized now why he did so, but it begged the question, why would Will bludgeon himself like that? And that spurred her to wonder, if she could be the catalyst for painful memories, then couldn't she also potentially be the catalyst for helping Will get himself to a place where he could begin to deal with the tragic loss he'd suffered?

Pippa couldn't imagine that if Will was thinking clearly, he'd want to block his son from pursuing a connection to his late mum. That said, she felt awful that she'd somehow been complicit in helping Jake do an end run around his father's wishes. She should have noticed something wasn't right, but she'd been so busy trying to sort out how to get Jake the lessons he needed, without having to explain why she wasn't willing to instruct him herself, she'd chalked up his nerves to the kind you get anytime you try something new. So, that much was on her.

Thank you for being the brave one.

"If you only knew," she muttered, as Seth's words echoed through her mind yet again. She'd put herself out there first, said the words first, and it had been terrifying, yes, but at the same time, not. The kiss they'd shared on the steps of her cabin had certainly gone a very long way to putting to rest any remaining questions she had. So she wasn't sure how brave she'd been, really. But he thought she had been, which meant he might not have been able to make the same leap, had it been left solely up to him.

She stopped dead in her tracks, her eyes widening as the lightbulb moment came to her. By putting herself out there first, she'd helped Seth to get to the place he already wanted to be. Maybe she could find a way to do the same for Will. "But how?" she murmured.

She continued her pacing. Surely Will didn't want to be conflicted and raw over his wife's passing for the rest of his life. It had already been a long time, perhaps a decade or more, because Jake was thirteen and had been so young at the time he couldn't recall his mum at all. And in all that time, Will truly hadn't moved on. And as she knew all too well, the deeper you went down that well of fear and despair, the harder and harder it became to climb back out of it. But he would want to, wouldn't he, if he could find a way?

She stopped and sank down on the couch. "Maybe he'll never do it for himself," she murmured. *So, who else does he care about more than himself?* "Jake," she whispered.

If Will was going to heal himself for his own well-being, he would have done so by now. When Jake was little, Will could control the narrative for his son, too, keep his pain tucked away, unaddressed. "But now Jake is a young man, and he's only going to grow more independent," Pippa pondered out loud. She propped her elbows on her knees and rested her chin on her curled fingers, then closed her eyes and tried to think. *What would open Will's eyes so he could see that his son needs his father more than his father needs to cling to his pain?*

Her eyes blinked open. She simply didn't know.

She flopped back on the couch and blew out a long breath. Maybe it wasn't her problem to solve. "And maybe you need to let Will's problem go and work on solving your own." Was that what she was doing? Focusing on Will's problem, and Jake's problem, so she could put off dealing with her own? "Probably," she said dryly, then grabbed a pillow and put it over her face, wanting to vent her frustration into it with a nice, healthy scream. And not daring. She slapped the pillow down in her lap. "Exactly. Who's the coward now?"

Wait. Wait just a minute.

She sat forward on the couch, clutching the pillow against her stomach, her mind racing as the solution started to tumble into place. Her smile came slowly, and was in no way confidant; in fact there was a growing knot in her stomach that wasn't so much excitement as a big ball of dread. The only way for her to help Jake was to put herself in Will's shoes. To ask no more of him than she was willing to ask of herself.

Yes, that's it. That is exactly it! That she finally had a solution, one that would help both her and Will, made her grin. It also made her want to throw up.

A half hour later Pippa was at the hospital, sitting by Mabry's bedside. He and Addie Pearl had been in Blue Hollow Falls longer than anyone she personally knew. Addie Pearl was next on her list.

"Aren't you a pretty sight for sore eyes," Mabry told her when she'd entered the room moments ago.

Pippa had taken a seat in the chair next to the bed, and scooted it a bit closer when Mabry held out his hand to her. She held it between her own, surprised to find it warm and strong, and not cold and frail, as its pale, bony appearance had led her to think it would be.

Mabry squeezed her fingers. "How are things up at the farm?" he asked her. "Maggie won't tell me the truth, of course. She's afraid the stress of any bad news will slow down my recovery."

Pippa smiled. "To hear the nurses tell it, they're having to strap you to this bed to keep you from trying to do too much, too soon."

Mabry made a sour face. "These dang fool bed exercises—horizontal physical therapy, they call it or some such—aren't getting me on my feet again."

"You have to let things heal before you start dancing a jig," she told him.

"My bones are past eight decades old; how long could they take to heal? Can't be much left to them at this point." He held out his arms. "Dang hospital food has whittled me down to nothing, so it's not like they have to support much."

Pippa tried not to laugh at that. Mabry did look pale, and much older than he had before the accident. He definitely was thinner, too. But his old eyes were on fire as he spoke, his voice was back to being steady, and his mind was as sharp as ever, which counted for far more in her book. "As I understand it, the nurses have confiscated more contraband food from this room than any other on this floor." She lifted her eyebrows. "Pretty much every one of those occasions has happened right after the twins come to visit. What a coincidence." She smiled. "There's talk of strip searches the next time they arrive. Does their mum know about this?"

"It turns out their mother, my sainted only daughter, has been turned to the dark side by those same nurses," he grumbled. "Co-conspirators, all. My grandsons are my only hope at this point."

Pippa did laugh then. "And here I thought you were the favorite patient here," she said.

"Yes, well, I think I've long since worn out my welcome.

You'd think they'd conspire to get me out of this joint, not keep me in."

"I think that's the end goal for everyone," Pippa said, gently squeezing the back of his hand. "We all want to see you back on the farm, but the best thing is to do what they say, so you get the full benefit of the recovery. Rushing any part of it might compromise you down the road."

Mabry let out a dry cackle at that. "I don't think I've much road left to travel, if you get my meaning. I'm wasting a good chunk of it stuck in this bed."

Pippa just squeezed his hand again and smiled. "Well, if being ornery will get you anywhere, I'd say you've got nothing to worry about."

That had him lifting his eyebrows and letting out a raspy hoot. "I'd forgotten why I like you so much. Now I recall."

Pippa laughed. "Good to hear."

"So perhaps those memories I've been having about you badgering me, none too politely I might add, while I had a jack shaft sticking out of my leg, weren't hallucinations either?"

Pippa's eyes widened at that, and her cheeks might have gone a bit pink.

"Quite the little bully," he said, then slipped his hand from hers, laid it on top of her fingers, and squeezed with more strength than she'd believed he had. "Thank you," he told her. "I should have said it sooner. But what you and Seth did for me saved my life."

Her eyes went misty and her throat tightened as she tried not to recall the specifics of that day. "I just did what anyone would do," she told him. Then, seeking to lighten the mood, she wiggled her eyebrows. "Besides, I really needed that truck. How would it look if I just drove off in it and left you pinned there?"

He chuckled at that, delighted, then squeezed her hands again before letting them go. "Can you help with my pillows?"

She jumped up and did as he asked and Mabry shifted to sit up straighter.

"So," he said, as soon as he was settled and she was seated back in her chair. "Seeing as we're being blunt, have you and Seth managed to figure out what the rest of us who aren't blind saw from the day you two met?"

Now it was her turn to look surprised and let out a choked laugh. "We're . . . making inroads in that direction."

Mabry looked pleasantly surprised, but was shaking his head at the same time. "Inroads? What in the blazes does that mean? Is that the younger generation's way of saying you're dating?"

"We're having dinner this evening, in fact," Pippa said.

"Have you come to me for dating advice, then?"

She grinned. "What've you got?"

"Well," he said, considering, "I've only got one thing to give you on that, but it's the only thing you need to worry about."

Pippa leaned closer, truly curious to hear what he had to say. "And what would that be?"

"Be honest about the important things, kind about the hard things, and whatever you do, don't give worry a leg up."

"Are we talking dating, or—"

"We're talking life," Mabry said.

Pippa nodded. "Okay. What do you mean, 'don't give worry a leg up'?"

"Worry gives you nothing, it only takes, and what does it take? It takes the most precious thing you have. Time." Mabry reached for her hand again, and this time he held hers between his own. "Don't waste time, Pippa. You young people think you have endless amounts of it, but none of us do. I had more than sixty years with my sweet Annie, and it wasn't long enough." He shook her hand slightly, and held her gaze. "Don't give your time away to worry. Go after life. You hear?"

Pippa hadn't known what to expect, but it hadn't been that. She felt her eyes water for what seemed the hundredth time that day. This time in gratitude. "I won't," she said, her throat full once more.

Mabry nodded, but didn't let go of her hand. His gaze turned shrewd and he leaned forward a bit when he added, "Will you promise this old man something else?"

Pippa nodded and blinked back the moisture in her eyes. "If I can."

"Apply that bit of advice to every part of your life. Do you understand my meaning?"

Pippa swallowed past the lump in her throat, feeling more foolish—and more indebted—than possibly at any other time in her life. "I will do my best," she whispered. "I promise."

Mabry held her gaze another long moment, then rested his head back on his pillows. "I plan to be around awhile, so I'll be keeping track," he said. "Don't disappoint me."

She laughed at that, and wiped at the corners of her eyes. "That's all the motivation I need."

"Good." He folded his hands on his lap. "Now, since I'm stuck here with nothing better to do than fill in those endless word-search books and harass the hired help, all while suffering the indignity of allowing other folks to do the work I was put on this earth to accomplish, what other problems of yours can I fix?"

Pippa perched her hip on the side of his bed. "Actually, I was hoping you could give me some help with another situation." She grinned. "Now that you've gotten my life sorted out."

Mabry lifted his hand, gesturing her to go on, but there was a twinkle in his eyes now.

"It's actually rather serious," she said. "I've made a muck of things. Not on purpose, mind you, but I want to set things right. It's about Wilson McCall, and his son, Jake. Do you know them?"

Mabry frowned. "I do. Wilson has helped me on more occasions than I can count. Mason by profession now, former military man, as was my brother. I've yet to find a thing Wilson can't mend. Jack-of-all-trades, I suppose you'd say. Fine fiddle player, I hear, too, once upon a time, though you'd never know it."

Pippa brightened. "So, it's common knowledge then, that he played at one time?"

"I don't know how common it is, but I know it's true. His mother, Dorothy, grew up here, you see. Everyone called her Dot. She was a bitty thing. She was Dorothy Lankford back then. My Annie and Addison Pearl were both childhood friends of hers, though they were in different grades in school. Not many kids in the Falls back then, so they were close, despite the age difference."

"That much hasn't changed," Pippa told him, charmed by the discovery. "Will's son, Jake, has become very good friends with Sawyer Hartwell's stepsister, Bailey Sutton. They're a few years apart, but they're two peas in a pod."

Mabry nodded, looking pleased by that. "Well, Dot met Jack McCall in college, married him and followed him around the globe for years. Military wife. Never met the man, but have heard only good things. They just had the one child, Wilson. Used to come visit Dot's folks in the summer when he was little. Dot, Annie, and Addison kept in touch, though. Wrote letters, sent postcards. Addison Pearl was most responsible for keeping that going, I think. Dot was gone a long time, but she was always Blue Hollow Falls family, you know."

"I do," Pippa said softly. "Where I grew up, it's much the same way. It's good she always had friends back home."

Mabry nodded, then sighed, some of the twinkle fading from his eyes. "Jack—Wilson's father—was killed in combat.

Wilson was serving by then, too, I think, but I'm not sure. Dot came back home after Jack died, lived out the rest of her life here. Will married, had Jacob." Mabry smiled. "Named after his grandfather. Jack was a Jacob, too." He chuckled. "Dot would go on and on about her only grandchild. Passed photos to anyone who'd look at them." He sobered then. "Then Wilson's wife passed. Dot went off for a while to help with the funeral and such, help out with Jacob. When it was said and done, Will was still serving his country, so she brought Jacob here, where she could look after him. He was just a little thing back then, barely out of the crib as I recall." Mabry sighed and shook his head. "No shortage of tragedy in that family, I suppose."

"What happened?" Pippa asked. "To Wilson's wife. If you don't mind telling me." She didn't want to drag Mabry through sad memories, but thought it might help her understand Will better.

"Car accident. Drunk driver." Mabry shook his head. "Annie knew more about it all than I did. Addison Pearl would, too. And her memory is better."

Pippa smiled briefly. "I don't know, you seem to be doing pretty well. I appreciate your sharing this with me. I didn't mean to dredge up sad memories. I wouldn't ask if it weren't important. Can you tell me anything else about her? Will's wife, I mean."

Mabry took in a slow breath and took a moment, searching his memory. "Well, though I never met her, word was that girl could sing like an angel." He looked at Pippa. "Don't know if she had any ambition to go and make something of it like you did."

Pippa smiled when he sent her a meaningful look. "So, you've heard about that, have you?" Since Mabry had gone into the hospital the day after meeting her, Pippa hadn't thought he'd have learned that bit of news. Maggie knew, though, so of course she'd probably mentioned it to him.

"Oh, there isn't much I don't hear about," Mabry said, looking pleased.

"Will's wife just sang locally, from what I know, but made a splash when she did. That's what she was doing the night she died. Coming home from singing for some Christmas holiday program on base, I believe."

"Oh, no!" Pippa gasped. "At the holidays? That's awful."

"Will was overseas, as I recall, stationed somewhere where families couldn't go." He shook his head. "Can't imagine getting that kind of news at that time of year."

Pippa shook her head, understanding more and more why Will had been so deeply affected by his loss. "Where was Jacob?"

"No idea. With a sitter, I'm guessing."

Pippa nodded, feeling heartsick for Will, and for Jake.

"And you know the rest," Mabry said. "Dot got sick a few years later. Jacob was in school by then, so five or six years later at least. It took a while, but that gave her and Will time to plan. It was sad, but merciful when her time came. Will got out of the service after that, moved here full time."

"You're right," Pippa said quietly. "That's a lot of grief and loss for one family."

"Lot of love in that family, too," Mabry countered. "All in how you want to look at it."

Pippa looked up then, pulled from her thoughts. "I suppose you're right."

"Ask me, I'd much rather someone sum up my life by all the good there was in it, than the sad. Live long enough and loss is unavoidable. You can choose to mourn what you don't have, or be thankful for what you did."

Pippa sat back in her chair and let that sink in. Only she wasn't thinking about Will and Jake. She was thinking about Seth, about the choice they'd just made to be thankful for what they might have. She hoped she'd be strong enough when the time came, to remain positive and thankful, after it was over.

She thought about her future, too, about her voice, and the choices she'd yet to make. Was that what she'd been doing all these months? Mourning what was gone? Instead of focusing on what she still had to be thankful for? She thought about what Mabry had told her earlier, about not giving valuable time away to something as fruitless as worry. She knew he was right, about all of it. *You just have to find the strength to do it.*

Pippa looked back at Mabry and saw that he was dozing. She hoped dredging up those memories hadn't tired him out too much. She gathered her purse and stood, leaning over and pressing a gentle kiss to his forehead. "Thank you," she whispered.

His eyes fluttered open briefly as she turned to leave. "Was that of any help?" he asked, sounding a big groggy now.

"More than you'll ever know," she told him with a warm, affectionate smile.

He nodded. "See?" he said, his eyes already drooping closed again. "More to put on that good list."

Chapter Fourteen

"Change of plans," Pippa said over the phone, but she sounded excited rather than regretful.

Seth pinned the phone between his shoulder and his ear so he could tuck the towel in around his hips. He sat on the side of his bed, his wet hair dripping down his bare back, and palmed the phone again. "Okay. What's the new plan? No dinner?"

"Yes, dinner, but not at Bo's." She paused, then said, "Could you meet me at Addie Pearl's house?"

Surprised, he said, "Sure. You know, if you're thinking we need a chaperone, I really won't carry you off to my cave like a Neanderthal. Earlier behavior notwithstanding."

She giggled at that, and whatever worry he had about what had prompted this detour instantly smoothed out. He wondered how long it was going to take to not worry every other minute that she would change her mind. *Now who's afraid of flip-flopping?* he thought, knowing Sawyer would be largely entertained by what he was putting himself through. The answer was that he'd stop worrying when her time in Blue Hollow Falls was up, and they knew what they were going to do going forward.

"Well," Pippa said, "I'm fairly confident I could take care of myself if you went all Viking on me. Stunt driving isn't the only thing Brae taught me."

"Having grown up with four sisters, even without special training, I believe you," Seth said, chuckling. "So, why are we inviting Addie Pearl to crash our date?"

"Because I have a plan to help Will and Jake. And if I hold off putting it into motion, I'm afraid I'll lose my nerve."

Seth's smile instantly changed to a look of concern. "Pippa, I really don't think we should meddle—"

"*We* won't be," she said. "It'll just be me. But I need Addie Pearl's help, and I would like your input, too. I promise, this is a gentle plan, Seth. I wouldn't risk hurting either of them any more than they've already been hurt. I'll explain it all when I see you. Same time, and Addie Pearl said to bring a bottle of your wine."

"I'm not making wine yet," he said.

"Addie said you've been playing with grapes and making test batches since back when you first bought the place."

"She did, did she?"

"Mm-hmm. Addie Pearl told me you've given a few bottles away as Christmas presents, but she drank hers." Pippa laughed. "Looks like we have a lot to discuss this evening."

"I'll bring the wine," Seth told her, shaking his head but grinning as he did. Pippa was a lot to keep up with, all by herself. Putting her in cahoots with Addie Pearl, however, might be more than even he could handle. "Is it just the three of us?"

"Yes," she said. "Bailey is out with Sawyer and Sunny tonight. And I'll make it up to you. Dinner at the cabin to-morrow?"

"I can't," he said, surprised but pleased by the offer. "The distributor ended up not being able to wait for me the other day, so he's coming back tomorrow. I'll be happy to let you borrow my kitchen, if you'd like. I make a mean tossed salad, and I can chop things up fairly decently. So I could play sous-chef."

"That's a date," she said, sounding more than pleased.

They ended the call and Seth tossed the phone on the bed, then lay back and closed his eyes. It actually wasn't a bad idea, having a chaperone that evening. Be it Addie, or the entire town watching the two of them dining at Bo's. They'd at least have a prayer of not ending up eating breakfast together tomorrow morning. Pippa wanted to move slow; he'd move like a snail if he had to. That said, dining at the chalet, with the bed he was presently sprawled over just a few yards away? They were adults, he reminded himself. Adults who'd had adult relationships in the past. It wasn't like ending up in bed together would automatically change things before they were ready for that change. He opened his eyes. "Who are you kidding?"

It would change everything. At least it would for him.

He sat up, then stood, snagging the damp towel that had come untucked from where it lay on the bed before walking back to the bathroom. He was going to have to change the venue for their next date—that's all there was to it. *And how many more after that?*

"Yeah, there's a question for you," he muttered, then twisted his hair up in a knot and finished the beard trim before getting dressed. They didn't have the luxury of forever. The clock was already ticking for them.

Seth arrived at Addie's twenty minutes later, two bottles of wine in hand, and a knot in the pit of his stomach. Which was ridiculous. "You're not sixteen here, bro." In fact, if anyone who knew him could see him now, standing there on the stoop, practically in a cold sweat because he was about to go on a first date—one chaperoned by a seventy-three-year-old woman no less—worried that he would somehow blow it and Pippa would change her mind . . . "Yeah, Sawyer, this one's for you," he muttered.

He was the smooth one, the flirty one, the one who was always at ease with the opposite sex. He was the world's best wingman. He realized now why he'd never once felt that kind of easy, smooth flirtatiousness with Pippa.

Because no one else has mattered until now.

It was the truth. And the fact that she'd talked about them starting something with the caveat that it would either work or it wouldn't, and they'd just figure that out when the time came for her to leave . . . Yeah, not exactly a balm to his ever-increasing anxiety.

"Are you going to go on in, or stand there like a wet-behind-the-ears twelve-year-old? Jake McCall has more swag than you."

Seth turned to find Addie coming up the walk with an armload of firewood. "What do you know about swag?" he asked, chuckling.

Addie was a short, septuagenarian hippie, with narrow shoulders and sturdy legs, who favored tie-died T-shirts and cut-off olive-green army shorts, the bottom edges of which ended below her bony knees but above her laced up leather hiking boots. She wore her long gray hair in a braid that dropped all the way past her wide waist, to brush her flat-as-a-pancake fanny. The top of her head might barely come to his chest, but she was a force to be reckoned with. "I was born with swag, sonny," she said, then sent him a wink.

Seth had already put down the wine bottles and hopped off the porch so he could relieve her of the load. "I thought Sawyer got you that firewood wagon thing."

"Thing's one word for it," she said. "I've carried wood inside my house all of my adult life, and a good couple of years before that. I don't need some silly trolley designed for yuppie campers. I made a planter out of it. Looks real nice out back. The day I can't fill my own wood-burning stove—"

"Is the day you let Bailey do it," Seth said, then slipped the stack from her arms and winked at her. "Or me. I think you've earned the right to delegate the heavy lifting."

She just waved his comment away, but went on up the walkway in front of him. She pushed open the front door, then picked up the bottles of wine and held the screen door open for him.

Seth leaned down and brushed a kiss on her cheek as he went by. "Beautiful as ever," he told her. "Swagalicious."

She swatted him on the backside as he passed, and didn't hold back, either, but he heard her chuckling. "If you'd just sweet-talk Pippa like you do me, you'll do fine, trust me." She followed him in and closed the door behind them.

Seth choked a little at that. Addie wasn't one for beating around the bush. Too late he realized that maybe he should be more worried about the chaperone than his date. He stood and brushed his hands on the legs of his jeans. "I'll have you know I've been nothing but charming."

Addie opened one of the wine bottles to let it breathe. "I should hope so. She's a lovely girl."

"She is, indeed," Seth said, walking over to the kitchen to peek over her shoulder. "Something smells like heaven."

She swatted him away from the bubbling pots on the stove. "Make yourself useful and pour us a glass."

"Happy to," he said, chuckling. "You didn't have to cook, you know. I'm not sure what Pippa's big scheme is, but something tells me we're going to be owing you the dinner, if she's planning on your helping in some way. Where is she, by the way?"

"She was still down at the mill when I left. She was talking to Sawyer before he and Sunny took off. Then she had something else she needed to do there, not sure what.

She'll be here shortly, I suspect." Addie stirred one pot while blowing across another to help keep the boil from frothing over the edge.

"Pippa said Sawyer and Sunny were taking Bailey out for the night?"

Addie nodded. "All the way up to Valley View for a gallery showing. I know it's Sunday and a school night, but I figured one late night would be okay. That child finishes her homework on the bus ride home from school more than half the time, so I've no doubt she's prepared for class tomorrow. I'll help her with the sheep in the morning."

"I'm sure she appreciates getting to go," Seth said. Turtle Springs was the nearest town to Blue Hollow Falls, with basic shopping amenities and other support systems that the Falls lacked, like the hospital. Valley View was the closest city that could truly be called that, and was close to two hours away. "Valley View, huh? Sounds fancy. Who's the artist?"

"Paper sculptor. Builds these amazing portraits by stacking together folded pieces of paper. I've never seen anything like it. Tremendous talent. She's considering moving to the area and wanted to talk to me about seeing if some of our artists could make hand-milled and hand-dyed paper for her for a big project she's working on for her next show."

"Sounds like that might be a good fit. Interesting craft. So, were you supposed to go? You should have said something. I'm sure Pippa wouldn't want you to—"

Addie waved a spoon over one of the pots. "I've every faith Sawyer will make a deal with the artist and I'll have plenty of opportunities to see her work up close and personal later. Who better to charm her than Sawyer?"

"And Bailey," Seth said, then laughed. "Poor woman doesn't stand a chance."

Addie Pearl smiled at him over her shoulder. "And I

figure once Sawyer closes the deal, I can convince her to come teach a seminar or two."

Seth lifted his wineglass in her direction. "Always thinking."

Addie nodded, taking the compliment in stride. "Besides, Pippa said this was something to do with that tiff I heard about at the mill yesterday, between Will and Jake." She laid the spoon down and wiped her hands on the towel she'd tucked into the pocket of her apron, then turned to Seth. "Doesn't sound like the Wilson McCall I know at all. So of course I want to help if I can."

Seth took a seat on one of the stools that fronted the workstation in the center of the kitchen. Addie Pearl's cabin was log-over-log, much smaller than his but similar in the open floor plan with the loft overhead. The large picture window behind him on the other side of the dining-room table framed a breathtaking view along the mountain range. Or as Addie put it, "the kind of art only God could paint."

Seth slid her wineglass to her. "It was definitely out of character," he agreed, "and then some. I was with Will and Jake more days than not when we were all working on the mill. Never once did I see him get so much as irritated with Jake, much less display the fury he put on show yesterday. He's the steadiest, most patient man I've ever met. To a fault at times." Seth shook his head. "I felt as bad for him as I did for Jake."

Addie Pearl nodded. "Pippa said it had to do with Jake bringing one of Will's fiddles to the mill, hoping for some lessons?"

Seth nodded. "She'd arranged for Drake to talk with him a little, go over a few basics, see if it was a passing fancy or truly something he wanted to pursue."

"Seems harmless enough."

"On the surface. But Jake should have gotten permission,

for the fiddle and the lessons. Pippa thought he had. And that's not at all like Jake, either."

Addie sipped her wine. "Mmm," she said, eyes widening in pleasure. "You're on the right path with this batch."

Seth smiled, nodded his thanks. "High praise, indeed," he said, meaning it. Addison Pearl was picky about her wine.

She set her glass down and held his gaze. "I imagine Will has a good reason for being ticked off like he was, about that fiddle. And not just because he'd made the thing himself." She smiled. "I know you've never heard him play, but oh, Dot—Wilson's mother—used to just go on and on about his fiddle playing. Did you know it was her daddy who taught Wilson how to play and to make his own instruments?"

Seth shook his head, surprised. "I didn't, no."

"Well, once his mama passed and he moved here for good, I can't tell you how often I tried to get that man to play, or even give us a little talk about how he came to build fiddles, talk about his daddy, maybe discuss the ins and outs of the procedures he uses." She smiled, but it was more rueful than anything. "He tolerated my busybody ways for longer than he probably should have. He's a gentleman, after all. But one day he finally stepped aside with me and very politely, but firmly, told me that fiddle making, and fiddle playing, were in his past, and that I'd be doing him a great service to refrain from asking him about either of those things ever again." She sighed.

"And did you refrain?" Seth asked, in a tone that suggested he might not think her capable of such a thing.

Addie Pearl gave him an aggrieved look and swatted his hand. "Of course I did. That man was in a world of pain. I could see he hadn't made the request lightly. Most likely he'd only put up with me asking as long as he did because he knew telling me to back off would just spark my curiosity." She picked up her glass again and sipped, her unique lavender-colored eyes gleaming mischievously at him over the rim.

"And it most certainly did." She cradled the glass in both hands. "But I'm a patient woman. I knew someday the moment would come along when I would find an inroad on the subject and we'd talk about it. I admit, it's taken a bit longer than I expected. I thought maybe during the mill renovation, but no." She smiled and poured herself another partial glass. "And now along comes Pippa, barely here for a minute, and things have been all stirred up again."

"I'm still not sure if this is something anyone needs to be interfering with," Seth cautioned her. "You should have seen him, Addie. I think he'd have come to blows with me if I'd blocked his path any longer."

"Let's listen to what Pippa has to say," she counseled. "Something tells me she's going to be asking as much of herself as she is of Will. Or at least that's the impression she gave me."

The sound of tires crunching on gravel interrupted their talk.

"There she is now," Addie said, and bustled on over to the front door.

Seth realized he was holding his breath, waiting for Pippa to step into the cabin. *What the hell is wrong with you?* He wasn't sure if the nerves were because he was looking forward to being around her for the first time without having to pretend his interest was strictly platonic. Or because he was wondering how Pippa was going to act, now that she could do the same. Or because in the back of his mind, all he could hear was *tick tock, tick tock.*

Then she walked into the cabin, with that bright, sunny smile, laughing at something Addie had said, and when she saw him, that smile went even wider and her gorgeous blue eyes danced with excitement and pleasure.

Whatever else happened, Seth knew, in that moment, that when it came to letting her go, or going after her, he damn well wasn't going to watch her walk away from him again. *Well then, laddie, best get on up and do something about that.*

Seth stood and met her in the middle of the room. He bent down to kiss her on the cheek, noting Addie's eye roll at such a chaste hello. He smiled at that, then smiled down into Pippa's happy face. "You look like a woman on a mission, and that mission is taking shape. Care to fill us in?"

She tipped up on her toes, wrapped her arms around his neck, and urged his mouth down to hers for a quick, solid kiss.

Seth caught Addie's smile of approval as she turned back to the stove; then he looked down at Pippa, who was still smiling up at him.

"I hope you don't mind," she said. "I've decided I'm not giving any more of my time away to worry."

He grinned. "I don't mind at all."

"Good," she said brightly, then slipped her hand in his and tugged him with her over to the center work island in the kitchen. "I need some wine before I lay the plan out."

It was like grabbing on to the tail of a comet, Seth thought, and grinned. At least it would never be a dull ride.

He poured Pippa a glass of wine, and waited for her to take a sip.

Her eyes grew wide as she did the little mouth swish and swallow. "That's wonderful." She put her glass down and picked up the bottle. Her expression melted when she saw the label. "It's Dex!" She looked at Seth. "I love this. Llama-rama Wine."

Seth smiled. "I had one of the artists at the mill do a sketch and watercolor for the label and business card. I haven't really had the chance to use it much yet, but I think it sums up the mood I want for the vineyard."

The label had a blue wash background, with a space in the middle to put in the specific type of wine it was and any other name he wanted to give it. Below was the winery name and info, which appeared hand lettered rather than typed. On one side was a trellised vine with bunches of plump grapes, with the vines crawling across the top of the label. Peeking in from the other side was Dex's neck and head, as he nibbled on the grapes at the end of the crawling vine. All the art was hand sketched and painted in a soft wash with watercolors, giving it a look that was both whimsical and beautiful.

"I love everything about it," Pippa said, finally putting the bottle back on the counter so she could take another sip from her glass. "Mmm. This really is amazing. Why aren't you bottling yet?"

Seth set his own glass down. "Gilbert Bianchi unearthed a chart that Emile had hand drawn, showing what grapes he'd planted where." Seth smiled. "It was in French, and Gilbert only spoke English and a little Italian. He had it translated and made up a more formal chart. A good part of what Emile had planted had died off, mostly due to neglect and weather. But a surprising number of vines remained, though they were out of control by the time Gilbert came along. He didn't want to plant as many acres as Emile, so he transplanted a lot of what was salvageable in the fields he planned to use."

"So, does that mean they're all mixed up out there?" Pippa asked.

"A little bit," Seth said with a grin, then lifted his glass as if in a toast to Gilbert. "He did try to chart it as best he could, but then he passed on and things went to seed again. So I really need to take at least a season or two to see what produces. I won't plant as many acres as Emile did, but I'll want more than Gilbert. There's just no point in expanding until I see what I've got."

"But you've been experimenting already," Pippa said, and took another sip.

Seth nodded. "A little. Mostly to hone my own skills as a

vintner. I want the chance to play a bit more before I commit to specific blends that will have my name on it." He smiled. "Or Dex's, as the case may be."

"Did Gilbert's wife know?" Pippa asked. "About the label?"

Seth nodded. "She knew I was going to change the name of the winery from Bianchi Vineyards to Bluestone & Vine, and she liked the new name and the reasoning behind it. She'd made a passing comment when we were discussing the sale, made in jest, really, about how Dex should be considered an ambassador for the brand, not an albatross." He shrugged. "One thing led to another."

"I know that had to have made her happy," Pippa said, beaming.

Seth nodded. "I think it did. I wish she'd made it long enough to get to taste the wine."

Addie reached over and covered Seth's hand and squeezed. "She knows. You've done right by her and her husband. She knows."

"Thanks, Addie," Seth said, touched. He looked at Pippa. "So, your turn."

Addie interrupted him. "How about we get this meal on the table? Then we can plot and plan."

Pippa laid the table with woven mats and the hand thrown, mismatched plates and antique silver—none of it alike, either—that Addie had stacked on the work island. Seth carried over a variety of crocks and serving bowls filled with wild rice, green beans with almonds and mushrooms, creamed corn, and stewed apples, while Addie carried the carving plate and roast to the head of the table.

"I think my taste buds have already died and gone to heaven, and I haven't even taken a bite yet," Pippa said with a contented sigh.

"Could you get the jam and butter from the fridge?" Addie said to Pippa, and went to get the biscuits from the oven. She also brought tumblers and a pitcher of cold sweet tea to the table, along with the wine.

"You're going to have to roll me out to my truck later," Seth warned as he finished carving the roast. "That is, if I'm not already fast asleep on your couch."

"I promise I won't disturb your beauty sleep," Addie Pearl told him with a wink. Looking quite pleased with herself, she took a chair at the end of the table, and Seth and Pippa sat across from each other at the same end, making for a cozy threesome as they passed the serving dishes back and forth.

"I don't know which is more life-changing," Pippa said, "this amazing meal, or that view." She was on the long bench seat that framed one side of the cedar plank table. Seth was seated in one of the mismatched high-back chairs across from her. "I can't think of a better way to spend a lovely spring evening." Pippa lifted her wine glass in a toast. "To good food, good wine, and good friends." Addie and Seth lifted their glasses and they clinked them together.

Food was served and appetites quickly fulfilled as they enjoyed Addie Pearl's feast. The conversation was kept to things like the spring heat wave they'd just had after the brutal, snowy winter, gossip about the mill, and a few new crafters Addie Pearl was hoping to bring on board as they each enjoyed several servings of both food and wine.

The sun was setting when Addie Pearl passed the biscuits for one last round, then set the empty basket in the middle of the table. "Well now, we've managed to put it off long enough." Addie waved her butter knife in Pippa's general direction. "Out with it."

Pippa and Seth shared a raised-eyebrow smile; then Pippa wiped her mouth with her napkin and took a breath. "As you know, this is about Will, and about Jake, but it's also about me. I need to start there, if that's okay."

"Of course it is," Addie Pearl said, her lavender eyes crinkling at the corners and her smile warm and encouraging. "You go on, and take your time."

"Thank you," Pippa said sincerely, but looked only fractionally relieved. "Seth knows this first part, and my sister Katie knows, but no one else does," she began. "Pretty much everyone knows about my ruptured vocal cords. So, I had surgery on them exactly one year ago, next week."

Seth's gaze sharpened at that. When she'd first arrived, she'd mentioned the surgery had been eleven months ago, but he hadn't put that together with the fact that she had been in Blue Hollow Falls for a few weeks.

"The surgery was a complete success. I followed all the protocols to the letter during my recovery, and I was given the green light to begin singing again some time ago. In moderation of course, and there are certain exercises I've been cautioned to do as an ongoing thing. I hired someone who specializes in that kind of thing to help me proceed in the smartest way possible." She looked down for a moment, then slid her hands to her lap before looking back at the two of them. "And I haven't done any of the exercises. Haven't sung a single note. Because, you see, I'm petrified it will happen again."

"That sounds like a perfectly normal reaction," Addie Pearl said.

"Maybe. But the longer I've gone without trying, the more scared I've become. I even went to see a therapist about it, but his advice was basically to just sing, and I'd see I was fine."

"Sounds like you needed a better therapist," Addie grumbled.

"Possibly. Probably," Pippa amended with a smile. "But I also realized that no amount of encouragement from a stranger was going to get me there, either." She picked up her napkin from the table and began folding and refolding the corners as she spoke. "The thing is, I used to not be able to *not* sing. By that I mean, if I wasn't singing, I was humming, or I'd hear music inside my head all the time. My world was always scored with a running soundtrack. So I guess I just thought that not singing would be the hardest part of the surgery. And once I was healed, it would be there waiting for me. It's like a . . . compulsion. No, that's not the right word." She looked at Seth, and said, "Singing is like breathing to me."

He reached across the table and took her hand in his, rubbing his fingers over hers, wishing he could give her all his strength, wishing he could win this battle for her.

"But, since the surgery . . ." She lifted her shoulders and slid her hand from his, bringing it back to her lap. She looked at Addie, then to Seth, and held on to his gaze, as if maybe summoning her strength from him after all. "I haven't heard the music," she said quietly. "I don't hum, I don't sing, my throat doesn't just tighten and automatically produce music as I go about my day." She took another sip of wine, pausing to find her words. "At first, I just assumed it was because of the surgery, and the pain, and all the healing that had yet to happen. But it should have still filled me up inside, like it used to. Only there was just . . . silence. As time went on, it didn't come back." She smiled then. "And that really freaked me out."

"I think sometimes fear can make us shut off parts of ourselves, and we think that means they're no longer there, but they are," Addie told her gently. "You've probably been worried that your voice might not be the same, or that you might hurt it again, so your subconscious mind did what it had to do to protect you from wanting to use it." She fluttered her fingers. "And poof, no music." Now she reached over and covered Pippa's hand. "Don't be so hard on yourself. It's a lot of trauma, both physical and emotional."

Pippa squeezed Addie's hand. "Thank you," she said

sincerely. Then she smiled and her eyes were filled with so much warmth and affection, it made Seth's heart squeeze in his chest when she turned that gaze to him.

"Actually, someone really special said almost the exact same thing to me."

Seth winked at her, silently sending her all the strength he had. Addie Pearl reached under the table and gave his knee a strong squeeze and a pat as well. He exchanged a quick glance with her and knew she was rooting for Pippa every bit as much as he was.

Pippa looked back to Addie Pearl. "As time went on, it was harder to just relax and try to let it come to me naturally. The whole world was watching, waiting. I had a lot of people who were also being absolutely amazing to me, so much love, so much support. But it still felt like I was under a microscope. The more time passed, the more speculation and rumors circulated. The gossip-rag insanity began to take off with the most outlandish rubbish you've ever heard. And though I've grown used to that, as much as any person can, when it was attached to this particular issue, well, I admit it did play some mind games with me."

Seth watched Pippa as he listened to her, and felt like he was having a little of that out-of-body experience he and Pippa had talked about when she'd first arrived, which seemed a lifetime ago now. He was watching the Pippa he knew, the warm, generous, funny, confident, ball of energy who'd turned his whole world upside down. But he was listening to a completely different Pippa. Not the vulnerable one—that woman he'd begun to know as well, who tugged so hard at his heart. No, this was Pippa the musician, Pippa the concert performer, Pippa the world-renowned singer. He hadn't as yet met that woman.

He also felt like a fool. Not only for not grasping—not truly—the totality of what she was really grappling with, professionally—but also for not realizing what hung in the balance for her when making a decision to get involved with him, an American with a life half a world from hers. And she thought *she* lacked courage?

"Then Katie—my sister—came to me, asking if an old friend of hers from uni could use the home I'd bought in our village, where I'd grown up," Pippa was saying, "while offering me the chance to come here on a sort of house swap deal that would be completely under the radar and off the grid . . . and I jumped at it. It was the perfect escape." She looked at Seth and smiled. "I couldn't have known how perfect."

Seth hadn't known it was possible to fall in love and feel his heart break all at the same time. She was it for him. He was done questioning that. But how on earth did he think he'd be able to hold on to her? He belonged to a small plot of land in the mountains of Virginia. She belonged to the world.

She held his gaze for a moment longer, her smile faltering just a bit at whatever she was reading in his eyes. He immediately grinned and winked at her. She didn't need his worries and fears right now; she had enough of her own. Just as instantly, she winked back.

Her shoulders relaxed a little as she looked to Addie. "And it's working," Pippa told her, banked excitement creeping into her voice now. She leaned closer and rested her arms on the table, her big eyes sparkling. "I've finally heard the music, Addie Pearl. Standing beside Big Stone Creek, watching the waterwheel, hearing the sound of the falls blend with the rhythm of that big, beautiful waterwheel."

Addie took Pippa's hands and gripped them between her own, her eyes sparkling as well. "I knew you would," she told her.

Pippa beamed and the transformation was brilliant. "It

was like a gospel sounded inside my head, and the skies parted, angels singing." She laughed. "Ridiculously over-the-top descriptions do not do the moment justice, trust me. It was, in the truest sense of the word, awesome." She laughed again. "And such a huge relief, I don't mind telling you."

Addie laughed and beamed herself. "It was in you all along, honey. You just needed the right key to unlock it."

Pippa looked at Seth, her eyes shining. "I did, indeed." Addie Pearl still held her left hand and Pippa reached across the table for Seth's hand and held on tight to them both for a long moment, before finally letting go. She let out a long, happy breath and fanned her glistening eyes with a little laugh, then took another sip of wine.

Seth might have had a little something in his eye as well, and noted Addie Pearl was experiencing a similar difficulty.

"And so, it's all begun," Pippa said. "I didn't know where that first moment would take me, but it's happening, and I'm just along for the ride." She turned to Addie Pearl. "The other night, sitting on the steps of my cabin, the night Bailey was there for our movie night, I sang the line of a song when I was talking to Seth," she said. "And I wasn't even aware of it." Her eyes wide, she laughed again as she lifted her hands. "How crazy is that? A whole year of all but wrapping my throat in cotton batting, and then I just go blithely singing along without even knowing it?"

"And how was it?" Addie asked, though the twinkle in her eyes said she already knew the answer.

"Absolutely fine," Pippa said. "I mean, I think I sound a little different now. My speaking voice is huskier these days." She shrugged. "That might work for me, who knows?"

"And what about now?" Addie asked. "Still singing?"

Pippa's smile faded a bit at that, back to the more self-deprecating one from before. "Not yet."

Addie looked dismayed. "Child, you need to—"

"I know I do, Addie. I truly do. But it was like, the moment

I realized I'd sung, everything clamped up inside me again. And singing a line, or even a song to myself is one thing. I do sound different, and there's . . . a lot to process."

"You can't process what you aren't doing," Addie said, not unkindly.

"Right," Pippa said with a sigh. "I know." She took a breath and squared her shoulders, looking at Addie, then Seth. "And *that* is precisely where my big plan with Will and Jake comes in."

Chapter Fifteen

"What on earth were you thinking?" she murmured under her breath, as she parked Bluebell in the driveway in front of Wilson McCall's sprawling ranch-style home.

Wilson came out on the front porch as she turned off the engine. He didn't lift a hand in a welcome wave, but neither did he look anything like the furious man who'd stormed into that music classroom.

She took a shaky breath, then another one, then forced herself to let go of the steering wheel and slide out of the truck. It was a beautiful spring day, though the breeze was a bit nippy. It was past the halfway mark in April now and the days had been mostly warm and sunny, with the occasional fierce thunderstorm tossed in to keep things interesting. She loved those days the most. The trees were budding out and starting to bloom lower down in the valley, but up here things took a little longer to get started.

As she walked up the stone pathway, itself a work of art, she noted the rows of pretty purple and white crocuses sprouting cheerfully all along the front of the holly shrubs planted in front of the house. She smiled at the perky little blooms and tried to will their jaunty cheer into her body.

She finally looked toward Will as she drew close enough

to see his expression. He'd been short with her on the phone when she'd called and asked to see him, but he'd agreed. So it was no surprise that he didn't seem overjoyed to see her, but at least he didn't appear to be angry. *Well, there's a start.*

"Beautiful place you have," she told him, smiling as she closed the last of the distance between them. The home was a sprawling single level, just outside of Blue Hollow Falls proper, so not as high up as Seth's place, or Addie's, or her cabin, but still well above the valley. She could hear a rushing sound and realized it was water. "Is that Big Stone Creek?"

He nodded. "Just down the hill out back." His expression remained impassive.

She extended her hand. "Let's start over, okay? Pippa MacMillan. Please call me Pippa."

Will took her hand and gave it a simple but decent shake. His palm was work-roughened and there were more than a few scars marking the back of his hand and his forearm, but she supposed that came with the territory for a stonemason. "Wilson McCall," he said a bit gruffly. "Will is fine."

"I'm guessing you did the stonework. It's gorgeous." The house was stained wood, stone, and glass, with a shaker roof and stacked stone chimney. The variety of materials blended together organically, and set deep in the trees as it was, the combination looked strong, earthy, and welcoming. It was an older-looking structure, but the remodel was breathtaking. Pippa paused before walking up the steps to the door to admire the inlaid stone landing in front of the bottom step. It was a sunburst, made entirely out of cut stone. She glanced to Will. "Your design?"

He nodded. "A present to my mother some years back."

"It's beautiful. I bet she loved it. Mabry Jenkins told me this place belonged to your grandfather?"

Will looked a bit caught off guard, and just nodded. "How's Mabry doing?" Will asked, as he gestured for her to go on up the steps.

"Pretty well, everything considered," Pippa told him. "He's going to be moved to a rehab facility next week to start physical therapy." She smiled as Will opened the front door for her and ushered her inside. "He's a little grumpy about that, but the attitude will serve him well, I think, as long as he's not too impatient."

Will motioned her through the small foyer and living room toward the back of the house. "I thought we could sit on the back porch. I made some coffee."

She smiled, surprised and encouraged by the effort. "That sounds perfect. You didn't have to go to the trouble."

He didn't say anything to that, but led the way through the kitchen, where he picked up the pot of coffee sitting on the warmer, and nodded to the mugs, the small pitcher of cream, and the sugar bowl sitting on a little tray next to them. "If you wouldn't mind."

She scooped them up and then followed him out the sliding back doors into a deep, screened-in porch that extended out a good several yards off the back of the house. She quickly realized that the place had two stories as there was a basement below. The property fell away from the back of the house in a steep pitch down to the creek. So the porch was really more of a screened-in deck that ran about two-thirds the length of the house and provided a spectacular view of forest and hills behind the house. The sound of rushing water from the creek mixed with the bird calls and other forest creatures. She set the mugs down on the wicker coffee table that fronted a thickly padded wicker couch and walked to the fully screened-in wall in front of her. Small planters filled with various herbs lined the wood beam that separated the top half of the screen from the bottom.

"This is spectacular. So peaceful and serene." She turned to him and smiled. "Jake described it pretty well, but I don't know that any amount of words could do it justice."

Will nodded, and motioned for her to take a seat.

Procrastination time was over.

She sat on the wicker couch facing the scenery and he sat in one of the two Adirondack chairs that faced the wicker couch on the other side of the coffee table. She offered him a mug but he waved it off. "I'd like to say something before you get into whatever it is you've come to discuss."

Pippa set her mug down untouched and folded her hands in her lap. "Sure," she said, trying to quell the sudden uproar of butterflies in her stomach and being entirely unsuccessful.

If she'd been expecting a more direct apology regarding his behavior at the mill—and she hadn't necessarily been— then she was destined to be disappointed.

"Jake and I have talked about what happened at the mill," he began.

"Mr. McCall, you don't have to—"

"Will," he said. "And I'd like to." She nodded and he went on. "Jake has apologized for not talking to me about his plans, and I've apologized to him about coming in the way I did. He's still grounded, and my decision stands on that."

Pippa nodded again. "Understood," she said. "I'm not here to talk you into letting Jake off the hook. I'm as disappointed in him in that regard as you are."

That seemed to surprise Will a bit. *Good*, she thought.

"Given what you said at the mill, I know you're familiar with my music and it's come to mean something to you," she went on, apparently surprising him again with her directness. With that, she gained a little more confidence. "I know that might be more about who my voice reminds you of than me personally, but I'm touched nonetheless." She paused, and though she saw him tense, he didn't immediately escort her out, so she went on. "From one fiddle player to another, that's high praise."

His expression began to shut down at that, as she'd anticipated it would, so she hurried on.

"If it's okay with you," she pushed on, "I'd like to tell you a bit about what's been going on with me this past year."

His expression was unreadable now, but he motioned for her to go on, and picked up his coffee mug, which she took as a good sign.

Pippa told him pretty much the same things she'd told Addie the night before. She didn't give him much, if any room, to comment, nor did he seem inclined to do so, but he appeared to be listening, and that was all she could hope for.

"I guess you can hear from me talking to you that my voice isn't the same as it was before, so that adds to the anxiety," she said, as she concluded her story. "I think it will be interesting to find out how it affects the songs I want to sing, the stories I want to tell, but there's also the chance that it won't be a sound that will resonate with the fans of my past music. So that adds to the worry."

"At the risk of sounding rude," he said, finally interrupting, "what does any of that have to do with me? Or Jake?"

Pippa could feel the tremors in her fingers, and her knees, and carefully set the mug back on the table. *Moment of truth time.* "I know everyone was a little taken aback when you came into the music room that day. It was obvious you were angry, and that there was pain behind that anger." She leaned forward then, and her voice softened. "But what I latched on to wasn't the anger, or even the pain. It was the other thing I saw that I recognized right up close and personal. Fear."

Will put his mug down and started to rise.

"Please," Pippa said quietly. "Please just let me say this— then you can toss me out and I won't bother you again." She looked at him until he met her gaze, and she let him see everything she felt, all of it, including the utter terror she'd experienced in the past year. "It's been a lot longer for you, since you closed yourself off. And I fear—feared—that's exactly where I was headed."

Will sat back in the chair, but there was nothing relaxed about him now. His gaze was fierce and agitation fairly radiated off of him.

"I'm not passing judgment on your choice. I know it sounds like I am, but that is something I would never do. The difference between us is, I don't want to be closed off. I want to confront the fear." She clenched her hands into fists as her tone became more intent. "I want to conquer it! I want to stomp it down until it can't ever scare me like that again. Music, song, was my best and closest friend, it was my companion and my protector. So I simply won't let it go," she said, heat rising now in her own voice. "And yet, here I sit, a full year later, and what have I done to thwart the fear? Not a single thing."

She rubbed her now damp palms against the legs of her trousers. "Until I came here." She looked at him, her walls and defenses completely down. "It felt like my last chance. To figure everything out, or just give up. But how do you make your music come back? Sure, I could just up and force myself to start singing again, but I couldn't force the music back into my head, or into my soul."

He was listening now, and despite the tight set of his jaw and his shoulders, the ferocity in his gaze was tempered now, with compassion. And yes, maybe with a little empathy, too. It was more than she'd hoped for and she felt instantly humbled by it.

"Deep down," she continued, "I honestly didn't think coming here would make a difference. I did it because my sister Katie really wanted me to, and I wanted her to think I was really trying. I didn't—don't—want to let her down, or any of my family, though they'd support me if I never sang again. At first, I was just so . . . relieved to be here, to not be back home in the midst of everyone tiptoeing around me, waiting to see if I'd sing again, that I was happy. And then I immediately got caught up in the life here." She paused then, and took a sip of her coffee. She'd been speaking so earnestly, her throat was tight to the point of feeling raw.

Will said nothing, just waited for her to continue, and for the first time, she thought maybe putting herself through this might actually help someone other than just herself.

"Blue Hollow Falls reminds me of my home in County Donegal. Not the mountains, but the farms, the slower way of life, and most definitely the people. Everyone pitching in, doing for others, gossiping their fair share, too," she added, trying for a smile, but too caught up to wait for it. "People willing to give whatever is necessary to help a neighbor. Meeting Mabry, Seth, Noah, Bailey, and your son, I felt instantly welcomed and immediately part of things." She set her mug down again. "Then Mabry had his accident, and I got caught up taking care of goats and making friends with a llama. I got to see the mill, meet all the artists, and I got so swept up in everything that I didn't have time to feel sorry for myself, or worry about what would happen if I never sang again. And then . . . to my utter shock, my music came back. Or it's started to. I want to build on that before I can chicken out, so it won't disappear on me again."

She stopped talking then and just looked at Will. When he realized she was waiting for him to say something, he said, "I . . . appreciate your being so forthcoming with me." He sounded sincere, and there was a surprising thickness underlying his words. He paused and cleared his throat. "I can relate, as I suspect you're aware, to some of the issues you're going through, only mine weren't so much physical."

It was all Pippa could do not to get up and hug the man. He looked genuinely miserable now, and she felt awful for pushing his own memories on him by talking about hers. But she let him take his time to find his words, as he'd done for her.

"I guess what I'm not sure about, is what, exactly, you're asking of me."

"For me? Nothing. You've made your choices, about your gifts, both in playing and in making your instruments, and those choices are only yours to make. If you're at peace with them, then that's all that matters." She took a slow breath, and forged her way into the hardest part. "How you reacted to Jake borrowing your fiddle—and you know him, so you know he'd never harm it—suggests you're not really at peace with any of it. And maybe peace is too big a thing to ask for, given the losses you've suffered. That is something I have no experience with, so I would never presume to say I understand, or know how you feel, or even what I'd do in your shoes, because I don't know."

"Pray to God you never do," he said quietly, perhaps a bit forcefully, but not angrily. And her heart broke even more for him.

"So, I'm here not so much with a request, but an offer," she said. "If I could ask for anything, I'd ask that you consider—just consider—going on this path with me. Me to get back to composing and singing, you to playing. Maybe creating." She lifted a hand to stall his immediate response. "I said if I could ask anything. It's my wish, that's all. I thought it might make it easier, or at least be helpful, to both of us, to have the support of someone who is also facing such a monumental task, trying to get back a part of themselves they thought was forever lost, or forever closed off. Maybe we could do it together."

She'd been looking at her lap, at the fingers she was twisting together, subconsciously rubbing at the spots that used to have calluses. She looked up at him now, not expectantly—she didn't think she'd get an answer—but just to connect with him.

He didn't say anything at all, and eventually ducked his chin and broke eye contact.

She let out a shaky sigh. *I laid my heart down on the table. I can't do more for him, or myself, than that.* "Thank you for listening," she said. "For agreeing to meet with me."

He nodded, but didn't look up as yet. She had no idea what was going through his mind, but his shoulders weren't so rigidly set now. She suspected he was just trying to hold himself together.

She stood up, knowing she'd intruded enough. She turned toward the door to the kitchen, then stopped and looked back. "I might not have been entirely truthful about one thing."

He looked up, his expression as bleak as she'd ever seen on anyone, save herself, and it was like a sucker punch to the gut.

"I'm sorry," she whispered, the words out because she couldn't not say them. "I am."

He nodded, then took a breath. "What untruthful thing?" he asked, and his voice was like gravel now.

"I do have one request. It's a big ask, but it is one I truly hope you'll consider."

"What, you want to use my fiddle for your big comeback?"

She started, and her mouth dropped open, she was so surprised that that was the mental leap he'd made.

"I appreciate what you're doing. I don't know why you're doing it, but I know you're sincere," he said. "But the way to get to me will not be through that fiddle. That I can guarantee."

"I appreciate that. I wasn't . . . trying to be tricky. I'm a direct person. I think we can both agree on that." He nodded and she went on. "I wasn't asking for the fiddle. Not because I wouldn't be honored to play it. But this isn't about getting to you. I've said all I can say on that."

That seemed to surprise him.

"I have my own fiddle," she told him. "One I've played

since I was a little girl. It's special to me, as I know you can well imagine. If—when—I get back up on stage and sing again, she'll be with me."

He nodded, as if he did indeed understand that much. A frown furrowed his brows. "Then what is the 'big ask'?"

"You've made your choice, about creating instruments, about not playing anymore." She softened her voice. "Shouldn't Jake get to make his own choices, too?" She immediately put her hand up to stall his response. "I'm not asking for him to get to play your fiddle, either. I would never do that. Just as I'd hope no one would ever assume I'd lend mine out." She held his gaze. "Even to someone I love very much." She worked up a smile, a gentle one. "Jake wants to play. Or he wants to learn to play. I don't know if this is because he wants to connect to you or his family history. Or if he simply has that desire in him, like you did, like I do. Like his mum did."

"What are you asking?" Will said, jaw flexed again, but his tone was surprisingly quiet.

"Just that you give him permission to learn. I'll teach him, if you'd rather Drake didn't, but we're both willing. I wasn't planning on charging him anything, because the selfish side of this is it would help me, too. I enjoy spending time with your son." She smiled. "He's a wonderful young man with a great big heart. I can't think of anyone I'd be happier to have along on my journey back into music." Her voice got softer still. "Save maybe his dad." She took a shaky breath. "I guess I'm hoping that maybe by teaching him, I'll find my way back to it in a way that's not so . . . terrifying." She let her smile grow. "One squeaky note at a time."

Will stood up. "Miss MacMillan—"

"Pippa," she said, and hurried on before he could end the conversation. "I have it worked out so he doesn't have to play here, if that's a concern." She hitched her purse strap over her shoulder and smoothed her damp palms over her hips. "Jake knows nothing about this," she told Will. "And I won't ever say a word unless you give your permission." She held his gaze more steadily now, pushing for Jake's sake, if she couldn't push for Will's. "I don't go around tooting my own horn, but if it helps to sway your thinking, your son has the chance to learn how to play the fiddle from one of the better fiddle players in the world. I'll provide the fiddle and the place for him to learn and play. All you need to do is give him your permission. Your blessing, too, if you find it in your heart. He's growing up, Mr. McCall, and I think his thirst is real. I know, and you know, how that feels. If he thought you supported him—"

"He's never once told me," Will said, somewhat abruptly. "That he wants to learn."

Surprised by the sudden comment, Pippa looked down for a moment, then back up to him. "I think it's possible he didn't think you'd take it well?" She dared to let a hint of a smile curve her lips.

Will closed his eyes at that, but perhaps the tiniest flicker of a smile twitched the corners of his mouth, rueful though it might have been. Then he ducked his chin and shook his head. She thought she might have heard him swear under his breath. She waited for him to look up again and extended her hand.

"I'm really glad we had the chance to meet and talk. I wish things were different, because I'd be all over you about that fiddle Jake brought with him the other day. You do gorgeous work, Mr. McCall. And I'd love to hear you play someday."

"Will," he said, a bit gruffly. "And thank you. That part of my life is over, but . . . I'll give some thought to your request." He looked directly at her then. "I know it wasn't easy, doing what you did here today. I appreciate it, for my sake and for Jake's. It was kind of you, as well as generous. And I'm not sure I deserved your kindness, much less your generosity, after the way I behaved the other day."

Pippa had to work to keep her mouth from dropping open at the utter sincerity in his quietly spoken words. The anger was gone now, replaced by resignation, but also by an attempt to make things if not right, at least better. This was the Will McCall she'd been hoping to meet, the one everyone had been telling her about.

He took her hand and shook it, then held on a moment longer. "I don't know how I feel about Jake playing. It's mixed up with . . . a lot of other stuff. And I won't lie to you, either. I really wish he wanted to do anything but that." He let her hand go. "It's an honor, what you've proposed, and I'm grateful. I just . . ." He looked away then, and she could see this was a torment for him, wanting to do what was right for Jake but trying not to torture himself more in the process.

"I do understand that. That's why I said it was a big ask." She smiled. "I surely won't think less of you if you say no."

He surprised her further by chuckling at that. "I'm not sure you could think any less of me at this point."

"That's where you'd be wrong," she told him. "You've served your country, you've been a loving husband, and you've raised a wonderful young man. I couldn't hold you in higher regard." On impulse, she reached up on her toes and shocked them both by giving him a quick kiss on the cheek. "And you like my music," she added with a grin. "So how bad could you be?"

She dashed at the corners of her eyes, thinking one of these days she really had to stop being so leaky, and left the porch, walking through the house and out to the front steps. She turned when she was on the stone pathway, heading to her truck, to find Will standing on the top step of the porch. She lifted her hand in a wave, and felt a sense of relief and rightness when he lifted his in a brief reply. It wasn't a yes, but she believed he would think about it, and that was more than she'd dared hope for when she pulled up.

She strapped herself in and turned the key, then patted the dashboard. "Well, Bluebell, we're one step closer than we were before." She smiled and pulled out of the drive.

Chapter Sixteen

Seth looked up from his monitor when Pippa came walking into the stone barn. He checked the time on the screen, then looked back at her. "That didn't take too long." He tried to gauge the success of her mission by the look on her face, but she was already striding over to give Dex some love and check in on Elliott.

He hadn't seen her since they'd gone their separate ways after dinner at Addie's the night before, but they'd talked that morning before she left to go talk to Will. He got up and crossed the open area of the barn.

"How did it go?"

Pippa straightened from leaning over the stall gate, cooing to Elliott and laughing as he butted his head against her hand, and turned to Seth, her expression serious now. "I'm not sure. We sat out on his back porch, with that amazing view, and talked. Well, I talked. A lot. But I think he listened." She looked up at him. "Actually, I know he did. He seems like a very kind and thoughtful man. I finally got to see that side of him, before I left."

"He's one of the most solid men I know. I'd trust him with my life."

Pippa nodded. "It's just so sad and awful, that he's never gotten over losing his wife," she said quietly. "I wanted to hug him."

Seth wanted to pull her into his arms, hug her, comfort her, then remembered he didn't have to resist that urge any longer. "Come here," he murmured.

She went immediately into his arms, wrapped hers around his waist, and pressed her cheek against his chest. He wrapped her up closer and pressed a kiss on the top of her head. She felt good in his arms. Perfect, actually. "So, I'm guessing it was a no-go on getting him to agree to work with you on the two of you getting your music back?"

"Aye. He was pretty clear about that," she said, disappointed.

"Do you think he'll let Jake take lessons?"

"I honestly don't know," she said, then lifted her head to look up at him. "I hope so." She leaned up then and kissed him.

She lowered her heels, but he lifted them right up again, and kissed her slowly and with great attention to detail. When he finally broke the kiss, they were both a little breathless. "Hi," he told her, smiling.

"Hi, yourself," she replied, and her eyes were somehow both bright with happiness and dark with desire. "Have I told you, you're good at this whole not-pretending-anymore thing?"

He grinned. "I have to keep reminding myself I don't have to."

She raised her eyebrows at that. "We should probably get more practice then, until it becomes second nature."

"Have I mentioned I'm a fan of these plans you come up with?"

She shook her head, all innocence, then batted her lashes for good measure. "How big a fan are we talking?"

If he pulled her any closer against him, she'd feel just how big, but that might be a little too much, too soon. "Your biggest," he said, and instead made a gesture to the difference in their heights, making her giggle.

"So, why did you ask me to come up?" she asked him. "I could have told you how the meeting with Will went over the phone. I know you have a lot to do. Did you see the distributor finally?" she asked. "How did it go?"

"Yes, I saw Denton, and it went very well. Looks like we have a deal."

"That's fantastic." She beamed and gently tugged the bottom of his beard so he'd lower his mouth to hers again, making him chuckle just before taking her mouth in a decidedly no-holds-barred kiss.

"Well then," she said, quite breathlessly this time when they broke apart. "I'd say practicing is definitely the way to go. You're making swift improvements on that second-nature thing."

He grinned. "Full disclosure, I asked you up here mainly because we can't do that over the phone." He slipped her arms over his shoulders. "But also because we haven't had the chance to spend much time alone together."

She wiggled her eyebrows. "Have I mentioned how big a fan I am of *your* plans?"

He chuckled again. "Why, ma'am, I'm not sure what you're suggesting. I just wanted to go for a little walk. Maybe have some lunch, if you've the time."

She looked surprised and charmed. "Truly? What a lovely idea."

Seth had been thinking a lot about what Mabry had said to him, about living life. Seth's to-do list that day was longer than his arm, and both legs, for that matter. But every day was pretty much that way. And it wasn't like the workload was going to lessen once the winery was actually, well, a winery. If he was going to have a life beyond being a vintner,

then now was the time to start establishing a few ground
rules and carve out some time for something other than vine
and livestock tending. Now that he had a reason for wanting
some time.

"I can help with the goats or the sheep later when Bailey
gets here." She smiled. "Assuming my barn privileges have
been reinstated now."

"Bailey won't be here until tomorrow. But yes, you're
officially welcome to invade any and all parts of my world."

She batted her eyelashes again at that, and his body reacted
like she'd stripped naked. *Yeah, you might want to pace yourself there, big guy.*

"I can keep busy if you need to finish up," she said, nodding toward his makeshift office. "It's a bit early for lunch
anyway."

In response, Seth slid her arms from his shoulders and
slipped his fingers through one of her hands. "That's why I
thought we'd walk first. Build up our appetite."

The irises in her eyes bloomed wide at that, and he realized maybe he wasn't the only one who needed to rein it in.
Which helped his efforts not at all. He slipped his hand
free and tucked her arm through his, leading her out the
back of the barn toward the vines. Before they both ended
up sprawled in the sawdust, ripping each other's clothes off.
"Shall we?" he said with a short bow.

"I believe we shall," she said, and he finally got his curtsy.

He could have sworn she was gazing at him a bit meaning-
fully, but that could just be wishful thinking. "This way, then."

The unusually high temperatures had returned that morning. The sun climbed slowly in a cloudless sky the same
color as the periwinkles that grew alongside the stone path
leading away from the barn. He led Pippa toward the rows
of vines, thinking if only Sawyer could see him now, and
grinned. He knew his best friend hadn't meant for Seth to

take his words so literally, but the image had struck him, and stayed with him. Besides, he wanted to share this part of himself with her.

"Not exactly a walk in the park," he said, his hand laced with hers now. "But I thought you might enjoy seeing what I do up close."

"Very much so." She glanced up at him, her cheeks a bit pink. "Although I do have a confession to make."

"Do you?" he asked, grinning at the naughty smile that curved her lips. "Please, tell."

"You recall when you were trying really, really hard to be anywhere but in sight of me?"

He winced. "In my defense, well, I had no defenses around you."

"So, purely self-defense then," she teased.

"Purely," he said, glancing down at her, noting the merriment in her eyes. "And what a waste of time that was."

"Time," she said softly, and held his hand a little more tightly. "Yes, let's not waste any more of that."

"Hear, hear," he said. "So, about this confession?"

"Right," she said, then looked a little sheepish. "The day you absented yourself entirely, I might have taken that opportunity to have a little stroll out here." She looked up at him. "I didn't touch so much as a single leaf, I promise."

He was surprised by the confession, but touched as well. "Because you wanted to know more about growing grapes?"

She slowed until they stood facing each other, hands still clasped. "No, because I wanted to know more about you. Feel closer to you."

He leaned down and kissed her, then pulled her into his arms and kissed her again.

Her eyes were filled with happiness when he finally lifted his mouth from hers, maybe a bit dazed by need. He was certain his looked much the same.

"I must say," she said, her voice throatier than usual, "I feel much closer to you this go."

A slow grin curved his mouth. He brushed at the strands of hair the light breeze had wisped across her face, then ran the side of his thumb across that plump bud of a lower lip. Her eyes darkened, and she gently tugged the end of his beard until his mouth was on hers once more.

"We're not going to work up much of an appetite this way," he murmured against her lips.

"Speak for yourself," she said, and nudging his lips apart, took the kiss deeper still.

She was straining on her tiptoes to reach him, so it seemed the most natural thing in the world to just scoop her up so she could wrap her legs around his waist and her arms around his neck, letting her match her mouth perfectly to his.

"I had all these plans," he murmured against her mouth.

"I was thinking about a new plan," she replied, then gasped as he kissed along her jaw, giggling when he nibbled her earlobe and his beard tickled her neck.

"I think I'm already on record as being a big fan of those," he murmured, working his way back to her mouth, his palms sliding up her thighs so he could cup her backside, pressing her more snugly against him.

She moaned softly and began to squirm. "Aye, and I'm beginning to realize just how big."

He let out a laugh, which ended on a groan as she wriggled against him. The mix of playfulness and seduction came naturally to them, and he thought it was the most erotic thing he'd ever experienced.

"Do you think lunch could wait?" she whispered in his ear, then nibbled his earlobe.

His fingers reflexively sank into the soft curves of her backside, urging her tighter against him. "I think we could manage that." What he wasn't sure he could manage was getting them all the way to the house before embarrassing himself. To that end, he nudged her legs from around his waist, letting her feet drop to the ground. Then he turned his back to her and crouched down.

She figured out his intentions without his having to ask. She hopped up on his back and wrapped her arms around his neck, nibbling at his ear again as he wrapped her legs arounds his waist until she could hook her ankles in front. Then he covered her hands with his own and pulled them down, turning his head to the side until their lips met. "Hold on," he said, then kissed her again.

"I don't plan on letting go," she said softly, looking directly into his eyes.

Please don't, he thought.

He started back down the turf strip, while Pippa nibbled at his ear and kissed the side of his neck, then giggled when he reached back and pinched her backside. They made it as far as the outside of the stone barn. Then she slipped off his back and turned him around to face her, tugging his shirt front down until they were hungrily kissing again. He lifted her up against him, then pressed her back against the gray wood slats, sliding her up so she could wrap herself around the front of him again.

He framed her face with broad palms, fitting her mouth more perfectly to his so he could take and be taken. They dueled with their tongues, as she slid her hands up and pulled his hair loose, then ran her fingers through it, raking nails against his scalp, making him shudder, testing his restraint.

"Hold on," he growled, and kept her right where she was, wrapped around him, kissing him, nibbling his earlobe, biting the side of his neck as he all but jogged them the rest of the way to the house.

They burst through the mudroom door and he was tempted to set her on top of the dryer and take her right there. *Slow your roll*, he schooled himself. But that was hard when she kept moaning softly every time she shifted against him. So, very, very hard.

He carried her through the living room and down the hallway, then stopped.

"Seth," she said, half begging, and just hearing his name like that was enough to push him right to the edge.

"Houston, we have a problem," he murmured in her ear, then regretfully let her go.

"Who is Houston and what is his problem?" she grumbled, when he took her by the hips and turned her so her back was to him. "Oh," she said as she looked at the set of wrought iron circular steps that led up to the loft. "That would be tricky now, wouldn't it?"

He grinned. "You should try it with feet the size of mine."

She giggled, and pointed up. "So, your bedroom is up there? I wondered what was in the loft."

"I like to spread out, and the rooms down here are too small for my bed."

Her eyes widened at that. "My room was a pretty decent size," she said. "How big are we talking?" She craned her neck to look up through the middle of the stairs. "And how on earth did you get it up there?"

"Dismantled, pulley system over the rail, reassemble."

"Ingenious."

He turned her in his arms. "Would you like to see it?" Now that they'd stopped kissing and fondling each other for five seconds, he was able to take a breath and get a bit of sanity back. "I know you didn't want things to go too quickly." He smiled. "Hence the walk and lunch plan."

"And we see how well that worked out for us," she said with a grin.

"True. Perhaps we should have taken Dex along as chaperone."

She looked up at him. "I think I'm all done needing chaperones."

His pulse bumped right back up again. "Are you now?"

"I'm tired of being afraid, Seth. Tired of worrying about what comes next. I'm not being cavalier here," she told him. "In case that's what you're thinking. I'm not just throwing caution to the wind. I can't change myself that much."

"Pippa, we don't have to—"

"Speak for yourself," she said, her tone gently teasing this time, but there was so much warmth in her eyes when she looked at him, he wasn't sure what to do with all the feelings she evoked in him.

"So, I look at it this way," she went on. "It's true, I don't know where this goes, or how we manage it, beyond this time we have right now. That's no small thing."

His heart slowed to that hard thump. "That's the part I'm having a hard time with, too."

Her eyes filled then and she reached up and stroked his face. "See, that's why I don't want to walk away from this, from you. You're such a good man—honest. True. I don't know how we go forward. What I do know, without a single doubt, is that I'll regret it every day for the rest of my life if I don't try."

He pulled her into his arms. "Then try we will," he said, and kissed her.

The kiss was different this time. The heat was there, the hunger, too, but it wasn't simply a connection born out of passion and constrained desire held in check for far too long. Now he knew where her heart was, that she wanted what he wanted, enough to risk heartbreak. *Isn't that what love is? Reaching for the best life has to offer, even while risking the worst?* He'd always thought falling in love would be the easiest thing in the world with the right person. And he'd been right. No one had ever told him, though, that it would also be the most terrifying thing.

Holding his hand behind her, Pippa led them up the spiral staircase to his bedroom. He wanted her like he wanted his next breath, and not just in his bed. He wanted her across the breakfast table, sitting cross-legged in the middle of his barn, driving Bluebell mostly on the right side of the road, cooing over Dexter, helping people close to him because she couldn't stand to see them suffer, being willing to suffer herself in order to do so. All of it, all of her.

And yet . . . at the same time, could he imagine himself in Ireland? Sitting offstage, watching her play to an arena full of screaming fans, fitting himself into the spaces of her life between her tour schedules and studio time? Being all those things for her that he so readily wanted her to be for him?

His thoughts drifted to Mabry, who still celebrated the love of his life every day, despite her being gone, and Will, who'd boarded his heart up in fear of ever letting love in again.

Who do you want to be?

He smiled to himself. *How about someone who falls in love with the girl next door instead of the girl next continent?* But it was too late for that.

Pippa gasped as they stepped up into the loft. It was deceptively bigger than she'd imagined looking up from below. The space covered not only the part of the living and kitchen area below, but extended back to cover both of the back bedrooms on one side and the spare office space on the other. Two of the walls were actually the eaves of the roof, steeply slanted, with exposed beams that soared all the way up to the peak. But her gaze wasn't on that—it was on the bed.

She turned to Seth. "It's the size of a modest playground,"

she said, all but gaping. "Does it need specially tailored sheets?"

"I like to stretch out," he told her, "but now that you mention it . . ." He took her hand and drew her over to the bed, then pulled her down on the broad platform mattress he'd had specially made for him the moment he'd left the service—and every cramped, too-short cot, bunk, and hammock—behind him for good.

She rolled to her back and splayed her arms and legs. Even with him lying next to her, her toes and fingertips didn't reach near the edges of the bed. "It's like being in the middle of an ocean." She pretended to do the backstroke, making him laugh. She arched her neck and looked behind her at the louvered screen that filled most of the back wall behind the bed. "Oh," she gasped. "Will you look up there. That's lovely." She rolled over and sat up. "Stained glass?"

Seth nodded. "That was already here when I moved in."

"It's stunning. Is the rest a window?"

He nodded. Though there was bright sunshine outside, it was dark and shadowy in the loft with the louvered blinds closed. The window just below the stained-glass triangle at the peak was an enormous, three-panel affair. "I had the blinds installed on the windows—Will custom built them for me, actually—because I can't sleep when it's light out, and my hours here aren't always in sync with the sun rising and setting." He rolled off the bed and pulled on a cord, which opened the blinds, then pressed a button and they began to rise.

Pippa got on her knees and gaped as she crawled to the wrought iron headboard. "And I thought my bedroom in the cabin had the window to the world," she breathed. "Will you look at that." They were well above the tree line as the ground fell away not far behind the house in a gentle downward slope. She could look down and see the round barn, and the topography of the ground around it. The top floor of the barn was level with the ground in front; then the land fell sharply away on the sides, so that the bottom of the three-story building had a ground-floor walk-out in the back. Beyond that were rows and rows of vines; then the ground rose up again, in wave after undulating wave of pine-forested ridges and peaks.

She glanced from the view, toward the railing and the soaring glass window at the front of the house. "So, the sun being on the front of the house now means you have the sunset view." She looked at him as he sat on the edge of the bed again. "And the stars . . ." She looked back to the view. "I've been wanting to get a chart, so I can learn them. But if I can see a good portion of the sky from my little cabin, you must see the whole galaxy."

Seth pulled off his boots, and shifted to the middle of the bed with her, pushing the pillows up against the open pattern of the iron headboard and resting his back on them. "The Milky Way does put on a pretty good show, most nights."

"Oh." She sighed in envy, then turned to him. "I don't think I'd ever be able to close those blinds. I'd be up here all day long, staring."

"Long about five o'clock when the sun is beaming in here like a death ray, you'll probably change your mind," he said with a chuckle, then reached for her, pulling her to him until she straddled his thighs. "Although far be it from me to discourage you from spending as much time up here as you'd like."

"Be careful what you offer," she said. "You know how easily I just move right on in and make myself at home."

He rolled her to her back, eliciting a surprised squeal from her, and pinned her hands next to her head. "I do know," he said, "and I'm counting on it."

Her eyes widened in mock surprise. "So presumptuous."

He grinned. "Let's just say I'm hopeful."

"Until I displease you and you banish me back to the wee cabin in the woods?" she teased.

He rolled to his back and pulled her full length on top of him. "I didn't banish—" He broke off at her look of admonishment. "Okay, so maybe I did." He covered her hands, pulled them up between them, and kissed her knuckles. "But don't worry, everything you do pleases me."

When he nipped her knuckles, she squealed, pulling her hands free and tugging on the end of his beard just hard enough to make him wince.

"You fight like a girl," he teased her, while carefully extracting his beard from her fingers before she could tug again. "Stop gaping at me," he said with a laugh. "As a man with four sisters, I say that with complete awe and the appropriate level of abject humility. My fellow Rangers could have learned a thing or three about hand-to-hair combat from them."

Pippa snickered. "Hand-to-hair combat." She giggled again. "I wish I could refute that, but I also have sisters, and you wouldn't be wrong." She lifted a lock of his long hair and carefully wound it around her finger, then leaned down until her lips were a breath away from his. "It's just so tempting."

He grinned at that, then framed her face and pulled it down to his. "Come here," he murmured. "Let me see if my distract-and-disarm training still works." He kissed her slowly, like a man who had all the time in the world to learn every last nuance of her mouth, her lips, her tongue. And if he was very, *very* lucky, he would.

Chapter Seventeen

Pippa could feel her pulse throbbing like it was connected to a single wire that linked to every one of her pleasure points. Seth's seduction wasn't hurried. In fact, he seemed perfectly happy to continue kissing her indefinitely . . . and she was in no rush to stop him.

They were both fully clothed, and his big, broad hands framed her face, his fingertips weaving into her hair. Yet her entire body was so alive she felt it would set off sparks if he so much as breathed on it.

She'd never been filled with want to the point of physical pain, but her nipples ached, and the muscles between her thighs had clenched into such a tight knot of need, she wanted to beg him to put those big hands on her there, that clever mouth of his, too, and that devilishly wicked tongue that was doing amazing things inside her mouth. One touch, one taste, and she was pretty sure she'd come apart . . . and love every explosive second of it.

It would be easier if he were wearing something she could unbutton to urge his attentions in that direction, or if she were. It turned out long-sleeved T-shirts really weren't made for seduction. She'd think that through better next time. *If I survive this time*, she thought, as she squirmed.

Something of her thoughts, or her wriggling, must have transmitted themselves to him because he lifted his head and smiled down at her. This time he curled a lock of her hair around his finger, then traced the curled ends over her lips. "Ha'penny for your thoughts," he said, his voice now a deep, gravelly baritone that sent a thrill racing through her.

She smiled and ran her hands over his shoulders and down his arms. She was half pinned under him at the moment, and she wanted to feel more of him on top of all of her. Just the thought of him, naked, moving over her, made her tremble in anticipation.

He felt her response and his slumberous, leonine eyes flared instantly to life, making her gasp. She felt her hips rise of their own volition. "Would it be bad form," she began, her own voice barely more than a husky whisper itself, "if I were to suggest that we remove a few articles of clothing? Merely to allow us to be a little more . . . unencumbered, of course."

His low, rumbling laugh was, in and of itself, a seductive thrill. "Of course." His eyes twinkled—no, they glittered—with amusement and a fierce light of desire she'd never witnessed before. All for her. It was both a little daunting and a lot exhilarating.

In answer, he levered himself off of her just enough to reach behind his neck and pull his long-sleeved Henley off in one, over-the-head maneuver. He tossed it behind him without looking to see where it landed.

His chest, his shoulders—*dear, sweet Lord*—his entire torso lived up to every single Nordic Viking fantasy she could have conjured up, and she'd conjured a few since they'd first met. "Oh," she gasped, and ran her fingertips across the flat, defined planes of his pectorals, over the deeply bunched muscles of his shoulders, then down along the rigid vein that lined the thick, long bulge of his bicep. She heard his rumbling, almost growling response, felt the muscles bunch and quiver under her touch and looked up to find him staring down at her, the gold in his eyes molten now.

It was too much to take all at once and she teased him out of reflex, trying to find her balance. "Who knew being a vintner was such a good workout," she said, keeping her gaze on his pecs. His beautiful, perfectly defined pecs.

She glanced up in time to see those molten hot eyes of his widen in surprise. He clearly had not at all expected that response. The accompanying laugh was more a hoarse rasp, but he understood, just as he always understood her, and pulled back, just a little. "More like ten years in the Army, followed by a year or so of banging that mill into shape." His voice was all gravel now.

It made her toes curl, and she honestly didn't think her nipples could get any tighter, but they did.

"Fair warning though, as soon as this place is up and running, I plan to hire good help, drink wine, and get lazy."

She held his gaze for a full five seconds, then burst out laughing. "Yes, I can totally see that happening."

He tossed his head back in a dramatic pose. "So, you're saying you only want me for my beauty? I feel so . . . used."

She giggled, but his antics were exactly what she needed to get her equilibrium back. She was doing this. *We are doing this.*

Well then? She pulled her own shirt up and off, along with the sports bra she'd worn under it. "I think the more important discussion is going to be about these." She motioned to her breasts, which were not only not bountiful, they barely qualified as breasts. "You can always work out, or bench press farm animals to maintain your God-given gifts. Me, on the other hand, not much I can do to enhance these. So, if you were hoping for more, I'm afraid I'm going to be a deep disappointment."

She was teasing, of course. Mostly. Boldly putting herself out there the only way she knew how. There was no way he hadn't already been aware of her utter lack of curves. But that didn't mean she wasn't more than a wee bit self-conscious. And just because she'd decided to handle her anxiety by brazening it out, didn't mean she wasn't holding her breath, just a little.

Seth had straightened out of his joking pose when she'd pulled her shirt off, then looked momentarily surprised by her direct proclamation. But with barely a moment's hesitation, he proceeded to handle the moment in perfect Seth style. His expression grew very serious. "Well, you see," he said, gathering his hair and pushing it behind his shoulders. "I don't really judge breasts by their size."

"No?" she said, trying to play along, but the word had come out quite breathlessly.

He gently pushed her back to the bed, and levered himself up so his body was next to hers, his chest brushing her arm. She gasped at the contact of his warm, bare skin on hers. He lifted the arm that was pinned between them and draped it over her head, then trailed his fingers back along the inside of her arm.

"What makes a woman's breast tantalizing," he said softly, as he lowered his head, "is how responsive it is." And then he closed his lips over her nipple, and ran the tip of his warm tongue over that tight, needy tip. She cried out, bucking hard off the bed, fairly certain with a few more strokes, he could actually make her come by doing nothing more than that.

He lifted his head and met her gaze, his eyes right back to molten, only this time, she was so tautly aroused she didn't want him pulling back. She wanted to beg him to hurry up and get on with it.

"Hmm," he said, and the rumbling sound felt like a vibration skimming over her heated skin. "I believe these will do just fine." Then he shifted and traced his tongue over her other nipple, while running the tips of his fingers over the still damp one.

She moaned long and low and writhed against his touch, wanting him to drag every last stitch of clothing off of her and *hurry up about it*. Dear God, she wanted him more than she wanted her next breath. And the one after that, too.

She reached for his shoulders, but he pinned both arms over her head with the weight of one arm. "I'm not done yet," he murmured.

"I'm going to be," she breathed, letting out a half-shocked little laugh at the truth of it, her back arching again as he continued his delicious torture.

He raised his head and waited for her to lift hers to meet his gaze. "Oh, I wasn't planning on stopping at just one."

She let her head drop back to the bed. "Marry me this instant."

He chuckled at that, and she could feel his lips were still curved in a grin as he slowly started to work his way down her torso to the waistband of her trousers. He unzipped them and slid them down her legs, panties and all, then moved up between her thighs . . . and at that point, any remaining threads of rational thought fled altogether.

The instant his tongue brushed over the most sensitive part of her body, she was catapulted straight over the edge into an orgasm so strong it made her scream. "Oh my God," she panted, as her body started to spiral back down again, still pulsing and clutching and shooting little sparks of pleasure throughout her body. "I didn't think you could actually see stars." She laughed when he lifted his head and she realized she'd said that out loud.

He kissed the inside of her thigh, then her navel, then the tip of her breast. "I'll try harder next time," he said in mock seriousness, pulling her hands away from where she covered her face.

"If you try any harder, I'm fair to certain I won't live to

see morning," she told him, her brogue such that it made him pause and grin; then their gazes caught and they both snickered. Then he started to chuckle, which set her to laughing. "I'm just a wee lass, after all," she went on between gasps, making her brogue thicker still. "I don't know how much my poor, wee nipples can stand, now can I?" And that put them both over the edge. They were lost to the laughter, until he had to roll to his back beside her to catch his breath.

They lay there, side by side, not daring to look at each other, and in that moment, she knew she was having the singularly best moment she'd ever had in her life. And the literal screaming orgasm had been the least of it.

Then she felt his hand find hers among the now bunched-up duvet and linens that covered his ocean of bed. He slid his fingers through hers, then pulled her hand up to his mouth and kissed the back of it. She turned her head to one side and found him staring at her. The look in his beautiful, beautiful eyes was a mixture of desire, joy, amusement, affection, and something else she dared not put a name to. And she thought, *No, this is the best moment.*

And then he pulled her to him, and their smiles remained even as their actions became more serious and deliberate. He undressed the rest of the way, found protection in the bed stand and put it on. She didn't even look at the rest of him as he angled his body over hers, careful to keep his weight balanced on his forearms so as not to crush her. She was too caught up in his eyes, in the intent look she found there, the way he searched her eyes. She knew what he was asking, without saying a word. She nodded and pulled his mouth down to hers and kissed him.

Moments later, he took over the kiss, exploring her gently, intently, taking care, such care, as he drew her more deeply in, pushed her farther, then farther still, until his heart was drumming so insistently she could feel it against her skin even though he was barely pressing against her. When he finally nudged her thighs apart it was the most natural thing in the world to wrap herself around him and take him inside of her body. The utterly glorious feel of him slowly filling her up made her cry out. He paused, but she rose up to meet him, tightened around him, and he groaned deeply, and started a slow, steady rhythm that felt so good it made her eyes well up.

She felt him kiss the dampness from the corners of her eyes, then press a salty kiss to her lips. They started to climb then, and she felt him gathering and wrapped herself even more tightly around him.

"Pippa," he said, the word hardly more than a rasp.

She opened her eyes and found his gaze on her. It was a moment so potent, she couldn't find words to describe it. It was as if their bodies paused on an endless moment of anticipation, as if time actually stopped, just so they could be in that space a moment longer, together. She saw everything she'd ever hoped to see right there in his eyes. "Seth," she whispered, and the words she wanted to say to him came to her lips, begging to be said. But the moment she whispered his name, his eyes closed and the world started moving forward again.

Their bodies rose and thrust in rhythm as he finally went over the edge, and the force of it, that look in his eyes when he did, all served to pull her right over after him. Panting now, he slid his arm under her and pulled her to him, so her back arched off the bed, and he held her there, suspended, cradled against him, for long, heart-pounding moments. He kissed her, and she opened her eyes, looked into his, and smiled. He smiled right back, and it was this perfect moment of intimacy, their bodies still joined, their gazes locked in that private, secret moment, that she wrapped up and tucked inside her heart, for safe keeping forever.

He rolled to his back, keeping her close, still inside her, and cradled her on top of his body. Her cheek was pressed against his shoulder, her hands curled on his chest as he wrapped his arms around her and she felt him press a kiss to the top of her head.

They lay like that for a long time, until he finally slipped from her, and gently slid her to the bed beside him. He kissed her cheek and her eyes were already drifting closed. She felt him roll off the bed, and pulled a pillow under her head. Smiling, she didn't fight the wonderfully sated, drowsy pull of slumber. She remembered opening her eyes briefly as he walked back toward the bed moments later, the warm sunlight coming through the big window casting him in a golden glow, and thinking, *My Viking, indeed*, before sleep claimed her.

It was the death ray that woke her up for good. Pippa blinked her eyes open and immediately squeezed them shut again, pulling a pillow over her head to block out the daggers of light that threatened to sear her corneas. "He wasn't kidding," she mumbled. She sat up, careful to keep her back to the window before daring to remove the pillow.

She looked over, expecting to see Seth's beautiful frame sprawled among the sheets and pillows, as contentedly spent as she'd been after their last round of lovemaking, but she was alone. There were remnants of the picnic lunch they'd had hours earlier, right there in the middle of the bed, now scattered across the floor. She smiled at the half empty bottle of wine on the nightstand, then leaned over and turned the bottle around. "Sorry, Dex. How rude of us," she said with a laugh.

She slid her legs over to the edge of the bed and realized she was still wearing Seth's T-shirt. It was the very same one she'd worn the first night she'd slept in his house, she realized now. She'd donned it to help him carry lunch up the circular staircase and hadn't pulled it off again, even when he'd seduced her with succulent grapes, and even more succulent kisses. Seth had been propped up against the headboard at the time and had merely pulled her astride his lap. She closed her eyes and let out a soft little moan as she remembered how that had turned out, how they'd looked into each other's eyes all the way through, right up until he'd pushed her gloriously over the edge.

She wrapped her arms around the pillow she still held, missing him already. Then she spied the rolled-up piece of paper he'd slid into the scrollwork of the iron headboard. Grinning, she leaned forward and slid the paper tube free and uncurled it.

Come find me in the vines, Sleeping Beauty. S.

Using the whole pillow to shade her eyes from the glare, she rose up on her knees and turned toward the window. Looking down at the fields she could see from her perch, she began searching for him, then broke out in laughter when she saw the arrow he'd made with white feed buckets, pointing toward the vines in front of the stone barn, out of her range of vision.

She climbed off the bed and immediately hit the button to lower the blinds. She made the bed, which, it turned out, was quite the undertaking. It was a big task for just one person, especially if said person was her size. Once done, she scooped up her clothes and shoes and went downstairs, looking for his bathroom, and shower. Then she remembered the one out back. *Could I?*

Bailey had insisted it was perfectly private and said she'd never ever shower indoors again, given the choice. *Hmm.* Grinning like a child about to do something naughty, Pippa did a little exploring and found the rather enormous bathroom at Seth's end of the house, and sure enough, there was a door just out the back, into the private little cubicle.

She stepped outside and put her clothes on the bench that lined the little entryway behind the taller-than-she-was privacy screen and turned on the spray. Then she went back into the bathroom for a towel. She pulled off Seth's tee and tiptoed back outside, like some kind of cat burglar, then laughed at herself. With the sun heading toward the horizon, the air was nippy. The steam from the shower billowed up in the dusky, early evening air and she sighed as she stepped under the hot spray. She let it pummel her back as she looked up at the deep purple streaks spreading across the sky. She felt . . . primal.

Her mind naturally played through the events of the long, lazy afternoon, and she was delighted to discover there was no trepidation, no *Did I do the right thing?* internal debate. Her smile softened. For her, the highlights of their time up in that amazing sea of a bed weren't the orgasms or the delicious care he'd taken to find and exploit every last one of her pleasure spots. No, the best parts were the whispers they'd shared, the mischievous smiles, and the laughter. Oh, dear God, had they laughed. The reason she had not a single doubt that she'd made the right decision was that she knew she'd made love with her best friend.

It wasn't until she'd rinsed the soap from her skin and turned her face to the spray that she realized she'd been singing under her breath, probably the entire time. The way she'd done all the time. *Before.* She stopped as soon as she realized it, her hand covering her throat—her perfectly fine throat—and she closed her eyes against the instant grip that clutched her gut into a tight, queasy knot. The fear swallowed her up, in that moment that she'd sworn she'd never let herself think about again.

She stood there, stock-still under the hot spray, and thought, *NO! Not this time you don't!* She was all done with being afraid now. She was going to face down her inner demons. She wasn't going to endlessly relive that terrifying moment on stage, wasn't going to allow the past to control her present. *I'm going to sing, dammit!*

"Pippa."

Her eyes flew open to find Seth standing just beyond the spray, amid the clouds of steam, as if in some kind of dream. She reached for him without a second thought and felt no shame in needing him. He was her partner, her lover, her safe space. Her best friend. He stepped under the spray, fully clothed, without hesitation, and pulled her against him, letting the shower beat on his back, shielding her face from the spray.

"I saw the steam and thought perhaps I'd come join you," he said quietly. "Then I got close and I heard you singing."

She went to pull away again and he held on fast, not allowing it.

"And I just stood there, transfixed by it," he said, his lips pressed against her temple, his broad palm stroking down her back as she began to tremble. "Such a gift, Pippa. I didn't know. Hadn't let myself know. Not truly. I was afraid it would make it that much harder to say good-bye."

She looked up at him then, eyes wide, confused.

His gaze met hers, and everything was there, laid bare for her to see. "What an idiot I was," he murmured, his lips curving upward. "Who in their right mind would deprive themselves of listening to that?"

"I'm such a coward, Seth," she confessed, and felt a certain release at saying the words out loud. "I know I have to do it, I was doing it, am doing it. But when I think about it . . . I freeze up. I'm being so stupid."

He pulled her back into his arms, pressed her cheek against his chest, and moved them both under the spray, deep into the billowing steam. It filled her lungs, soothed her tight throat, worked its relaxing magic as he simply held her. "So," he said after a bit, "don't sing for you." He stroked her hair, her cheek, kept her tucked deep into his arms. "Slide your arms around me," he said, and she did, then held on tight. "Close your eyes," he murmured softly, and she did. "Feel my heart beating," he said. "Feel the water, the evening air. Sing for the trees, for the stars." He leaned down and kissed the side of her neck, and in a whisper only she could hear, he said, "Or sing something only to me. I won't let anything happen to you, Pippa. You're safe."

Her first instinct was to curl into herself, to tell him all the reasons she couldn't do as he asked, that nothing had changed. But everything had changed. Her outlook, her life, this new partnership . . . and her music had come back. It was all there for her now, waiting for her to make the conscious decision to reach for it.

"Not singing won't save you," he said, and put his back to the spray again. "You know that. Your music is back, and it wants out." He slowly pushed the hair from her face, traced his fingers over her cheekbones, then slowly ran them down, along her jaw, then lower, until they rested at the base of her throat. She shuddered, hard, but he gently caressed her, sliding his thumb gently up and over her throat, then back, repeating the action until she stopped shuddering, stopped shaking. "So you might as well give in to it and see what happens next."

Exhausted, she rested against him in defeat, trying to empty her mind, trying to do as he asked. "I want to," she said. "Desperately. I just don't know how anymore."

"Don't think about singing," he said, his voice a low hum. "You said it's your soundtrack. Think about life. Feel it. Your music will do the rest."

He continued to hold her, stroke her, and let her try.

He made her feel . . . anchored.

She let in thoughts of the day, let herself relive those moments, feel those moments, let them inside of her . . . and gradually they took over, and she wasn't thinking about the knot in her gut, or the fear, or singing, or any of it. She was thinking about that morning, about talking to Will. She let herself see the emotions play across his face, and felt them tug as sharply at her heart now as they had then. She thought about walking hand in hand with Seth through the vines, about him piggy-back-jogging her to the house, and only making it as far as the barn. She thought about how he'd posed in bed, how they'd laughed so hard they couldn't even look at each other. She thought about how she'd stripped her shirt off . . . how he'd made love to her breasts, then made love to her.

She thought about the man, standing fully dressed in a hot, steam-filled shower, holding her close, yet giving her all the space she needed . . . and how she knew without a single doubt in her heart that he'd stand there until the end of time if she needed him to.

The music found her then. And, with it, so did her song.

Chapter Eighteen

It was a moment he'd never forget for the rest of his days.

Four weeks had passed since he'd stepped, fully clothed, into that shower. May had come and almost gone, and with it the mountains were turning green and lush, and his vines were once again surging to life. It felt like a lifetime ago now, but he found himself thinking about it all the time. Four weeks since she'd sung those first shaky notes, her whole body trembling so hard he couldn't soothe her. She'd sung so softly, he'd barely been able to hear her, but it hadn't mattered. He'd been thankful for the shower spray hitting him square in the face. Then he could pretend it was shower water tracking down his cheeks from the corners of his eyes.

Seth walked the last row of vines, checking his cuts, looking at the new growth, but his thoughts stayed with that monumental moment. He found himself grinning, then chuckling as he remembered the instant he'd realized what it was she was singing. He'd begun chuckling then, too, and hadn't been able to stop.

She'd lifted her head, standing there in his arms, for all the world like a wee drowned thing, water running all down her face, and stared at him in stunned shock. "Are you honestly laughing at me?" she'd demanded. "What happened to this being my safe space?"

"I'm sorry," he said, wrapping his hands around her fists before she could pummel him. "But are you singing 'The Itsy Bitsy Spider'?"

"Well, you didn't expect me to sing you an aria, did you now?"

He remembered he'd shaken his head. "No, why would I think that?" Then he'd leaned down and kissed her, and kept kissing her until she finally relented and leaned into him, kissing him back.

"You can sing me anything you like," he'd said against her lips. "I'm quite partial to 'The Hokey Pokey.' Do you know it?"

And she'd looked up at him and said, "Is that the one where you put your right knee in?"

He was pretty sure she'd been the first one to snicker. But it might have been him. They'd both laughed, of that much he was certain. She'd pulled his head under the spray as payback, while fiendishly giggling, and he'd just opened his mouth to say the three words that had come to him so easily it was as if he'd been telling her he loved her for years. But the small propane tank heating the water had chosen that exact moment to bottom out, sending them both racing out from under the ice-cold spray and back into the house.

They'd gone up to the loft to find dry clothes and he'd apologized to her there, quite sincerely.

"It was the very first thing I learned to sing as a little girl," she'd told him quite primly, in that way she had. "It seemed . . . a fitting place to start."

"It was perfect," he'd told her, and meant it.

Seth grinned and he finished inspecting the last vine on the row, then walked around to the next and last row, feeling his body tighten all over again as he recalled how they hadn't come back downstairs again until well after the moon had risen in the sky.

Fifteen minutes later and still smiling, Seth started up toward the stone barn, intent on stowing his tools and clipping bucket before heading down to the round barn to help Bailey. When he saw Jake walking along the stone path from the driveway, Seth stopped and lifted a hand in a wave to Will as he backed his truck around. Will lifted a hand briefly in return through the open window, but didn't pause, and drove on back down the drive.

It was the first time Seth had seen Will since Pippa's little talk. "I guess that's a start," Seth said under his breath, then turned to look at Jake. "Are you back?" he asked Jake as he got closer to the barn.

Jake nodded, looking sheepish. "I need to apologize to you," he said. "I'm sorry I put you in that situation with my dad."

"Jake—"

"I need to say it," the boy told Seth. "And not because I have to. This is coming from me, not my dad." He shuffled his feet, and Seth gave him the time to find his own words. "I shouldn't have taken the fiddle," he said. Then he looked up and met Seth's gaze. "I shouldn't have let you or Pippa think I had permission, either. I know it's important to him. He made it for my mom." Jake's voice cracked on that last part and it made Seth's heart hurt.

Seth wanted to tell Jake he didn't need to say any more, but it wasn't his place to tell the boy anything at that moment.

"He'd been teaching her to play. My gramma said she was really good at it, too. So Dad made her a fiddle for Christmas. But . . ."

"It's okay, Jake," Seth said gently, unable to bear letting the boy torture himself any further.

Jake's eyes grew a little glassy, and his voice was more croak than not, when he added, "Gramma Dot told me he burned his own fiddle, right in our fireplace. After . . . you know. I don't blame him. I don't. Not one bit. Gramma

didn't either. She just told me so I'd understand about . . .
everything. But Dad kept the one he made for Mom. Even
though she never saw it. So, I know I shouldn't have taken
it. No one's ever played it." He dashed at his eyes again and
cleared his throat, then straightened his shoulders. Seth
could swear the kid had grown another two inches since he'd
seen him last, or maybe now that he'd started the painful
journey toward becoming a young man, he simply looked
taller because of it.

"It's just . . . I've been thinking about her. My mom.
A lot."

"Do you and your dad talk about her?"

Jake shook his head. "Gramma did with me, all the time,
so I know tons of stories about her. And we have loads of
photo albums. Gramma made those, too. I hadn't looked at
them in a long time, not since before Gramma Dot passed.
But I have been lately. I'm not sure why really. I don't remember her, so it's not like I miss her." He sighed. "Bailey
says I'm trying to figure out who I am. And I guess if anyone
should know about that, it's her."

Seth nodded. "She's a pretty wise young lady."

"Right?" Jake said, sounding both impressed and annoyed,
as only a teenager could, and they both laughed.

"I know it's stupid," Jake said. "And I don't know why
I thought it was a good idea, but I got to thinking that if I
learned to play the fiddle, the fiddle he made, then maybe
that would take away some of my dad's . . . hurt, I guess?
Like, I know I can't replace my mom or anything, but I'm
the one person left in the world that he loves as much as he's
ever loved anyone, so who else could do it but me? I just
didn't think it through."

Seth had to curl his fingers inward to keep from hugging
the kid tight. "Did you tell him that? What you just told me?"

Jake shook his head. "I've never in my whole life seen
him that angry. Or angry at all. We're okay now, him and me.

He said he was sorry for coming in there like he did and I apologized for doing what I did." Jake smiled then, and looked more the little boy he had been than the young man he was becoming. "I did my time, served my sentence," he said, then lifted his shoulders. "And now, we're back to where we were. I don't want to mess that up."

Seth took all that to mean that Will hadn't said anything to Jake about Pippa's offer. She'd be so disappointed, but Seth wasn't really surprised.

"I'm sorry I left you without help," Jake said. "My dad said I could come up every day for the next two weeks to make that up to you. I'd like to, if that's okay."

Seth nodded. "I'd be happy for the help. Bailey's already down in the round barn. We've moved the goats down there so I can start the barn renovation." He'd given the greenlight to the local contractor he'd hired to go ahead and start working on turning the barn into a tasting room, despite not having anything bottled as yet.

In the past few weeks, Seth had been rethinking his decision to hold off on doing any pressing or fermenting from the upcoming crop. The bottles he'd been making as testers really were coming out pretty decent. It meant a much more accelerated schedule than he'd been planning, but what the hell? More of that *living life without fear* mantra that he and Pippa were embracing.

"Is Pippa up here?" Jake asked. "I mean Miss Pippa," he corrected. "Except she calls me Master Jake when I call her that. Bailey said she's spending more time up here now." The blush that came into his cheeks and turned the tips of his ears bright red suggested Bailey had been a bit more blunt in her description of the new direction Seth's relationship with Pippa had taken. But he appreciated the boy's discretion in how he'd chosen to frame it. "I need to apologize to her, too. I know she and my dad have talked, but she still needs to hear it from me."

Seth's attention snagged on that last part. "Your dad told you about that?"

Jake nodded. "He told me she came over to talk to him and apologize, which she totally didn't have to do. I mean, it wasn't her fault. But I am glad they talked." He looked down at the dirt he'd been scuffing into a little pile with his toe. "He doesn't play her music anymore," Jake said quietly. "And I'm sorry for that." He looked up. "Don't tell Pippa, okay? She—it would only hurt her feelings. It's not about her, I'm sure. It's just my dad."

"I won't say anything," Seth promised him. "I'm glad they talked, too. Pippa likes your dad a great deal. She said it was a really good conversation. I don't know why your dad may have decided not to listen to her music, but I'm pretty certain he and Pippa are just fine."

Jake nodded, but didn't look entirely convinced. "I asked him if he was nervous, meeting someone famous like her." He let out a short laugh. "I remember how nervous I was. It feels stupid now, because, you know, she's just Pippa. Like, it's hard to believe she's the other Pippa, you know?"

Seth nodded. "I do know," he said, and tried to ignore the knot that tightened in his gut, as it always did when he thought about the other Pippa.

"Bailey also told me something else, but I'm not sure whether or not I'm supposed to say. I mean, Pippa didn't tell her not to say and it's not like you probably don't already know, since you're, you know . . . together." His cheeks flushed scarlet and he snapped his mouth shut.

"It's okay, Jake," Seth said, chuckling. "We are together, and it's a really happy, good thing. Nothing to be embarrassed about. Maybe check with Bailey about the other thing, or better yet, Pippa, and make sure it's okay to tell me."

He nodded. "Will do. So, where is she?"

"She's at the cabin," he told Jake. "She'll be here a little later, around three. She's cooking supper. You're welcome to stay if you'd like. Addie Pearl's coming to get Bailey and they're both staying to eat. Give your dad a shout. I'm sure it would be fine if he comes, too. Pippa always cooks like she's cooking for a family of eight anyway. If your dad can't make it, Addie Pearl or I can take you home after. We'll get you back in time to finish your homework."

"Already did it," Jake said. "And that'd be great. I'll text him and let you know."

"Why don't you head on down to the barn," Seth told him. "We've had four goat babies in the past week, so I know Bailey's got her hands full. The sheep are out, and Dex is with them, so no worries on that."

Jake nodded and turned to head down the hill, then stopped and looked back at Seth. "How come Pippa's at the cabin? I thought—Bailey said—I mean, I thought she was here now?"

Seth swallowed the urge to chuckle. The poor kid was going to turn permanently pink. "She is, but she kept the cabin, too." He wanted to tell Jake that Pippa had kept the place as her private little music studio, but that was for Pippa alone to say. She'd explained to Seth that the small size, the comfort, and the joy she felt there, along with the complete and utter privacy it provided from everyone, himself included, made it the perfect spot to shut down her active brain and focus inward on her songwriting brain.

It made as much sense to him as it could to someone who didn't write music and lyrics for a living. He was just happy to see her writing again, singing again. She didn't sing much around him, though she swore to him it wasn't because of what they now referred to as "the shower incident." She was simply keeping it to herself, she'd said. "Getting reacquainted," was how she'd described it. He understood that.

He'd overheard her singing along to the Disney tunes she always played when she was brushing Dex late at night, after Bailey had gone home, or playing with Elliott and the new baby goats. He often heard her in the outdoor shower when she got up at dawn along with him; and very occasionally, late at night, while in bed with him, she'd sing bits and pieces of new verses under her breath, revising them, trying out different emphasis or tones, while she thought he was asleep. He'd never heard her sing full out yet, only in moderation, but he suspected she'd need some time to get past the fear of really letting herself go.

And none of those things could Seth share with the young man standing in front of him. Seth was still the only one in Blue Hollow Falls who knew she was singing again.

Seth was grappling with what excuse to give Jake as to why Pippa had kept the cabin, when the boy said, "Oh, that's cool. Well, when she gets here, let me know, okay?"

"Will do," Seth said and watched Jake lope down the hill toward the round barn. He chuckled, thinking Bailey was right, adults really did make things so much more complicated sometimes than was necessary. "Most of the time, more like," he said, and shaking his head, went on inside the stone barn. Seth had decided to keep his office out in the barn and was in the middle of revising the tasting-room floor plan to include a formal office space. He'd spent all morning the day before looking at the property, trying to decide if he wanted to plant more vines this season, or keep to his original plan. He'd started the rough outlines for repurposing another one of the outbuildings into a reception hall of sorts. Maybe he would go ahead and mow down the overgrowth around the small pond that was down past the round barn. Sarah Bianchi had pegged that as the perfect spot for wedding ceremonies. Adding a trellised arch, or a pergola. Seth thought she was probably spot-on with that.

He sat down behind his desk and chuckled. "And man, you've got weddings on the brain these days." He turned on his computer and pulled up the tasting-room designs, but his thoughts were already wandering down the very familiar path he found himself working harder and harder to steer clear of. The thing was, his life felt like it had come full circle. Everything seemed pretty damn perfect. He was doing something he loved, he had a wonderful woman in his life. It made him feel happy and content, knowing Pippa was over at the cabin, pursuing her own passion.

Seth loved waking up with her, and looked forward to the end of each day now, too. It made him feel grounded, made life feel more balanced. They dined together every evening, taking turns cooking depending on who got done working first, cooking together when they could. He talked over his new plans for the winery with her, and she talked about the music she was discovering, and how it was taking a different turn now. Her voice was definitely smokier than it had been, which he knew, as he'd now listened to pretty much everything she'd ever recorded. She told him it still startled her when she opened her mouth and sang, but it sounded gloriously rich and full to him, which he'd told her countless times.

She'd told him her songwriting was changing too, and that didn't surprise him. Given her injury, the surgery, and everything that had come after, it seemed natural that she'd have different stories she wanted to tell. She told him her time spent in Blue Hollow Falls, and her time with him, was influencing her songwriting, too. That made him happy, and though it was maybe kind of weird to imagine someone writing songs about him, he'd been flattered and more than a little abashed. He knew she was working hard to find a way to meld the songs in her head with the voice she now had, and he had every faith she'd not only find it, but her fans would be knocked out of their collective socks when they heard the result.

What they very carefully didn't talk about was how they were going to manage his going after his dreams, getting the winery up and running, when she finally reached the point where it was time to get back into a studio and start recording again. She'd be going back to performing, touring, recording, and the myriad of other things that came with it, which he'd only had the barest whiff of as yet. He'd overheard her on the phone with her assistant, Julia, her manager, her agent, her record label, checking in with them, handling the business details of her life, which went on even when she wasn't actively recording or setting up tour dates. It was hard for him to wrap his head around the fact that his Pippa was also that Pippa, even as he watched them finally become the same person, right there in front of him. When the two of them talked about any of that, though, or the future at all, it was always in the abstract, as if it was going to happen so far down the road, there was no need to figure it out now.

The other thing they didn't talk about was love.

It had gotten so he silently said those words to her multiple times every day. And given the way she looked at him, the way they made love to each other, if she didn't love him right back, she was doing a damn fine impression of someone who did.

But they didn't talk about love. Not because they were afraid to say the words. Or he wasn't, in any case. Hell, he wanted to hire a skywriter, and tell the whole world. But he didn't say those words, and he was pretty sure she didn't either, because then it would make everything they were doing all too real and not some dream-sequence timeout from reality. Which was ridiculous, and yet . . . there it was.

Seth wanted things to stay exactly the way they were right now. And he knew that couldn't happen.

He had just punched the button on his keyboard to open the most recently saved version of the tasting-room schematic, possibly with a little more force than was necessary, when his phone rang. Seth knew that ringtone and immediately picked up his phone. "Mouse," he said with a grin. "About time you checked in. I'd begun to think the leprechauns had spirited you away."

"Katie told me," Moira said. "You're hooking up?"

Initially, he and Pippa had decided not to tell his sister, or hers, to avoid this very conversation, but that had been a month ago now. Pippa hadn't mentioned that she'd told her sister, but for all he knew it had just happened five minutes ago, and she hadn't gotten the chance to let him know.

"I told you not to get involved," Moira told him, sounding more worried than scolding. "Seth, she's—"

"Someone I love very much," Seth interrupted, feeling as if some huge pressure had just been released inside his chest and he could finally breathe again, now that he'd finally gotten to say that out loud. "Mouse, it's okay."

There was a long pause, and he could hear her long exhale of breath. "Promise?"

"As much as I can, yes. I don't know what Katie has told you, or what Pippa told her—"

"They just got off the phone. Pippa told her she wanted to tell you first, before Katie said anything to me, but she and I were texting when Pippa called, and I kind of wheedled it out of her. Don't be mad at Pippa."

"I won't be. Wouldn't be."

Moira paused, then said, "So, you love her? The real kind of love?"

Seth smiled. "Yes," he said without hesitation. "The real kind of love."

"She loves you back?"

Seth chuckled. "Don't sound so surprised."

"I'm not," Moira hurried to say. "I'm just . . . I didn't expect this. It's a lot, Seth. Like huge, big-time a lot."

He knew it was, just as he knew Moira was talking about more than love. She was talking about him being in love with Pippa MacMillan, singer. "I know," he said.

Moira's voice was softer when she continued, and he heard the worry, and all the love. "Are you ready for all that?"

Seth felt the first tiny fissures start to crack the bubble. He wasn't ready yet. "As ready as I can be." Which was the first lie he'd ever told his sister. "How has your time gone?" he asked instead, shoving his own feelings aside with phenomenal force of will. "Have you gotten much studying done? What do you think of our ancestors' homeland?"

"It went by too fast," she told him. "Katie's family is amazing, so much like ours, Seth. And the countryside is more breathtaking than you can imagine. Everyone is so lovely."

She paused then, and Seth could hear some other thread in her voice, one that wasn't quite as joyful. "But?" he asked.

"You always know," she said, and her voice broke just the tiniest bit.

"What happened, Mousie?" he said, instantly concerned, but careful to keep his voice gentle. "Are you okay?"

"I'm fine. Or I will be." She let out a watery attempt at a laugh. "Turns out you weren't the only one to have a little fling."

Seth wanted to correct her: what he and Pippa had was no fling, and the vehemence with which he felt the need to do so told him he really did need to have a talk with Pippa. About a lot of things. "What happened?" he asked her again. "He didn't hurt you in any way, did he?" He felt his stomach knot and his temper—rare as it was—start to rise, but she hurried on.

"Just my heart, Seth," she assured him. "And that's not even his fault. He's a lovely, lovely person. Generous and kind. I just . . . well, I fell, and . . . he didn't." Her voice broke on the last word. "It looks like you found your Kate Winslet after all," she added gamely. "While I didn't get so lucky with my Jude Law." She was trying so hard, but he heard the sniffle, the catch in her throat, and, with four sisters, he knew what was coming next

Seth hated it when anyone cried, but he especially hated it when it was someone he loved. He felt so damn helpless. "Listen to me, Mousie. You know you're perfect. You're lovely, smart, and every bit as kind and generous. If he couldn't realize the gem he had in his hand, then he's both a fool and an idiot. He lost out, but you haven't. You want the guy who sees that about you, not the guy who doesn't."

Moira gave a watery laugh. "See? This is why I love you. Why I always turn to you. You always say such lovely things, even if they aren't true." She sniffled again. "The truth is, I don't feel like any of those things right now. I feel stupid. He told me he wasn't interested in starting up anything, but did I listen? No, I did not. I mean, I tried, but we were having such a lovely time, and he was the one pushing things along—not like that," she hurried to add. "I just mean, he wanted to see me, he'd set up our dates, and we had so much fun together, Seth. How could he not want more of that?"

"I don't know, Mouse. Not everyone is made for commitment. Or it could be he's just not mature enough, or where he wants to be in life. I don't know. It could be a dozen different things. But know it's not you."

"It sure feels like it's me." Her dry delivery and laugh sounded a bit more like herself. "He even broke up with me the right way, if there is a right way. I made some silly comment about trying to work it out to stay a bit longer, and instead of being happy about that, he was a little concerned. Which surprised me, but that's when I knew." She paused, and he heard her breath hitch again, but she didn't start crying. "He gave me the most beautiful little speech, because he really is lovely. But he made it clear he wasn't falling in love, and while he enjoyed being with me and thought I was delightful—his words—he'd just assumed we were having some fun together. He told me he'd never meant to hurt me, and I swear, Seth, we both cried. It was both beautiful and awful, all at the same time."

"I'm really sorry, Mouse." Seth half wished the guy had been an ass so she could be angry instead of heartbroken. Or maybe so he could be angry instead of sad on her behalf. "There's nothing easy about that. He does sound like a good guy."

"Right?" she said, her laugh a bit sadder this time.

"Well, I suppose you could console yourself that your instincts are good and you didn't fall for some jerk."

"I feel loads better already," she said, the wry note back, and they both laughed.

"When are you coming home?" he asked.

"Oh, I am home. I'm back at Mum and Dad's."

He smiled at her use of the Irish word for mom, and at the hint of brogue he detected in her voice. "I'm sorry you came back early. You should have stayed and enjoyed the rest of your time."

"I didn't come back early," she said, sounding surprised.

Seth flipped the calendar up on his computer screen. His smile faded as he realized Moira was right. It had been more than six weeks since Pippa had popped up over the ridge and plowed into that snowbank. *Your time is running out.* "Right, right," he said, trying to stomp down the surge of panic. But it was too late; the bubble had already gone from having tiny, little fissures to big, huge cracks.

"I am glad I went," Moira told him. "All in all, it really was a wonderful time. Once I get over having my heart being stomped flat, I'll have only fond memories. I'm sure of it. Katie's even talking about coming to see me when I move back to California."

"You ready for the bar?" he said, feeling like he was having a dual conversation. The nice, calm one he was having with his sister, and the panic-fueled one in which he scrambled to figure out how he was going to save his nice, grounded, perfectly balanced life.

"I still have a bit of time," Moira was saying. "The exam isn't until July. But I've already registered, so it's going to happen."

"I know you'll nail it," he told her, meaning it. "And I know how much you'll love moving back to California."

"Actually, that's happening now," she told him. "Mom and Dad have been great, but being in Ireland, and yes, having my heart broken, I just feel like I can't stay in this weird purgatory any longer. I need to take action, move on, get started. I've found a place recommended to me by another friend from back in my Stanford days. It's short-term, but it's a place to crash until I find the right spot."

Seth frowned and his focus returned solely to his sister. "Will you be able to study there?"

"I'll be fine. If the apartment is too noisy or whatever, and seeing as I'll have three roommates, it probably will be, I can use the libraries on the Stanford campus since I'm an alumnus. I have a few other friends I may end up crashing with, if the room thing doesn't work out."

"You sure you wouldn't rather wait until you have something more permanent lined up?"

"No, it's time to get on with things."

"Well then, you've got my support," he said, smiling even as he felt lingering concern for her. But that was pretty much par for the course in his relationship with his youngest sister. "Knock 'em dead."

"Thanks, big brother. I love you."

"Love you back."

"So," she said, sounding relieved and a tiny bit refreshed, "back to you. What have the two of you worked out for when she goes back to Ireland?"

"We haven't sorted that part out yet," he admitted.

"Really?" she said, sounding truly surprised.

"Really," he said, mildly annoyed, but mostly with himself, because it was true. "Don't worry, okay?"

"Oh, I'm not. I mean, I trust you. I was just surprised because, well, from what Katie said, Pippa's got almost enough music written to start thinking about her comeback album. And I haven't a clue what-all is involved in going from writing music to making a record or anything, but I guess I assumed she'd want to be back in Ireland when she did it. Are you going to go with her? What about the winery? This is your first big harvest before wine making. Did you get the distributor deal?"

"Whoa, slow down, slow down. The winery is fine," he said, his brain really doing double time now. "I'm actually thinking about pressing some of the grapes from this crop. The distributor can't take them all, and though I have other avenues to sell to other vintners, I think I might just dive in and get started. A limited edition run."

"Wow, that's wonderful!" Moira said. "I'm so excited for you. So, Pippa will be staying with you, then, I guess. I mean, that makes more sense when you think about it. You have all those random buildings on your property; she could probably just turn one of those into a recording studio, right? Wouldn't that be cool? I mean, why does it matter where she records? Artists record in places all over the world. And you have some of the best musicians around right there in the Falls." She gasped. "Oh my God, Seth. Wouldn't it be awesome if she recorded her comeback album there, with the guild musicians? Given she wrote the songs there, it seems kind of fitting. Oh!" she added, on a roll now. "That would be amazing for Blue Hollow Falls and the mill, too. Everybody wins!" She squealed and he held the phone away from his ear. "I'm *so* happy for you. This helps me so much, big brother. There's nothing better than a real love story. When are you going to propose? Can I come out? Wait, duh! I'm guessing I'll be in the wedding. Or I hope I will. She has a lot of sisters."

Seth let Moira ramble on excitedly in his ear, her honest joy making him surprisingly happy. More than happy. Because out of the mouths of babes—or in this case, his twenty-six-year-old sister—he might have just come up with the perfect solution.

"Moira," he said, breaking into her excited babble. "Mouse," he said, more loudly. "Listen, I need to go."

"Okay, okay, but you have to call me and tell me everything when you can. And thank you for your shoulder. Sorry I got it all soggy. Again." She wound it back down then, sounding quieter and sincere when she added, "I love you so much. You're always there for me, Seth. I know I always say I'll repay you, but I don't know how that will ever be possible. You're the very best."

"Actually," he told her, grinning now, "I think we're beyond even. Thank *you*, baby sister. I love you right back." He hung up, then leaned back in his chair and propped his hands behind his head. "Adults do make things so much more complicated than they have to be." He got up and paced his little office stall, trying to force his brain to process everything in a linear fashion, wanting to have it all thought out before he said anything to Pippa. Surely there had to be a glitch he wasn't seeing. And yes, it wasn't a perfect solution, and sure, she'd want to spend time in Ireland. He hoped he would, too. At some point. He just had to hope she was willing to not spend all of her time there.

Seth turned in his pacing to find Dex standing on the other side of the stall door, giving him his classic baleful look. "I know," he told the beast. "I just have to go ahead and do it." Then he grinned and thought, *Yeah. Just go ahead and do it.* Before he could change his mind, or God forbid find that glitch, Seth grabbed his wallet and his phone, then opened the stall door and kissed Dex square on the snout. Then immediately grimaced and wiped his mouth on his sleeve. "Buddy, you really need to grab a mint." He waved to Jake and Bailey, who were just coming through the door on the other side of the barn.

"Sheep are up. We just have to do the last feeding for the goats," Bailey told him. "Then we'll go bring the hay up to the top level of the round barn."

"Dad can't come, but he said I could stay for supper," Jake added.

"Great, on both counts," Seth told them. "Listen, I have to run over to the cabin for a few minutes. Maybe a half hour."

Bailey wiggled her eyebrows at Jake.

"Stop being forty and be a ten-year-old for just a few more months," Seth told her. "Okay?" When she just smiled and rolled her eyes, he said, "Pretend. For me."

"Will do, boss," she said, then did a perfect Pippa curtsy.

"I'm going to grow old before my time," he muttered, but the grin was already edging back.

"You don't need to hurry back on our account," Bailey told him. "Addie Pearl just called and said she's coming up a little early. Probably in the next half hour. I think she's planning on commandeering your kitchen. She said something about a new recipe she wanted to try and how it was easier to make it here on your big fancy range."

"Even better," Seth told her. "Tell Addie *mi* kitchen *es su* kitchen. We'll be back long before supper, so no worries."

"Mm-hmm," Bailey said doubtfully as she and Jake started over to the stalls where the baby goats were still being housed.

"Ten," Seth reminded her as he went back in the stall and shut down his computer. Then he took off toward the house.

There was something he needed to pick up first.

Chapter Nineteen

Pippa sat cross-legged on her bed up in the cabin loft, facing *that view* as she always thought of it, and strummed the guitar for a few notes, then stopped, made a few corrections on the blank sheet music she was filling in, then played the same riff again, changing the last note. "Better," she murmured. She flipped the page back to the beginning, and softly sang the lyrics she'd been fine-tuning all day. As she moved into the song, her gaze shifted from the notes and lyrics she'd penciled in, to the view beyond the window.

She let a little more body come into her voice as she got to the refrain, then a little more on the second run. She hadn't, as yet, cut loose and sung full out. Her throat felt good. More than good, actually. It felt perfectly fine. She was babying it, doing all the warm-up exercises. She'd even talked to the vocal coach she'd hired and never used, and gotten some additional pointers on how to start pushing herself back toward her full vocal range.

Panic didn't lock her throat up tight like it used to, but she and fear were still doing daily battle. Some days she won, some days she didn't. Her legs still began to tremble when she started to push it, but she sang anyway. Just not very loud. *Baby steps*, she told herself. "Shoot, any steps," she murmured, as she paused and erased a few words on the last line, then thought for a moment, pencil poised. She ended up putting the pencil down and played a little with that part of the lyric, filling in this word or that, then finally reached for the pencil when she found the right one.

She might still be struggling with the performance part, but her music was having no such baby-step issues. Her music wasn't just back. It was back with a vengeance. It was like she had a year's worth of pent-up soundtrack inside of her, trying to rush out all at once. It pushed her and prodded her, filling her mind up night and day, until she had to put it down on paper. There was no point in fighting it, and the truth was, she didn't want to. For all that the slow singing progress was making her nervous, the music she was producing was good. Really good. And that gave her some much needed confidence. She might have lost faith in her ability to sing without restraint, but she hadn't lost her faith in knowing when she was on to something good, something right, when it came to the music itself.

Pippa still hadn't gotten the fiddle out yet. She wanted the songs polished first, before she worked on that part and started orchestrating the rest of the music for each song. It was all there in her head, so she knew there was no reason to worry. Not about that part anyway. It was really just a matter of whether she'd be able to actually sing the new songs as intended when it came time to finally record.

Don't mourn what you don't have. Love what you do. Mabry's words came to her often these days. That was her mantra.

Pippa smiled, thinking about the time they'd spent together the day before. Mabry was still living full-time in a rehab facility, but he'd made great strides, quite literally, in the past two weeks. He was on his feet, or able to be on his feet. There had been a lot of nerve damage due to the puncture wound and from the emergency surgeries as well, so the progress was slow, but he was getting ever closer to going home again. Yesterday they'd gotten him in the indoor pool for the first time as part of his physical therapy, trying to help him build up his leg muscles faster. "Water aerobics," he'd told her over the phone in disgust, not at all happy with that turn of events. Especially when he found out he'd be the only man taking the class.

Pippa had teased him about being the most popular guy in the pool, but she knew he was self-conscious about having to be seen in swim trunks, not at his finest. He was embarrassed, though he'd never admit it.

So Pippa had gone online and found him one of those old-fashioned men's bathing suits from the twenties, the kind that would cover his torso without impeding his leg movement too much; then she'd gone down and gotten in the pool with him. He'd initially been mortified at her seeing him like that, but she'd gotten him past it. Mostly. Enough that the therapist had invited her to come back two days from now, and though Mabry had poo-pooed the idea, she planned to be there.

She looked down at the music book and flipped over to another song she'd been working on, about an apple farm and the wisdom to be found in the trees. She hoped Mabry liked it. She planned to sing it for him someday. She'd settled the guitar on her lap and started to strum it again, when she heard the sound of gravel crunching in the driveway below.

She set the guitar aside and crawled off the bed to peek down from the dormer window. Every part of her filled with pleasure when she saw Seth climb out of his truck. She liked his hair wild and loose, but she had to admit, when he braided it snugly down the back of his head, like he had today, it did show off his angular cheekbones and jawline, and showcased those beautiful eyes of his, and the neatly trimmed beard would forever draw her eyes to his mouth.

Oh, that lovely, lovely mouth, and all the pleasures it had brought her.

She was so caught up, it took her a second to realize that he was carrying a fistful of what looked like wildflowers in his hand, and her heart melted a little more. "Whatever is he up to?" she murmured, and climbed down from the loft. If he thought to distract her from her work with a little afternoon frolic, *Well, he might just be successful,* she thought, her body already perking up in happy anticipation.

When she opened the door, though, it wasn't to the confident, flirtatious, gregarious man she'd come to know and love. Actually, he looked a bit pale. "Are you all right?" she asked, taking him by the wrist and gently tugging him inside. "Has something awful happened?" She took the flowers from him and laid them on the small dining table.

"Those are for you," he told her.

"Aye, yes, and they're lovely indeed. I'll get them into some water in a moment. But first sit down before you go down in a dead faint." Her brogue always got thicker when she was worried.

"I'm fine, really, I just—"

But she'd already nudged him back until he sat down on the small couch. She perched on the coffee table directly in front of him. "You've been working too hard and not getting enough sleep. Maybe I should sleep here a few nights a week." She let go of his arm and leaned forward so she could feel his forehead. "You don't feel warm, so that's a good sign."

He took her hand from where she'd pressed it to his cheek, then tugged her forward until she was in his lap. "I'm fine," he told her gently.

She looked into his eyes. "What is it then? Not bad news?"

"I sure hope not," he said under his breath, then took in a breath and let it out again, very slowly.

Looking worried still, she placed her palms on his big

shoulders and put her nose to his. "Out with it." She leaned back and folded her arms.

Finally, his grin surfaced, and he was back to looking a bit more like himself, despite the high color that had suddenly risen to his cheeks. "I realized on my way over here that perhaps I didn't plan this out exactly the way I should have," he said, "but I just want to go on record now as saying I didn't see it going quite this way."

"Didn't see what going what way?"

"I don't know why that surprises me," he went on. "It's not like we've done any other part of this relationship like normal people."

"Like normal peop—" She broke off and her eyes went wide. She swiveled her head and looked at the flowers on the table, then back to his neatly showered, braided, and trimmed appearance, knowing that wasn't at all how he'd normally look in the middle of a workday.

Then he unfolded her arms and took one of her hands in both of his, and her other one flew straight to her mouth. "You're not," she whispered behind her fingers.

His grin returned, broader now, and it seemed the more flustered she became, the calmer he got. He took her other hand from her mouth and held that one, too. "I know our time here, living like this, can't last forever," he began.

And instead of the rush of anticipation and disbelief that had filled her suddenly, she felt like someone had punched her directly in the chest. *Wait.* He wouldn't have gotten all neatly pressed and picked her a fistful of posies if he'd planned to end things and send her on her merry way back to Ireland, would he? There wasn't a cruel bone in Seth Brogan's body, but then whatever—

He leaned forward and whispered, "It's all good, relax."

Her face crumpled into a smile then. No, he wasn't cruel. He was perfect. "I love you," she said on a shuddery breath as tears gathered once more. *Of course they did.* That was all she did these days. But there'd be no holding any of it back, not anymore.

His eyes went dark and hot and she immediately wanted to squirm. He squeezed her hands so tightly she had to wriggle them a little to get him to loosen his hold. And every part of his reaction had been better than the perfect response she'd hoped for.

"That's . . . really good to hear," he said, the words thick with emotion. "It'll make this a little easier."

"Go on," she said, her breath catching, her thighs trembling a bit now as tears glittered on her eyelashes.

"You've found your music now, and your life isn't here in the mountains. Or it wasn't, before you met me." He paused and held her gaze. "I want you to know, I would travel the world over for you. And I hope you'll show me your Ireland. I hope to find my place there, in your life, and come to love it, like you've come to love my home."

"Oh, Seth—"

"Seeing as I'm tied to this land that I love, to these mountains, and to the people who live here, I'm hoping we can find a way for you to fit here, as I'm willing to fit there. It might take me some time before I can push the work off here for someone else to handle for long stretches of time, but that's one goal. I hope you can find a way to do the same. I have some ideas about that. Actually, Moira was the one with the ideas, but they're pretty bloody brilliant ones, if you ask me, and I think maybe, since you're already writing here and composing here, that they'll work for you, too."

She could hear the nervousness climbing back into his voice as he spoke, feel the hands covering hers growing a little damp, which was so beyond charming, she could barely stand it. And she understood now, how he'd grown stronger when she'd grown flustered, because she felt the same now, as his face got a little warmer. He'd always be strong for her, want to care for her, and she would always be and do the same for him.

"Seth," she said again, her heart already in a puddle, and when she could see he wasn't sure what she was going to say, that he was truly worried, she leaned forward, met his gaze with her own and whispered, "It's all good, relax."

He grinned then, a bit crookedly this time, and she watched as his beautiful eyes grew a little glassy. Maybe it wasn't her knees trembling, but his legs that were shaking a bit. More likely, it was both.

"I want to make this work," he said. "And I'm willing to do whatever that will take. Because I love you, too, Pippa Mavreen MacMillan."

How he knew her middle name, she had no idea, but her breath had caught in her throat now, because he'd finally said the words she'd wanted to hear him say to her for what felt like forever now.

"So I think, if we're going to put in all the effort that it's going to take to find a way to make our very different lives fit together, it would be best if we started out on that adventure truly united." He let go of her hand and fished in the pocket of his pants, then came out with an old, worn, black velvet box.

And her hands flew right back to her mouth again.

"This is my great-grandmother's ring," he told her. "She lived to be one hundred and five and was married for more than seventy-five of those years. Would have been longer if my great-grandfather had lived as long as she did."

"Oh, Seth," she whispered shakily.

"She left this to me." He grinned. "I always was her favorite."

"Of course you were," she said, her voice no more than a rasp, and they shared a short laugh.

His voice was shaky and the sheen in his eyes was brighter still. "I know she'd have loved you, and I know this would make her happy. But it will make me far happier still if you'd agree to be my wife."

He opened the little box and the most impossibly tiny little ring sat wedged into the worn, yellowed satin. There was a small amethyst in the middle, set on either side by two delicate little diamonds.

"I know there's not much to it in terms of size, but I thought it suited you. It needs a good cleaning," he said, "and possibly a fitting, though your hands are small like hers were. We can change—"

"Not a single thing," she breathed, then looked from the sweet, heartbreakingly delicate ring to the man who was going to be her husband. "It's perfect," she told him. "And I will wear it proudly, cherish it greatly, and hope I can come close, someday, to honoring the memory of the woman who first wore it. You're going to have to tell me all about her."

"Is that a yes, then?" he asked her, and she swore she could hear his thundering heartbeat echoing in the space between them, or perhaps that was her own.

"Aye," she said softly, "that's a yes, then." She wrapped her arms around his neck and he slid her fully into his embrace. "That's a forever yes."

Epilogue

Pippa cleared her throat and leaned closer to the mike. "Thank you, everyone, for coming tonight." She looked out across the sea of smiling faces that had crowded into Sawyer's pub. The whole mill was jammed full as well, as were the grounds outside, where people were enjoying the warm, late July evening. They'd be able to see and hear her, thanks to the big screens and speakers that Seth and Sawyer had set up both inside and outside the mill, with the help of her crew.

She knew it felt like a big crowd to them, but to her, it was intimate and personal. Just how she wanted it. She knew every single face she could see.

Everyone in Blue Hollow Falls was present. Except for Mabry, though Maggie and her husband were there. The twins were with Mabry, helping to live stream the event for him, via their parents. Pippa hoped he could hear her okay, as she planned to debut his song that night.

"Now, we're going to be recording this," she told everyone, "so you have to be on your best behavior."

There were some hoots and hollers, including some from Drake and several of her own bandmates, who were seated on stage with her. "I can see already that I'm going to need to hire a really good sound editor," she said, and the audience chuckled. "As you all know, I've said yes to this handsome bloke when he asked for my hand." She wiggled her hand with the engagement ring, which had, of course, fit her perfectly. Fate was like that, she believed. The crowd erupted in cheers and applause, and she looked down at Seth, who winked at her while accepting hearty pats on the back. "I think we might need to expand the space for our wedding reception," she told him, and the resounding roar from both inside and outside the mill fair to shook the walls.

"But tonight," she said, when they'd settled back down, "it's about the music. The songs you'll be hearing were inspired by these beautiful mountains you live in, and by some of you personally as well. So many of you have become good friends, and all of you have welcomed me with open arms, and open minds"—she glanced to Seth once more—"and some of the most amazing wine I've ever tasted."

A mix of laughter and cheers filled the air and she paused to sip from the water bottle she'd set on her stool. She took a deep breath then and let the tension release from her neck, then across her shoulders, and on down her spine. She felt . . . good. Better than good. She felt bloody brilliant. All the familiar vibes were rushing through her, the energy was amazing, and she knew from their rehearsals that the music was going to be fantastic. She wanted to hold on to this feeling forever—she was so grateful that she was having the chance to feel it again.

She didn't have to belt it to the rafters tonight, or go on jamming for hours. Here, all she had to do was sit on her stool, pull the microphone close, let the music come, and enjoy the ride. Here, in Blue Hollow Falls, she was safe.

She introduced her three bandmates one by one, then thanked Drake and the two other local musicians who were also onstage, who'd be sitting in with them that night. When the cheers and whistling died down, she turned back to the crowd. "I have someone else who'll be joining us tonight. This is his first time performing in public, so give him a warm welcome. Come on out here, Jake. Jacob McCall, everyone."

There was a moment of silence and maybe a gasp or two, and folks craned their necks, looking around. She knew they were looking for Will. Then Jake stepped up on the back of the stage, squinting at the bright lights, and gave his bow and a little wave. The thunderous applause, she knew, was for him, and it was for his father.

Pippa knew that Will was back in Sawyer's office, where he could watch the whole thing on Sawyer's computer monitor, and hear it live perfectly well, given he was only a dozen or so yards away. Will had told her that he hadn't wanted to take anything away from Jake's debut. And Pippa knew he simply wasn't up to being among people, especially people he knew, when he heard Jake play for the first time.

Will had come to her about a week after Seth had proposed, well over a month since they'd first talked. They'd sat on the tiny porch in front of her cabin, and Will had told her he wanted Jake to have the chance to pursue playing the fiddle if he truly wanted to. He'd also informed her he'd be paying her for the lessons, and wouldn't take a no on that.

Pippa had been perfectly fine with all of that. In fact, she'd been downright thrilled.

Will had gone on to tell her he'd be keeping the fiddle he'd made for his wife, explaining it had been designed for a woman's hand, and he'd rather Jake begin with an instrument that he could continue playing as he got older, if he was so inclined.

Pippa hadn't been sure if that was his real reason, but it didn't matter. It wasn't anyone's business but Will's what he did with that fiddle. He'd also asked Pippa if she or Drake could take Jake down to Turtle Springs and help him pick out a secondhand fiddle and bow from the music store down there. If music turned out to be something Jake was good at, Will would see that he got a better one eventually.

That was when Pippa realized that while Will was giving his okay, he was still far from comfortable with any part of this. It was only his love for his son that was making him step outside the walls he'd built around himself, around his heart. She admired him greatly for that, and felt only sorrow that he couldn't find a way out from under his past pain for himself.

As it turned out, Jake was his father's son. He'd taken to the fiddle like a fish to water. She knew everyone would be astounded by his performance tonight. What they didn't know, what even Will didn't know, was that Jake was his mother's son as well.

Other than herself, only Will, Seth, Drake, and Bailey had known anything about Jake's lessons. Well, and Addie Pearl, because Pippa had learned early on she knew pretty much everything that was worth knowing. Jake had been the one to request their keeping quiet about his lessons. If it turned out it wasn't for him, or he just wasn't any good at it, he didn't want the added pressure of the whole town knowing about it. Jake had already put enough pressure on himself, because he knew his father wasn't thrilled that Jake was playing, and Jake didn't want to let him down.

Still unwilling to give up on the father, Pippa said a silent prayer that when Will heard his son play, maybe, just maybe, it would unlock something inside of him, and set some part of him free.

Pippa smiled at Jake and he smiled back, looking a bit more comfortable up there already. She leaned closer to the mike and addressed the crowd. "Before we dive in, I have one last little announcement. I'll be using some of tonight's performances, along with others I'll be recording out at our new little studio, out at Bluestone & Vine, for my next album. We'll be releasing it sometime around the end of this year, hopefully by the holidays, if everything goes well. I'll be calling it *The Sessions at Blue Hollow Falls*." The crowd erupted in whoops, hollers, stamping feet, and hands drumming on tables, so loudly this time she thought the place might vibrate right to the ground.

Pippa finally made a motion with her hands to quiet the crowd, and they did. Mostly. The murmur of conversation through the crowd would not be silenced. "One last thing, I promise," she said with a smile. "I wanted to add that what you all are doing here at the mill—the artists, the musicians, the painters, the weavers, the woodworkers, every last one of you—is keeping alive traditions and skills that might otherwise be lost. Being from Ireland, where we have one or two of those, I know a little about how special that is. I can't tell you how much I admire all of you for what you're building here."

Spontaneous applause broke out again, and she took another sip of water. "To that end," she said, "I'll be donating the proceeds of *The Sessions at Blue Hollow Falls* to the guild, for the purpose of creating a music venue here, expanding on what you've started with your love of music here at Sawyer's place, and hopefully bringing your music, and your passion, to any and everyone who wants to come to Blue Hollow Falls and fall in love." She looked at Seth and smiled. "Like I have."

If she'd thought the place couldn't get any louder, she was wrong. She laughed and covered her ears as the thundering response went on for many long minutes. Finally, Drake did a loud whistle, and slowly the room, then the rest of the building, settled down.

"Okay then," she said. "Let's play some music." She turned to pick up her fiddle, and noticed it wasn't resting by her stool where she'd put it. She looked at Drake, then at her bandmates. Drake nodded toward Jake. A hush fell over the room as Jake stepped off the stage, then climbed back on again.

Pippa knew immediately what he had in his hands. "Oh, Jake—" she began, shocked that he'd do something like this, on tonight of all nights.

Jake smiled and handed her a small folded card. "It's okay. This is from my dad," he told her, his voice getting picked up by the mike. "And so is this." And he handed Pippa the case she knew held his mother's beautiful fiddle.

Pippa immediately covered her suddenly full throat with her hand, her eyes too blurry to read the words on the card. A moment later, Seth was up on stage beside her, his hand on her back. She covered the mic. "Did you know about this?" she asked in a hoarse whisper.

"No," he told her, then slipped the card from her hand and read it to her, and only to her. "'As I said to you before, this was made for a woman's hand. And you were right, it was meant to be played. I know your fiddle is special, too, but even if just for one song, Zoey would have been so honored to know her fiddle was being played by you. I admire you, Pippa, and your music, but even more, thank you for being the friend my son needed, when he most needed one. Blessings to you, and play her well. Wilson.'"

"Oh boy," Pippa said, then fanned her face. Drake stepped over and handed her a napkin so she could dab at her eyes. "How on earth can I sing now?" she said, laughing and sniffling at the same time.

"Like you've never sung before," Seth said, and kissed her, making the crowd erupt in cheers all over again. "I love you," he whispered in her ear. "Go knock 'em dead."

Pippa nodded, then tugged Seth back as another thought struck her. "Could you go back and slip a note under Sawyer's office door—don't bother Will—but let Will know I want to see him after the show, please? Or whenever he's up to seeing me? I can't not thank him for this. Thank you," she whispered when he nodded and gave her a wink. She reached up, tugged his beard down, and kissed him hard and fast on the mouth.

The crowd broke into hoots and whistles. Grinning, Seth waved to them as he hopped down from the stage.

Pippa opened the case and took out the fiddle. It was a stunning piece of craftsmanship, and Pippa was both humbled and more than a little thrilled that she was going to have the chance to be the one to make her sing.

"It's all tuned, just like yours," Jake told her nervously. "I hope you don't mind."

"Are you kidding?" she told him. Then she dragged his stool next to hers. "Come on up here." She settled on her stool, and waited for him to settle on his. She leaned over and whispered to him the name of the song she wanted to play, then turned around and told her band as well. She propped the fiddle on her shoulder and picked up her bow, then looked to Jake, who did the same.

Then she looked at the audience, and at Seth, and she leaned forward, as if she was going to tell them all a secret . . . and she sang.

Back in Sawyer's office, Will watched on the monitor as Pippa played Zoey's fiddle as if she'd been born with it in her hands. No one could have honored it, or the memory of his wife, any better. He watched his son play and didn't even recognize the young man he'd become. Will sat, stunned, at just how good Jake truly was, and felt a rush of shame that he'd ever considered keeping his child from following his dreams, just to hide from his own pain.

Then Pippa rested her bow and leaned into the mike to sing. Her voice was so different now, haunting and rich. She didn't sound like Zoey anymore, which should have relieved him, but instead, it caught at his gut. As if, somehow, that last tenuous connection he'd had was gone forever.

Then Jake lowered his bow and leaned into the same mike alongside Pippa and shocked Will into utter stillness as his son opened his mouth . . . and sang. There Zoey was, only this time, it was an actual flesh-and-blood, living, breathing part of her, singing with a voice so clear, so true, Will felt something break apart inside of him.

And while their bows danced across the strings, and they sang a duet about apples in springtime and the wisdom of the trees, Will laid his head on his arms and did something he hadn't been able to do since the night his wife died. He cried. Shuddering, wracking, soul-rending sobs. And as he let out eleven long years of pain and anguish and bone-deep loneliness, he could have sworn he felt her hands on his shoulders, and her voice whispering in his ear what she always said when he told her he loved her: "I love you to the moon, my fiddle-playing man, and I always will."

Read more about Blue Hollow Falls
in the holiday anthology *A Season to Celebrate*,
available now!

A BLUE HOLLOW FALLS CHRISTMAS

by Donna Kauffman

"Weddings on Christmas. There should be a law."

"For or against?"

Moira Brogan drained the last of the Coke from her glass until the straw made a slurping sound, jiggled the ice a bit, then found one last sip. *Because you need more sugar. And more caffeine.* Ignoring her little voice, as she had been all day—*week, month, year*—she glanced up at the bartender, pondering the question with all the gravity of the attorney she was. "Against, your honor. I mean, who wants to share their anniversary with Santa's big day? It should be all about him."

"Unless you don't believe in Santa," replied the bartender.

The bartender—Sally, according to her hotel name badge—looked about five or six years older than Moira's own twenty-seven, and eons wiser.

"Even if you don't, it should be recognized that many people do," Moira countered, warming to the debate. Debate she understood. Debate she knew how to win. Life outside the courtroom? Not so much with the winning there. Case in point? Sitting in a rural hotel bar drowning her sorrows in a gallon of carbonated sugar and caffeine instead of dancing the night away at her brother's lovely and beautiful wedding reception up in Blue Hollow Falls. "Those people, the believers," Moira went on, perhaps more doggedly than required given the judge and jury was bartender Sally, "might, and quite probably would, construe a person marrying on such a day as being . . . well, sacrilegious. Or, at the very least, unimaginative. Like, said person could only improve on the most celebrated day of the year by getting married on it. Somewhat self-aggrandizing, don't you think?"

"Point taken," Sally said, judiciously.

Gaining momentum, Moira said, "I mean, I suppose we might include a clause for people like my wonderful and completely besotted brother, who are just so madly in love, they think what could be more festive than getting married on Christmas? Because, really, what could be?"

"Getting married in Disney World?"

"Ha," Moira said with a grin, raising her empty glass in toast. "Point to the prosecution." Then she caught the look on Sally's face and set her glass down. "Oh my God. You didn't. Did you? Was Mickey Mouse the justice of the peace?" A splutter of laughter threatened and Moira tried to frown it into submission. Firstly, because it would be rude to her new friend Sally, and secondly, because she knew she was one-too-many-insomnia-riddled-nights away from the kind of laughter that would quickly devolve into a run of convulsive, bordering-on-hysterical giggles. And she doubted Sally would join in, given it was her nuptials that had triggered them.

"Not me, your honor." Sally smiled and lifted a hand, as if she was being sworn in. "Maid of honor."

"Me, too!" Moira replied, perhaps a little too loudly. In addition to far too little sleep, she was definitely way too hopped up on wedding cake. "Well, co-maid of honor, anyway, with the bride's sister."

"Yeah," Sally replied with a smile and a nod toward Moira's outfit. "I gathered."

Moira looked down to the strapless, silk and organza, emerald green formal she was wearing. She probably should have changed when she'd first gotten back to the hotel. She'd left the reception right after Seth and Pippa had taken off for their honeymoon in Ireland. She'd done her due diligence, smiled and laughed her way through all of her sworn duties. But once her brother and brand-new sister-in-law were gone, Moira had wanted nothing more than to be alone with her stupid, self-pitying misery. She was not proud of herself, of her apparent inability to get over her latest life disaster. Either of them. But the romantic disaster had been last spring, for God's sake.

Only when she'd gotten back to the hotel in Turtle Springs, itself a tiny town tucked into a curve of the Hawksbill River, in the shadow of the Blue Ridge Mountains, she'd realized the very last thing she wanted was to be alone.

She just hadn't wanted to be with people who knew her. People who would expect her to be overcome with joy and happiness for her brother, Seth, and his new bride, whom Moira adored almost as much as she adored her older brother. And she was quite sincerely thrilled for them. She was. It was just the host of painful memories watching them say their I Do's had roused up, coupled with the recent collapse of all her future career plans, that had her escaping the family-clogged reception like Cinderella from the ball.

She didn't know which had made her more miserable, the tough love "oh, come now, Mouse, get on over yourself, lass" looks from her oldest brother and sister, Aiden and Kathleen, the "you poor, wee thing" pats on the shoulder from her dear Aunt Margery, or the endless variations of "don't you worry, you'll get married, too . . . someday" comments from what felt like every last one of the rest of her relatives and family friends. And given she was the youngest of six, as were both of her parents, their collective clan was a small army. And that was just the Brogan side.

Pippa's family, straight over from Ireland, was just as prolific when it came to propagating the family tree. *And they brought those lovely, awful accents with them.* Lovely because that beautiful lilt was still music to her ears, and her heart. Awful because she still missed that particular lilt and the man it had belonged to, and hearing it all around her, in conjunction with a wedding no less, had doomed any chance she might have had to avoid reliving every moment of their whirlwind love affair. All the good parts, which had been every moment of it, and the very, very sad parts . . . which had only been right at the end of it. Because it had been the end of it.

And no one in her family even knew that her big, bold career plans of being a trial attorney in Silicon Valley had suffered an equally swift and demoralizing demise when she'd learned she'd flunked the bar exam. *Yeah, won't that be a fun reveal.*

So, she'd fled back to the small hotel she'd booked herself into, claiming she'd be fine there as all the lodgings in Blue Hollow Springs were fully taken by her family and the equally extensive MacMillan clan. In truth, she'd been relieved for the excuse. She'd liked knowing she had an escape route, a bolt hole, somewhere to hide, if needed.

Upon her return, the small hotel lounge had been packed to the gills with reporters from all over the globe, along with a fair number of the less-than-savory paparazzi, who'd all rushed to the rural mountain region—in most cases, judging by the bevy of accents in the room, from far, far away—in hopes of getting photos or footage of Moira's new sister-in-law, Pippa MacMillan. Well, Pippa Brogan now, she presumed. It just so happened, Pippa was a very famous Irish folk singer. The reporters hadn't been successful, though. Blue Hollow Falls had well and truly adopted Pippa, and they protected their own. The ranks had been locked up tight, and not so much as a single long-range lens had intruded upon the happy couple's special day.

From the raucous noise level inside the hotel bar, Moira presumed the collective journalist horde had apparently decided to drown their defeat as well, only in something far stronger than her Coke.

Moira took another long sip of her soda, the fizzy bubbles tickling her nose, absently realizing that while she'd slipped back into her melancholy, Sally had refreshed her drink. Moira continued to sip while she watched Sally deftly handle the gaggle pressed up against the bar. Moira shifted away, into the shadows where she had tucked herself at the very end of the bar.

The only reason she had a stool at all was because Sally had spied Moira edging her way around the periphery of the dimly lit place and had slid one under the exit gap at the end of the bar. Sally probably kept one on her side of the bar specifically for forlorn-looking creatures such as herself. Sally had even taken Moira's long, winter coat and tucked it back in the office, making Moira initially wonder if perhaps the bartender was angling for some kind of wedding scoop herself. But, even sleep-deprived and on a cake frosting high, Moira was pretty good at reading people. Bartender Sally was a good egg. She'd bet her one and still only law license on it.

Moira really didn't want to think about that second law license, the one she didn't have. The lack of which had crushed all her future plans. Instead, she tilted up her glass, intent on crunching a few pieces of ice, only the full cluster slid down and splashed her in the face. Sally appeared like the magical genie Moira was beginning to suspect she was, and proffered a clean napkin to Moira while quickly mopping up the spill. "Thanks," Moira said, checking the front of her gown, relieved to see she hadn't stained the fabric.

She caught Sally checking out the dress, and held her

arms out slightly. "I thought the bride did a pretty good job picking these out," Moira said. "I mean, they're tasteful, and they don't make me look like I'm playing dress-up as a Grecian goddess or anything." She looked back at Sally and sighed. "It still has bridesmaid written all over it, though, doesn't it?" Lifting a hand to her short mop of auburn curls, she said, "At least I don't have the teased and lacquered beehive up-do to go with it. It could be so much worse."

"Actually, you look great. Amazing even," Sally said, appearing quite sincere. "The green dress, with your red hair, and fair skin? And don't get me started on the green eyes, which I'm just going to pretend are colored contacts, because, honestly, so not fair."

Moira blushed and laughed at the same time. "If you're angling for a bigger tip, done. I'll just be emptying my wallet on the bar right now."

Sally laughed, waved her hand. "Just being honest. But I'd have known it was a bridesmaid dress no matter what it looked like. This is Turtle Springs, Virginia," Sally added dryly. "Out here, we don't have much call for formal anything." She pulled another two beers from the tap, put them on a tray and handed them to one of the waitresses, while taking three more orders from the other waitress, which she'd already started filling with her free hand. People jammed up against the bar shouted their orders non-stop and somehow Sally managed to pull their drinks, smile and joke with them, all while continuing the conversation with Moira as if they were seated at a café table alone together, dishing over wedding gossip.

"You're very good at your job," Moira told her, vaguely wondering what kind of money a bartender made. Maybe she needed to completely rethink her life. *And maybe you need to steer clear of the caffeine and sugar and get more than a catnap at night.* She prudently pushed her once again empty glass away.

"Besides, it's not like your brother's wedding was flying under the radar," Sally continued, taking the compliment in stride. "It's been front-page news pretty much everywhere since the moment they got engaged." She nodded to the throng. "Hence this insanity."

"Well, they did initially try and keep the wedding date under wraps," Moira said. "In truth, I think Seth thought that having it today would kind of throw everybody off. Like, who would get married on Christmas? Because he'd never want to compete with Santa, either."

"Who would?" Sally offered.

"Right? But there was no way to keep it from getting out. I mean, you know all about it, everyone knows all about it." She waved at the crowded lounge. "The whole world knows about it, because, you know—"

"Pippa MacMillan," Sally finished for her, nodding, as if nothing else needed to be said. And it didn't.

"It's such a happily-ever-after story, too." Sally, who had seemed so pragmatic and seen-it-all, clearly wasn't immune to the Christmas fairytale wedding, either. "I mean, Pippa finally returns to the music scene just when speculation reached the point that everyone was convinced she'd never come back from her injury, and then she's getting engaged after a whirlwind romance during her secret hideaway trip to the States? And they're getting married on Christmas? Even Mickey Mouse has to bow to that." Sally let out a self-deprecating chuckle. "Listen to me, getting all sappy." She wiped down the bar and went to refill Moira's glass but Moira waved her away. "But, you know what, a gorgeous holiday wedding up in the mountains here? What could be more romantic than that?"

Falling in love while you're on a whirlwind trip to Ireland, was Moira's immediate thought. *Finally allowing yourself to consider having a personal life after years of studying, and studying, and more studying. Maybe even picturing your own wedding day for the first time.*

Only her whirlwind romance hadn't ended with the fairy-tale wedding, holiday or no. Nope. Hers had just . . . ended.

"I mean, they seem perfect for each other," Sally went on. "I bet it was a really beautiful ceremony, too, up at your brother's winery. What with the recent snowfall and that view. I went to a tasting up there in October. It's gorgeous." She filled another set of orders and began drying a few freshly washed glasses that someone had just brought out from the back. "I know you probably can't talk about it."

Moira had promised Pippa and Seth not to talk about the ceremony to anyone outside the family and invited guests. And she wouldn't. She just wished she didn't have to picture it in her own mind. Because it had been stunning and beautiful and perfect. Sally was also right that Seth and Pippa were perfect for each other. So much so, it made Moira's newly mended heart ache all over again, reliving their sweetly intimate ceremony in her mind.

She'd felt selfish and ridiculous, thinking about her own heartbreak while they said their I Do's. But how was she supposed to watch them, their love shining so brightly as they shared both laughter and tears while speaking their personally written vows to each other, and not wonder what might have been for her? Maybe it wasn't selfish—she was sincere in celebrating their happiness after all—so much as simply human.

"If they'd really wanted to keep it secret, I guess they could have eloped," Sally said, then handed two more trays of beers over the bar.

Moira laughed at that. "Maybe, but it would have been a toss-up over which clan would have disowned them first. Turns out the only family more traditional and excited about all family events than the Brogans is the MacMillans."

Sally laughed along with her, then nodded toward two

swarthy, good-looking men who'd pushed their way to the bar, laughing and jostling each other, while a third man, a bit older and quieter, moved in behind them. He was also good-looking, but of the tall, blond, and chiseled variety. He wore a beautifully tailored suit that didn't fit in with the relaxed throng.

"What'll you fellas have?" Sally asked. "That you haven't had already, that is?"

The two younger guys started flirting outrageously with Sally, despite being easily a decade her junior, their accents pegging them as French, maybe Belgian. Sally handled them with easy aplomb, and appeared just a little flattered by the attention. *Beware the accent,* Moira wanted to warn her. *That's how they get you to lower all your defenses and act like an idiot.* Never again, she vowed. No more pretty men from distant lands with beautiful accents.

Mr. Tall, Blond, and Chiseled decided to turn his attention toward Moira. He appeared something of the brooding hero type, big and broad shouldered, with darker eyebrows, sharp cheekbones, and a sensuously shaped mouth. His hair was painfully perfect, and his eyes were a deep, dark brown, but there was nothing warm in them.

Moira shifted away from him on instinct.

His smile was slow and did nothing to warm his gaze. "Member of the wedding party, I see?" he said, his accent thick as well, but decidedly American. By way of the south. Texas, she guessed, noting the expensive Stetson he carried in one hand.

Ha-ha, Karma, Moira thought. *Touché.*

Her lack of immediate response was all the invitation Texas needed to insert himself way too deep into her personal space.

Moira hadn't been genetically gifted in the stature department, topping out in the eighth grade at a few inches over five feet. However, as the youngest and shortest of six children, she'd long ago learned how to hold her own. She managed to slide her elbow onto the bar as she turned only her head to look directly at her would-be lothario, creating both a barrier to his intrusion while simultaneously making it clear she was not welcoming his attention. Unfortunately, not enough of a barrier to keep from smelling the alcohol on his breath. "Observant," she said, not unkindly, but not kindly, either, then pointedly turned back to her soda. Which she belatedly remembered pushing away earlier. It now sat right in front of Texas.

"Looking for this?" He picked up her empty glass. "Why don't I buy you another and we'll get to know each other a little better." His smile deepened, but his eyes remained cold. She caught a flash of what looked like irritation at her lack of a positive reaction to his overture. When she saw his smile change to something darker, as if she'd just issued him a challenge he intended to meet, the first tinkling of alarm prickled at the hairs on her neck. Moira was suddenly glad she was sitting in a public place, filled with people. A lot of people.

"Who knows, darlin'," he added, picking up the glass and jiggling the ice, his gaze directly on hers now. "If you're real lucky, maybe we'll hit it off and someday you can upgrade that bridesmaid dress to the real deal."

Moira knew the best response was no response of any kind, but he'd caught her so off guard with that decidedly misogynistic bon mot, her mouth dropped open before she could stop herself. "How do you know I'm not married with three kids?"

"No ring."

"I'm liberated."

"I'm Max," he said, his gaze dropping to the front of her strapless dress, then back up to her eyes. "Nice to meet you, Libby."

The predatory look, along with the smell of stale alcohol

that he seemed to wear like some men wore cologne, made her shudder involuntarily. Moira turned to look for Sally, but she'd joined her fellow barkeep at the far end of the long, scarred, oak bar to help him break up an argument. Which Sally managed to do rather handily, Moira noted. "I want to be her when I grow up," she murmured under her breath.

"I have something that wants to grow up," Texas said, his hot breath now right next to her ear. "And you're just the one to help me with that."

Moira had to lean way back when she turned to look at him so as not to actually come into contact with his body. So far back she almost fell off her stool. She could have simply slid to her feet and put more space between them, but for one, she wasn't letting this guy back her up. And secondly, she stayed seated because the high bar stool put her closer to even height with him. Standing, even in the heels she was still wearing, she'd have been at a sore disadvantage. "Max," she said, quite sympathetically, "I know this will come as a big disappointment to you, so I'm apologizing up front, but I'm afraid I'm already spoken for."

He made a big show of looking around. "Funny, I don't see anyone."

"I know," she said, helpfully. "And that's okay. I just didn't want to take up any more of your time."

He looked confused, which had been her goal.

"Now you're free to go dazzle someone else. Or maybe get a cab and call it a night?" Moira wasn't sure if Turtle Springs even had cabs. "Or an Uber." They were everywhere, right?

Texas surprised her again by neatly sliding his arm through hers and tugging her off the stool. Caught off balance, and now from a standpoint decidedly lower than his six-foot-plus height, she staggered a step or two. He took that as an excuse to put his other hand on her hip to help steady her. His fingertips were hard and dug into her flesh.

"Let's go outside and you can help me with that, too," he said, the cold light of what looked like victory gleaming in his dark eyes.

Moira felt a brief wave of nausea, and knew it was only partly due to her instinctive reaction to him and the sudden, untenable situation she'd somehow gotten herself into. She hadn't had a full night sleep in longer than she could remember, and the catnaps she'd convinced herself were enough, had just been proven woefully inadequate.

"Your other gentleman caller will have to wait his turn," Texas told her. He let his gaze dip to the front of her dress again, and that light in his eyes, when he looked back up, had gone from victorious to predatory. The kind of predator who looked like he'd take great pleasure in claiming his prey, and not necessarily in a way the prey was going to enjoy. "First come, first get, right, darlin'?"

"First—get?" Moira repeated, trying not to splutter. Okay, now she was done being nice. Actually, she'd been done the moment he'd put his hands on her. She tried to tug her arm free. "What on earth gave you the idea that I would ever—"

"You're a bridesmaid, sitting in a bar, drinking alone." This time he raked his gaze up and down the full length of her body. "What other idea would I get?"

Fair point, Moira conceded, and yet, that still didn't give anyone license to put their hands on her. "I've said I'm not interested. Please respect that, and remove your hands," she said in her best courtroom voice.

He merely stepped in closer, forcing her to look up at him to maintain eye contact. "When I said first come," he began as he leaned down closer, making her almost gag with the stench of his breath, "I didn't mean me. I'm a generous man, Libby. You'll get yours, too."

Moira's long dress made kneeing the guy impossible. Even if her knee would reach up that high. She wasn't averse to the idea of using a balled fist to get the same point across. Being short did have its advantages, and, due to her size, her brothers had taught her how to fight, and not always fairly. However, Max still had her arm in one hand and his other hand tightly gripped her hip, blocking her from getting in a good left hook.

Moira preferred to fight—and win—her own battles, but, given the day she'd had, on top of the week she'd had, and the month, and the year, well, right now, she'd settle for expediency. She glanced down the bar, knowing Sally would set Max here straight in two seconds flat. Only now there was some other argument going on, this one not so easily controlled. Moira's eyes widened as she saw Sally pull a silver whistle out from under the neck of her shirt, while the other bartender reached under the bar and came up with a thick, wooden baseball bat. *Uh oh.*

Moira supposed it shouldn't have surprised her that things would get out of hand. She suspected the hotel lounge had seen its share of bar fights, but she'd bet they'd never once been overrun by this many people all at the same time. And most certainly not from such a global community of travelers. Not to mention it was also Christmas Day.

Voices were being raised in multiple languages now, and the mood had begun to shift from overly festive to something far less jovial. Then Sally put the whistle in her mouth and the resulting series of shrill blasts instantly silenced the room. For about two seconds.

Max also noted the disturbance and tightened his hold on her arm to the point she was sure he'd leave marks. "I believe that's our cue to go find somewhere a little quieter, and a lot more private." Without warning, Max tugged her into the crowd, heading in the general direction of the door that led to the side parking lot of the small hotel. Her car was parked out front. Dressed as she was, and given their height and strength differences, she didn't like her chances for making a clean getaway once outside.

So, there was only one thing to do. The moment he'd let go of her hip to pull her into the crowd, she'd snagged her clutch from the bar. She slid her hand to one end of the long, tubular shaped bag, then clutched it in her fist like her own little satin-and-pearl encrusted bat. *It might not be thick and made of wood, but then my target is probably a lot smaller.*

When he turned to move them sideways between two clusters of shouting patrons, she swung her bag right at the zippered front of his trousers. Any other impact site might result in an immediate retaliatory response. Her brothers had taught her that there was one particular spot guaranteed to make a man drop whatever he was holding and immediately cover the injured area with his hands. Do it well enough, he'd be on his knees while cupping himself.

Moira only needed Max to let go of her. She could lose herself in the crowd in an instant, and they'd never lay eyes on each other again. The only question would be whether it was better to head upstairs to her room, or to run to her car, so she could drive back to the Hollow and the security of her family.

An instant before impact, however, she was spared from having to make that split-second decision when a large, warm hand blocked her shot. His palm was broad enough to encompass her hand and her bag, which he proved by gently but firmly wrapping long fingers around them both. "There you are, sweetheart," he said, swinging their joined fists neatly downward, appearing for all the world like they were simply a couple holding hands. "I looked at the bar for you."

Pinned as she was between her errant Good Samaritan and Max, with the crowd pressing in all around them, Moira couldn't turn her head enough to see much more than a flash of what looked like . . . a white lab coat? She could feel his large frame behind her like a big, sturdy wall of support, however, and unlike Max's egotistical slithering, this guy's somewhat Neanderthal approach didn't make her feel threatened at all. Quite the opposite.

"Sorry I'm late," he added, then shocked her by leaning down and pressing what felt like a kiss to the top of her head. She quickly realized it was an excuse to put his mouth closer to her ear when she heard him whisper, "Go with me on this and I'll have you out of here in a jiff."